TWO MEN . . .

They sat quietly watching the evening news on television—two of America's most powerful men; the President of the United States and his chief advisor on foreign affairs.

> *"A late bulletin has just arrived on the situation in the Far East. A surprise Japanese naval and air attack on units of the Soviet fleet anchored in Vladivostok harbor has apparently caused serious damage to a number of ships. The exact extent of the damage is not known, but observers onshore say that at least a dozen ships and submarines were sunk. Oil storage tanks and ammunition dumps were also hit, and the military area of the harbor is in flames. We'll be back with the latest bulletins later in the program."*

As a hair-spray commercial flickered back on the screen, Thompson snapped off the TV. "It's very close to getting out of control," he said. "Too many countries and people are involved. Everybody's gonads are beginning to swell. And the Soviets must be getting a little desperate. This is when somebody could make a really serious mistake."

"And they almost always do," the President said.

THE CHINESE ULTIMATUM

Edward McGhee
&
Robin Moore

PINNACLE BOOKS   NEW YORK CITY

THE CHINESE ULTIMATUM

An original Pinnacle Books edition, published for the first time anywhere.

ISBN: 0-523-00974-7

First printing, September 1976

Printed in the United States of America

PINNACLE BOOKS, INC.
275 Madison Avenue
New York, N.Y. 10016

THE CHINESE ULTIMATUM

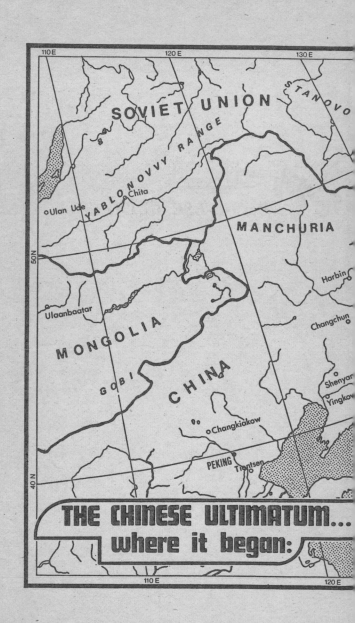

THE CHINESE ULTIMATUM...
where it began:

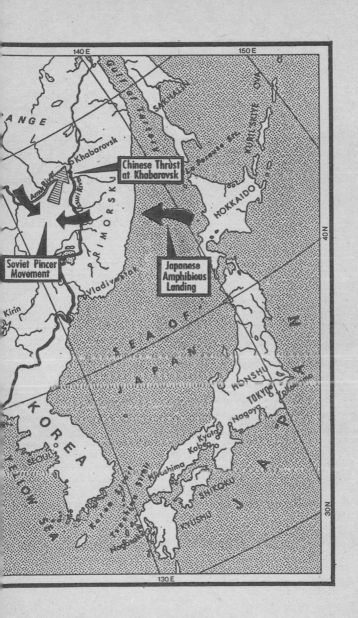

1

Jacques instinctively braced himself as the president's foreign affairs advisor entered the restaurant. He motioned toward the small corridor facing the cloak room where favored clients were brought in ahead of those waiting patiently at the red plush barrier to dine in the company of the capital's great. Alec Thompson slipped through the door into the main dining room and was led to one of the eight tables overlooking Lafayette Park and the White House. It was generally argued that this was the finest view in Washington and almost made up for the destruction of the quietly charming old hotel torn down a few years before. The new Hay Adams, a chunk of red brick neo-Federal architecture topped by the glass façade of the Brasserie Lorraine, squatted on the site like an oversized transparent outhouse.

"You're late, Mr. Thompson," Jacques said, an ever-so-slight edge in his voice.

"I know I am, Jacques. You should have given the table to someone else," Thompson said, smiling at the little Frenchman.

Jacques and his partner, Athène Sauvignon, had been in Washington for twenty years working in the shifting sands of the capital's fashionable French restaurants before founding the Brasserie. They had opened the restaurant with the arrival of the present administration, now seven years old; and their success was assured when the new chief executive's staff, led by Presidential Counselor for Foreign Affairs Alec Thompson, had gravitated to it. Now, on any given day, the eight tables facing the park would be occupied by the great and the near great of the capital. By unspoken accord, his table, the third from the corner, was held until one o'clock every day, at which point it was assumed he would not arrive. It was one-ten now, but Jacques had held the table, anyway, probably because his secretary had surreptitiously called.

Thompson threaded his way through the tables exchanging greetings with senators, congressmen, cabinet members, lobbyists, lawyers, and newspapermen. For more than six years he had held a job at the very vortex of power. With this power came such intangible perquisites as a table at the Brasserie, a chauffeured limousine, flights in the sleek presidential jet, and, last but not least, the attentions of beautiful women attracted to what one of his predecessors had described as the aphrodisiac of power.

You paid for that power, of course—in sixteen-hour days, stomach linings, shattered marriages, heart attacks, Byzantine intrigue, and brutal ruthlessness. Some men left the job broken and shattered. Others, the ones with iron nerves and a kind of amoral cynicism that insulated them against pain, survived to

2

become elder statesmen. But all lived under the same daily tension, the knowledge that their power depended totally on the whim of the man in the great white mansion across the park. They were twentieth-century courtiers and grand viziers of foreign affairs with no constituency and a tenure that lasted only as long as their usefulness.

Thompson and Jacques understood each other. It was a symbiotic relationship of exquisite balance. By suffering a calculable financial loss in holding a table empty for him, the restaurateur confirmed his importance in incalculable ways in the eyes of every other powerful man in the restaurant. By habitually eating at the Brasserie, Alec Thompson conferred on the restaurant the priceless cachet that meant the difference between its being the capital's indispensable eatery and just another good French restaurant where the chef seldom made a decent Béchamel.

"I'm expecting Miss Wilson, Jacques," Thompson said as the waiter, unasked, placed a pale glass of manzanilla in front of him.

"She's here, *monsieur*," the Frenchman said, glancing across the restaurant toward a table where a striking blonde was talking intently with Sam Cassidy, editor of the *Washington Herald*, and Dan Crane, the paper's diplomatic correspondent. Crane, a tall, slender man with a mane of prematurely graying hair and a boyish face, had just returned from the Soviet Union, where he had interviewed the Soviet premier. It was his third such interview in five years, and each time the Soviet leader had used it to float a new policy balloon. There wasn't much doubt in Thompson's mind what Crane would be writing for tomorrow's paper, and the thought of it made him wish for a martini instead of the manzanilla.

Suzanne glanced over her shoulder and waved be-

3

fore turning back to the conversation. Either Crane was telling her something, or she was letting everybody in the room know that she could keep Alec Thompson waiting. The games bored him these days, although he played them reflexively. He hadn't done it well in the beginning. The little tricks had come hard: holding the file in such a way that the man you were handing it to had to reach for it; arranging for the chair in front of your desk to be so low that anyone sitting there would be looking up; all the business with doors and cigarettes; and the protocol of cars, telephones, seating, and rooms. It was all childish and ultimately senseless. You didn't grab the brass ring riding on tricks. It took brains, guts, and ruthlessness—the willingness to go the last mile, the last yard further than the next guy, to put him to the wall and watch him break. Smiling all the while.

He motioned to the waiter and ordered lunch as Suzanne materialized. He stood up. "Hello, darling," she said, kissing him lightly on the cheek, the merest hint of expensive perfume enveloping him. "Did I keep you waiting?"

"I don't mind. But you cost Jacques about ten dollars a minute. Have you ordered?"

She shook her head, glancing up at the patient waiter and saying in exquisite French, "Just a salad of some sort, Michel. You know what I like. And bring us a bottle of the Pouligny Montrachet. The '78. Not too cold."

The waiter stopped, pen poised, and turned to Thompson, eyebrows raised. "It's all right, Michel," Thompson said.

Suzanne giggled. "Oh, shit, Michel," she said. "Have I gone and violated your Latin mores again?"

The waiter did not smile as he collected the menus. "No, *madame*. But *monsieur* is having steak."

4

Suzanne looked at him across the table, her green eyes searching his face. "You never really let the non-essentials bother you, do you, Alec? You just don't give a damn what you drink, since you won't drink much, anyway. And it doesn't make any difference at all that I might have diminished you in the waiter's eyes." The smile slipped away from her face. "And you don't really much care what I think, either, do you, darling?"

"What did Crane have to say?" he said, ignoring the question.

"To me? A Federal Broadcasting commentator? Are you kidding? He's got something big, though. I could feel it. He and Sam were sitting there grinning from ear to ear. Old whoosits in Moscow must have planted another one of his bombs. Dan says he talked to him for three hours, most of it off the record. Even got one of those Kremlin lunches. What's up, darling? You must know. You're on the phone with them every day. There are rumors, you know. It's all over town. There was a meeting between the Russians and Chinese at some town on the border." She snapped her fingers impatiently.

"Svobodny," Thompson said, finishing the last of the Spanish wine, feeling its cool dryness shrivel the edges of his tongue. He wished she hadn't ordered the Pouligny. It would taste like toilet water after the manzanilla.

"So it's true," she said, surprised at his telling her.

"It came over the AP ticker about ten minutes ago."

"You bastard," she said affectionately. "I should have known you never let anything slip." She reached a long, slender hand across the table and laid it on his, playing with the wiry black hair on his wrist. He met her green eyes, accented by eye shadow, and

5

was surprised to note the beginning of tiny crow's feet at the corners. She must have been up late last night, he thought, wondering with whom, pushing the thought out of his mind.

"Are you very busy, darling?"

"No."

"Am I going to see you tonight?"

"I'll let you know. If there is anything to this Sino-Soviet meeting, I may not be able to get away," he lied. On his desk was a Russian-language Telex from Moscow giving the transcript of the meeting. Relays of translators were putting it into English at the National Security Board translation service, but a quick glance at the original had told him all he needed to know.

"Call me after the seven o'clock show," she said. "I'm going to Senator Clarence's house for dinner. Joan says she'll set an extra place for you if you can get away." It happened all the time. He and Suzanne Wilson had been sleeping together for a year now. More or less automatically, when she accepted an invitation, she asked if Thompson could also come. He almost never did. In the second year of the president's first term, he had begun to turn down all invitations except from old friends or people essential to the smooth functioning of presidential foreign policy. It saved his energy and time, and it avoided alienating the capital's powerful.

"If I can't, I'll see you at home."

Before she could answer, Outerbridge Dean sauntered over, breaking an unwritten rule at the Brasserie, and leaned on their table. "I've got to see you, Alec. Jan has picked up something over at State that is dynamite." Thompson motioned for a chair. He liked Dean, who, at sixty, was one of the most astute journalists in Washington. He and his paunchy partner, Jan Kempka, were a startling contrast in styles:

Dean, Ivy League, smooth, low-keyed, and graceful; Kempka, a greasy, rude, unpleasant bully who was probably the most effective investigative reporter in town.

Thompson suspected Kempka had a line somewhere into the National Security Board's Eastern European setup, a disgruntled code clerk or a junior officer passed over for promotion. He had long since given up hope of keeping anything secret that more than three people had access to. The president himself was one of the worst offenders.

Dean looked at Suzanne Wilson. "Okay, okay. I've got to go to the john. But don't take too long."

"What is it, Kip?" Dean's middle name was Kipling, given him by an eccentric father.

Dean leaned forward in his usual conspiratorial pose, his almost hairless skull speckled with freckles. "There's been a meeting between the Chinese and Russians at Svobodny on the Siberian border. Something really big is going on. I've heard the Russians are mobilizing. What's up, Alec?"

Thompson sipped the Pouligny Montrachet and filled a glass for Dean. "I don't know anymore than you do, Kip. The part about the Russians mobilizing sounds a little farfetched. Hell, they've got two million men in place in Siberia right now. They can't supply anymore than that, not even with the new rail line. Why would they mobilize?" Thompson knew Dean was fishing, but he was one of the three most powerful journalists in Washington. He had to be handled with exquisite care. He never betrayed a confidence, and he never held a grudge. But if you screwed him, he paid it back when the chance came, dispassionately and with a certain sly relish. Thompson tried not to lie to him, and occasionally he would

7

throw an exclusive his way. In return he sometimes got a notice of an impending attack on the president, for which they could prepare.

Dean shook his head impatiently. "Cut the crap, Alec. I know you can't tell me what's going on. All I want to know is this: Is is really big? If it is, we'll gear up for it. If it isn't, we'll quit wasting our time."

Thompson answered without a moment's apparent thought, lying easily, watching his pulse and respiration rate with inner amusement. "Kip, I'd tell you if I knew. We're supposed to get something from Moscow on it sometime today. They're not giving us the full dope on this one. My own feeling is that it was some sort of procedural meeting at most. If it was important, Evgeny would have been there, and he was in Moscow yesterday."

Evgeny Nabokov was a Russian Politburo member and minister of foreign affairs. The press had taken to calling him Thompson's counterpart in Moscow. He wasn't, but Thompson was happy to have the idea accepted by the world press. The man he dealt with was both more intelligent and more dangerous than the old diplomatic hack who was serving out his time on the Politburo as a figurehead for Soviet diplomacy.

Dean didn't believe him. "So you don't think there is anything in it?"

Thompson shrugged. "Sure. There's always something to it. Any time they sit down and talk, it's important. Hell, Kip, they've had three major outbreaks since 1975. We hear the Russians lost fifty thousand men in that battle near Aihui last summer. God knows what the Chinese losses were. Maybe they're trying to avoid another slanging match."

"Fifty thousand men? Dead?" Dean was surprised. This was the first time anybody had come up with a figure even approaching this for the series of actions along the Siberian border the previous summer. "Can I use that?"

Thompson looked grave. "Look, Kip, I don't know that it's true. It's an estimate. I let it slip. You know my personal rules. You squeeze something out of me when we're not on deep background, and it's yours. But I'd rather you didn't print this. Not now. In two weeks, without attribution. Okay?"

Dean bought it. It sounded sincere. Thompson was human. He made mistakes. He was a good man. Under lots of pressure. And, anyway, it wasn't much of a story by itself. Using it as a lever, Kempka might be able to get more. "Okay. I'll hold it," Dean said, getting up and raising the glass of pale wine to Suzanne Wilson as she came up to the table. "To the prettiest competitor in the business," he said, bowing low.

Suzanne picked up her glass and touched his. "To a man who knows a bitch when he sees one," she said. Dean cackled and drained his glass, then departed.

"What did he want?" Suzanne asked.

"Same thing you do—a pipeline into the president's mind."

She shook her head. "I wouldn't come to you for that."

"Meaning the way to a man's mind is through his crotch, I suppose?"

Her green eyes sharpened and he instantly regretted the crack. She knew him too well. When he let the razor show, it was because his famous control was slipping just a touch. He wondered if his nerve was beginning to go a little. Six years in this job was a long time. He'd noticed recently that, late at night, he was having trouble bringing his mind up to the fine edge of concentration. And he sometimes caught

9

himself not listening. That was bad. You had to listen, even to the fools. When you quit listening, you lost touch with reality and began to live in that dangerous intellectual world of logic and reason unleavened by stupidity and irrationality. That was what happened to Henry in the end.

"Alec, your hand is trembling."

He glanced down at the wine glass, moving almost imperceptibly in his hand, and restrained himself from stopping it. "It always trembles, darling, especially when I'm with you."

"You need a vacation. Why don't we take off and go down to that new hotel in Cuba everybody is talking about? I hear it's glorious. Some New York gangster is running the casino, and it's supposed to be just like Chicago in the 1920s."

"Harry Taliaferro," he said absently.

"You know him?" She was surprised. Since she'd known him, he'd seemed interested in only one thing other than work.

"I served in Vietnam with him."

"Of course. I'd forgotten. You were some sort of exotic spook, weren't you? What did you do there, Alec?"

"Assassinated Vietcong leaders," Thompson said, regarding the steak in front of him with disinterest. Harry Taliaferro was the agency's covert man in Havana, one of the best in the business. It had taken half a decade to build his cover.

"Mr. Thompson," the waiter said, holding a telephone that was plugged into a wall circuit two tables down, "the White House."

"Yes. What is it, Lucy?" His secretary's voice was packed in ice, modulated to a pitch so calm that he realized she must be on the verge of hysterics.

"The boss wants you right now."

10

"Thanks, Lucy. It can wait." He hung up and dug into his steak, eating slowly, hands not trembling now.

"You've got to go, haven't you?"

He grinned at her over the wine glass. "Yes. But I'll see you tonight, crisis or no crisis."

Dimitri Stashevsky lit his fiftieth Marlboro of the day and glanced once more at his watch. It was two P.M. in Washington. They would have the message translated by now, and the president and Alec would be meeting. The combined chiefs of staff would have been alerted. The CIA, the Department of State, and the National Security Board staff would be preparing assessments. The whole cumbersome machinery of the American government would be focusing its computers, its committees, and its brains in order to present them with options. None of this meant anything, of course. Alec already knew what the options were; the machinery would simply confirm them. He would have seen to that. Bureaucracies give power the answers it wants.

Stashevsky leaned back in his deep leather swivel chair, a relic of his father's days at the Soviet embassy in Washington, and stared across the room at the blown-up photograph of his American opposite number. The question was which option Thompson would back.

Stashevsky opened the folder updated that morning by the most recent intelligence reports and leafed through the biographical data on the presidential counselor for foreign affairs.

Born 1931, Madison, Georgia. Graduated University of North Carolina, 1951, majored in international relations. ROTC. Marine infantry lieutenant, Korea, 1951–54. Participant, battle of

11

Chongsan Reservoir. Silver Star. 1954–55, Paris Ecole Libre des Sciences Politiques. 1955–57, Guggenheim Fellow, University of Vienna. Doctoral thesis on Frederick the Great, published by Columbia as "Buntzelwitz, the Turning Point." 1957–59, Department of Soviet studies, Columbia University. Published in 1959 "Bismarck and the Russians: 1876–1890." 1959, recruited by CIA, assistant station chief, Soviet Union, 1959–63. 1963, posted to Vietnam. 1964–66, chief, Third Special Severance (Assassination) Team. Resigned 1966, accepted post of assistant professor of Soviet studies, Princeton University. 1967, published "Vietnam: Rape of American Liberalism." 1969, associate professor with tenure. Published "A Foreign Policy for the 1970s." 1971, full professor. 1974, published "Detente and Its Aftermath." 1976, special presidential assistant for international relations.

Stashevsky smiled as he read a summary of conversations tapped with a bug placed in Suzanne Wilson's bedroom. Thompson showed near genius in leaking only the information that would polish the administration's image. And his own. He did not, the Russian noted with mild regret, show much erotic imagination.

Stashevsky let the folder close on a list of publications that had skillfully attacked the Nixon-Kissinger foreign policy of the '70s while offering alternatives that had gradually been implemented when a new president took office in 1977. It was, Stashevsky had long since decided, a brilliant foreign policy. Tactically astute, strategically impeccable, it defined U.S. interests in terms of minimum and optimum attainable goals, and it was sufficiently flexible to react to the unexpected with speed and imagination. After a crisis was resolved or defused, Thompson, with patience and a fierce force of will, once again would attempt to bend events to his country's advantage. He could compromise, and he could be brutal, cold, ruthlessly sacrificing traditional friends and alliances under the cover of pious hypocrisy, all in the pursuit of a national self-interest conceived in the broadest and most subtle terms.

If Thompson alone were making the decision today, Stashevsky could be confident that his assessment of likely U.S. actions in the next three days was accurate. He had talked with the American for hundreds of hours over the past six years. Each had read every word the other had ever written. Each knew the other's personal life and peccadilloes in stupefying detail, due to the incredible ability of both countries' intelligence organizations to collect prurient trivia.

And, given what he knew, Stashevsky was sure that the decision would be favorable to the Soviet Union if Thompson had the final voice. But there had been rumors, slivers of information, hints, that after winning the election overwhelmingly, the president had decided to take his foreign policy out of the hands of his counselor for foreign affairs and conduct it himself. Perhaps Thompson had let his tact slip, had allowed that note of deference essential to any courtier to atrophy over the years. Power, or the appearance of it, is the fertilizer of arrogance. He might have forgotten, for a split second here and there, that he had no real power, that his influence was only an extension of the president's and could be used only by exercising the most subtle intellectual dominance. The job took nerve, shrewdness, and a penchant for self-abnegation rare in a man of such intelligence. Stashevsky lit his fifty-first cigarette and glanced compulsively at his watch. There could be no decision for hours. Washington could not be prodded.

13

He moved across the room to a refrigerator and bar concealed as a wooden bookcase and took out a bottle of chilled Polish vodka, filled a small glass, and knocked it back, savoring the sudden artificial warmth at the back of his throat. He was drinking too much. He had been for months. The pressure had been building all around him. The old man was leaning on him more and more, which was good as long as he was right. But one major mistake could ruin him. Not like in Stalin's time, with death or a labor camp. Those days were past, thank God. No. But something almost as bad. A minor post in the embassy in Albania. Trade delegate to the Central African federation. Ambassador to Somalia. Stashevsky grimaced and filled the glass again, looking down on the stream of cars on the wide boulevard below. As he watched, a big Mercedes turned in a circle at the point reserved for official cars and cut through traffic, coming to a stop at the foreign ministry door.

The German ambassador had been called in to meet with the foreign minister. In a few hours the whole world was going to know. Already the foreign press office was clogged with inquiries about the meeting at Svobodny. Washington and Bonn were both notorious sieves where secret information was concerned. Borsov had told him recently that he had a source on the National Security Board and four more at a level just below it. Borsov was a liar and a braggart, but there was no question that the KGB's information had been uncannily accurate lately. Stashevsky went over the eleven members of the board, idly wondering which one it was. Borsov would never tell him, of course, and he would not ask.

The door opened and Nadia entered as he filled the small glass once again, replacing the bottle in the miniature refrigerator, a gift from the French foreign

14

minister during an official visit of the president two years before. He looked at his secretary with frank lust. God, he thought again, what a glorious creature. Even after a year of taking her whenever the mood was upon him, his groin shriveled at the sight of her. Borsov maintained it was only his peasant snobbery, because she was the granddaughter of a Czarist general. A skinny nothing, he said. But Borsov did not know.

"Yes?"

"There is a telephone call from Washington, from Thompson."

Lieu Shen sat contemplating the modest spray of flowers on his desk, a gift from his staff. It was his birthday today, April 22. He was seventy. An old man and very tired. Very soon now he would have to leave this office and retire to the small house in the mountains near Kunming to die. He had selected the house five years ago before the death of his wife, expecting to spend a few years of peace and quiet there with an occasional visit from his children, then to die the gentle death of old age, reading Confucius and listening to his beloved Haydn.

Shen's leathery face creased in a wry smile. What was that marvelous American expression: "There is no fool like an old fool!" And the other: "Those who live by the sword die by it." Not exactly Confucian in profundity, but in philosophy, as in all things, Americans were eminently practical. The Chinese persisted in pretending that age was a time of wisdom when it was, in reality, a time of fear and paralysis of will, an ebbing of strength not only in the loins but in the withered remnants of the mind.

The pain came in slow waves, stabbing at his stomach, bending him over the massive teak desk until

15

his forehead almost touched it. He fought it for a full minute, counting off the seconds as perspiration splotched his forehead. Then he fumbled in the pocket of his uniform for the pill and waited for the relief. The pill was a miracle. It worked almost instantly, attacking the nerve centers that controlled the pain reaction, leaving only a dull ache where once there had been a tearing, ripping pain. But it also affected other things, veiling his mind in a mist of languid disinterest, forcing a major effort of will to face the task at hand.

For the next few days he was going to need all his will, all his concentration. For they were about to gamble everything they had won with so much blood, sacrifice, and hard work on the weakness and indecision of their enemies. He and Teng had made the plan fifteen years before, and, with that infinite patience that the Occidentals so justly attributed to them, they had played their game of diplomatic "Go" until it had reached the crucial point. If their analyses of their opponents were accurate, a massive victory would be theirs, altering the course of human history, restoring China to its preeminence among nations and wiping out the humiliations of two hundred years. But he would have to make the last few moves alone. Teng had suddenly grown very old and fragile, and his fine sharp mind now sometimes clouded over at crucial times.

Lieu touched a bell on his desk and waited for the tea to come. It was one of his few luxuries, the rare Theezan tea. That and his passion for calligraphy. Even during the worst times of the cultural revolution, Teng, who had not been able to protect him, had seen to it that the tea arrived at the commune. The tea and the books he needed to continue his work. The young fools who had imprisoned and humiliated him had also indulged him. After all, the old man had been a hero of the revolution. He had fallen into error, but he had repented, abjectly, on his knees in front of them, his forehead touching the ground. Let him play with his books, they had said.

When the soldiers came to free him, they brought a small box from Teng. In it was his old Luger from the war days. Lieu had leaned back in the chair, sipping the tea. He had held the gun and looked at his young former captors, feeling the sweet taste of vengeance, smelling the sour odor of their terror. How many had he killed with that gun in the days when death had been as common as spring rain? Two dozen? Three dozen? But always for the revolution. Never for personal vengeance. The young had been puzzled when he spared them, thinking him sentimental and weak. Perhaps when they were old they would understand.

But he must not reminisce. It was an old man's weakness. It distracted him. He glanced at the antique clock on the wall. The Telex from Washington would soon begin to chatter, and they would know whether they had won the first crucial part of the gamble.

2

"And now Suzanne Wilson with today's news." Thompson swiveled in his chair and turned up the volume as Suzanne's face appeared on the center tube, flanked by the commentators from the other two networks. He had long since learned to listen selectively and quickly concentrated on Suzanne.

"Good evening. The Soviet Union and China were on the verge of war tonight. Following the failure of their talks at the obscure little Siberian border town of Svobodny, armed skirmishes between units of the Chinese Twelfth Army and the Soviet Fifth Corps escalated to the level of a major battle today, with both sides acknowledging casualties in the hundreds before the engagement was broken off. Chinese units are continuing to probe the Soviet defenses along the entire seven-thousand-kilometer frontier with heavy concentrations of troops along the Ussuri and Amur rivers.

"Soviet commanders have massed defensive forces at critical points on the Chinese border at the expense of strategic reserves normally stationed near Leningrad, Kiev, Moscow, and in the Caucasus. Reliable reports from Berlin, Prague, Warsaw, Bucharest, Sofia, and Budapest indicate that significant withdrawals of Soviet occupation forces have reduced garrisons to skeleton levels. The Soviet general staff is reportedly demanding immediate general mobilization. German sources close to the BND, the West German CIA, report that a meeting of the Warsaw Pact countries is scheduled in Moscow tomorrow. The Soviet Union is rumored ready to demand troops and other military aid from its allies.

"With the military situation reaching crisis proportions, the general secretary of the Soviet Communist Party, Alexei Kharkov, has requested Secretary General José Lerin to seek an urgent summit meeting with Chinese Foreign Minister Lieu Shen on neutral territory.

"The Chinese leader has refused to negotiate without prior Soviet acceptance in principle of border rectification. Kharkov has refused. For an analysis of the roots of the conflict, the Federal Broadcasting System brings you Willoughby C. Pepperdine."

Thompson frowned as the seamed and weathered visage of the former Harvard political scientist appeared on the tube. Pepperdine had appeared on a network panel show a few years back and left his opponents in shreds. The Federal Broadcasting System had taken him on as an occasional commentator, and he had soon eliminated his competitors with a combination of Machiavellian guile and a ruthlessness so total that even in the television jungle he was regarded as unique. For the past several years he had

19

attacked administration foreign policy with an informed brutality that enraged the president.

"Good evening," Pepperdine began in a voice like a rusty razor blade. "The core of the Sino-Soviet conflict is land—millions of square miles of land in Siberia. Beginning in the late 1950s, the Chinese have repeatedly demanded that the Soviet Union return to them large chunks of Siberia that they ceded to Russia during the nineteenth century when the old Chinese empire was breaking up. These demands became more strident in the 1960s and resulted in several armed outbreaks along the Ussuri and Amur rivers.

"Since then the Chinese have periodically restated their demands, only to have them rejected by the Soviet Union. In the late 1960s and early 1970s, a faction in the Soviet military is reliably reported to have urged a preventative military strike against the Chinese nuclear facilities at Lok Nor to prevent their developing an offensive nuclear capacity.

"In 1975 a serious border incident took place near the Siberian town of Obluchye. Accurate, unbiased information on the incident is not available; however, it is believed that five divisions of Chinese troops overran an undermanned Soviet outpost and killed more than a thousand Russian troops before being driven back. Again in 1976 a similar outbreak occurred on the Ussuri River near Vyazemski, where a pitched battle between Soviet and Chinese army groups raged for five days before both sides withdrew.

"The most serious incident occurred last summer near the town of Aihui. Again it is wrapped in secrecy, but American intelligence has reason to believe that more than fifty thousand casualties occurred on both sides.

"At present there are reported to be five million

Chinese troops massed along the seven-thousand-kilometer border facing two million Russian soldiers. It is an explosive situation complicated by the fact that both sides possess nuclear weapons capable of totally destroying the other's heartland. American military strategists believe this will limit any conflict to conventional warfare in which, they point out, the superior Soviet firepower and mobility would be offset by the immense Chinese manpower resources and closeness to their bases of supply. Soviet supplies must move along the single-track trans-Siberian railroad or by air transport. The new northern line will have little effect, since it ties into the rail bottleneck farther west. Western military experts do not believe the Soviet transport system could support a sustained campaign lasting throughout the summer.

"The Russian dilemma is acute, and the Chinese are undoubtedly using every pressure point to force territorial concessions in Siberia. Specialists in Chinese affairs are divided over how serious the Chinese threat is. Professor William Chalmers of Harvard persists in believing that the Chinese strategy is to keep up maximum psychological pressure on the Soviet Union, moving from one position of tactical and strategic advantage to another until the weight of its superiority becomes so overwhelming, as in the famous Chinese game of 'Go,' that the enemy finds himself surrounded and forced to surrender. Professor Chalmers points out that this is the classic form that Chinese warfare has taken in the past. He does not believe even a limited war is likely at this time.

"There are others who are not so sure. They think that there is a more profound purpose behind the Chinese strategy of the last twenty years. According to this school of thought, led by the Morgan Institute's Charles Weaver, China is seeking to regain its ancient position as the major world power, first among equals. To do this it must first break the will of one of its major opponents and humble it. The obvious choice, according to Weaver, is the Soviet Union, which is also the major immediate danger to China. According to this line of reasoning, a humbled Russia would leave the Chinese free to confront the United States without fearing for its rear.

"Weaver points out that the recent economic integration treaty with Japan makes the two Asian powers, together with Indonesia and their other Southeast Asian dependencies, the second largest economic power grouping in the world after the North Atlantic community. All evidence now points to an ever closer cohesion between the new Marxian Socialist regime in Japan and China, a classic example of economic symbiosis leading to political integration.

"If Professor Weaver's analysis is correct, the United States is faced with perhaps the most important decision in its history tonight, for both the contending Communist powers must be looking to us for support. The decision our leaders make, if the situation in the Far East is as serious as it now appears, could decide the fate of the world for several centuries.

"Thank you and good night."

Suzanne Wilson replaced Pepperdine on the screen in a transition the trade had labeled "Beauty and the Beast." "Thank you, Willoughby. And now to our correspondent in Vienna, Bill Jackson."

"Good evening. News of a new crisis between China and the Soviet Union has overshadowed all other events in Eastern Europe this evening. However, recent reports of growing unrest in Polish coal-mining areas following this month's increases in food prices continues to arrive in Vienna. Polish Communist Party First Secretary Georg Wozniakowski is reported to have met with leaders of the dissident miners in Katowice for four hours today. There are also reports of Polish army units . . ."

Thompson touched a button on his desk, shutting off the set. He picked up the phone and punched a direct line. "Jim?"

"Yes?"

"Does CIA have anything on this business in Poland?"

"Just that the miners are really pissed off this time. There hasn't been any pork in the stores since Easter, and there's another coffee shortage. Some dummy in the Ministry of Trade misordered for the spring quarter, and they've practically run out of coffee."

"What does State think? Who's our ambassador there? Sanderson?"

"Yeah. You know him? He's one of those elegantly tailored nonentities State turns out these days. All his reports keep saying it's nothing serious and will go away once the next load of Danish pork comes in."

Thompson drummed on the desk with his fingers. He was waiting for an opinion. "What do you think, Jim?"

It always amused him to feel the tension build up in his staff when they had to go on record. He had picked the best he could find from the spooks, State, the universities, and the military. But they all had the same training and outlook. You staffed it all out, you set up the options—and you let somebody else bite the bullet. Jim Holland cleared his throat.

"Well, on balance, I'd say they'll keep it under control. Wozniakowski will probably give them a raise, and the Danish meat shipment should start arriving any day."

"Okay, Jim. But stay on top of it. The Russians are going to be very uptight at any problems developing in their rear right now." He glanced at his watch. General Phillip Samsun, chief of military intelligence, was briefing the National Security Board and the president on the Siberian military situation. There was nothing new. They had all heard it half a dozen times. The briefing was simply an excuse to avoid coming to grips with the problem.

When he entered the conference room, Samsun was summing up. He was a brilliant off-the-cuff speaker with a phenomenal memory and a superb gift for instant synthesis. Listening to him, you became hypnotized with the elegant mathematical logic of his presentations.

"So, gentlemen, we feel the situation is in delicate military balance, and that an all-out conventional war would result in a stalemate over the short term."

"Define 'short term,' Phil," the secretary of state requested.

Samsun replied instantly, which was one of the reasons Thompson distrusted him. "Five months. Until winter paralyzes any possible offensive action by either side."

The chief of the Joint Chiefs of Staff, a tough old four-star general who began his career leading platoon action in North Africa in 1942, looked up from a collection of medieval forts he had doodled on the lined yellow pad lying in front of him. "Phil, I think you're full of shit," he said in a deep Southern accent.

The president slumped deeper in his big chair at the head of the table, covered his mouth with one hand, caught Thompson's eye, and grinned. General Craig Pruitt had a faculty for reducing interminable sessions of the National Security Board to a one-word scatological summation.

Samsun had stiffened to attention, his elegant profile white with rage. "Sir?"

"You don't know what the hell is going to happen," Pruitt said, waving toward the charts lined in neat arrays across the briefing wall. "Nobody's fought a major war over that terrain since the Han dynasty. Neither of these armies has ever been in battle. The Russian generals were all shavetail lieutenants in World War Two, and the Chinese fought with pick handles. There isn't a man on either side who has handled as much as a division in combat, except for a couple of skirmishes. Their logistics are almost certainly all fucked up. There is an immense amount of sophisticated weaponry on both sides in the hands of soldiers who have hardly ever had a chance to use it because it's too damned expensive to practice with." He shook his head.

"There is one thing we'd better keep in mind, however. If the Chinese lose a major action, they just split up in small groups and fade back into the interior, leaving the weapons behind. There they can regroup in the heartland and go back into action. If the Russians lose, they've got two thousand miles of forest and steppes full of basically hostile subject peoples across their line of retreat. And resupply is one hell of a lot harder for them, first because they need five men to keep one in the field, whereas the Chinese can do it with two, and second, because they're three times as far from their supply center.

"The fact is, Phil, this is a new kind of war. And every time a new kind of war has been fought, the experts were full of crap, especially military intelligence and the generals. I think we'd better take into account the asshole variable here."

"What's the asshole variable, General?" the president asked, grinning openly now.

"It's when you get everything planned down to the
25

last paper clip and you can't lose. And then some asshole screws it all up."

The president nodded. "What you're saying is we'd better take into account the possibility of one side winning big." His voice was deep and resonant, impacted with a kind of animal force and vitality which, as Suzanne Wilson once described it to Thompson, oozed semen. "We've done that around this table a hundred times in the past five years. And, unless somebody has come up with a better answer, we decided each time that we had no self-interest in either China or the Soviet Union gaining a preponderance of power over the other. Does anybody want to debate that one again?"

Thompson had dropped into a chair on the president's left, and he now leaned over and gave him a quick sotto-voce rundown on the evening television news shows. The president nodded, listening with half an ear to Gordon Wiseman, the CIA director.

"Mr. President, I don't think the problem is who is going to win a war, but whether there is going to be one. This is the seventh time in the last twenty years the Chinese have precipitated a crisis. Each time, they have pushed a little harder, gone one step further toward the brink, and each time they have pulled back. Before we get involved or even consider it, it seems to me we've first got to decide how serious they are. If it's another bluff, another square in an elaborate game of 'Go' being enclosed, then it seems to me we'd be better off staying out of it altogether."

Wiseman was another glib one, Thompson thought. He marshaled his thinking in neat little Cartesian syllogisms, and unless you could cut the legs out from under him on a basic premise, he'd slice you into salami.

"Okay, Gordon," the president said, always patient,

"We've been over all this. Are you people prepared to say flatly that there isn't going to be a war, that the Chinese are just clawing the Russians a little, drawing a little blood covering one or more psychological square, as you call it? Can you guarantee me that? The Russian minutes of the Svobodny meeting are pretty categorical. They have made specific territorial demands and implied they will attack if the Russians don't give them satisfaction. You think it's a bluff, but can you guarantee it? If you can, I'll go play poker up on the hill with a clear conscience."

Wiseman didn't squirm. They were all used to being nailed to the wall by the president, whose one great talent was in cutting through the verbiage to the heart of a problem. He didn't expect an answer, and if Wiseman had given him one, he would have raised his thick black jutting eyebrows in surprise. Meetings of the National Security Board were not the place for serious decisions to be made. They were only useful as open sparring matches where good minds threw up ideas, solutions, questions that other good minds could attack, support, or probe. If Wiseman knew something, he goddamned well knew better than to wait for an open meeting to tell the president.

"No. I can't guarantee anything. But based on what we've got, I don't think they'll fight. Oh, maybe a heavy skirmish like last summer, but nothing . . ."

Craig Pruitt's voice exploded. "Heavy skirmish? Fifty thousand Russians and Chinese got buried after that 'skirmish.' Do you realize there are only nine other battles in history where fifty thousand men died?"

Wiseman shrugged. "Thermopylae was a company-sized action, Craig," he said gently, "But it was more important than the battle of the Marne."

27

Pruitt subsided. He knew better than to take on Wiseman in a battle of historical analogies. The man's mind was a fucking computer.

The president looked around the room, waiting for somebody else to speak. Nobody did. "Well, gentlemen, we're back to square one. There is a bomb lying here in front of us ticking away. The chairman has every right to a reply. We've got twenty-four hours. I'm going to have Alec get on the hot line to Stashevsky. Meantime, I want every one of you gentlemen to take one more hard look at the situation. If you come up with any new ideas, have them into Alec's office in writing by eight o'clock tomorrow morning. I think we all know what we've got to do, but I want to sleep on it. There's always a possibility we can sit tight, as Gordon suggests, and not get ourselves committed. As of right now, however, it looks as if we're going to have to take a stand." He got up, a big, powerful man who exuded confidence and controlled masculinity. "Come on, Alec, let's talk."

The president stripped off his coat and threw it over a sofa in the big Oval Office. He dropped into his heavy leather chair and propped his feet up on a desk that had once belonged to Andrew Jackson. He held a sheet of bond paper in one big hand and read it once again, half-moon reading glasses perched low on his nose.

"Let's go over the options, Alec. First, there's Gordon's. Do nothing. Let them sweat and hope they both back off." He looked up over the half rims, blue eyes quiet and speculative. "You don't like it, do you?"

Thompson shrugged. "He could be right. It could be just another tough bluff. Chou and Lieu have done it before, although Gordon's figure of seven crises is phony. I agree that this is just one more move in a policy they've been developing for twenty years or more. We can follow the broad outlines with no trouble at all. Put more and more pressure on the Soviets, economic and political as well as military, until they're willing to make at least some territorial concessions. The question at issue here is, where are we? Just another turn of the wrench, or the final crunch?"

"And you think it's the crunch?"

"A crunch. I'm not sure there is a *the* crunch in the Chinese political lexicon. Our reading of Chou and Lieu is that they're immensely subtle, cautious old men who believe patience combined with nerve and a willingness to go to the brink time after time will eventually soften up the opposition's willpower and lead to victory. But they're both capable of putting up with momentary humiliations and major loss of prestige when they think it's to their advantage to back off. You're just not dealing with the Western mentality where, at some point or other, a leader's balls swell and machismo overtakes judgment." He paused. "All this kind of reasoning is dangerous as hell, of course. I don't for a minute think any of our analysts have gotten inside Lieu's head. Let's not even talk about Chou, who is as wily as a snake."

The president grinned at him. "You're pretty greasy yourself on this one, Alec. Where are those crisp, decisive recommendations you always give me?"

"Keep reading, Mr. President."

"The Soviet option," the president read aloud, "The Soviet Union has requested us to bring all possible pressure to bear on China to avoid an armed conflict. If a serious conflict breaks out, the U.S. should stand ready to tell the Chinese that it would participate in a Soviet-American naval blockade of Chinese and Japanese ports to shut off the oil supply."

The president grimaced in distaste. "That's decisive

29

enough, all right. But I'm not sure it's an option at all. The entire NSB is against it, especially the military. Nobody can see our interest in maintaining stability and the status quo drawing us into a Sino-Soviet war, especially with the Japanese ready to come in. It could escalate out of control."

"So could a prolonged Siberian war. If I thought the threat of a naval blockade wasn't enough to stop the whole business, I wouldn't even have suggested it," Thompson said.

"I know, I know," the president said, his big voice muted. "I've read the Weaver thesis that it's all a game of 'Go,' too. But it's an immense risk. After all, they've got a ninety-day supply of oil. Before that's exhausted, the issue could be decided."

"There's a third option," Thompson said, his voice tight.

"Yeah, I know," the president said, flipping the paper back onto the desk. "If we make the assumption that the Chinese really mean it, let them fight it out and weaken each other. Then, after they're exhausted, we offer to mediate. It's theoretically brilliant, but it's also dangerous as hell. What if one of them wins big? We've then got a genuine monster on our hands instead of a triangular world power setup that has been working fairly well now for fifteen years."

Thompson nodded to the paper. "There's always the fourth option."

"You're not serious." The president was incredulous. "Bring pressure to bear on the Soviet Union to make territorial concessions? Good Lord! Do you realize what the effect would be on the Soviets?"

Thompson nodded. "The fact is that we don't have much room for maneuver. There isn't any clear-cut move we can make that won't damage some of our interests."

"Okay. Let's cut out the horseshit, Alec. What do you recommend?"

"You know my feeling. Over the long term, China and Japan in close alliance are by far the biggest danger we face. They've already got effective economic hegemony over all of Southeast Asia—Indonesia, the Philippines, Indochina. Their economic power is projected as being equal to Europe and the United States combined within twenty-five years. The new Marxian-socialist-Indian regime is about to enter into a treaty with them, which will put well over half of the world's population under effective Chinese dominance. I just don't see how we can contribute to the weakening of the Soviet Union, which has become, although it may not know it yet, our natural ally."

The president was silent, his big hands fiddling with an ornate Chinese letter opener, a gift from Chairman Teng at their meeting last year. "You think the Sino-Japanese alliance is locked in concrete, then?"

"Yes. Our best economic intelligence estimates show that the progressive closing of our markets and those of Europe to Japanese goods have forced them into such close integration with Chinese and Southeast Asian markets and raw material sources that they have no economic options. There's a symbiosis between China and Japan that has developed much more rapidly than we thought possible ten years ago. Our own fault, of course. But our economists just didn't realize how certain market imperatives were going to work. Also, the discovery of the vast new Chinese oil reserves and that mountain of high-grade iron ore in Sinkiang province will make the Sino-Japanese combination virtually autarkic in energy

31

and ore by 1985." Thompson shook his head. "They're locked into each other like Siamese twins."

"We've been over all this about a dozen times, haven't we, Alec?"

Thompson nodded, smiling faintly. "If you like, we can do it a dozen more. I can put the Russians off another day. The Chinese ultimatum doesn't expire for another forty-eight hours. Letting everybody sweat a little longer might not be a bad idea. They must be getting pretty nervous as it is."

The president shook his big head, his thick, graying hair moving slightly as he did so. "No. No games. We're going to have to live with them once this is over. I think one of our big assets is that we've never played games with them. We don't really want anything but stability, and they know it. So if we come down one way or the other, it's got to be done so that we arouse the least possible hostility. I'm looking beyond this crisis to the conference that is going to have to come sooner or later. There's got to be as much trust left as we can possibly manage. We've got to be able to play the honest broker at least once more."

Thompson said nothing. The American politician was a creature of his environment, and no amount of intelligence or experience in that environment could make him quite accept that there was another, different, world where his values were looked upon with bewilderment. The concept of trust among American politicians was an accepted conceit, and Thompson had seen it work again and again among men whose normal concept of honor or honesty was at a level of the bedbug. It was sine qua non of a working democracy. But it had little or nothing to do with international politics.

The president had lit a long green Cuban cigar and

was smiling once again at Alec over the glowing tip. "Why don't you get the hell out of here tonight and forget about the whole thing until tomorrow morning? Call Dimitri and tell him we need some more time. Then go out and get drunk. This is one time I'm going to let it go down to the wire. What's that gorgeous creature of yours doing tonight, aside from ripping pieces off my hide?"

"Senator Clarence is giving a dinner party."

The president took his feet off his desk and stood up. "Go to it, Alec." He was grinning impishly now, his streak of fraternity-house humor taking over. "Go to it and tell your goddamned office to deliver no messages short of an ultimatum. The Chinks and the Sovs will know where you are within half an hour and really begin chewing their nails. I can see old Kharkov stomping up and down trying to figure out what the hell we're doing."

Thompson nodded. It wasn't a bad idea, the wait. Over the years he'd come to the conclusion that more problems were solved by neglect than mindless activism. But he had a feeling this wasn't going to be one of them. . . .

Senator James Clarence grunted painfully as he pulled the thick elastic band up over his bulging belly until it flattened the pot and squeezed a couple of inches off his waistline. His wife watched in the mirror as she slipped a diamond earring into a pierced earlobe.

"Tell me, darling, how much do you think Suzanne Wilson would give to know that you wear that thing? I mean, can't you just hear her on television saying, 'The chairman of the Senate Foreign Affairs Committee, Senator James Clarence, popped out of his corset last night at a dinner party for the French

33

ambassador. His five-hundred-dollar Savile Row suit split from crotch to . . .'"

"For Christ's sake, will you shut up, Joan. You're getting more and more coarse in your middle age."

The woman swung around to face him, her handsome face focusing on him with quiet contempt. "After twenty years with a phony slob like you, what do you expect, Little Red Riding Hood? Which reminds me. Will you just for a change tonight try to keep your paws off Suzanne's round little ass? She isn't interested, you know. That particular little slut belongs to Alec Thompson."

Clarence's handsome tanned face stared back at him from a full-length mirror as he tied a subdued striped silk tie especially made for him at a little shop in Paris. He was getting jowly, no question about it. The daily workouts and jogging weren't enough. He was just going to have to cut back on the food and the booze . . . starting tomorrow. "I thought you didn't give a damn what I do."

"I don't, you vain jerk. But I've spent twenty years getting you where you are, and I'm damned if I'm going to watch you kick it all away by slobbering all over some ass-twitching little tramp and making a public spectacle of yourself. You're letting yourself go, Jim." Her voice softened ever so slightly now, the steel draining out of it. "If you hang in there for another two years, the nomination will be yours. Nobody can stop you. The president is going to back you. But you've got to cut out drinking so much and quit making a fool out of yourself with your secretaries and anything else you can lay your hands on."

Clarence nodded. "Yes. The president will back me. You fixed that, didn't you?"

"Oh, for God's sake, Jim. That was ten years ago. Anyway, what difference does it make now?"

34

"None. None at all. Only I don't intend to live like a monk, not even to become president so you can get your jollies hard-assing all the other dried-up bitches in this town."

She stood up, a tall, slender woman who looked closer to thirty than forty-five, her pale blonde hair piled high on an exquisitely chiseled face. She wore a vaguely Chinese dress with a high collar to cover the incipient wrinkles in her neck and cut very low in the back to reveal a tanned expanse of smooth, youthful skin.

"Come on. They'll start arriving any minute."

"My God, Alec, how marvelous!" Joan Clarence said and got up as she spotted him through the dining room doors. "The world's blowing up around our ears and the president's man of confidence comes for dessert." She slipped an arm through his and led him into the high-ceilinged dining room of the old Georgetown house. "I'm sure you know everybody. Be careful of our two wicked journalists. Kip and Suzanne have been pumping everybody all evening."

"Not true, Joan," Kip Dean said. "Nobody here knew as much as we did until our saturnine friend here arrived."

"God, Kip, let me get him a plate before you start in on him. Are you hungry, Alec?"

He shook his head. Besides Kip Dean and his wife, the guests were French Ambassador Charles de la Margerie, his tough, lovely wife, Claude, and Representative Caleb Sutpen of North Carolina, an aging widower who headed the House Foreign Relations Committee.

Sutpen grinned at him from around a giant Cuban cigar, his gnarled old face a map of more than half a century of scheming political chicanery and personal degeneracy. FBI files reported that he was a steady visitor, at eighty, to one of the elite bordellos specializing in black girls who catered to very special tastes. "Well, now, Mr. Counselor, I can't think of anybody I'd rather see than you right at this point. I figger you and that slicker you work for gonna be needin' a little hep from some of us old poker players up on the hill before this hand has been played. Ain't I right, Jim?" Sutpen was Phi Beta Kappa from Yale and a cum laude Harvard law graduate, but his accent was pure and unadulterated cornpone.

Clarence nodded across the length of the long table, his handsome, florid face flushed and animated, then turned back to Suzanne Wilson on his left, one hand stroking her arm as he talked.

"How's your hammer hangin', Colonel?" Thompson asked, imitating the old man's Southern drawl to perfection. Sutpen had been a colonel in the reserves and treasured the title. He and Thompson were regulars in the twice-monthly game in the ornate Anabasis Club, once described as the oldest floating poker game in the capital. At least five presidents had played in it at one time or another.

"Well, it ain't driven any nails lately, that's for a fact," the old man said, cackling.

The French ambassador, a tall, slender, elegantly tailored man with the face of a corroded razor blade, leaned across the table and smiled. "My congratulations, Alec. It confirms my faith in you, *mon chéri*. It will make a nice footnote in the history books. On the night before the Soviet Union and China went to war, the American counselor for foreign affairs attended a dinner party with utter unconcern. I shall make it a vignette in my memoirs."

"Well, you know what Talleyrand said: '*Surtout pas de zèle.*' " He had disliked the Frenchman for thirty

36

years, and the feeling was returned with interest. Behind the man's polite aristocratic mask and impeccable British accent was a hatred and contempt of the United States that bordered on paranoia. His dispatches, which Alec read regularly, thanks to a French embassy code clerk who had been recruited by the CIA after he was caught smuggling a kilo of heroin into the U.S., were perversely elegant, distorting the American reality enough to give a thoroughly astigmatic view of U.S. policy to a French government eagerly prepared to believe any perfidy.

Joan Clarence had put him next to Kip Dean, and the journalist turned away from the smoky beauty of the French ambassador's wife with vulpine anticipation. "You sure picked a hell of a place to spend the evening—the congressional foreign affairs establishment, two of the least friendly journalists in Washington, and de la Margerie. You're a glutton for punishment, Alec."

"You know what Masoch said. If you're going to get beaten, you might as well enjoy it." And Thompson was enjoying himself. Years ago, he had, when he found himself intellectually cornered, begun making up frivolous quotes and attributing them to famous names in history. Never once had anyone questioned him in a quarter century of playing the little game.

"Yeah," Sutpen said. "But what does that con man in the White House say?" The old man's voice was hard now. "Jim and me been tryin' to see him for three days. I got news for you, sonny. There hadn't better be any decisions taken about this business until we've been cut in on it. Congress is not gonna put up with any one-man foreign policy. And you better take the word to him, just in case my message hasn't been gettin' through."

The old man's message had gotten through. They

had debated having the two committee chairmen in to brief them on the situation. Sutpen could be depended on to keep his mouth shut, but Clarence had twice leaked what had been discussed at top-secret briefings within minutes of leaving the White House. All other things being equal, it was better to get the two men's cooperation. But the real power was in the White House, and they all knew it, Sutpen perhaps better than any of them, since during his fifty years in the House he had watched congressional authority over foreign affairs wither away to impotence. Only for a brief period in the post-Watergate era had the legislative branch wielded any real power, and that had soon disappeared with the election of a strong president.

"We're not really sure what's going on, Colonel," Thompson said. "When the situation clears up, we'll set up a briefing."

Sutpen shook his head. "Listen here, boy. We been hearin' talk about the United States takin' a hand in this game. And I got news for you and him, too. This country is not ready to get involved with either side." His Southern accent was almost gone now, and there was no more cornpone in the old voice singed from a lifetime of whiskey and cigars into a dark, rasping weapon. "If they want to kill each other off, more power to them. It is not up to us to take sides. You tell him that. Tell him that's what the people think."

Thompson counted slowly, neutralizing the irritation, smoothing his voice. He smiled deliberately, looking the old man in the eye. "Colonel, he's president of the United States. If anybody knows what the people think and want, it's him." The silence around the table was an invisible wall of tension. The old man met his stare, rolling the ridiculous cigar between his fingers.

"Meaning you're gonna do what you damned well please, and Congress can go to hell?"

"No, Colonel. You know what it means." He'd won the exchange and his voice was low, almost inaudible. "Foreign policy formulation is the president's job. He listens to every expert he can find, weighs his alternatives, and makes a decision. He then communicates that decision to you. But he's got the responsibility. And he's got the authority. And he'll use them. You wouldn't want a weakling in the job, would you, Colonel?"

"Well, we sure as hell ain't got one," the old man said sourly.

"Okay. So we've got a decisive president. What's he decided?" Kip Dean asked. "Are we going to take sides, or do we just sit back and watch the fight?"

"Christ, Kip, why do you newsmen always have to lay it out in such smooth black-and-white terms? First, nobody knows there is going to be a fight. Second, even if there will, taking sides, as you put it, might not be the best policy for us. We could offer to arbitrate or use our influence to stop the thing before it got started. There are a half a dozen other options that you can think of as well as I can."

Dean leaned forward, his thin, aging athlete's face pointed very much like a hunting dog in search of a bird. "That's baloney, and you know it, Alec. If you can't say anything, okay, I understand. But don't take me for a fool. If we have to take sides, it'll be with the Soviet Union. That much is clear. The only question is whether it's worth it right now. Maybe the sensible thing is to let the Chinese bleed them a little and then come in behind them after they're wounded. Gain us some gratitude."

"Who was it who said that gratitude is an emotion of cravens?" Thompson asked, smiling inwardly.

"Chesterton," Sutpen said. "Dean's got a point. It's one we take in Congress. Why should we pull the Soviet Union's balls out of the crack? Goddamn it, they've been screwin' things up for us around the world for the last forty years. Let 'em sweat this time."

Thompson shrugged. "You may be right, Colonel. That may be the best policy."

De la Margerie watched them all with a thin, super-cilious smile. "You gentlemen are leaving something out of the equation here, I believe."

"What's that?" The Frenchman was a perverse son-of-a-bitch, but he was also a brilliant political mind. Thompson listened.

"Our sources tell us that the Visigoths are restless. There was a secret meeting in Krohnheim today be-tween Beck and Gerhardus. Nobody knows the topic, but it must have something to do with what is going on in the East, *n'est-ce pas?*"

"What about that, Alec?"

"First I've heard about it. French intelligence is always much better than ours where the Germans are concerned. We have always regarded them as our friends and didn't bother much penetrating them," Thompson said, cursing Wiseman for not having got-ten the information to him. What in the hell were the East and West German prime ministers doing meeting now? That damned fool Beck was capable of any idiocy.

Joan Clarence listened as a waiter leaned over her and called down the table to Thompson. "Telephone, Alec. You can take it in Jim's study."

Thompson excused himself and heard Wiseman's voice as he picked up the instrument. "Hello, Gordon. What the hell is going on in Germany?"

"You want it in the clear?"

"Yes. Everybody but me seems to know about it, anyway. Clarence's phone is clean."

"Beck and Gerhardus met last night. Alone. No advisors and no minutes. Nobody knows what they said. State has queried the West Germans about the meeting and is being stalled. I don't see how we can find out what they talked about unless they want us to know. You're aware that they were in the same platoon in the last war? Joined the Communist Party together in the 1930s as kids and managed to stay together throughout most of the war."

"Yeah," Thompson said drily. "Both won the Iron Cross, first class."

Wiseman laughed. "Beck has been a respectable member of the Socialist Party since 1946. We've never found any hint that he isn't what he says he is. Hell, Alec, you're getting paranoid."

Wiseman had misunderstood him. He wasn't worried about West German Prime Minister Horst Beck's being a secret Communist, something that had obsessed Washington at the time he became head of the Socialist Party. He was more concerned with the possibility that he and Gerhardus had come to some sort of agreement to take advantage of the Soviet embarrassment in the East to shake loose concessions. There had been persistent intelligence reports of secret meetings between general staff members of the two nations in recent months. Beck had admitted one such meeting, saying that it had been held to make sure there was no friction during East German army maneuvers near the frontier.

"Listen, Gordon, you've got to find out what's going on. We can't afford to have the Krauts getting in the middle on this one. It's already very close to being out of control. Can you switch me to the president?"

41

The president came on the line almost instantly. "Gordon told you?"

"Yes. It makes things a hell of a lot more complicated. Beck is as unstable as nitroglycerin. He may see an opportunity in the situation. And his relations with Gerhardus are almost too good. We hear that he has some kind of a hold over him from their wartime days."

"Yeah. And the thing we never want to forget is that they are Germans. That's what old Kharkov kept telling me last time we met. He hammered on the table, got red in the face, and said they had killed twenty million Russians, and he'd be goddamned if he'd ever let them reunite."

Thompson grinned, remembering the scene. "I've been half-expecting Beck to pull something. It's the obvious time for it. I think maybe we had better send the ambassador in for a talk with him and tell him this is one time he'd better keep his fat fingers out of the pie."

"Alec, you can tell him. But there's no guarantee he'll listen. It might just push him into action. You know what a nut the man is, especially about reunification."

"You want me to come back in?" Thompson asked.

"No. This isn't anything new. And, anyway, it doesn't alter what we've got to do tomorrow. I want you to get a good night's sleep and come in fresh. I'm going to do the same. We've got a couple of tough days ahead. We've got to be reasonably rested."

Thompson hung up and rejoined the party, which had moved into the living room that Joan Clarence had furnished with American antiques from the eighteenth and nineteenth centuries, giving the room great warmth and an air of solid practical comfort. She took Alec by the arm and led him over to a comfortable chair, perching beside him, a soft hip flattened against his shoulder.

"God, Alec. Nobody ever sees you anymore. You've become a monk up there in the great white monastery. Your swinging image is beginning to suffer."

"It was always more image than reality, Joan."

Claude de la Margerie came over and sat on a low stool in front of him. "I had a letter from Janine the other day, Alec."

"How is she?" He seldom thought about his ex-wife now. For a decade her absence had represented an almost physical void. But the last few years had blurred the old images and dulled the pain. In addition to being an aphrodisiac, power was also apparently a narcotic, he thought wryly.

"She sends you her love. She and Herbert are spending the spring in Corsica. One of your beautiful sons is with them; Harry, I think."

"He's the pilot, isn't he, Alec?" Joan Clarence asked.

"Yes." His younger son was a navy pilot doing a tour of duty on a carrier in the Mediterranean fleet.

The woman next to him shivered slightly. "God. Do you think there will be another war, Alec? It is all so senseless. Who gives a damn about that frozen wasteland in the middle of Asia? Why do the Chinese bother?"

"Oil, minerals, prestige," Thompson said mechanically, letting his eyes wander automatically up the exposed leg of the French woman to the darker stain of the pantyhose where they joined her hip. She followed his glance with amusement, her brown eyes meeting his with a gleefully lascivious question. Thompson almost laughed. He had known Claude de la Margerie since his student days in Paris when the choice had been between her and his wife. At forty-five she had hardly changed; the wiry, boyish body

43

seemed as firm and arrogantly handsome as it had when she was twenty.

"You two seem to have something going here," Joan Clarence said. "I think I'll go rescue Suzanne from my slobbering husband." She headed across the room to an alcove into which the senator, his bulky body straining forward, had boxed Suzanne Wilson.

He had been walking down the street in London on the way to a meeting of the European Political Union, where he was to lecture on "Convergence: A Function of Economic Determinism" when he heard her voice.

"Alec, what a surprise!" It was 1968, a sour year. His marriage was shot. Three years in Vietnam had left him with fragile nerves and a shaken confidence in his political intelligence. Nothing had happened as he'd expected it to. The logical imperatives of power politics had split wide open on what one of his colleagues had called "the shoals of hysterically emotional responses." But if emotion could overpower logic and move events, then political science had goddamned well better program in the emotions along with the logic.

"Claude." She had been lovely standing in the pale sun in a light gray tweed suit and sensibly black walking shoes, a cloud of dark hair framing the triangular Gallic face with the slightly slanting eyes. "What are you doing in London?"

"I came over to shop for a couple of days. Charles is off in Africa at some boring conference." They had gone for lunch to a little French restaurant in Soho. It had been like old times in Paris in the mid-1950s. The good memories had come back to both of them in a flood of reminiscences.

"Remember the time Charles came to your room

in that awful hotel you lived in—the Daneois or some-thing—and imitated Janine's father?" She giggled at the memory of Charles de la Margerie pounding on the door and demanding that the seducer of his daughter come out and meet his fate.

"It made Janine frigid for a week," Thompson said, remembering its momentary effect on his own virility. He had for one panicky moment contemplated trying to climb down from the fourth-floor window of the rickety old hotel.

She had come back to his room after lunch, and they had made love. He had been amused at the neat pile she made of her clothes, carefully arranging them over the back of a chair to minimize the folds. The total unself-consciousness of a French woman in the presence of her body had never ceased to astonish him. It was an instrument of pleasure, detached from her emotions and her spiritual well-being, a tool to be used to obtain maximum effect.

But in the course of the day as they exhausted themselves with repeated bouts of lovemaking inter-spersed with champagne and the odd little sandwiches the British made so well, something happened. Their hands grew gentler, their kisses less demanding, the pleasure deeper.

"My God, Alec, you are a gentle brute," Claude had said drowsily, running her fingers through the thick, curling black hair on his chest, letting her hand move slowly down until she held the limp remnants of his virility in a small paw. She turned her lean body onto his and began to kiss him, letting her lips glide down over his chest, along his side, and across his stomach, until she took him gently in her mouth, crouching over him until the erection appeared. "I'll promise I'll leave you alone after this," she said, giggling, as her body covered his and began, once again, the slow rhythm.

For four days they hardly left the room, except to eat and wander hand in hand in the immense park across from the run-down old hotel. He had delivered his paper and had never gone back to the conference. Then, on one of the pale spring Sundays when London seemed like a copy of a Turner painting, she had said good-bye, kissed him gently, thanked him with a smile, and returned to Paris and her family.

3

Suzanne Wilson stood over them, fists on her hips, unsmiling. "Are you going to take me home, Alec, or does duty call? The senator has volunteered if you have to get back to the White House."

"I have to get back, Suzanne," he said. "I can drop you off, if you like."

"No, thanks. The senator has practically insisted that we all drop by the Chocolate Club for a nightcap. There's a new singer who's got it all together. Are you coming, Claude?"

The French woman shook her head. "No, I am afraid I am much too old for the Chocolate Club. The lines are bad enough even after ten hours of sleep. After five I don't dare face the mirror in the morning."

Thompson stood up and slipped an arm around Suzanne Wilson, walking her toward the door. "There's nothing I can do, Suzanne."

"I know. Only this is beginning to be a little ridiculous. If I wanted to be a nun, I'd join a convent. When do you think you'll be free?"

He shrugged. "Two, three. I don't know. Maybe not at all."

Senator Clarence broke in on them, red face tumescent as he put one heavy arm around Suzanne Wilson and drew her to him. "Wife can't make it," he said, leering, an aura of good Scotch and Old Spice enveloping him in a cloud.

Suzanne planted a bored elbow in his corseted gut and jammed it home. "In that case, let's go give some old bat an item for her gossip column tomorrow." He was a front runner in the presidential sweepstakes. It was only sensible not to play along.

The executive offices were quiet when Thompson arrived at the White House at midnight. The president's secretary was cleaning her desk as he walked in. "He's gone to bed, and he said you should do the same, Alec."

Thompson nodded. Jane Cleveland was an arrogant, efficient, crotchety female who had been in love with the president for twenty-five years. Her protectiveness was a legend in Washington. It was also a pain in the ass.

He took the proffered sheaf of presidential cables and reports and dropped into a chair, aware of a great weariness and a small neuralgic pain in his left shoulder. The British cabinet had met to consider the possibility of a Sino-Soviet war and had agreed that there was little, if anything, that they could do to influence events. Evacuation procedures for the British subjects in Hong Kong were discussed in the event of nuclear attack on the mainland.

The French president had sent a personal message pointing out that any U.S. action would have to be cleared with its European allies and suggesting a meeting, preferably in Paris, among the British, French, German, and American heads of government to take concerted action.

There was nothing from the German government.

A cable from the embassy in Poland cited rumors that the Polish army had informed the party secretary that it could not answer for its troops in any confrontation with rioting workers and had requested that it not be used to put down a strike by Silesian miners. The miners, the embassy cable said, had taken a secret vote to strike if their wage demands were not met. The Polish Politburo had been in a marathon session since the previous afternoon as a battle raged between hardliners demanding that the paramilitary riot police be used to crush the miners and a group led by the Silesian provincial party secretary urging caution.

At the bottom of the pile was a cryptic note from the U.S. military advisory group in Germany noting that West Germany had placed its armed forces on red alert. The advisory group had been asked to make sure that its men with the alternate trigger mechanisms for the jointly controlled tactical atomic weapons, including intermediate-range ballistic missiles capable of reaching Moscow, Leningrad, and Kiev, also be in a position of instant readiness.

Thompson stared down at the piece of paper, reviewing the conditions for the use of those weapons. Only in the event of a joint decision by the heads of government of both nations and the NATO commander could atomic weapons be activated. The activation required the insertion of a coded trigger mechanism in each weapon by a German and an American officer. There was simply no way the Germans could use the atomic capability without Ameri-

49

can concurrence. And without the atomic weapons they were helpless militarily, even if confronted with a greatly reduced Soviet presence in Western Europe. Sometime during the next few hours the president was going to have to talk to Beck and lay it on the line. The man was too unstable to be left to his own devices in a situation as delicate as this one.

The president's phone jangled in a peculiar beeping rhythm, and both Thompson and Jane Cleveland started slightly at the sound. It was the Moscow line. "The White House," Jane said, her voice taut. "Yes, I can put you through to Mr. Thompson." She handed him the phone, hand covering the mouthpiece. "It's Stashevsky."

Thompson took the phone and, speaking virtually unaccented Russian greeted his opposite number in Moscow. "Hello, Dimitri. How's the weather there?"

"Clear and cool; a typical spring day," Stashevsky said. "How are you, Alec?"

"Sleepy."

"Yes, I can imagine. Alec, there is great anxiety here. The chairman asked me to call you to find out when we can expect an answer. It's urgent that we hear soon. We cannot wait much longer. There are preparations that cannot be put off, and once things are in motion . . ." His voice trailed off. "Well, you understand. Accidents can happen. Our communications in the Far East are not the finest. Units may not be informed in time."

"Dimitri, I understand. We are trying our best. You're not asking for a cup of coffee, you know. We have to consult. A decision just can't come in one day. Too many people have to be brought in."

"Alec, that is bullshit, and you know it." Stashevsky had lapsed into the colloquial English he had learned during two years at Stanford University. "You are talking to nobody but the president, just as I am talking to the chairman. It is a tough decision. We know it. But you don't have any choice. The chairman has asked me to repeat that this time we are positive it is not a bluff. We have people very close to the top in China who are with us. And they tell us Chou means to go through with it. I must tell you, Alec, the situation is very grave.

"The chairman has asked me to inform you and your general staff that a first strike cannot be ruled out. We are in no position to allow them to obtain a tactical advantage. With their superiority of numbers, it is imperative that we obtain the initiative immediately, which means an attack. We know where they intend to strike. If we do not hear from you within twelve hours, I cannot guarantee that our military can be restrained. The chairman expects an answer. The Chinese ultimatum is about to run out."

Thompson picked up another phone and dialed a Pentagon extension. "Phil? Alec. How are you?"

The chief of military intelligence sounded exhausted. "I was about to take a nap. What can I do for you, Alec?" His polite upper-class voice was blurred. Thompson wondered if he had been hitting the bottle. After the scene with Pruitt, he wouldn't blame him.

"Phil, review for me quickly where the Chinese attack will come."

"Have you got a map handy?"

"Yes."

"Well, the major Chinese troop concentrations are opposite two vital railheads, Skovorodino and Khabarovsk," the general said as Thompson located the two obscure towns in eastern Siberia. "We think an attack on Skovorodino would be made solely to tear up the railroad and disrupt Russian supply efforts.

51

The main attack will come at Khabarovsk at the junction of the Amur and Ussuri rivers. The Chinese will attempt to crack through the river barrier and, keeping the Amur on their left flank, seep north to the port of Nikolayevsk. This will enable them to cut off Vladivostok and the maritime province. I don't need to tell you what this would do to the Russian naval effort in the Pacific."

"Their whole communications setup for the Pacific is in Vladivostok," Thompson said, thinking aloud. "It would put their submarine strike force out of operation for weeks."

"Worse than that," Samsun said. "We've all become so dependent on electronic aids of all kinds that, without that Vladivostok center, the Soviet defense effort would be flopping around like a bird with one wing. They've got a backup setup at Irkutsk, but it would take weeks to get trained personnel in place and operate it effectively."

"So they'll put everything they've got into holding at Khabarovsk?"

"It's difficult to get into old Korzybsky's head. You'd expect him to give ground as the Chinese attack, pull them into the river crossing, punish them as they crossed, and then, when they've got about half their forces deeply engaged, hit them with all he had on the flanks."

"What makes you think it won't happen that way?" Thompson asked.

He could feel the intelligence expert's hesitation on the other end of the line. Finally Samsun seemed to shrug. "Look, Alec, nobody's fought a major war in thirty years. In the meantime we've developed a whole spectrum of weapons that have been put to the test only in small-scale battles, such as the Israeli-Arab wars and a few skirmishes in Siberia. The firepower available to one infantryman today is about thirty times what it was in World War Two, even if all he's carrying is a rifle. Add to that the electronically guided high-explosive anti-tank weapons, and a three-man team can give you the equivalent of a 155-mm gun. There isn't any way to get a realistic picture of what's going to happen until it does."

"You think one of these weapons may turn out to be the longbow of it's time, and the tanks the medieval knights?"

"Could be," Samsun said. "Or it could work out just the opposite. These new tanks are awesome monsters, and some of the electronic jamming devices are damned effective. But the biggest variable here, as always, is the human factor. The Russian generals have at least had tactical combat experience and the chance to refight World War Two over and over again in maneuvers. They almost certainly have better logistics and can handle large masses of men in combat more effectively. The big question mark is the Chinese military leadership."

"Thanks, Phil. Let me know if you get anything from the satellite that might change the military picture."

"Will do."

Thompson glanced at the series of small clocks lined up on Jane Cleveland's desk. The Chinese ultimatum expired in thirty hours. They couldn't keep the Russians waiting much longer.

A messenger from the communications center came in with one of the characteristic red-bordered envelopes signifying the highest security classification. Jane Cleveland handed it to Thompson without a word. The cable was from the Berlin CIA station chief.

Persistent reports coming in indicating contact between East and West German staff and line officers down to regimental level. Minefields in East and West Germany being cleared on emergency basis. Tank barriers have been dismantled. Both armies fully mobilized and standing to battle stations. Russian ambassador has demanded meeting with East German Party Secretary Gerhardus, but repeatedly put off. West German contacts report highly erratic behavior of West German general staff. Stringent security precautions in effect, confining all staff officers to base.

Thompson handed the cable back to Jane Cleveland, feeling the neuralgic pain stab at his shoulder again. "Jane, get me General Harris in Frankfurt. Wake him up if you have to."

The call came through in about thirty seconds. "Harris here."

"Bill, Alec Thompson here. How are you?"

"Fine. What's up?" The general, an old hand approaching retirement, was wary. It was the first time the presidential counselor for foreign affairs had ever called him, although they had met at conferences over the years.

"We're getting reports of erratic behavior by the West Germans. Mobilization orders. Red alerts. Also, we've heard that Beck and Klein had a meeting. What's going on?"

Harris cleared his throat. "Well, it's true that they've gone on red alert. But it's mainly because they're worried about the Sino-Soviet business."

"Bill, what's that got to do with mobilization?" Thompson asked, his voice very gentle. "The last thing the Soviets are likely to do right now is present a risk to Europe. Mobilizing is a direct challenge to them."

"I know," Harris said heavily. "Fact is, I can't reach anybody. Even the lower-echelon liaison staff is avoiding me. They've made a point of wanting us to have instant readiness on the big-bang weapons. But that's standard, anyway. We're always on red alert, if you want to call it that. But they've moved up security troops around the installations and even blocked off some roads. No question about it that they're concerned about something. And they're not letting us in on it."

"Thanks, Bill. Let me know if you find out anything that might give us a line on what's bothering them." Thompson frowned as he hung up. Beck was definitely not rational. You could never depend on his doing something sensible under pressure. The mobilization could simply be a sop to his ego, an attempt to prove he was important in the world chess game, and, of course, an attempt to make the Russians nervous.

Jane Cleveland handed him another cable, this time from the Paris CIA station chief.

Head of Service de Documentation Extérieure et de Côntre-Espionage, Jean Saracin, reported confidentially that Chinese ambassador met secretly with German Premier Horst Beck February 1 in Baden-Baden villa for five hours. Second meeting occurred February 28. A third lengthy meeting took place on April 1. Saracin volunteered that French most concerned with German mobilization and contemplating limited call-up of reserves.

"Shit."

Jane Cleveland's head shot up, an astonished frown on her face. She had never known Thompson to be coarse.

He didn't believe it, of course. It was probably a meeting Saracin made up. It simply didn't make sense that Beck would get himself involved with the Chinese in an attempt to squeeze the Soviet Union. Even wholly embroiled in the Far East, Soviet conventional forces in the West could crush the German army overnight, unless tactical atomic weapons were used. And those were firmly under American control.

The peculiar ring of the Moscow hot line sounded again. Jane Cleveland, about to turn her desk over to the night-duty secretary, raised her eyebrows. "Christ, they really are uptight. It's Stashevsky again," she said, handing him the phone.

"Hello, Dimitri. You're going to have one hell of a phone bill."

Stashevsky's voice was grim. "Listen, Alec, something very serious is going on in Germany. We've been hearing about it for days, but nobody took it very seriously until now. Beck is crazy and Klein is a fool. But we are not going to put up with any amateurish nonsense. The situation is altogether too serious for idiots to be allowed to play stupid games. The chairman has asked me to have you contact Beck immediately and tell him to demobilize the West German Army and send it back to its barracks."

"You know we don't have this kind of control, Dimitri. He'd tell us to go to hell."

Stashevsky's voice was grim. "The fool has been talking with the Chinese. We found out about it only within the last few hours. Alec, the chairman is in a rage. I must warn you that he is even considering the possibility that the U.S. may be involved."

Thompson's knuckles were white around the phone. "Dimitri, we just found out about the Chinese meetings ourselves. The president will talk to him first thing in the morning."

"Very well. But please keep us informed. And, Alec, tell your Germans we will not put up with any game-playing. Their ambassador has been here today. He was torn to shreds by the foreign minister. So they'll be prepared for you tomorrow."

Stashevsky signed off abruptly.

"You want me to wake him up?" Jane Cleveland asked.

"No. There isn't that much of a rush about it. But we're going to have to make that son-of-a-bitch Beck pay for this one."

"That's what you've been saying for years," Jane Cleveland said dryly. "Why don't you go home and get some sleep? You look terrible."

Thompson nodded. All of a sudden he was very tired. It was two A.M. He was going to have to be back at seven. "I will. Make sure he sees these first thing when he comes in, Jane."

"Did you think I was going to burn that?"

He grinned and threw her a mock salute. He left the White House by the front gate and walked along Pennsylvania Avenue the four blocks to the new high-rise apartment house where he lived. The armed door-man greeted him with a leer. "Your friend's upstairs, Mr. Thompson. She said it would be all right."

"Thanks, Jim." Thompson punched the elevator button with a sudden feeling of overwhelming weariness.

She was curled up in the center of the big bed, the sheet pulled into a wadded mass, leaving her round, nude behind uncovered, one leg drawn up. She breathed deeply, sleeping with a profound health. Thompson undressed and slipped into the bed, falling back on the pillow carefully, trying not to wake her. The bed sank in and rolled her body against him. She turned in her sleep, one arm and leg draping across him as she did so. Her small, firm breasts were pressed into his arm and side as she stirred sleepily.

"Alec?"

"No, George."

She came awake instantly, half sitting up, leaning on one arm, looking down at him. "Hmm, you don't look like George. He's fat and he always sleeps with a cigar in his mouth. What time is it?"

"Two-thirty."

"Tired?"

"No." He lied, slipping an arm under her and pulling her down against him. She kissed him gently, her lips moving across his face down his neck, fingernails gently scratching his stomach.

"We don't have to make love, darling."

He grinned in the dark. There was no question about it. Fifty-two-year-old men and twenty-nine-year-old women were mismatched. He gently turned her on her back, willing back the fatigue and the age. "How else would I get to sleep?" he said.

"You no-good bastard. So all I am—the beautiful, witty, famous Suzanne Wilson—is Alec Thompson's sleeping pill?" She giggled as she pushed him off her and onto his back. "Lie still. I'll take you the way the Women's Liberation Movement used to recommend that all sex be performed—with the female in the dominant position."

"I understand it's hell on the knees," Thompson said, stifling a yawn.

4

"Christ, you look terrible, Alec," the president said. "I told you to get some sleep."

"I'm okay," Thompson said, accepting a large white mug of coffee proffered by Jane Cleveland. "Something new?"

"The chairman called me personally half an hour ago. He practically accused me of betraying him. I finally cooled him off, though. We went over all the options. He told me flatly that only the threat of an oil blockade is going to have any effect."

"He's really trying to nail us to the wall."

The president nodded. "Yeah. We've been living in kind of a dream world for years. But now, as ole Lyndon used to say, we've got to shit or get off the pot. If you had to do it right now, what would you do, Alec?"

"You know how I feel. Since the early 1960s our self-interest has paralleled that of the Soviet Union.

The initial problem was that the Soviet leaders were unable to bring themselves around to an understanding that Russia has become a conservative power whose interest was in maintaining the status quo. Not surprising, since the United States should have come to the same conclusion before World War One. But the rhetoric of revolution and democracy and all that crap obscured our self-interest until well after the end of World War Two."

"Okay," the president said; "so our self-interest is parallel to theirs. And now they know it."

"The aggressive expansionist powers are Japan and China." Thompson recited his theory in a monotone. The president had heard it all before. But he always listened without impatience. "On their periphery are potential powers or economic reservoirs such as India and Indonesia which have, or will, logically, combine with them. Despite Japan's economic clout, it's really a 'have not' power, inextricably bound up with the suppliers of its raw materials. For the foreseeable future, these Asian powers are going to exert pressure on the borders of the Western hegemony. We don't have any choice. We've got to resist."

"You think the threat of an oil blockade will stop them?"

"It will this time. Those new Chinese fields are ten years away from full production. Phil Samsun says they've been stockpiling oil, but it won't last more than ninety days. Then they'll have to quit. A ninety-day war doesn't make sense."

"A hell of a lot of things don't make sense," the president said. "What's this fucking Beck up to?"

Thompson shrugged. "Christ knows. Maybe he thinks Germany is a world power again. Who knows? The guy's unstable."

The president propped his feet up on the desk and

nursed the big white mug of black coffee. "Yeah, you and Gordon keep saying that."

Thompson stiffened and opened his mouth to say something, then stopped. One of the major insights that had come to him over the years was the uselessness of confrontations with no payoff. It didn't matter who was right about Beck. All that mattered was an accurate appraisal of what he was likely to do. The president was watching him, smiling.

"Just because we can't figure out what the son-of-a-bitch is going to do doesn't mean he's a nut, Alec. It just means he's using a different wave length."

Thompson shrugged. "As far as I'm concerned, his circuitry is fucked up. Where's his self-interest in sticking his oar into this one?"

"What does he want? That's where you always start an analysis, isn't it? Seek out the sources of power, define their motivations, and forecast their actions—isn't that what you keep telling me? Where does he come out using that system?"

Thompson sipped the coffee. "He's the power. His motivation is the reunification of Germany, and through this, the practical hegemony of Europe. Any action he takes will be directed toward those goals." He sounded like a professor in elementary geopolitics.

"Okay. It's a classic case. The Soviets are in trouble in the East. So you pressure them in the West. What's so nutty about that?"

"Nothing," Thompson said, "except that the Soviet Union could crush him in about forty-eight hours. They know it. He knows it. His mobilization and all that crap is just playing with himself—fun, but not productive."

"Horst Beck, the great masturbator." The president slapped his leg and laughed his big, booming laugh. "Goddamn it, Alec, I don't know what I'd do without

61

you. Okay. Let's leave him out of the equation for the moment. I've got a call in to him right now, and I've promised the chairman I'd get his tin soldiers back in the barracks.

"But right now Beck is just a minor nuisance, Alec. We've got to try to defuse this thing and give everybody a chance to come out of it with some dignity left."

Thompson stared impassively at the president. China and the Soviet Union were about to go to war, and the head of the U.S. government was going to handle it like a dispute between two petulant cabinet secretaries.

The president read his mind, not particularly liking what he saw.

"Okay, maybe nothing will work. Maybe this time both sides have checked out the options and decided they are going down to the wire, but I can't believe we're going to wind up with a nuclear conflagration, Alec. They'll fight. But before they walk over the brink, they'll quit. And we'll be there to arbitrate. So what do we do now? We build up our credibility for later. Both powers are our friends. We sympathize with the Chinese position and agree that it might have some historical merits. But guns are no way to resolve it. We suggest the whole problem be submitted to a special international court for arbitration."

"The Russians have already refused to do that," Thompson pointed out.

The president nodded. "I'm trying to work out the basis of some sort of compromise they'll both buy. If Chou is willing to talk, I'll pressure the chairman into going along, if only for the sake of delay. I'm just not quite ready to go your route, Alec—not without making one more try." His resonant voice hardened now, and Thompson realized that further argument was useless.

"You may be right, Alec," he continued. "I'm inclined to think that you are. But I don't see any self-interest in taking sides in this until I absolutely have to. So what we're going to do is send Chou a message telling him we want to delay a confrontation to enable him and the chairman to meet with me personally in Geneva or wherever he likes and we'll talk the whole thing over. A solution may still be possible."

"And if one or the other winds up saying no, what then?"

The president shrugged. "Then we've tried and failed. But it's cost us nothing. And the longer the Chinese delay their attack, the more likely moderate forces will take over within the regime and stop it altogether."

Thompson refrained from pointing out that Chou and Lieu were the moderate forces. The younger leaders were, if anything, even more eager to rush for an armed solution.

"I'll draft the messages. Shall I call to warn them what will be coming?"

The president shook his head. "No, I will. No details, just that a proposal is on its way. Ask Jane to get me Kharkov. I'll talk to him first, then to Lieu."

Horst Beck stared out through the vast expanse of glass that covered one wall of the new building housing the office of the West German chancellor and dug his fingers into the ridge of flesh on his left shoulder, where a Russian grenade had torn loose the muscles. He'd have to get down to the sauna more often. The old wound bothered him almost continuously these days. The doctors were after him to go under the knife again, but after each operation he seemed to have less feeling in the arm. He'd rather live with the pain than lose any more control. He was sure they had cut some nerves the last time, although they swore they hadn't.

A light on the console on his vast, gleaming, almost empty desk flashed. "Yes," he said into space. Gudrun's voice came back, softened, disembodied by the electronic circuit.

"Dr. Boehm is here."

"Send him in."

Boehm entered with his usual deferential sideways slither, bowing and walking at the same time, his gold-rimmed glasses slipping down over his nose. He came to a stop in front of the big desk, a sheaf of papers clutched in his right hand. The left was an empty sleeve.

"Well?"

"It's all moving according to plan, Chancellor," Boehm said, his thin, intelligent face creased by a diffident smile. "Our agents assure us that the miners will go into the street tomorrow morning. The army will not move. The gendarmerie will, but there are simply not enough of them to contain things. Poland will be paralyzed by this time tomorrow. Once the miners are in the streets, the dock workers and the railway men will join them. Within twenty-four hours there will be a general strike."

"And Wozniakowski? Are we absolutely sure of him?"

Boehm was silent.

"Well, man, speak up. Are we sure, or are we not?"

"He's a Pole, Chancellor. One can never be sure with these people. But he is as sure as anything is in this uncertain world. I think his patriotism, his ambition, and the fact that this may be their last chance for a century will keep him in line."

Beck's thick face broke into a broad grin. "Willy, by God, it's going to work! Do you realize what we are doing? We're bringing Germany back from the abyss to its proper place in the world. Think of it, Willy. Think of our place in history." He heaved his broad body, thick with muscle under the layers of fat, out of his chair and moved with surprising lightness and grace to a sideboard where he selected a decanter of clear liquid and two tiny crystal glasses.

The two men drank in silence, Boehm's thin, pale face flushing with the alcohol. "You are sure, Horst?" he said, dropping the tone of a servile functionary and using the familiar "du." "You are sure that nothing can go wrong? What if the Russians move?"

Beck shook his head, his thick neck straining at the stiffly starched collar biting into the folds of fat. "Willy, they cannot. There is no way. We have planned it down to the last millimeter. Nothing can go wrong." He refilled the glasses, his hard, light blue eyes boring into his friend. "And if it does, what have we lost? This is our only chance for a hundred years. Do you want your grandchildren's children to live in an enslaved Germany, a Germany deprived of its rightful place, a Germany sniveling and groveling to the Americans, and, God help me, even to those arrogant French and English bastards? Not to mention the Slavs. Willy, we have to take the risk. After us there is nobody with the willpower or the guts to do it. Once we show the way, once we take back the power that is rightfully ours, then the young will follow. Nothing attracts the young like power and success."

Boehm nodded. "I only wonder if the country will follow you, Horst . . . if the memory of the last war is not too strong."

"For a reunited Germany? A Germany with the

power it should have had in 1918 and again twenty years later? You underestimate the people, Willy. Germans are not wornout Frenchmen or Englishmen, or silly assed Americans afraid to use the power they have, trembling like women at the sight of blood. No, by God. And the Russians know it. They've known it for five hundred years, and with the Chinese at their back, they will hesitate just long enough . . . until it's too late. Get the message to Klein. No, you go personally. Nothing must go wrong at the last minute because of a misunderstanding."

Georg Wozniakowski stared at the map of Poland spread on the massive conference table in the meeting room of the Politburo of the Polish Communist Party. A pale April sun streamed in through the glass curtains, shutting off the room from the old town outside its windows. He shivered. The heat had been cut off on April 1 in accordance with regulations, but spring was late in coming and the massive rooms of the rebuilt royal palace were frigid.

"What's this?" Wozniakowski demanded, planting a thick peasant finger on a red circle near the coastal city of Gdansk, looking up at the general who stood with him at the map.

General Witold Lulienski, chief of the Polish general staff, answered. "Central radar control for the SAM and Yakov missiles. It has to be taken intact. If we can get it undamaged, we can use the missiles ourselves; otherwise, our whole anti-aircraft defense structure is useless."

"We have no independent capability?"

Lulienski shook his head. "None. We've managed to set up a few primitive local radar centers that are wholly untested. If we'd tried to run them, the Russians would have caught on instantly. They're useless."

"What are our chances of capturing the center in working order?"

Lulienski shrugged. "If our liaison officers can capture or kill the commander before he gives the order to destruct, no problem. If not, the charges will be set off, destroying them."

"What is the situation in East Germany?"

"The same, except that the East Germans built the Soviet radar equipment and have undoubtedly got a complete duplicate air-control center hidden somewhere, fully tested. They have to test all the new equipment, anyway, and they can keep their own system in top shape by running it on a simulated test basis. We think it's near Lübeck, since we occasionally pick up a stray signal in that area.

Wozniakowski stared down at the map with its little red circles enclosing the Soviet units occupying Polish soil. "So if we don't get the center, we'll have no air protection at all."

The general hesitated and finally spoke. He had served with Wozniakowski in the Polish resistance, and he dropped the formality. "Georg, that is irrelevant. Even with the radar center we would lose control of the air within the first twenty-four hours if we have to fight. Our success depends on a correct reading of the political situation. If we're wrong, we'll lose in any case. If we win, we need no weapons after the opening phase of the operation."

Wozniakowski nodded. He was a short man, compact, with the quick, springy step of an athlete. Startling light gray eyes dominated a deeply lined, oddly sensitive face. "It's a tremendous risk, Witold. If it doesn't work, it means the destruction of Poland."

Lulienski shrugged. "We've known that all along.

It's the same choice Poland has had half a dozen times in its history: live as a slave to Germany or Russia, or fight and be free . . . except this is almost our last chance. If the Soviets manage to settle things with China, they will lock us in tighter and tighter. We'll be a province of the Soviet Union. And the Germans won't stop, Georg. They're going ahead, with or without us."

Wozniakowski nodded. "I know. There is no turning back. I only hope the people don't have to suffer as we did, Witold. The young know nothing of war."

"No. They know only a comfortable life as serfs of the Russians," General Lulienski said, heavy face contorted with emotion. "We can't back down now, Georg. We must take part; otherwise, we will be treated with contempt. We'll be like," he groped for a word, then spat it out, "like the Czechs."

Wozniakowski nodded. "Yes. We had six million dead in World War Two, and the Czechs lost a few hundred."

Lulienski shrugged. "Everybody dies. The important thing is *how* one does it."

"Good God, Lulienski, you sound like those maniac cavalrymen who were attacking tanks with spears in 1939. You're not some romantic Polish nobleman out to save his honor. You're a peasant from Galicia who only learned to read and write in the resistance."

The general stiffened, face congested. "Perhaps I am not an aristocrat, Comrade Secretary, but I am a man and I am a Pole, and I say we fight like men and not grovel like dogs."

Wozniakowski grinned and slapped the general on the back. "Relax, Witold. We will neither grovel nor will we fight. The Russians are not fools. They will accept the situation. They have no choice. Once the Chinese attack, they won't worry about us."

He stared down at the map. "I've informed the Russian ambassador that you're mobilizing to put down the strikers. He has agreed. We're calling the strike leaders together for a meeting a few hours before you are scheduled to move. They suspect nothing, but when they know what we plan, there's no question that they'll agree. Provoking the strikes was a brilliant cover for the operation. The Soviets can't object to our mobilizing to put them down." He turned away from the map and moved over to the long, elegant windows overlooking the statue of Jan Sobieski, the savior of Vienna from the Turkish hordes, and the rebuilt medieval old town of Warsaw, remembering the flattened ruins of the city in 1945.

"This time we had better be right, gentlemen."

Dan Crane's interview with Chairman Alexei Kharkov began on page one of the *Washington Herald*. A banner headline proclaimed:

KHARKOV WARNS CHINESE THREATEN WAR

In an exclusive interview with this reporter on Monday, Soviet Party Chairman Alexei Kharkov said that China had threatened the Soviet Union with war.

During a series of meetings at the Siberian border town of Svobodny last week, Chinese Prime Minister Lieu Shen told Soviet negotiators that China could no longer tolerate the occupation of its territories by foreign troops. He presented the Soviet side with a series of detailed maps outlining Chinese territorial demands.

Chairman Kharkov, slamming a fist on his massive Kremlin desk for emphasis, told this reporter that the Chinese demands were absurd.

Essentially, according to Chairman Kharkov, the Chinese have called for the return to China of the independent republic of Outer Mongolia and the establishment of a frontier beginning at the northern tip of Lake Baikal and extending to the town of Ghumikan on the Sea of Okhotsk.

The Chinese base their demands on the Treaty of Nerchinsk signed on August 27, 1689, between the Russian commander in Siberia, Fyodor Golovin, and Chinese Prince Songgotu. Although geographically vague, the treaty assigned much of the disputed territory to China, which continued to administer it until Russian incursions began in the middle of the nineteenth century.

Mongolia, they maintain, has been an integral part of China since the second millenium B.C.

Chairman Kharkov, stressing that the Soviet Union had no intention of negotiating or compromising over one foot of the disputed territory, pointed out that the Chinese demands included the Russian city of Vladivostok and well over one million square miles of Soviet territory.

The chairman said the Soviet Union had massed more than three million troops along the disputed border facing twice that number of Chinese. He warned that war was imminent, emphasizing the grave problems such a conflict could cause for the United States and the rest of the world.

Asked if the Soviet Union would use tactical nuclear weapons to offset the Chinese advantage in manpower, Chairman Kharkov said his nation would use whatever means were necessary to defend itself from aggression.

Thompson skimmed the rest of the story, which outlined the historic Soviet claim to the territories and defended the Mongolian republic as a sovereign, independent nation.

He picked up a sheaf of notes and crossed to the door, which opened directly in the Oval Office. The president was sprawled on a long couch, tie undone, a mug of coffee resting on the rug beside him, watching a rerun of the early morning television news. "See that goddamned Crane article?"

Thompson nodded.

"Kharkov is trying to pressure us," the president said, sitting up and propping his shoeless feet on the coffee table. "Get everybody all worked up so we'll be forced to lean on the Chinese and Japanese." Both men watched Suzanne Wilson's cool, almost chilly presence on the center screen.

"Meanwhile, in the Middle East, the situation continues to remain tense.

"Israel has announced that a further increase in the price of Saudi Arabian and Libyan crude oil would be posted in the early summer. The EEC ministerial group has called an emergency session of the community's economic council to consider possible retaliatory measures.

"Simultaneous street riots in Damascus and Cairo were ruthlessly suppressed by Israeli security forces yesterday with eleven reported dead in Syria and fifty in Egypt. Ten hostages were executed in Jidda by the puppet regime of Sheikh Sharbatly following the knife slaying of an Israeli occupation official.

"Israel has announced that the long-expected test of its hydrogen bomb will take place in northern Yemen in July. The Israeli defense ministry said it would issue a map of the danger areas by early May. Fallout from the underground blast is expected to be minimal, although the Israeli Atomic Energy Commission conceded some venting is possible.

"In West Germany the Ministry of Defense has

71

denied press reports of a general mobilization. Defense Minister Hans Richter said certain reserve units were being activated on a provisional basis to participate in regular spring maneuvers. He added that similar reports of East German mobilization were gross distortions of the facts and called on the press to exercise discipline and restraint during a tense period in history. False reports, he said, could lead to dangerous situations.

"The Japanese prime minister, Admiral Yashima Nagoya, today informed parliament that the nation's mutual assistance treaty with the Chinese People's Republic specifically excluded border incidents similar to those in Manchuria and Sinkiang. Only full-scale war would trigger the alliance mechanism, he said. Under heavy questioning from pro-Soviet factions in parliament, the admiral conceded that all twenty-five of Japan's nuclear missile submarines were on station. Japan's three hundred fifty land-based intercontinental 'Kamikaze' missiles were also on full alert, he said. However, Nagoya described these as measures of simple 'prudence,' given the tense world situation.

"In Cuba, President Juan Carichal informed rioting students that he would not hesitate to close the universities and eject them if peace and calm were not reestablished. Observers in Havana said the situation in the Cuban capital was as tense as it had been at the time of the assassination of President Fidel Castro.

"In southern Rhodesia, Premier Ian Smith announced that another five thousand South African border rangers had entered Rhodesia at his request to help combat guerrilla infiltrations along the northeastern border with Mozambique. He said joint operations were planned with South Africa to stamp out once and for all what he described as the Communist-supported bandit bands.

"In Spain, Communist and social democratic trade unions threatened a general strike today to protest a government decision to dissolve parliament and govern by decree. The decree, read to a tumultuous session of parliament by King Juan Carlos, allows the center-rightist regime of Dr. Francisco Alvarez to rule the country for six months under Section Fifty-seven of the Constitution. This will be the fourth time since General Francisco Franco's death that Spanish governments have used the device to circumvent a chronically deadlocked national assembly. Diplomatic sources in Madrid say, however, that the left-wing parties fear Alvarez will now institute a permanent authoritarian regime with the aid of the army."

The president flicked off the set with a remote-control switch and turned back to the press summary. It was the regular nine A.M. ritual. Fifteen minutes or so with Thompson on foreign affairs and the press, then a similar short session with his two domestic advisors before beginning the day's meetings. Shortly before noon he called in the press secretary and the same early morning group to go over what might be brought up at the regular twelve o'clock news briefing and give guidance. These four men, more than any others, ran the government by virtue of access to the final source of power. Cabinet ministers, powerful congressional barons, the masters of the myriad independent agencies—all these saw him when there was a need. But the inner circle saw him daily, hourly if need be, and it was this that gave them power.

"What else is new, Alec?" The president asked, his voice betraying the weariness of a virtually sleepless night.

"Our embassies continue to suffer from the myth of the central position. The world continues to revolve around their navels. The French are getting nervous. The foreign minister called Ambassador Morgan in and demanded that France be kept informed of any U.S. demarche in the Far East. He said, and Morgan quotes him, 'France cannot and will not be left out of a consortium to settle the fate of the world.'"

"Shit," the president said. "What did that moron Morgan say?"

"He invited the foreign minister down to his vineyard in Burgundy for the weekend."

The president grinned. The scion of a famous banking family had contributed half a million dollars to his last campaign. Paris had been his reward.

"What's next?"

"The secretary of state wants to see you today."

"Why doesn't he call Jane?"

"He did. She said you were too busy."

"All right. We'll have to talk to him. Set it up with Jane in the afternoon. Are you telling his people anything?"

"Not much. The goddamned place leaks like a sieve. Every foreign service officer has his own foreign policy and tells the press how bad ours is."

"Well, make an effort. After all, they are supposed to be running it." Both men grinned. Thompson treated the flatulent old former senator who was secretary of state with a certain surface deference. But there was no time to waste on him now.

"The shah sends his thanks for your long explanatory cable on the Far East situation, and he has put his occupation troops in Bahrein, Kuwait, and the Trucial Sheikhdoms on twenty-four-hour alert. He reports that the local guerrillas don't seem to be any more active than usual. His fleet is leaving port and putting itself at the disposal of Admiral Clark near Diego Garcias."

"Anything more?"

"Just the usual elaborate professions of friendship. And one more report from Israel."

Both men stared at each other across the massive white coffee mugs, remembering another crisis. It had been very close that time. As the Israeli tank columns swept across Syria and Egypt to take Damascus and Cairo, the hot line had been in continuous operation. The Sixth Fleet had positioned itself off the Egyptian coast to prevent a landing by Soviet marines on the war's tenth day. An Israeli flying column had pushed into Cyrenaica and taken Benghazi. Tunisian troops occupied the rest of Libya. Three days later Israeli paratroopers had taken Jidda and the Saudi Arabian oil fields without firing a shot. The airborne forces had struck with such ruthless speed and efficiency that the fields were virtually undamaged.

World opinion had been enraged, of course. The U.N. had voted to censure Israel, the Security Council called for sanctions, and the Soviet Union threatened a nuclear holocaust. But within two weeks the Common Market countries had issued a pious call for peace and an urgent plea for the flow of oil not to be interrupted. On the day Jidda fell, the shah, with the tacit approval of the United States, had taken Bahrein, Kuwait, and the Trucial Sheikhdoms in the Persian Gulf virtually without the loss of a man. A short, bloody war with Iraq had resulted in total victory for the shah, and that country was partitioned between Iran and Turkey, which had earlier occupied most of northern Syria when an Israeli victory had been confirmed.

Israel had quickly set up puppet regimes in Syria, Egypt, and Saudi Arabia. Jordan and the Sinai peninsula had been incorporated into Israel. The forced resettlement of the Palestinian refugees as well as Arabs occupying the Israeli "heartland" had begun almost immediately. Now, a year later, there were none left living in camps. Emigration had raised Israel's population to nearly five million. U.S. economic aid, plus the revenues from the captured oil fields, had financed the resettlement efforts, ridding the country of almost all its former Arab inhabitants.

Israeli occupation troops, now reduced to token forces, fraternized freely with the Arab populations of the puppet states. The regimes maintained themselves without great difficulty with the help of efficient Israeli-trained secret police and small indigenous paramilitary detachments that brutally repressed any occasional demonstration or terrorist outbreak. A network of highly paid informers repeatedly infiltrated resistance organizations and led to their destruction.

The Iranian occupation of the Persian Gulf had been much messier. Several dozen sheikhs and traditional religious leaders had been liquidated by the shah in the initial period, only to be replaced by much more efficient Marxist-oriented guerrilla groups, some supported by the Soviet Union and others by the Chinese Communists. A continuing low-level political fever enveloped the region and had begun to infect the Iranian mainland as the shah's losses mounted. There were rumors of disaffection in the middle levels of the army. The CIA had already uncovered three plots and reported them to the shah, who crushed them ruthlessly.

"What does Lev have to say?"

"Be careful, we are with you," Thompson said, grinning. In his years as national security advisor to the president, he had managed to win or get a draw in just about every international encounter except with the Israelis. Their orchestration of the American Jewish minority, combined with steely nerves and the negotiating instincts of an Armenian rug peddler, had sucked American foreign policy along in their wake like a whale being towed by a trout. That their self-interest had usually been that of the United States' was cold comfort to mounting frustrations and a bruised ego.

"Yeah," the president said. He shared Thompson's weariness with their Mediterranean ally. "What about Beck, your favorite psycho?"

"Have you seen the cables?" The president shook his head and Thompson glanced through his notes and read:

> West German troops are mobilizing. All reserve units have been called up. Civil defense units have been put on red alerts.

Thompson glanced up. "That means a condition of war." He read on:

> Defense Minister Richter met with leaders of the armaments industry in a secret session Wednesday, and all senior German police officials were called in to a meeting at the Interior Ministry several hours later.

The president frowned. "What the hell does the son-of-a-bitch think he's doing? Who in Christ's name is he going to attack, East Germany?"

Thompson shrugged. "Doesn't seem very likely. We've got another report that his *chef de cabinet*, Boehm, met secretly with East German Party Chairman Gerhardus yesterday."

"What's your feeling, Alec?"

"All the evidence points to some sort of deal between East and West Germany to take advantage of the Soviet Union's problems in the Far East. But it's an idiotic game. Without atomic weapons they would be helpless against a Soviet attack. I can only assume that Beck is bluffing, knowing we'll have to bail him out if he gets in too deep."

The president picked up the phone. "Jane, how is that call of mine to Germany coming? They *what?*" He replaced the receiver, his face a mask. "He's taking a nap. They won't wake him up."

Thompson grinned in spite of himself. It wasn't often that this modern emperor got an answer like that. "He obviously doesn't want to talk to you. I think we'd better get a cable off to the embassy and have them make a formal protest about the mobilization. You promised the chairman you'd try to get Beck's troops back in the barracks."

The president shook his head impatiently. "That's no good, Alec. I told the chairman I'd lean on him, and I intend to." He picked up the phone. "Jane, get me the German foreign minister. If he's not available, you go down the protocol list until you get somebody to come to the phone. Tell them the president of the United States wants to talk to somebody in authority. And call the German ambassador in here right now. Get him out of bed if necessary."

Two minutes later the president's secretary came in, frowning. "The German ambassador is on a hunting trip in West Virginia. Nobody knows exactly where."

"What about the foreign office?"

Jane Cleveland shook her head in disbelief. "I keep getting told that all the circuits are out. Some problem with the communications center in Germany. I tried the army line, but they can't get through from headquarters in Wiesbaden. I've never heard of such a thing."

Thompson felt a crawling sensation along the surface of his skin. Something was wrong, goddamned wrong.

5

General Phillip Samsun awakened precisely at seven o'clock, the alarm bell built into his brain ringing virtually as the second hand passed the hour mark. He lay on the thick leather couch in his office for perhaps thirty seconds before sitting up. The stale taste of sleep and cigarettes fouled his breath. An old back injury from a jeep accident in World War II made it an effort of will to bend over and tie his shoes. Thirty-five years ago his doctor had told him to wear a slipper-type shoe and use a long shoehorn to get into it, but Samsun had refused. There was too goddamned much self-indulgence in the world as it was, and, anyway, he had to present some sort of model for the younger officers. Slipper-type shoes, for God's sake. They'd be wearing tassels next, like some goddamned corseted Rumanian colonel back in 1925.

Samsun got up and went into his private bathroom,

stripping off his shirt and undershirt, looking at his image in the mirror with satisfaction. Goddamned fine figure of a man, fifty-eight or not, he thought, grinning at his vanity. It wasn't vanity alone that had kept him working out two hours a day for four decades, jogging doggedly on the Pentagon track, playing squash, and watching his diet. It was ambition. To make it, you needed a certain image, that look of calm athletic confidence. He'd been lucky, of course, to be able to keep that thick mass of graying hair and flat stomach. Anyway, it had all been worth it. That goddamned pussle-gutted Pruitt, with his jowls, bad teeth, and rumpled uniform, was a disgrace to the service. Samsun opened the worn leather case in front of him and selected the straight-edged razor marked *"donnerstag"* and prepared to shave. The German razors had belonged to his grandfather, an officer in Stonewall Jackson's army. Their very touch made him feel secure.

Fifteen minutes later he strode into the main military intelligence briefing room, a vast, windowless cavern walled by military situation maps and dominated by an immense backscreen projector covering an entire wall. Smaller map tables covered almost every inch of space, and young officers bent over them, converting the latest military intelligence into men, machines, and ideas.

"Good morning, Jim," Samsun said to the night-duty officer. "What's the prognosis?"

Colonel James Bowman, number one in the West Point Class of 1964 and reputedly the finest military intelligence officer of his time, motioned to one of his assistants, and a large-scale map of the Sino-Soviet border appeared on the screen.

Using an electronic pointer, the younger officer

81

moved a spot of light across the map and gave a crisp, detailed description of the Chinese and Soviet forces. "The Chinese have concentrated more than two million men inside the Khabarovsk salient with some twenty-five thousand tanks and armored vehicles in the assault group. Pontoon bridges have been massed behind each crossing point and heavy artillery and rockets to cover the crossing are emplaced. The reserve, more than a million men with heavy armored support, is concentrated at Fuchin and straggles back as far as Shwangshan."

Samsun nodded. "It's obviously intended to move up against any Russian breakthrough along the flanks at Vyazemski or Leninskaya."

"Yes," the colonel said in agreement. "There doesn't appear to be much subtlety involved. It'll be a frontal attack against well-entrenched Soviet forces with superiority in armor and probably in effective artillery throw-power."

Samsun stared at the map. "It looks suicidal. The Soviets will have tactical air superiority and will blast those bridgeheads unmercifully. Their armor will cut the landing force to bits." He shook his head. "I can't believe Wang Chin would attempt anything so absurd. What do the Soviet dispositions look like?"

"Nothing's changed," the young colonel said, adjusting his rimless glasses and motioning for another map. "You'll note that most of their armor is at Vyazemski. They'll go for a hammer-and-anvil effect, driving with masses of armor at the flanks of the Chinese army and hammering with massed artillery from Leninskaya." He indicated a bulge on the map. "That salient will be a slaughterhouse within forty-eight hours. It's a death trap unless the Chinese can make a quick breakthrough, and even they'll have one

82

hell of a time keeping the Soviets from closing those pincers. It just doesn't make much sense militarily."

Samsun nodded. "I suspect the Soviets will punish the crossing attempt but allow them to get maybe half their troops across before counterattacking in force. Once the entire Chinese front is engaged, they'll close in on the flanks. It's a tank general's idea of paradise. Pruitt must be having some orgasms at the sight of my battle plan."

"I get my orgasms on a different field of battle, Phil," Pruitt said. The army chief of staff had entered the intelligence briefing room and now stood at the table beside Samsun.

Bowman ran over the briefing again, pinpointing the headquarters of each army corps for Pruitt as the maps flickered across the screen in quick succession. It was all done in cryptic military shorthand, half-finished sentences, and map coordinates spat out in rapid bursts.

Pruitt listened, blunt forefinger tracing positions on the table map, noting terrain features, asking mono-syllabic questions about roadbeds, logistics, and the latest estimates on running time for the new Chinese main battle tank. Finally he looked across at Bowman and demanded, "What's the latest from the bird?"

Bowman shrugged. "Nothing really new. We're a little surprised at the amount of heavy artillery they've brought up behind the assault group. They're holding it too far back to be of much use in the attack."

Pruitt glanced up from the map, frowning. "Let's have a look."

Bowman flashed a large-scale photograph on the screen, seemingly showing nothing but a verdant countryside. Then in a series of flicks the pictures concentrated on smaller and smaller segments until, as if by magic, a battery of 122-mm guns suddenly

83

emerged from the camouflage. "Bring it down more," Pruitt barked.

The photograph was progressively enlarged until the last picture, covering the whole wall of the briefing room, showed the long, slender barrel of a gun lying virtually flat behind a sandbagged revetment. Pruitt stared at the picture intently, chewing on the butt of his cigar. "Bring it back up," he said softly. As the picture changed he nodded. "Looks as if they're bringing in the ammo under the barrels of the guns," he said, indicating a muddy track running along just beneath the flat barrels of the fifteen-gun battery.

Colonel Bowman stared at the map and smiled. "The terrain tapers off at the rear, General. They ran the road there because it was too much trouble to bring it around behind the guns. The Chinese don't much bother with such minor efficiencies."

Pruitt removed the ragged cigar from his mouth and stared at the colonel. "Sonny, cut out the bullshit. There is no artilleryman alive who is going to bring his ammo in under the noses of his guns and make his men lug the stuff another thirty feet. Show me some more of these batteries."

The pictures flickered on in quick succession, hundreds of guns massed for miles, all facing in the direction of the Chinese offensive, all barely within range of the opposite banks of the Amur and Ussuri rivers. And, in each case, the supply road ran under their muzzles. "What about the rocket sites?"

Bowman, small beads of sweat popping out on his forehead, snapped an order and massed rocket launchers appeared on the screen, row after row, deeply embedded in earthwork revetments. Again the access roads ran in front of the batteries. "Blow that one up. I want to see it in relation to the artillery." Bowman pinpointed through the camouflage the various batteries on the expanded photograph.

Pruitt glanced at the younger officer, impatience creasing his weatherworn face. "Listen, son, are you trying to tell me they've got their artillery sites behind the goddamned rockets? That picture must be backward. Those rockets will throw up to forty miles. Maximum range for a 122 is eighteen. What the fuck have you done, reversed the picture?"

Bowman grabbed for a phone and talked briefly with the projectionist before turning to the general. "The picture is not reversed, sir. Those are the Chinese dispositions."

"Well, Phil, what do you make of it? Wang's brought those guns up in the last few days, put them in deep revetments obviously prepared months ago, and, by God, they're fucking near out of range of the enemy. To top it off, he's got his rockets out in front."

Samsun nodded. "Doesn't make much sense. What about the forward guns, Jim—the ones designed to clear the landing area in depth?"

Bowman once again showed a series of heavy-artillery emplacements, these within five miles of the assault area, capable of punishing anything within fifteen miles of the landing sites on the opposite bank. "Son-of-a-bitch. Look at the ammo trails. They run behind the batteries."

All three men watched intently as a series of images flickered on the screen. Samsun nodded and let his breath out explosively. "Well, it's pretty clear that the second line of artillery is supposed to be turned around to hold off the expected counterattacks from the flanks. It almost looks as if they expect to be cut off."

Pruitt nodded, chewing on the dead cigar butt.

85

"Yeah, it does. Only Wang isn't damned fool enough to think he can fight in two directions at once. He's got to figure on putting every man he can across that bridgehead in as short a time as possible and spreading out on the other side of Khabarovsk, disrupting the Soviet rear and forcing them to pull back their pincers to contain him. He can't afford to immobilize that much artillery and the forces needed to defend it." He shook his head. "It's gotta be an elaborate feint. Wang must be figuring the Soviets will read their pictures the way we do and will figure those guns will be reversed, which means they're facing one hell of a defensive force at Wang's rear. He's trying to make them cautious, force them to mass more forces than they need, which will buy him a couple of more days to make the crossing."

Samsun nodded. "It looks like it. But it's awfully transparent."

"Yeah," Pruitt said sourly. "It sure as hell is, but I didn't notice any of your young geniuses around here coming up with it."

Samsun flushed to the roots of his carefully combed graying hair and shot a venomous glance at the intelligence colonel, who stood studying the map, frowning.

"What's the matter, son?" Pruitt asked.

"If the Chinese are expecting the pincers to close, that reserve is useless. They've got almost half their available tanks here." He indicated the towns of Fuchin and Shwangshan, south of the indicated Russian pincers movement. "Those forces won't be available to Wang's attacking force if he assumes his rear is going to be cut."

Pruitt nodded. "He's gambling that the Russians are concentrating their forces on the sides of the salient rather than in front. He thinks he can make the breakthrough in the center and roll up the flanks by fanning out and attacking the rear of the forces operating the pincers. If it works, he's got half his tanks fresh and ready to be committed."

"True, General, but the Soviets will have him cut off from his supply base, assuming they can close the pincers. It just doesn't sound like the kind of generalship the Chinese are noted for—cautious, conservative, and low risk."

"I agree with you, son," Pruitt said. "And if you come up with a better analysis of the dispositions, you give me a call. Meantime, it's the only reading that makes any sense. Now, how about their feint at Skovorodino?"

The young colonel ran through an analysis of the dispositions. More than a million Chinese troops faced half a million Russians across from the rail junction. Both armies were short on armor, much of which had been siphoned away from the major battle at Khabarovsk. "It'll be a battle of attrition. The Chinese will probably attack in human waves. The river isn't that much of a problem here and they have the advantage of being able to attempt a crossing at more than a dozen points. The Soviets will have to thin out their forces to meet all possible attacks. It seems fairly likely that the Chinese will be able to disrupt rail traffic drastically if they're willing to pay the price in lives."

Pruitt stared at the battle maps, grinding out his dead cigar absentmindedly. "There's something wrong, Phil. I can't finger it, but somewhere we're missing something. Wang is a brilliant general. It's his terrain. He's had half a century to study it. I just can't believe he's going to come up with something as simple as this. He's got to have something else going for him. He knows the Soviets are more maneuverable, their tanks are better, and probably their tactical ability in fluid warfare is superior. He's better off fighting a set-piece battle on the defensive where these new anti-tank weapons can chew up the Soviet armor and turn it into a battle of attrition. That way he might have a chance of grinding the Soviets down and taking advantage of their longer supply lines and that vulnerable rail link. The way he seems to have planned it just doesn't fit his capabilities."

Samsun nodded. "We're all agreed. All I can think of is that he's been told to mount an attack for political reasons and bleed the Russians badly. What the hell are the Russians going to do if they win, Craig, occupy China? Maybe the Chinese see the war as a first stage of a long campaign to wear down the Soviets and bring them to the conference table. Indications are that when the battle starts they're going to skirmish along virtually the entire seven-thousand-kilometer frontier. It'll be another Vietnam, only fifty times bigger. The Soviets can't escalate to a nuclear exchange, so they'll be forced to fight the wrong kind of war in the wrong place with the wrong weapons. What difference does it make if they win one battle?"

Pruitt stared into the arrogant, handsome face of his colleague and shook his head. "Phil, I've been around for a while, and I've fought and read a hell of a lot of war. And I've got news for you. I never heard of a general who went into a battle he couldn't win of his own free will. It doesn't work that way. Goddamn it, we've got to be overlooking something. Wang is not going to stick his head into a noose and pull it tight."

Samsun stood at semi-attention. "Our people are doing the best they can, Craig. We can't ignore the facts. As for history, you know yourself there have been fifty winning combinations in history that looked totally nutty until after the fact."

Pruitt shrugged. "Okay, Phil. Be prepared to update the president later today."

6

Dimitri Stashevsky stifled a yawn as Marshal Ivan Korzybsky outlined the military situation before a large-scale map in the Kremlin briefing room. He was seventy, far too old to be on active duty. And fat. Stashevsky wondered why all Soviet generals were fat and all American generals thin. "Yours eat more," his friend Thompson would have said in his dry, laughing way. Stashevsky wanted badly to be in one of those elegant restaurants in London, Paris, Rome, or Washington and fencing with his American counterpart instead of sitting here listening to a stupid peasant talk about tanks and air cover and logistics. There wasn't going to be a war. It was unthinkable. But if they continued to act as if it were inevitable, then events that were now only the fantasies of some old men living in the twilight world of unrealized dreams could become reality and he, Dimitri Stashevsky, might wind up a charred cinder like the rest of them. He glanced at his watch as the general droned on. Nadia Raskolnikova would be cleaning off her desk now, pale face angelic in its purity. He let his eyes close halfway and he began to undress her in his mind, lovingly lifting each piece of clothing off her body, feeling the muscles in his groin tighten in anticipation.

"Dimitri!" The first secretary never spoke in a normal tone of voice. It was always a low, menacing growl, even when he was telling a joke, which wasn't often. Dimitri thought it was one of the keys to his success, since, aside from a certain peasant shrewdness and a will of absolute steel, he had little to distinguish him from the seventeen other bureaucratic hacks on the Politburo.

"Dimitri!" There was rage in his voice now. "Have you been asleep again?"

Stashevsky yawned and stood up, sauntering over to the map, the hollow, dry taste of fear in his mouth. It was a taste he loved. This knowledge had come to him with a shock some years before when the affair with the minister of Heavy Industry's young second wife had almost finished him off. He only really came alive when danger threatened. His nerves steadied. His mind came awake. And his intelligence worked at full speed instead of idling along as it usually did.

"No, I have not been asleep. But Marshal Korzybsky is a man of such penetrating consistency that I felt he would give the same briefing he gave the last dozen times he visited us. He hasn't disappointed me. Nothing has changed." The irony in Stashevsky's voice was heavy now, slicing through the room like a new razor blade, but lazy, unaggressive. "We are asked to believe that the stupid Oriental, General Wang, has decided to pour his troops into the diabolically clever trap set by our esteemed marshal

91

and let them die like pigs in a slaughterhouse. You'll forgive a poor amateur if he finds it a trifle unlikely."

"Well, Dimitri," the general secretary said, "you are witty and sarcastic. But I don't hear you exercising your great military genius to come up with another answer to their dispositions." He loved his brilliant aide like a son, put up with his peccadilloes, and used him judiciously. But the country was on the brink of war, and it was no time to indulge in jokes and silly one-upmanship. Besides, the old marshal was a hero of the Soviet Union and deserved respect.

"No, I have no ideas," Stashevsky said, sensing the mood in the room and adjusting to it. "But there are times when no ideas are better than stubborn, unimaginative, and wrong ones. The situation isn't clear. But, with all due respect, Marshal, you are not taking into consideration that the enemy may very well have something up his sleeve that we know nothing about."

"Our intelligence has produced a copy of their battle plan down to the last detail," the old soldier said, yawning to show his contempt.

"Marshal, our intelligence has produced a battle plan," Stashevsky said. "No doubt their spies have a copy of ours, just as we do of theirs. But what we have seen simply does not make sense. You agree to that. They are walking into a sure defeat, or as sure a defeat as anything ever is in war." Stashevsky stopped and lit a cigarette from the end of the one he had smoked down to the elegant filter tip. "You are assuming stupidity on the part of people who have never been stupid before. It seems to me a bad premise upon which to go into battle. There has to be some other explanation for their dispositions."

"And what do you suggest, young man?" Korzybsky asked, his old voice thickened with rage and sarcasm.

92

He had been a major at the time of the purges in 1938. After spending three years as a woodcutter in one of the worst camps along the Siberian Arctic Circle, he was rehabilitated late in 1941 during the German invasion when the Soviet Army was in shreds and the prisons and camps were emptied to provide officers for the new divisions. He had fought through the war as a tank commander, getting his division in 1943 at Karsk and his corps in the final days before Berlin. He bore seven wounds on his thick body, and he was partially deaf from the continual pounding of artillery shells. He was marshal of the Soviet Union. He did not h   it in this room and listen to a lecture on   a young fool who had never smelle

"I   thing, Marshal," Stashevsky said, his v   tial now, glancing at the general secre—   was looking at the old man with admiration   erant affection. That was Russia's problem   than sixty-five years after the Revolution. It till revered age and tradition. He was the only man in the room under fifty. "I only wish to point out that the situation lacks a certain logic and that we should continue to probe the enemy's intentions." He had covered himself. If the Chinese took some unexpected action, as he fully expected them to do, he would be remembered as a genius. If they didn't, the incident would be forgotten.

General William Jackson Harris grunted explosively as he charged the little black ball, flailing ineffectively as it ricocheted off the left wall, touched the backboard just above the thin strip of tin, and skittered away just off the tip of his racket. Perspiration poured off his face and dripped onto the sodden mass of his gray speckled sweatshirt. His eyes bulged with effort and his thick, hard belly lifted and fell in massive heaves as he sought to suck enough air into his lungs to steady himself.

His aide, a smooth-muscled young paratrooper who had played cornerback at the Point on one of the academy's worst teams since the disaster of 1973, leaned against the wall and waited for the older man to catch his breath. His smooth black skin glistened with a slight patina of sweat.

"Shit, Henry, I've got to quit this fucking game. One of these days you're gonna have to carry me outta here in a basket."

"Yes, sir."

The general grinned. And you, you black bastard, you'd grin all the way to the graveyard, he thought. "Serve."

Before the young black man could move to the service line, the low door onto the squash court opened and a sergeant stuck his head through. "Message from your office, General. Flash—nodis."

"How many times have I told you to stay the hell out of here while I'm playing? All right, McHenry, serve." Harris had long since established that if anything was so urgent it had to be done within the next fifteen minutes, then the situation was probably hopeless, anyway. And, at fifty-eight, one year away from retirement with forty years of honorable service, he refused to be buggered about.

"Twelve—ten, General," the aide said, then proceeded to lose the next five points and the game.

Harris swaggered off the court, grinning, knowing full well the young officer had thrown the game, not caring. One of the privileges of rank and age was making the young ones bend to his will. If you could make the aggressive, slim-bodied young studs eat shit, well, that was good. He'd eaten enough of it in his time, and now he was dishing it out and loving every minute of it.

"All right, gimme the goddamned message."

He glanced at the paper and frowned.

Central Intelligence Agency reports West German Army moving to full mobilization status. Armored units are moving out of base areas to East German frontier in Order of Battle Formation 78654. All reserves called up and moving to staging areas. Air force bases and anti-aircraft units on twenty-four-hour status. East German Army on similar red alert, but forces are not concentrating Lübeck line in conformance with strategy outlined in contingency plan 304-Fx. Indications are they are moving to prepared positions along Polish frontier.

Harris glanced at his watch. It was eight A.M. in Washington. He and his officers were scheduled to have dinner with the German general staff that evening. He would get General von und zu Feiersdorf aside and find out what the fuck was going on. Meantime, he'd have to stop copies of this message from getting back to the Pentagon; otherwise he'd have a bunch of hysterical White House nervous Nellies on his back within the hour.

Alec Thompson listened to the pedantic voice of the American ambassador in Bonn with patient resignation. The man, a former professor of German literature at Harvard who had contributed two hundred fifty thousand dollars to the last presidential campaign, was an educated fool.

"Alec, I tell you, you needn't worry. Beck assured me less than an hour ago that the partial mobilization of the West German Army is simply a routine exercise. They do something like this every three or four months. It's ridiculous to think this has anything to do with the situation in the Far East. The whole German general staff is gathered at Schloss Krohnheim to celebrate the victory at Buntzelwitz, and General Harris has been invited to dinner tonight. You think they would be doing something like that if they were planning some," his voice faltered, "some adventure?"

"Willy, I don't give a damn what Beck is really doing. All I know is that he has got our friends to the East in an uproar at a time when we think it would be better to have them as calm and secure as possible in Europe. Now, you get Beck. I don't care how, but you do it, and you read him this note. Get somebody to take it down or put it on your recording machine."

Thompson waited for the recorder's mandatory click and read: "The government of the United States presents its compliments to the government of the Federal Republic of Germany and wishes respectfully to point out that the present military exercises being conducted along its borders with the German Democratic Republic have aroused concern among its neighbors. In view of the tense international situation and the possibility of serious misunderstandings in connection with these maneuvers, the government of the United States wishes urgently to suggest that they be suspended for the duration of the present crisis. The government of the United States wishes to take this opportunity to express once again . . ." The note trailed off in the archaic language of formal diplomacy.

"My God, Alec, I can't send that to Beck! He'll reject it out of hand. It's," he groped, "it's arrogant."

"Willy, I think it's time you got something straight. The Chinese and the Russians are about to go to war.

96

Once they start, nobody knows what the hell will happen. The Germans are mobilizing at the Soviet Union's rear. Now, Willy, even you and Beck can understand that this is going to make our friends goddamned nervous. I'd tell the son-of-a-bitch myself, but they're not answering their phones. So get over to the chancellery right now and report back in immediately."

Thompson glanced at his watch. It was almost two P.M. There had been no answer to the president's proposals for a meeting in Geneva from either the Chinese or the Soviets. His desk was littered with reports from Samsun's office indicating that military preparations along the Amur and Ussuri rivers had very nearly reached the point of no return. Almost six million men confronted each other across the Russian-Chinese frontier. Orders of battle must have already been issued. To stop the vast machine was going to be virtually impossible.

He punched a button on the desk console. "Get me Dimitri in Moscow." It was nine o'clock in the evening there, but Stashevsky was sure to be in his office. Within thirty seconds the communications miracle lit up a red button on the gray phone occupying a separate table behind his desk.

"Dimitri?"

The Russian's weary voice, sounding as if it were submerged in water, came back. "Good evening, Alec. Or should I say afternoon? I have good news for you. The Politburo meeting just ended after a six-hour session. We agree to the president's proposal for a meeting, provided the Chinese also accept. But you must let us know their reply as soon as possible. We will not touch our military dispositions until we hear from you."

"It's a big concession, Dimitri. The chairman is a

world statesman." For twenty-five years the Soviet Union had refused to discuss the Siberian border problem with the Chinese.

"Yes. We've done our part. Now you've got to get the Chinese agreement, Alec. You must move quickly." Stashevsky hung up and leaned back in the soft leather of his father's chair, put his feet up on the mahogany desk, a relic of Czarist times, and stared at Thompson's picture. He wasn't really comfortable in the ridiculous posture that he had copied from a roommate at Stanford, but Soviet psychologists in their recent studies on the intellect had evolved the theory that mannerisms and styles were a fundamental part of human thought processes. Thus, if you seek to penetrate the brain of a German banker, it was useful to assume the attitudes of such a man, both intellectual and physical. And he was trying to enter into the intellectual core of Alec Thompson, who seemed to spend most of his life slumped on his spine with his feet up.

He had some priceless information that was not in the file, of course—from Harry Taliaferro, the American agent he had broken into small, chipped pieces and put carefully back together again before returning him as a double agent. Taliaferro had been an unexpected prize. Stashevsky had been in Hanoi heading a team of KGB interrogation specialists in the early 1960s. His star had already begun to rise, and it was his last assignment for the bureau before being transferred to the chairman's personal staff. Maybe that was why Taliaferro had been such a challenge.

The Vietcong had picked him off a Hue street, intending to kill an American agent as a lesson to the special elimination squads that the CIA had set up. But the young Viet intelligence officer realized at the last minute that the man was a more valuable prize. Taliaferro had been in Hanoi for two months when Stashevsky met him. The Vietnamese had used their standard tactics, mostly inherited from the French: electric shock; dental drills; heavily lighted rooms that denied rest; continual interrogation by teams alternately humane and brutal. He had not broken, of course. Men like that seldom did. Suicide was much more probable as they reached the end of their resources.

Stashevsky had him taken out of the prison and lodged in a small hotel under heavy guard. In the United States KGB agents quickly located his family, and within days a folder was in Stashevsky's hands. Wife of extraordinary beauty, whom Taliaferro idolized. Son in medical school. Fifteen-year-old daughter of great promise and intelligence. Taliaferro had been amused when he told him the problem they both faced. He, Stashevsky, needed a great deal of information about the inner workings of the CIA. Taliaferro was in a position to give it to him. He was going to have to insist on cooperation.

The American agent, a slender man in his late forties, had grinned. He had wanted to know how Stashevsky planned to do this. They had begun with the wife, first, because it was easier, and, second, because despite Taliaferro's obvious love for her, it was the least of the shocks. An American KGB agent of immense sexual vitality and attraction to women had first tried to seduce her without success. He had then, rather crudely, Stashevsky thought, shown her eight-millimeter movies of her husband being tortured and explained to her that he could be of some assistance if the woman offered herself to him. The films of the subsequent sexual encounters had demonstrated the agent's immense aptitude for the genre. He had rapidly reduced a reluctant, even hysterical, partner to an enthusiastic participant in a variety of rather esoteric sexual adventures.

Taliaferro had watched the films impassively, turning at the end to Stashevsky with a smile. "Superb technique, huh?"

But he had known what was coming. And the act had begun to crack when Stashevsky explained in detail a plan to destroy his son's medical career by hooking him on heroin under the guise of a treatment for syphilis, which he would contract from a female agent. He broke completely when a film showed his fifteen-year-old daughter in deep conversation with a spectacular young black whom Stashevsky described, accurately, as one of the most successful pimps in New York. And, incidentally, he was a convinced member of the Party willing to place his peculiar talents at the Party's disposal.

"He will arrange for her to work in a crib in New Orleans catering to the tastes of aging black men, Mr. Taliaferro. I can assure you the whole business would be most distasteful to me personally. But with a man such as yourself, we have very little leverage. She would be destroyed within a matter of months."

Taliaferro had hardly changed expression. "Okay, let's get started."

The tapes had been a remarkable amalgam of truth and lies, as the man tried to give them what he thought they already had, while withholding or distorting the rest. It had taken two months to drain him. But the results were invaluable—almost their first insights into CIA operating techniques and the psychology of the agency's leaders. Incidental to this had been a profile of Thompson, the intellectual killer, the classic Renaissance man, combining a crisp, incisive, yet introspective intelligence with that dispassionate ruthlessness that characterized truly dangerous men. And, yet, through some quirk of personality, training, or pure genetics, he had retained enough of the humanist core to remain in contact with his fellowman. It was this quality that fascinated Stashevsky, for he recognized it in himself. Without it one became a Himmler or a Beria. With it, one could do what one had to and still survive.

The president opened the door connecting their offices and entered, face gray, and dropped a cable tabbed with a red "Urgent" sticker on his desk. "The Chinese Government respectfully wishes to thank the U.S. Government for its offer of mediation with the Union of Soviet Socialist Republics. However, the Chinese government is unable to accept the offer inasmuch as the U.S.S.R. has repeatedly given evidence of bad faith in the matter. Only following prior agreement to discuss in detail the following border adjustments will the Government of China consent to a meeting in Geneva." The list was long and detailed. It amounted to a demand for virtually all the disputed territory east of Lake Baikal and north of the Amur River.

"Jesus, it's the Chinese ultimatum."

The president nodded. "I think we'd better ask our military people to go on a medium-grade alert just to be on the safe side. I've decided to sit tight, Alec, and not interfere at this time. I'm going to talk to Kharkov now."

Thompson leaned back in his chair and propped his feet on the cluttered desk, letting the flood of weariness roll over him. For the first time since Vietnam, he had the hopeless feeling of being out of control, of events taking over as if they had an inner logic impenetrable to the men who supposedly were their masters. In Vietnam it had begun in the Vietcong-controlled village of Ben Hut in the Mekong Delta in 1963. The Cong had come into a government area two days before, taken over a crossroads town for ten hours, murdered the mayor and the chief of police, and slipped away before South Vietnamese troops could get through.

In Saigon the station chief had called a meeting of all top CIA personnel, the army general in command of the U.S. military assistance group in Vietnam, and the colonel commanding the Green Beret detachments. Stanford Cabot had looked more like a Wall Street lawyer than the top spy in Vietnam. He was a tall, slender, graying man with a lined, distinguished face who had begun in the business in World War II. His most famous exploit had been the destruction of the German Third Army intelligence headquarters in Lyon in early 1944. Dressed as a German Army officer, he had walked into the building carrying four plastic bombs concealed in a long circular map-carrying roll. More than fifty top German intelligence specialists had been killed in the explosions that followed. Twenty years later nothing much had changed.

"Gentlemen, you're all busy men, so I'll come right to the point. The South Vietnamese are beginning to lose this war. We all know why. The enemy is much more highly motivated and exceptionally well organized, and also utterly ruthless. The Vietcong cadres' strategy has recently begun to have a paralyzing effect in the villages. The systematic murder of village officials loyal to Saigon is causing the government cadres to melt away in terror. Something has got to be done to stop the hemorrhaging." Cabot spoke in the slightly nasal accents of Choate and Princeton, never raising his voice.

"We have, therefore, decided to adopt their tactics." He stopped and looked around the room at the eight CIA section chiefs. "The South Vietnamese have set up a clandestine organization to go into the villages and kill Vietcong cadre leaders." Somebody in the room snorted derisively.

Cabot looked up sharply. "Exactly. It will be penetrated within days, if not hours, and very little will happen . . . which leaves the job up to us. Alec, you're going to head the group. You'll begin in the village of Ben Hut." Cabot turned to the map behind him and indicated a speck on a large-scale map of the Mekong Delta. "We know that the cadre commander of this area has his headquarters in the village. A Cong defector has told the South Vietnamese that he'll be having a meeting of his group the day after tomorrow in the village chief's house. Colonel Sirica and fifty of his men, with the help of a company of South Vietnamese rangers, will secure the village, and you'll go in with your team and execute the cadre."

"How do we get there?" Thompson asked.

"We've brought in a special helicopter force to transport you. Surprise will be total. The whole operation shouldn't take more than two hours; if it does, you're in trouble. There is a battalion of Vietcong camped here." Cabot indicated a spot on the map about ten miles from the village. "There are fewer than a dozen Cong in the village itself. Any questions?"

Nobody said anything. After the first shock, the operation had seemed eminently logical. The choice of Thompson imposed itself because of his wartime experience in Korea. Preparation had been simple. Thompson and his top aid, Harry Taliaferro, had coordinated with the Green Beret commander, who told the South Vietnamese nothing about the operation. They had lifted off before dawn, the choppers sounding like giant mixmasters gone berserk. Ben Hut, a village of less than two thousand people, had been taken without a shot being fired. They had moved swiftly from the landing area to surround the chief's hut. No attack had been necessary. Four men in the classic loose-fitting black uniform of the Vietcong had surrendered along with the village chief and his family.

The Viecong informer, a cringing, twitching wreck following four days of interrogation by the South Vietnamese, had pointed to one of the four youths, identifying him as the cadre chief. A South Vietnamese ranger captain had machine-gunned the four as they stood in the village square.

It had been a crude operation, successful only because the helicopters had offered the element of total surprise. They were never able to duplicate it. Vietcong intelligence had been too good. Three expeditions had ended in near disaster before Cabot had ordered a change in tactics. Rewards were offered for the death of known Vietcong cadre leaders. Saigon's bandit gangs were recruited to send killer teams into the villages and bring out specific targets. Harry Taliaferro had shown an unexpected talent for the job.

The operation had become a routine part of the CIA's structure in Vietnam by 1965 when they had executed the informer. They had been forced, by the very nature of the job, to take on half a dozen Vietnamese specialists, translators, and guides, all given rigorous security investigations. But by the end of 1966 it was obvious that they were infiltrated. Finding the traitor had proved surprisingly simple. A series of expeditions was organized with only one of the Vietnamese participating. Three went off without a hitch. The fourth was wiped out.

Harry Taliaferro had come into Thompson's head-quarters with the dossier. "It's got to be Nhu. We checked it every way. Nobody else could have been involved." They had put two South Vietnamese security men on him. Another expedition was set up, with Nhu participating. The same day he was caught with a known Vietcong agent in a Saigon café.

They questioned him in relays for three days until he cracked. He was a Christian from the North. His family had fled to the South in 1954, leaving one of his brothers behind. The brother had come to the South and recruited him. No ideology. No revolutionary ideals. A family connection. He had cost them more than a dozen men betrayed to the Cong.

They had taken Nhu out into the Delta the next day, and Taliaferro had handed Thompson the .38. He was the commander. It was up to him to do the job. He remembered being surprised at how little blood there had been in the back of the man's head. They had come back, and the two Green Berets, he, and Taliaferro had gotten drunk. But it hadn't made much of an impact at the time. People were dying all around them friends, enemies, women, children. And there was a certain machismo about it all. You did what you had to do, no matter how brutal it was, and that was that.

But the press had begun to close in on them about this time, and the Nhu incident surfaced. Somehow the CIA had convinced the army to take the fall, and Thompson's name was never connected with the incident. The Green Berets were blamed, and the story died after a week. Most stories did.

Ten years later, during his first meeting with Chou after the 1976 election, he had caught the old man looking at him across the dinner table with an ironic smile. Finally, Chou had leaned forward, speaking his curious sibilant German and raising the miniscule glass of Chinese white lightning, and he said, "I drink to you, Mr. Thompson, as the only American I have met who is as ruthless as we old revolutionaries. It is a pleasure to deal with a man who knows death as we do; it makes him respect it more—and fear it less." He had only then remembered the old story of Chou's personal execution of seven Party defectors in Shanghai during the 1930s. He was supposed to have shot them in the back of the head with a Luger.

7

General William Harris walked up the steps of Schloss
Kronheim conscious once again, as he always was, of
how well the Germans did it. The sergeant who
opened the door of his Chevrolet had stood ramrod
straight, his boots gleaming like mirrors. The honor
guard had come to attention as his foot hit the first
step, polished World War I rifles moving as one unit,
heels coming together with a crisp leathery crack at
the sound of the young lieutenant's barked order.
Not an eye moved. Nobody but a soldier who had
seen men die by the thousands because of sloppy discipline and untrained green officers could appreciate
what it all meant. God, it made him want to cry at
the frustrations he'd lived through in his own goddamned army ruined by the fucking civilians.

General Fabian, Freiherr von und zu Feiersdorf,
met him at the top of the stairs, an imposing figure in
a blue dress uniform with gold piping. When Beck

took over as prime minister, the German Army officers had unobtrusively begun wearing their World War II decorations. Feiersdorf wore only one, the Ritterkreuz mit Schwertern und Brillianten, the highest decoration of the German Army. "My dear Bill, what a pleasure to see you." Feiersdorf spoke almost unaccented British English, a result of two years at Cambridge in the years just after the war. He had entered the German Army in 1938 as an officer-cadet and had ended it as a colonel in temporary command of the remnants of a division in East Prussia. When the Russians surrounded the German Army, Feiersdorf had taken a small sailboat and, with his adjutant, crossed the Baltic to Sweden.

He ignored Harris's salute and took him by the arm, leading him into the main hall of the old castle. It had belonged to an extinct branch of the Hapsburg family and in recent years had been converted into the ceremonial headquarters of the reconstituted German general staff. Battle flags of famous German regiments of the past hung from the rafters, and immense nineteenth-century paintings in the romantic style depicting the great battles of German history decorated the walls. Harris stopped momentarily in front of one showing the destruction of the legions of the Roman consul, Vara, in nine A.D. and von Feiersdorf grinned. "It's awful, Bill. In fact, the whole business is. Believe me, we were all a bit embarrassed by it. But you can't run an army without tradition, and for some reason the young ones are immensely awed by it all, even the phony armor we had made in an automobile body shop. There is one compensation—the cellar is excellent, and we have a fine chef who was trained at the Cordon Bleu in Paris."

The room was full of a glittering assemblage of German and NATO officers. The British and French contingent commanders were huddled with the German Air Force chief in front of an immense fireplace, and throughout the vast entry hall of the castle clusters of bemedaled figures sipped champagne and talked of old wars. The ostensible excuse for the evening was to pay homage to Frederick the Great's victory at Buntzelwitz. Long tables cluttered with exquisite linen, silver, and crystal were visible through an arched opening. The great pictures, the flags, the ancient armament, and the colorful crowd of officers below evoked innocent memories of the nineteenth century, when war was the sport of gentlemen rather than the suicide of the masses.

The British force commander detached himself from his French colleague and greeted Harris. "I say, Bill, good to see you."

"Hello, Harold," Harris said, extending a meaty red paw. He disliked the Brit, having long since detected under the forced heartiness a contempt and distaste for things American.

"Hear you've had a bit of a morale problem at the missile site outside Hanover. All's well now, I hope."

Harris nodded, annoyed. Some of his bored young officers had been playing the key game with their German counterparts and trouble had erupted. "Yeah, we resolved that."

The Brit slapped him on the shoulder. "A little more discipline, Bill, that's what your army needs. Know what we always say about morale: 'Grab 'em by the balls, and their hearts and minds will follow.' Just look at these chaps." He gestured to the respectful waiters standing at attention. "Mindless robots, but superb soldiers. Follow their officers into absolute hell. And what do we have? All that shit about individual initiative and improvisation. I saw it kill thousands of men in World War Two while these chaps fought with a disciplined calm that made one want to weep."

Harris didn't like the man, but he agreed with him. Over the past five years the West German Army had shaken off its attempt to "democratize" itself and gradually reassumed all the great old Prussian traditions. Discipline was savage. Officers were superbly trained and indoctrinated. An inner loyalty had developed with amazing rapidity, and there seemed no question but that the German Army, with its reconstituted general staff, was once again an autonomous entity within the nation.

As they entered the dining room, an army band struck up a medley of military marches from all the NATO nations, playing with an exquisite precision and delicacy that made the White House strings sound like a cow-town high school band. Feiersdorf led Harris to the head table and placed him at his right, aligning the other Allied commanders by rank and seniority with an unobtrusive but nonetheless firm hand. The meal was about what Harris would have expected: lobster in aspic; some sort of small game bird cooked in a Madeira sauce; a superbly delicate boiled beef with fresh horseradish and spring vegetables; an immense platter of cheeses; and chocolate cake. The service had been a little oppressive in its military efficiency, Harris thought, savoring the last of a superb Bordeaux as the fourth wine glass was filled with a white German after-dinner wine made from grapes that had been picked individually from the vines after they had partially dried to raisinlike consistency. It cost, Harris knew, sixty dollars a bottle.

Feiersdorf rose as the last dish was lifted from the table and tapped his wine glass with his signet ring. The bell-like tone of the crystal gradually reduced

110

the room to silence. "Gentlemen, we are gathered here this evening to honor a warrior king who was also a philosopher and an intellectual. He laid the groundwork on which Bismarck was later to build a great nation. But until this unique prince taught us what we were, the Germans had been nothing more than a scattering of anarchic tribes, prey to any disciplined force that chose to attack and loot us. It was Frederick who taught us that we were not only mindlessly brave, but that we could also organize ourselves, build up industry, conquer empires, and withstand with stoicism the inevitable defeats. I think, gentlemen, he would have been proud of the German nation and its army tonight. Thirty years ago we were a defeated and crushed people, ground under the heels of the victorious coalition that had attacked Germany from all sides." Harris glanced around him and noted the irritated looks beginning to appear on the faces of his Western European colleagues. The Dutchman was white with rage. "Tonight, Germany is the most powerful nation in Europe. Its industry is rebuilt, its army a weapon without compare. Yes, I think Frederick the Great would have been proud of us, gentlemen, as we are proud of him. And so I shall ask all of you to stand and drink to the greatest German of them all."

The Allied officers stood and drank, although the Frenchman barely made a pretense of raising the glass to his lips. Felersdorf remained standing as his guests took their seats. "One of the reasons Frederick was such a great warrior," he continued, "was his uncanny ability to recognize just the right moment to strike. He had what our American friends call superb 'timing.' And, above all, he had luck. Well, gentlemen, I hope he will have one more reason to be satisfied with us tonight, because I think our timing may also be superb—and all we will need is luck." He glanced at his watch as, unobtrusively, the walls behind the tables filled with soldiers of the guard of honor who had traded their ceremonial rifles for short-barreled submachine guns.

"At this precise moment, gentlemen, a joint announcement is being made over German radio and television proclaiming the reunification of our nation. The barriers between us are being removed, and German soldiers on both sides of the shameful border are embracing." He turned to Harris and the British and French generals further down the table. "I must apologize to our allied friends for not having been able to let them in on our little secret, but I'm sure they'll understand. I am also a trifle embarassed about the next announcement I have to make." His voice had hardened now and showed no trace of embarassment.

"I fear I shall have to ask you all to be our guests for a few days here at Schloss Kronheim. You see, German troops have at this very minute entered every Allied installation in Germany and disarmed the occupation troops. The holders of the duplicate key mechanism for the jointly controlled atomic weapons have been overpowered and relieved of their keys, which are now in the hands of the German Army. In other words, gentlemen, a united Germany is now a nuclear power with the means of utterly destroying the Soviet Union, should that nation object to our reunification."

Harris had risen from his chair, as had the other NATO representatives present at the dinnner. Nobody knew quite what to do. Harris cleared his throat. "Fabian, do I understand that I am your prisoner?"

The German smiled. "Good Lord, Bill, don't put it that way. We're just taking our country back." He

112

spread his hands. "After thirty-two years, who can blame us for that? And please understand," he said, facing his audience once again, "this has not been directed against our friends. They will stay with us for their own safety until the details of a new Atlantic Alliance can be worked out. Our East German brothers have surrounded the Soviet forces in their territory, and trains are even now being prepared to send them back to Russia. The Poles," he paused for dramatic effect, "are doing the same thing in their territory. Gentlemen, I ask you to raise your glasses to a free, united Germany. *Es lebe Deutschland.*"

The telephone jangled persistently, pulling Thompson awake. He leaned across the curled body of Suzanne Wilson and cradled the instrument against his shoulder. The luminous dial on his watch read five A.M.

"Alec?"

"Yeah, Gordon. What's up?"

The CIA director wasted no words. "Some sort of coup has taken place in Germany. The border barriers have come down and the two armies are fraternizing. Also, the Germans have taken over all our installations in Germany. Every soldier we have there is a prisoner. What's more, they've taken most of my people into protective custody. About the only ones who escaped were the zero teams." Zero teams were special groups of CIA agents known only to a control in Washington and separate from the normal field operations. "Otherwise, we wouldn't have known about this until we read the papers."

"What about the nuclear weapons?" Thompson asked, already knowing the answer, wondering how the hell he could have been so stupid not to think of it.

"The keys are in German hands." Wiseman paused, and Thompson could hear him take a deep breath. "They overpowered our men holding the duplicate keys at a prearranged signal. No destructive action was possible. It was a contingency we just never thought of. Hell, they were our most loyal and reliable allies. Now they've got an integrated nuclear capability—seven thousand warheads. Beck has informed the president that his people have secretly built more than a hundred IBMs with a range sufficient to hit any target in the world. And, of course, they've got the submarine capability. Overall, it's nowhere near as formidable as ours or the Soviets', but it's enough to destroy us or them if they felt like it. It's a credible deterrent to Soviet invasion, especially right now with the Chinese about to attack."

"Who led this? The Army? Beck?"

"We're not sure. I just told you, most of my people are in German jails."

Wiseman's bitterness came across the phone in a splutter of hatred. A warning flickered out of Thompson's subconscious. They will have to watch his reports from now on. He didn't like the Germans anyway and this betrayal would probably be enough to turn off any objectivity. "However, it looks as if Beck and Gerhardus set it up together. The army is just carrying out orders—with classic German efficiency. They had the entire Allied staffs for dinner at Schloss Kronheim and just kept them there—as 'guests.' No question about it, it was beautifully done."

"What about the Russians in East Germany?"

"The barracks were surrounded and the troops were disarmed. Our satellite scannners show them already being loaded onto trains. The Poles are in on it, Alec. Same thing happened there. They've obviously made some sort of deal with the Germans."

114

"Have you told the president?"

"Yes. He's waiting for you at the White House."

"Do me a favor, Gordon, send a car for me. I'll be there in ten minutes."

Thompson slipped out of bed, inadvertently pulling the covers off Suzanne Wilson's bare behind. He flicked the sheet back over her hips, feeling tired at the sight of them, and headed for the bathroom. Sooner or later he was going to have to get some sleep.

The president paced back and forth across the seal decorating the rug in the center of the Oval Office, his big ex-athlete's body coiled with tension as he pounded his right fist into the palm of his left hand, small explosions ricocheting off the walls of the room in the early morning silence. Wiseman and Thompson sat drinking coffee from the oversized white mugs decorated with the presidential seal. The man's brand was on everything, but at times like this it didn't seem necessary. When the shit hit the fan, it always became frighteningly apparent that all the power was concentrated in his big, meaty hands. He was thinking out loud, analyzing the situation and his options.

"It's brilliant, absolutely brilliant! Christ, the simplicity of it all! It's the one thing nobody ever really thought of! And so goddamned obvious!" He turned on Thompson and Wiseman, his heavy face lined with fatigue, blue eyes as hard as stone. "And you two geniuses have been telling me for years what a crock old Beck was. Unstable. Stupid. Thick-necked Kraut living in the past. Well, what do you think of him now?" Nobody spoke, and the president continued to pace. "Brilliant! That's what the son-of-a-bitch is! And he must have held it so close to his chest that no more than half a dozen of his absolutely top people

115

knew about it; otherwise, you would have found out, huh, Gordon?" He stopped in front of the head spook and stared down at him. Wiseman, the epitome of cool, had begun to perspire on his forehead and upper lip, although the room was cold. He said nothing. There was nothing to say. If you're the chief spook and you miss the big one, you're replaced. His days were numbered by the length of the crisis. Once it was over, he was finished.

"Well, what the hell do we do now?" The question was rhetorical. "Together they've got about a million men, one of the most powerful air forces in the world, and nuclear weapons capable of wiping out all our big cities. God only knows what they could do to the Soviets. Tell me, Alec, just what are our options?"

Thompson shrugged. "If you mean what can we do to Beck, the answer is nothing. He's got a credible deterrent. If we tried to mobilize the French, British, and NATO forces against him, they'd tell us to go screw. However, the longer I look at the situation, the less bad it looks."

The president stopped in mid-stride and looked down at him. "Just what the fuck is that supposed to mean?"

Thompson leaned back in the big overstuffed chair cradling the heavy white coffee mug and met the president's stare. "From our standpoint, just what does this mean? It means another nuclear power, which is bad. It means a Europe dominated by Germany, which it was pretty much anyway. And it means that the Soviet Union has another massive enemy right on its borders. Kharkov is bound to be dismayed. He's cornered now between two major world powers. Within a few hours the Chinese are going to attack."

"You're sure?" the president said, interrupting.

Thompson nodded. "No question about it now. That

meeting with the Germans the French reported must have happened. They set it up together. The Germans probably wouldn't have had the nerve to move unless the Chinese had agreed to attack. The Russians might have been just frightened or irrational enough to accept the possibility of a German nuclear attack and invade on the theory it would cost them less now than later."

"But you don't think they will now?" The president didn't sound so sure.

"No. I don't think they will. Maybe they will once they've disposed of the Chinese. If they can win a decisive encounter in the Far East, they may decide the Germans are just too damned dangerous not to hit now. They've got to figure that in five years a united Germany will probably be so powerful nobody will be able to take it on. It might be cheaper to take fifty million dead now and destroy them."

The president nodded, dropping heavily into a chair. "It all sounds eminently logical. Trouble is, everything we've been counting on has sounded logical, but it hasn't worked out the way we expected." Thompson felt a quiver of anxiety shoot down his spine. Wiseman might not be the only one looking for a job when this crisis was over.

"Kharkov doesn't have the horses to attack on both fronts at once," Thompson said, letting his voice slide a tone lower, pouring a soothing coolness over the tension filling the room like invisible viscid fluid. "He's got to accept the Chinese attack, deal with it the best he can, and play for time in the West. There's almost certainly going to be trouble in Rumania, Czechoslovakia, and Hungary. About the only satellite they can be sure of is Bulgaria. Kharkov is just going to have to face it. It's the breakup. The end of the postwar Soviet empire in Europe. The question we've got to ask is: Is this in our self-interest or not? When you're confronted with a new situation, the natural reaction is to assume the worst. But let's face it, this is precisely what our foreign policy was working for in the 1950s and 1960s. Just what the hell are we afraid of now?" Thompson sipped the strong, bitter coffee. "Christ, as I think about it, about the only thing that really bothers me in the situation is the fact that I've been working comfortably with the Russians for a decade, and now I've got to begin with people I don't really know and can't trust."

"You're suggesting that it's in our self-interest to have Germany and the Soviet Union confronting each other on terms of equality in Europe?" The president was incredulous.

"We don't seem to have much choice. The Germans have been waiting a long time and showing more patience than they have ever before. Let's face it, they've been the strongest nation in Europe since 1866. Their own impatience and stupidity robbed them of victory both in 1914 and 1939. If they'd waited, Europe would have fallen in their lap. This time they have waited, and it begins to look as if they might have won."

"There's a difference between recognizing that historical inevitability you like to talk about so much and welcoming a disaster just because it fits into a pattern." The president's voice had in it a certain rough contempt, the practical pragmatic politician confronted with scholarly theory.

Thompson met his gaze steadily. There wasn't much point in backing away here. He was paid to be right in situations like this. If the man quit listening, he was through. "It makes even less sense to piss into the wind."

The president stared at him for a split second before finally letting a grin spread across his face. "You know, Alec, you were beginning to worry me there for a minute with all the theoretical bullshit. Okay, let's quit pissing into the wind and figure out what we're going to do."

8

Colonel General Valeri Gorbykov listened to the rolling thunder of the barrage in disbelief. He had been too young for World War II, and his knowledge of it had come from innumerable bull sessions of his elders at a thousand mess tables over the past thirty years. But the reality was nothing like what he had imagined. Thousands of Chinese guns had erupted across the river, emerging from camouflaged bunkers like a mass of insects, and three miles in front of him incoming Chinese rounds were landing among the riverbank fortifications. His own guns were now beginning to reply. Chinese rockets were landing in salvos of six, beginning at the river's edge and "walking" inland at intervals of twenty meters. He had ordered most of the troops out of the bunkers during the night, leaving behind only a few communications and maintenance troops. Most would crack under the barrage. That was the experience of both world wars.

A few would run screaming from the protection of the concrete and be destroyed. The ones who remained would mostly recover. But some would be twitching wrecks for the rest of their lives.

Across the river the pontoon bridges were being pushed out into the river by amphibious tanks. His own artillery, operating on coordinates agreed on months, even years, before, was laying down a blanket of fire along the river's edge. He had never believed in the attack. There was no way for the Chinese to cross the river in the face of the kind of withering fire his guns could bring to bear. And if they did, the massed armor just over the ridge line behind him would rip them to shreds. Only a total idiot would engage in such a battle.

As Gorbykov watched, a wave of light amphibious tanks disengaged itself from the masses of pontoons emerging from their camouflage and headed across the river for the opposite bank. For a moment Gorbykov was puzzled at what seemed like strings of spaghetti hanging from the tanks until he realized that each of the amphibians was covered with the ant-like figures of Chinese infantrymen.

Gorbykov barked an order to an aide and the short-range artillery above the beachhead belched a hail of shells at the oncoming tanks. He realized that he'd made a mistake. Across the river Chinese heavy howitzers instantly laid down a withering return barrage. It would have been better to wait before revealing his artillery emplacements. Not that it made much difference; the guns were so deeply embedded that nothing would knock them out.

Chinese planes suddenly appeared low over the horizon, skimming the river at what looked like a meter above the water, laying down a thick layer of putrid yellow smoke in front of the oncoming tanks.

Gorbykov smiled and shook his head. His artillery radar would zero in on the tanks and pick them off one by one. An aide appeared. "General," someone called in an urgent tone, "that smoke has some sort of metallic particles in it. It's fouling up the radar."

The Chinese tanks were hitting the beach now, wave after wave of crab-like machines clawing at the tank obstacles as the Chinese planes made another pass. Four went down before the Soviet anti-aircraft fire, but the smoke was everywhere.

Reports from up and down the river confirmed a similar scene. Above the battlefield, the air forces of both armies were fighting a grim battle for control of the skies. At several points along the river hundreds of jet trails interweaved among each other like an abstractionist painting, and regularly one of the shark-nosed planes broke off in a blot of smoke and flame and spiraled downward. The sky was flecked with the parachutes of the victims. Just above their heads, wave after wave of rocket and cannon-firing close-support aircraft were attacking the oncoming Chinese tanks and the bridge builders across the river.

Gorbykov could see nothing through the mass of smoke and exploding shells. He motioned to his staff to follow and climbed the bunker steps to the roof, where a battery of six 40-mm anti-aircraft guns was spitting an unending stream of metal at the low-flying planes. The incoming howitzer shell hit the bunker squarely, its shell exploding on impact, killing the entire headquarters staff of the Soviet Third Army.

Thompson stared at his desk, awash with cables from virtually every embassy in the world. He had called Suzanne an hour earlier and warned her to get down to her office. Now as he flicked on the battery of television sets across the room, her face formed in front of him. He could imagine the chaos of the Federal Broadcasting studios as the news flooded in from AP, UPI, Reuters, Agence France Press, and their own correspondents. Film teams were being formed in twenty cities around the world, planes chartered, telephone lines leased, and satellite circuits overloaded—all for a thirty-second spot on a program watched by half-sleepy people hardly aware of where the unpronounceable and distant names were. Suzanne was in the anchorman slot, looking obscenely fresh and cool.

"And now a commentary on the news by Willoughby G. Pepperdine," Suzanne said, turning to the commentator.

"Good morning." Pepperdine's face was set in a stern mask. "It begins to look as if the postwar world order is coming apart at the seams this morning. The reemergence in Europe of a united, nuclear-armed Germany is a phenomenon that was inevitable in the long term, but exceedingly dangerous at this time. The destabilizing effect on Europe will be immense. The remnants of our troops in Europe, now surrounded and imprisoned by the German Army, will be sent home within a matter of days, according to German Premier Horst Bock. And that will mark the end of an era, an era during which the United States guaranteed the status quo in Europe and in fact dictated all major moves of the Western Alliance.

"The other half of that stability was the Soviet empire in Eastern Europe. For many years we mouthed a set of pious platitudes about 'freeing Eastern Europe from Communism,' but our statesmen never meant it. Only a fool would have preferred a collection of anarchic small states capable of any stupidity to Soviet domination in this vital region. Far better the benevolent despotism of the Soviet Union, which at least maintained stability, rather than the horrors of an unknown 'freedom.'

"Now Poland has revolted and declared its independence of the Soviet bloc. The Czech Politburo is in session, and indications are that a similar declaration will be forthcoming. Soviet troops are pulling back voluntarily from both Hungary and Czechoslovakia, and there is virtually no doubt that within the week there will be upheavals within the regimes of every Eastern European state except Bulgaria in order to bring power to men capable of making arrangements with the West to assure their security against the Soviet Union once it has dealt with the Chinese attack in the East.

"We will then be confronted with a fluid political situation similar to that which existed between the two world wars when a resurgent Germany dominated Central Europe economically and politically and a worried France and Britain combined with the Soviet Union to contain its power.

"In the East the frightening consortium of Japan and China is about to be joined by India. This inevitably means an Asian bloc encompassing every nation from Australia east to Pakistan and containing more than two-thirds of the world's population.

"The specter evoked by the great German historian Oswald Spengler has suddenly become a reality. If the Western nations continue to fight their petty internecine battles, he said in 1917, then they will go the way of the Greek and Italian city states that were unable to unite against the peril from without. The natural self-interest of all Western nations, including Germany and the Soviet Union, is to come together to defend the values of our civilization against the new coalition in the East. Otherwise, the 'Decline of the West' will become a fact as well as a forecast. And now here's Suzanne with the latest news."

Suzanne reappeared on the screen, her cool self-possession in sharp contrast to the rugged image projected by Pepperdine.

"We have more news from Germany. The American garrison in West Berlin fought a ten-hour battle with West and East German forces last night before being overpowered. More than two hundred of our troops were killed and a thousand wounded. Premier Horst Beck has sent a personal letter of apology to the president and has offered to pay an indemnity to the soldiers' families. The French and British garrisons surrendered after putting up a token resistance.

"The West German state-controlled radio has announced the formal reunification of the two German states with West German Premier Horst Beck becoming interim President and East German Communist Party Secretary Gerhardus becoming Prime Minister. The new government has announced that new nationwide elections would be held within two months. In the meantime, the nation will be ruled by decree. Both parliaments voted full powers to the regime before dissolving themselves.

"Trainloads of disarmed Soviet troops are now streaming across East Germany and Poland toward the Soviet border, and jubilant crowds are surging through the streets of Warsaw celebrating the nation's freedom from foreign control for the first time in nearly forty years.

"In Czechoslovakia, the Politburo of the Communist Party has been in continuous session for fourteen hours. Prague is calm and the Czech people seem indifferent to the situation. In Hungary, however, army tanks have rolled into Budapest and sealed off the city. The Hungarian Politburo, also in continuous session, has called for calm until the situation is clarified. Rumania, which declared its independence from the Soviet Union nearly a decade ago, has also stationed a large number of security forces in the capital city, but otherwise has taken no special precautions. Bulgarian Party First Secretary Valdimir Bazala has declared his nation's undying loyalty to the Soviet Union."

As Suzanne talked, the screen cut to film footage of each of the Eastern European capitals.

"On the Sino-Soviet border, fighting continues. The Soviet Union has accused the Chinese of unprovoked aggression in their attack across the Amur and Ussuri rivers near Khabarovsk. News of the actual fighting continues to be sketchy, although we hope the United States government will release pictures from its satellites later in the day, at which point it should be possible to assess the situation more accurately.

"And that's the news this morning. Our programming will be interrupted throughout the day for special news bulletins, so stay with us."

Thompson flicked off the set and leaned back in his chair, feeling a new wave of exhaustion roll over him. Sooner or later he was going to have to get some sleep. The inter-office buzzer jerked him erect and the president came on.

"Better come on in, Alec. Pruitt and Samsun are here."

Thompson greeted the two generals and accepted his third mug of coffee from Jane Cleveland. "Okay, what have you got, Craig?"

The big general sank into an easy chair and slurped up a mouthful of coffee. "Not much. The Chinese have launched a massive attack at the junction of the Ussuri and the Amur. Show him, Phil." Samsun unfolded a large-scale map of the battle area. "They're using pretty conventional tactics—pontoon bridges, amphibious tanks in the first wave, followed by armored landing craft and masses of motorized rubber boats. They're laying down smoke over the whole battlefield, first with planes, then from the boats as they cover the river. There's a massive artillery barrage designed to keep the Russians' heads down."

"How is the battle going?"

"The Chinese seem to be doing a little better than we expected. One of the Soviet Army commanders was killed and his staff wiped out with him. There was considerable confusion in his sector," Pruitt said, stabbing a finger at the map, "and the Chinese exploited it to get a foothold. They're pouring in troops at that point now, shifting their artillery fire to cover the bridgehead and moving forces from up and down the front to concentrate on the breakthrough. But the Russians are punishing them something fierce."

"What's the prognosis?"

Pruitt shifted the stubby cigar in his mouth and shrugged. "Same as it always was. You've got a numerically superior force with inferior weapons and primitive tactics attacking a highly mechanized modern army. As always, the attacker has an initial advantage. But the Chinese have got a big river at their backs, don't control the air, and have considerably less tactical suppleness than the Soviets. The only factor we can't assess is willpower, which, on a battlefield, can sometimes outweigh all other factors. But right now I'd have to say that the Soviets will mass their artillery and armor and turn that bridgehead into a slaughterhouse over the next four or five days."

"You agree, Phil?" the president asked, turning to the intelligence chief.

Samsun nodded. "The Russians are probably a little off balance right now. They obviously planned to stop the attack on the beaches rather than allowing bridgeheads to form. The destruction of the command elements of the first army gave the Chinese an unexpected chance. But it will wind up being a disaster. There's just no way they can mass enough armor to break out of that bridgehead before the Soviets massacre them."

"Still, they've done a hell of a lot better than you or the Russians expected. That means the Russians have got to be a little concerned."

Samsun glanced at Pruitt. "Well, we have noticed some movement of armor up from Vyazemski." He pointed to a town south of Khabarovsk where the main Russian counterattack at the Chinese flank had been expected. "If they weaken the assault group much more, it could have an effect on the counterattack. But I don't really expect that to happen."

"When do you see the counterattack coming?" the president asked. He had been a marine company commander in Korea, and his knowledge of military affairs had more than once given members of the Joint Chiefs some bad moments.

Samsun shrugged. "It may never come. If they blunt the attack across the river, the Soviets may decide it's not worth the effort. On the other hand, if they want to teach the Chinese a lesson, they'll never have a better opportunity. I'd say within a couple of days they'll have to move. There's bound to be a lot of confusion behind the lines as the Chinese move up reinforcements to widen the breakthrough. It's an ideal time to hit the flanks."

"Thank you, gentlemen. I want a briefing from one

of your subordinates every four hours. Every morning I want a full-scale setup in the situation room in all aspects of the military situation in China. If there is anything dramatic happening, wake me up. Now, what the hell is going on in Germany? I heard on television just now that those two regiments of ours in Berlin fought a battle with the Germans last night."

Pruitt took the cigar out of his mouth. "Yeah. The Germans infiltrated their barracks area under some pretext and overpowered most of the command without a fight. But General Masterson," Pruitt said, grinning broadly, "had put about five hundred men on special alert, just on a hunch. He hit the Kraut commander unexpectedly, took out about half his force, and got all of the German men free within about an hour. The Germans withdrew and surrounded the barracks. Our boys are digging in. I'd say they lost a good many more men than we did."

"Brilliant," the president said, his voice dripping with sarcasm. "Can you gentlemen tell me how this goddamned coup could have been planned for months without our knowing about it?"

"Better ask that brilliant spook of yours," Pruitt said sourly. "I doubt if more than half a dozen of the top German officers were in on it. They didn't need to be. With that army they've got these days, all you've got to do is give an order and it marches, right over a cliff, if necessary. Only the Israelis have anything comparable to it, man for man." Pruitt had trouble keeping admiration out of his voice.

"What do you suggest now?"

Pruitt shrugged. "You've got two choices. Send in the planes, lift our people out, and accept the situation . . . or nuke 'em."

"Jesus Christ, Pruitt, what the hell are you saying?"

129

The president's deep voice had sunk almost to a whisper.

Pruitt met his incredulous stare. "Look, Mr. President, I'm a general, nothing else. You asked me for our options. Militarily, that's all the choice we've got. Our conventional forces are a joke, have been for the last decade ever since the big move out of Europe after the mutual balance force reductions, which left us with ten thousand men on the Continent. The politicians gutted us, both at home and abroad. We can't put six divisions in the field. The Germans have the twenty finest mechanized and armored divisions in the world backed by some goddamned effective reserve infantry divisions. Plus, they've now taken over about a third of our tactical atomic weapons and a fair stockpile of arms."

"What about the British and French?"

Pruitt shrugged. "The French Army would last a couple of days against them. I wasn't aware the British had an army." The general's insolence was overt now. He was a few months away from retirement and obviously relishing his role.

The president remained totally calm, his big face impassive. "And what about the Soviets?"

Pruitt frowned. "The Soviets? What about them?"

"Could they handle the Germans?"

There was a moment of deadly silence in the room as the two generals' faces registered a kaleidoscope of shock and consternation. "Jesus, you're not suggesting we use the Soviets to knock out the Germans? They'd be sitting in the middle of Central Europe when it's over, which is just where they've always wanted to be and what we've most feared."

The president shook his head. "No, I'm suggesting that we and the Soviets together could give the Germans an ultimatum. Return to the barracks, give up the atomic weapons, revert to the status quo ante. A divided Germany occupied by the U.S. and the Soviet Union. Total German disarmament. We would put in three or four hundred thousand troops again."

Thompson rubbed his eyes, trying to hide his despair. He recognized beneath the apparent calm a man enraged beyond repair, a man on the verge of an illogical hostility that would be hard to control if it became reinforced with spurious logic. The two generals were no help. They had both been reduced to intellectual pulp by the sudden reversal of roles suggested by the president. Pruitt, his rebellion crushed, sat like a defeated old man, horrified at the prospect of his world—a world he had defended for more than forty years—coming apart before his eyes.

"Mr. President," Thompson said, speaking even more softly than the president, "maybe we'd better go over the options in private."

The president nodded. The two generals, dismissed, left hurriedly.

"I just talked to Kharkov, Alec," the president said. "He's ready to attack. He told me as much. He said he suspected us of being involved, and if it's ever proved, he wanted me to know that any cooperation between us on any subject would be impossible ever again. He was enraged. Foaming at the mouth. Talked about being stabbed in the back. When I told him about our troops being killed in Berlin, he was contemptuous. Called it a ruse and hung up. Well, you wanted to consult. What the hell are you going to recommend? More doing nothing and letting the dust settle, with a couple of hundred dead Americans in Berlin and that maniac, Beck, laughing at us? They're going to be after us like jackals on the hill this morning."

"That's exactly what I am going to recommend," Thompson said. "Better two hundred dead Americans in Berlin and an enraged Congress and public opinion than two hundred million dead here. The Germans have pulled a brilliant maneuver. We don't have an effective counter at the moment. The Russians are not going to attack anybody. Kharkov was bluffing. If they hit Germany, they themselves will lose a hundred million people from the nuclear missiles the Germans have taken over, and they know it. If they attack with conventional forces, given their engagement in the East, the Germans are liable to be in Minsk by Labor Day. Kharkov is no fool. He knows damned well we're not involved. His intelligence is too good for him not to know. And he's far too smart to go off half-cocked. He'll take care of China first and then turn to Europe."

The president nodded. "By which point he won't be able to do anything."

Thompson shrugged. "So what? We've got to redefine our interests in Europe. Let's face it, we haven't done too well with the Common Market over the last few years or so. Maybe a Europe under the domination of its natural leader, Germany, will be one hell of a lot easier to deal with than that impotent octopus we've been working with."

The president slumped onto his spine and lifted his size thirteen shoes onto the desk. "Okay, I'm calmed down. You can demobilize the army and navy and take the air force off alert." The irony was bitter. "So we sit on our dead asses and do nothing while that shithead, Horst Beck, takes over Europe and the Chinese and Russians fight a major war in Asia?"

"No. We lean on Beck with all the weight we've got, behind the scenes, and we stand ready to mediate in Asia."

"Lean on Beck? Christ, man, I can't even get him on the phone." As he spoke, Jane Cleveland stuck her head in the door. "It's the German premier . . . or president, rather."

9

Senator Caleb Sutpen climbed out of his black limousine and moved up the stairs with the careful splay-footed walk of an old man afraid of falling. The black maid opened the door as he reached it and she took him by the arm. It was an old house, built just after the Civil War when the land around Capitol Hill had been a cow pasture. As the area was developed, the big mansion was finally surrounded by three-story row houses attached to it like parasites. The maid led him toward the back of the house, where a large, airy room overlooked a miniature garden.

"How're you gettin' along, Letty?"

"All right, Senator. How are you?"

"Older'n God. You still retired?"

The woman grinned at him. She wore a white blouse and black mini skirt, her superb legs encased in black net stockings. "I haven't turned a trick in ten years, Senator. Got four kids and every damned one of 'em is going to go to college."

Sutpen smiled. "When they get old enough, let me know, Letty. Maybe I can get the brightest one into Harvard."

He hadn't been to the house in almost a year. He'd broken his hip on an icy spring day and been confined to his bed. They'd agreed to send the girls over, and it had been convenient. But somehow it wasn't quite the same thing. Too much like being married, he thought, grinning, surveying the whorehouse bedroom with satisfaction. The ceiling mirror, the pornographic etchings, and, behind the doors of the wardrobe, a unique set of instruments of minor, nonfatal torture. He wondered who it would be this time.

She came through the door smiling, a big girl, heavy black hair done up in a chaste bun. She was wearing a long-sleeved black jersey dress with a turtleneck and one simple strand of pearls. She held out her hand. "Good morning, Senator. I'm Stephanie Smith."

The senator took her hand. "Hello, Stephanie. Come over here and sit down. Tell me a little about yourself."

"You mean, how did a nice little girl like me get into a place like this?"

"Just lucky, I guess," the senator said as they both laughed. "No. I mean, what do you do?"

"I'm a student at Georgetown, Senator, taking a doctorate in international affairs. I'm going into the foreign service when I get my doctorate. I turn a trick now and then when I need a little extra money."

"And you asked for me when you heard I was a customer, because I might be good for a few lines in your thesis on 'The Senatorial Role in U.S. Foreign Policy.'"

135

She giggled and stood up, lifting the dress over her shoulders, revealing as it slipped free a pair of small, barely developed breasts. With a twist of her head, she freed her hair, which tumbled down over her shoulders reaching almost to her waist. A garter belt and black lace stockings were left. "They said that's the way you like it, Senator."

"Yeah, I guess I'm old-fashioned. Set for a spell, honey. An old man like me gets most of his pleasure just looking at a fine girl like you. Ask Letty to bring us some tea."

"You mind if I have a joint instead? It kinda turns me on."

"Go right ahead, honey. Anything that makes you feel comfortable." The amateurs had begun to come into the business in the late 1950s. First came a few middle-class housewives who had borrowed money from the loan sharks and were paying it off in kind. They had been a novelty, usually hating the job, barely able to restrain their tears. They had rebelled at the more arcane aspects of the whore's trade, but they had almost always wound up complying, albeit with a revulsion that had made it all the more titillating.

In the 1960s the runaways had begun turning up, fourteen, fifteen years old, picked up in bus stations by the pimps and turned to the trade. But, aside from their youth, they had almost nothing to recommend them. Psychologically disturbed, they were little more exciting than the old-style prostitute who was in the business because she was too lazy to work. Then, in the 1970s, a new phenomenon appeared. Young wives and single girls from good families in search of kicks or a little extra cash began to come into the houses for one-trick stands. It got so bad, as one of the senator's friends had said, you weren't sure you wouldn't be sitting next to the woman you screwed for a hundred dollars that afternoon at that evening's dinner party.

The girl came around the table and sat on his lap, undoing his tie, running a hand down inside his shirt over his paunch. "How old are you, Senator? You must be some sort of sexual phenomenon, I mean, at your age."

"Honey, the secret of eternal youth is eternal youth. Right now you're rollin' back about twenty-five years off my old hide. And you get that wicked little hand of yours down just a little lower and, by God, you might be takin' off thirty."

Steffie Smith giggled and was about to do as requested when the maid knocked. "Senator," she said, through the half-open door, "there's an urgent call for you from the White House. They told me they didn't give a damn where you were or what you were doing, but to get you to the phone."

"Shit," Sutpen said, gently removing his hand from the girl and the girl from his lap. "That man is gonna wind up irritatin' me."

Wozniakowski listened to the report of General Witold Lulienski, chief of the Polish general staff, intently. "There were no casualties, Witold? You're sure?"

"None. We took them completely by surprise. Every installation was overpowered before anybody knew what was going on. The Soviet commanders accepted our initial explanation of an 'exercise' and went along with it good-naturedly. Once we had the officers, there was no problem."

"What's happening now?"

"The trains are being loaded. Within twenty-four hours there won't be a single Russian on our soil."

"And at the border? What are the Soviet troops doing?"

Lulienski shrugged. "They're on red alert. And there is some evidence that the divisions in Minsk and Kiev are being prepared to move. But they've already denuded these troops of armor, anti-tank weapons, and close air support to beef up their forces in the Far East. They're also short of officers who know what they're doing. The fact is that for at least two years they've been pirating men, materiel, and weapons from these divisions. The Soviet High Command just couldn't see any danger in Europe and, since they had no intention of attacking there, they've cannibalized their forces."

Wozniakowski turned to his chief of staff. "You've been singing the same old song, Witold. I hope you're right. If you're not, and they decide to attack, how long can we hold out?"

Lulienski moved across to the map and picked up a heavy black marking pencil. "It would take them at least five days to get into position to mount an armored attack. They would strike from the border here at Kaliningrad, using the amphibious divisions based at Riga to interdict the Gdansk port area." Lulienski hesitated, reluctant to continue.

"Yes. Where else?" Wozniakowski was calm, but the tension in the room had risen perceptibly.

"They would attack along the rail line at Brest in an effort to take Warsaw and cut our rail links. This would be the major thrust. We have, for this reason, most of our forces concentrated here. A subsidiary offensive based on Lvov would probably follow the rail line to Krakow."

"How long could we hold them?"

"Within four days our armies would be destroyed," Lulienski said calmly.

"And if the Germans come to our aid?"

"It would take them a week to get their troops in position. They would probably not make an effort to defend a line east of Poznan."

"So if we can't stop them politically, there is no hope," Wozniakowski said.

"But we knew that," Lulienski protested. "We never anticipated fighting a war. The assumption has always been that, with China on their backs, the Soviets would never move."

Wozniakowski nodded and handed over a note on the heavily embossed stationery of the Soviet embassy.

The Soviet government wishes to inform the government of Poland that its actions in attacking friendly Soviet troops garrisoned on Polish soil in conformity with the provisions of the Warsaw Pact are regarded as an act of war. The Soviet government wishes further to inform the government of Poland that its troops in Poland must be immediately set at liberty, their arms returned, and the Polish Army disarmed and sent to its barracks, or the Soviet government will be forced to regard itself as being at war with the Polish state. The Polish government is accorded twenty-four hours to comply with these demands.

Lulienski whistled softly. "I've been trying to get the chairman by telephone. He won't answer."

"Have you talked to Beck? Gerhardus?"

"I'm meeting them in four hours at the border. The question now, gentlemen, is: Do we dare ask them for assistance, and if we do, will we be willing to pay their price?"

The twenty members of the National Security

Board and the foreign affairs leaders of the House and Senate rose raggedly as the president entered the cabinet room followed by Alec Thompson and the Joint Chiefs of Staff. "Hello, Caleb, Jim," the president said, shaking hands with the two committee chairmen. "Glad you could make it," he said, taking his place at the middle of the oval table.

"Well gentlemen, the shit has really hit the fan this time," the president said. "I've just finished talking to Chairman Kharkov and the new president of the United German Republic, Beck. They're on the verge of war, and Kharkov is just about out of his mind with rage. And he's blaming us. He thinks we've encouraged the Germans to move while he was at war with the Chinese, and he's demanding that we join him in sending an ultimatum to the Germans to dissolve this new united Germany, disarm its army, and force it to accept large numbers of U.S. and Soviet occupation troops." The president paused. "He just told me he would go to war with the new German state within twenty-four hours if these demands were not met. A similar ultimatum has been handed to the Poles."

Sutpen cleared his throat. "You talked to Beck?"

"Yes, finally. He avoided me for most of a day, but when I got through he was most polite, in fact, highly conciliatory. He apologized for the way he and Gerhardus had operated, but he pointed out that the interests of the German nation were paramount. He said we would never have permitted the reunification had we known, but now that it has happened, it serves our interests. I told him of the Russian ultimatum. He discounts it. He says it's all bluff. He has a Chinese guarantee that, if the Russians attack in Europe, they will initiate a nuclear exchange." The president stopped and stared around the table.

140

"Jesus!" Somebody exploded at one end of the table.

"Exactly. I'm not sure that Beck believes in that commitment. I've got a call in to Lieu now, but if we can assume that the Chinese mean what they say, then we are on the verge of a war that could destroy civilization, gentlemen. Beck assures me that the Chinese have weighed the strategic considerations just as he has, and that the Soviets have no choice but to accept the fait accompli in Germany and fight a ground war with the Chinese with conventional weapons, which Beck is convinced they will lose, especially now when they will be forced to keep large segments of their reserve in Europe to face the threat of a German attack."

"A German attack?" Senator Clarence asked, uncomprehending.

The president nodded. "Beck intends to maintain a threatening posture in order to keep the pressure on the Russians. There isn't any question that this will freeze their strategic reserves in Europe. We've always got to remember what the Germans did to the Russians in World War Two and their almost pathological fear of German power. Beck is sure this will be enough, and I agree. He assures me it's only a bluff, and for once I believe the treacherous son-of-a-bitch. The question now is: What do *we* do?"

Sutpen cleared his throat. "Why do we have to do anything? Why can't we just let the dumb bastards fight it out?"

"And wind up with a nuclear exchange? Caleb, the Chinese bombs are dirty enough to kill every living thing in the Northern Hemisphere." The president shook his head. "And, anyway, we can't afford to abdicate. If we sit back and let things slide on the

141

assumption that nobody will be enough of a damned fool to enter into a nuclear exchange, we'll be seen as a weak, vacillating power from now on. Our clients won't believe we have any power left. We've got to take a hand. The only question still open is when and where do we intervene."

Jane Cleveland slipped into the room behind the president and passed a note over his shoulder. He read it, thick black eyebrows shooting up. "It's a joint announcement by the Czech and Hungarian governments. They've surrounded and disarmed the remaining Russian garrisons on their soil and are sending them back to the Soviet Union. They, along with Rumania and Poland, have declared that they are no longer members of the Warsaw Pact." The president dropped the paper on the conference table and glanced around. "Gentlemen, it looks as if this is the breakup of the Soviet empire in Eastern Europe."

Dimitri Stashevsky rubbed his eyes and glanced at the clocks on the walls. It was seven P.M. in Moscow, noon in Washington. He pawed through the battle reports on his desk, finally locating Korzybsky's latest report to the Politburo.

The first twenty-four hours of the battle have proceeded according to plan. The enemy attacks at the junction of the Ussuri and Amur rivers have been repulsed in all areas except that of the Third Corps. The death of General Gorbykov and his staff in the first assault enabled the Chinese to throw a bridgehead across the Amur at this point and gain a foothold on the north bank. However, our artillery and air barrages are punishing them terribly. With increased visibility tomorrow morning, we anticipate interdicting supplies and the annihilation of the bridgehead before nightfall.

Meanwhile, the counterattack at Vyazemski is ready to move. The attack begins at dawn. Ten thousand tanks will cross the river in the first wave. Parachute troops will disrupt the enemy's lines, and our artillery and air preparations will have broken the enemy's will to resist. Within forty-eight hours, the Chinese armies will cease to exist as a fighting force."

Stashevsky threw the piece of paper down impatiently. No figures. No statistics on enemy losses or those of his own. No notation of just how far the Chinese had penetrated the Soviet lines. No indication of air losses or how effective the flak support had been. An arrogant old son-of-a-bitch who was telling them as little as he possibly could in order to avoid interference. The problem was that nobody could figure out how much of the bombast was true and how much was cover-up. He had persuaded the chairman to send four members of his personal military inspection staff to the old man's headquarters, but they were all generals and all stood in awe of the old man. They would learn nothing.

Nadia Raskolnikova entered the room and stood before the desk. "Will you need me any longer tonight?"

Stashevsky stared at her, feeling the sudden dryness in his mouth, the tightening in his groin. He stood up and walked around the desk. She turned to face him, her gray eyes meeting his. "It's very late, Dimitri. My mother is waiting outside for me."

"Let her wait," Stashevsky said, beginning to unbutton her blouse. She shrugged and stepped back, pushed his hands away, undressed quickly, and moved toward the leather couch. Stashevsky watched her, rage and lust intermingled. "Bitch," he muttered.

143

The girl looked at him and grinned. "You know the joke about the Russian girls, Dimitri. You can have my body, but you'll never get my soul. Well, come on, let's get it over with. My mother is waiting."

10

"Okay, let's go into the pit, Harry," Alec Thompson said to the press secretary as the two entered the press room for the White House noon briefing. Harry Concannon was a Boston Irishman who had started out as a police reporter on the old *Boston Globe*. He had come to Washington in the 1900s and wound up an administrative assistant to the president during his third term in the Senate. He was personable, well informed, quick witted, and usually drunk by five o'clock in the afternoon. Behind the press-room podium hung a poster advertising a long-forgotten DeMille epic showing Christians entering an amphitheater filled with lions.

"Good morning," Concannon said. "This morning I have the great pleasure of introducing my friend and colleague, Alec Thompson, who will talk to you about the events of the last twenty-four hours. He'll start with a statement and then take questions."

"Thanks, Harry. Good morning. You all know about as much as I do about what's going on. The Chinese attacked yesterday at Khabarovsk and seem to have a small foothold on the north bank. The Soviets are counterattacking. We've been in contact with the chairman and with Foreign Secretary Lieu in an attempt to get a ceasefire, so far unsuccessfully.

"In Europe, East and West Germany have agreed to merge. I understand that both parliaments voted unanimously this morning for reunification and have agreed to dissolve. New elections will be called within sixty days, according to President Beck, the former West German premier, who was elected president of the new nation with special powers to govern by decree until the election.

"East German Premier Klein has become prime minister ad interim of the new state. As you know, our troops were confined to their barracks and are now being airlifted home in accordance with the wishes of the new Germany."

"I'll take questions. Dan."

Q: "You left out the most important part. The Germans have taken over all the keys to the atomic weapons in Germany and now are a nuclear power. That's right, isn't it?"

A: "Yes."

Q: "Well, what the hell are we going to do about it?"

A: "What do you suggest, Dan? Shall we nuke them?"

Q: "No. But we sure as hell must have some options. As I understand it, they've developed their own intercontinental ballistic missiles secretly and have mounted some of the warheads from the intermediate-range missiles on them and can now hit just about anyplace in the world."

146

A: "You've got more information than I have. They have the warheads. Whether they have IBM's, I don't know. Bernie."

Q: "You don't intend to move against them?"

A: "No. It's not a particularly happy situation, but there are times when your options are limited. The German nation has been divided against its will for almost forty years. It was probably inevitable that it would sooner or later reunite. It's just unfortunate that they had to pick this time and this method of doing so."

Q: "How many Americans were killed in Berlin?"

A: "About two hundred. One thousand were wounded."

Q: "How many Germans?"

A: "I don't know, and I wouldn't tell you if I did. Ask them."

Q: "What's this going to do to NATO? Do the Germans plan to stay in?"

A: "President Beck has assured me that they wish to remain a part of both NATO and the Common Market. The Council of Fourteen is meeting in Brussels today to debate the situation. I understand there is a good chance that a reunited Germany will simply be accepted as a natural evolution. After all, as you know, East Germany has for all practical purposes been considered an economic unit with West Germany for some time. It won't change much."

Q: "Also, did you say it won't change much? You've got to be kidding."

A: "I never kid, Marilyn."

Q: "What you're saying is that we have no options as far as Germany is concerned? It's just too powerful for us or our allies to take on?"

A: "I'm saying that reunification has to be consid-

147

ered a natural phenomenon. It's just unfortunate that it had to happen the way it did."

Q: "What about Poland, Czechoslovakia, and Hungary? Do we agree with what they did?"

A: "We don't have a role to play as far as these nations are concerned. It's up to them what they do or don't do. It wasn't too many years ago that this government was publicly demanding freedom for Eastern Europe. Well, now we have it. I think it was George Kennan who said that the Soviet Union couldn't dominate these countries forever, since never in history had a primitive state managed to keep a more advanced one in permanent bondage."

Q: "What about Rome keeping Greece in bondage for four hundred years?"

A: "I quoted Mr. Kennan. I did not say he was right. Dick."

Q: "You don't sound very happy with events. You think it would have been better if none of this had happened? You think it would be better if all those nations would stay under the Russian yoke?"

A: "I said we were and are unhappy about the congruence of events, Dick. The result may turn out to be beneficial, but with the Chinese and the Soviet Union involved in what appears to be a major conflict, it just may not be the time to cause trouble in Europe."

Q: "In the past, it has been regarded as clever politics to attack your oppressor when he was having difficulties. Isn't this what the Germans and, to a lesser extent, the Czechs, Poles, and Hungarians are doing?"

A: "Yes, Kip, it is. But the world is a different place from the fourteenth and fifteenth centuries when Florence and Genoa went to war over trade, land, or glory. We simply have to face the fact that any conflict today can escalate very quickly into unacceptable dimensions and involve everybody."

Q: "What are we doing to stop the Russians and the Chinese from having war?"

A: "I wouldn't characterize this frontier clash as a war, Bruce. It's a serious conflict, but it is localized. As for our role, we're in contact with Chairman Kharkov and with Foreign Secretary Lieu. We'd like to see a ceasefire and have both parties sit down and talk it over."

Q: "Have we offered to mediate?"

A: "No, not formally. But I'm sure we'd be willing to serve in a constructive role if both sides felt the need for us to."

Q: "What about the United Nations? What are they doing?"

A: "Nothing that I know of. Nobody seems to have asked them to do anything."

Q: "The third World Caucus has demanded that both sides stop fighting and that the Germans dissolve their union since it represents a hostile economic unit."

A: "Really? Marvin."

Q: "How many people have been killed on the Amur?"

A: "I don't know."

Q: "Do you know the magnitude of the forces involved?"

A: "About six million on both sides."

Q: "And you call that a skirmish? Do you have any comment on the Israeli decision to increase the price of Saudi Arabian crude to twenty-five dollars a barrel?"

A: "We deplore the increase and think it is likely to disrupt international monetary markets."

Q: "Are we likely to cut off military aid to Israel?"

A: "Aid? We don't give Israel any aid, Bernie. We haven't since the last Middle East war."

Q: "I meant arms shipments. Will we cut them off?"

A: "That has not been discussed."

Q: "What is the position of Japan in this conflict, Alec? I understand she has said that she will honor her mutual assistance pact with China, since the Soviet Union was the aggressor in this conflict."

A: "I've heard the same thing, Philippe. I'm not sure what it means."

Q: "It means they could hit the Russians in the rear with naval forces."

A: "I don't want to speculate on that here, gentlemen."

Harry Concannon leaned across, interrupting Thompson. "The president wants to see you."

Concannon turned to the assembled press. "That's it for today. I'll see if I can't serve up another sacrificial lamb tomorrow."

The president was striding back and forth in his office, his tie loosened and heavy mane of hair rumpled as Thompson entered. "What's up?" Jane Cleveland handed him a telegram.

"Austrian parliament has voted to join as federal province with new unified Germany. Unable to contact prime minister, but government sources tell us Anschluss was agreed on a month ago in secret meeting between Herbaczek and Beck at Salzburg. Defense attaché reports German troops began crossing Austrian border five minutes after announcement to take up positions along Czech and Hungarian border. Popular reaction highly favorable, primarily because Austrian economic problems have resulted in standard of living at least a third lower than Germany. Unable to assess implications for relations with Yugoslavia, but indications are Czechs and Hungarians welcomed move, which strengthens their position vis-à-vis Soviets."

Thompson dropped into a chair and fumbled for his pipe. "Well, what do you make of that?" the president asked.

"It confirms my belief that Germany, as the strongest state in Central Europe, was ripe to begin exercising the rights power conveys. And they're doing it." Thompson lit his pipe, trying to keep his hand steady. "Austria is hardly a major power. Adding seven million people to Germany gives it about ninety million. It doesn't bring much strategic advantage, although, as our esteemed ambassador points out, it should make the Czechs and Hungarians breathe a little easier."

The president stopped pacing and stared at Thompson. "Listen, Alec, things are getting out of control. We're losing our leverage. The world is coming apart at the seams, and when the time comes to put it back together again I have the feeling we're not going to like the end product."

Thompson shrugged. "It isn't a question of our liking it or not. We've got to face up to the fact that our power has been progressively reduced vis-à-vis the rest of the world. It began about 1962 or 1963, after the Cuban mess. Soviet missile strength reached a point where a nuclear exchange simply became unthinkable. At that point, we—and they—were paralyzed in dealing with small conflicts that escalated onto the world stage. The Israeli-Arab wars, Pakistan-India, the Greek-Turkish conflict over Cyprus, even the disaster in Vietnam simply got away from us because there was no option short of a nuclear holocaust that would get us our way. And it's gotten progressively worse. Kissinger said it once in the early 1970s: 'We get along better with our enemies than with our allies.' It's true to a certain extent. At least we can sit down and bargain with them on the basis of power realities. With the goddamned Germans, we can't begin to do that. They know and we know that we could nuke them into the Stone Age. They also know that there isn't the chance of a snowball in hell of our doing it. So what kind of pressure can we exert?"

The president dropped into an easy chair, letting his bulk sink deep into the overstuffed cushions. "I take your point. But we aren't really dealing with Germany here. Germany is a sideshow. We're being asked to take sides in a conflict between the two most powerful nations in the world other than us. We can't stay out of it much longer, Alec. If one starts losing badly, the temptation of the loser to go to the big bang will be too great."

"Agreed. But that's maybe a week away. We can still sit tight for the moment. Once we move, we're committed. What's this about Japan, anyway? Nagoya isn't seriously thinking of going in?"

The president handed him a cabled report from Tokyo.

Intelligence sources report that Nagoya visited Peking for twenty-four hours yesterday for intensive meetings with Lieu. Chief Japanese general staff, chief of naval operations, and Commander of Fifth Army plus staffs accompanied. FYI: Fifth Army is only Japanese unit with amphibious landing capability. Fifth Army concentrated near Sapporo on second-class alert. Landing craft have been moved into position. Mission feels this activity is bluff intended to freeze large Soviet forces in coastal areas.

The cable went on to give strengths, capabilities, and degrees of readiness of various units.

"That's five hundred thousand men who could be landed in the rear of the Soviet armies massed to attack Vyazemski," Thompson said, moving to a battle map spread out on the president's conference table. "I wonder why Tokyo is so sure it's a bluff?"

"Logic. Why should the Japanese get involved? What's in it for them? Nagoya is a Marxian-socialist, but he's not an idiot. His alliance with China is based on economic imperatives. He needs China's raw materials and market, and China needs his industrial goods and technology. It's a perfect symbiosis. But that doesn't include getting into a war with the Soviet Union."

"Access to Siberian raw materials?" Thompson mused aloud.

The president nodded. "All projections indicate that no industrial nation is going to be able to survive the competition for energy and primary raw materials unless she controls them directly. This means, when you come down to it, that the Soviet Union, China, Canada, Brazil, Australia, and the U.S. are about the only actual potential major powers around. Japan hasn't got a chance. What would she get out of a Chinese victory, except having the source of supply move from one greedy hand to another?"

"That Morgan Institute survey suggests that over the next fifty years nonholders of raw materials, such as Japan and Western Europe, will inevitably have to move into the orbit of some major raw material source. They suggest some logical groupings: Japan with China, which would dominate the Pacific area, pulling in Indonesia and Australia as well as the Indian subcontinent; Europe and the Soviet Union would combine along with Israel, with its control of the energy resources, in a second grouping; Canada, the United States, and Mexico with, maybe, Central

America would be another; Brazil would extend its hegemony over South America; Africa and some of the fringe areas would drift between the major groupings."

"Meaning that Japan has a pretty concrete interest in seeing its ally win this one and take over a good bit of Siberia?"

"Yes," Thompson said, picking up the phone. "Get me our embassy in Japan, flash, will you please, Jane? I'm interested in why George seems so sure they won't go." The call came through within ten seconds.

"Hello, George, Alec Thompson here." He listened as the former Stanford professor of Oriental studies boomed a greeting. He was in a tradition of Japanese-speaking U.S. ambassadors married to Japanese women. The fact that Dr. George W. Collins was a woolly minded idiot who was unable to disassociate U.S. interests from those of his beloved Japan made him virtually useless as an emissary. He was, however, a great public relations man with immense personal charisma and heavy backing in Congress, which made him even more dangerous.

"Alec, it's good to hear from you. I hope you have been reading my reports. I want to stress that we have nothing to worry about from the Japanese. Nagoya has assured me personally that nothing will make him move. Nothing. I talked to him for an hour last night at the British reception, and I can assure you and the president that the man is utterly sound. He does not plan to get involved. The Chinese have told him they won't invoke the mutual assistance treaty."

"George, that's great. Just tell me one thing. Why is he massing troops and putting together an invasion armada at Sapporo if he's not planning to move? If

154

he's not careful, the Soviets will hit that fleet with planes before it has a chance to move."

"Just a bluff, Alec, nothing but a bluff. He's trying to take pressure off the Chinese by freezing Soviet troops along the coast. They had denuded their coastal artillery, you know. Stripped their defenses. He's just trying to get them to shift some troops back into the coastal fortifications."

The president had flipped a switch on his telephone console and was listening to the exchange. He now picked up a telephone. "George, this is the president. Listen to me, George. We can't have any mistakes on this. You get the spooks and every goddamned attaché you've got on it. I want to know every move Nagoya makes, you understand? You tell him from me that the Soviets are getting damned nervous. They may do something irrational if they find they're under any more pressure than they are at the moment."

"Mr. President, I've explained to him our policy of limiting the conflict, and he agrees completely. I have his word."

"Fine," the president said, then hung up and turned to Thompson. "What do you think?"

"Nagoya would lie to his dying mother," Thompson said. "But I cannot see him getting involved in this one. The Soviets seem sure to win it, and Nagoya has never been one to get on a losing side if he could help it."

The buzzer sounded on the console bank and the president flipped a switch. "Yes?"

"The chief of staff and the head of military intelligence are here."

"Send them in, Jane."

Pruitt and Samsun entered with an aide bearing an armful of maps. "What's the latest, Craig?" the president asked, addressing Pruitt.

155

"The Russian counterattack is poised to jump off tomorrow morning. They've massed everything they've got in the way of armor and aircraft. It's going to be a hammer-and-anvil attack, with the anvil anchored at Leninskaya." The general unfolded a large-scale map showing the triangle where the Amur and Ussuri rivers met, his stubby fingers jabbing at map coordinates as he listed the Russian forces and the Chinese opposing them. "Once they've cut through the Chinese line, they'll set up a defensive perimeter on the southern front and turn north to grind up the Chinese assault forces attacking at Khabarovsk."

"You think it will work, Craig?"

Pruitt rolled an unlit cigar between his lips, staring down at the map. "It's an idiotic battle the way the Chinese are fighting it. Recent reports are that they have lost more than a hundred thousand men in twenty-four hours in the Khabarovsk assault. My first impression was that they couldn't be serious, that it was a bluff. But they seem to be serious. That bridgehead is holding, incidentally. The Russians are moving in masses of reinforcements, including a good bit of the Vyazemski reserves to contain it."

"Will that have any effect on the attack?"

Pruitt shook his head. "They've got all the troops in place that they can deploy for the attack. It will only have an effect if they take really drastic casualties. And I'm inclined to think they won't."

"How long do you think it will go on?" the president asked.

Pruitt shrugged. "Depends on what the Russians will want to do. I can't see them heading for Harbin. On the other hand, they'll want to destroy the Chinese armies as thoroughly as possible. It could last for a few weeks if they decide to really do some surgery."

"What if the Japanese hit them from the rear with five hundred thousand troops and heavy air attacks?" Thompson asked.

Pruitt and Samsun exchanged glances. "Our information from Tokyo is that that's not very likely."

The president chopped the air impatiently with one meaty hand. "Listen, General, I don't give a damn what your information is. You've been wrong so often lately that we can probably figure on the opposite to happen of what your people forecast."

Pruitt reddened and opened his mouth to speak when Samsun interrupted, gripping him warningly on the arm. "We don't think a Japanese attack would have that much of an effect, Mr. President. It's a three-hundred-mile run from Sapporo to Amgun, where they would probably land. We figure it would take at least a week for such an attack to have any effect. By that time the battle around Vyazemski will be over."

The president nodded, losing interest in the war maps. "Okay, so we can figure on a Russian win here. Now, what about in Europe? What the hell does this Austrian move mean?"

Pruitt unfolded another map and smoothed it across the table.

"First, it puts heavy pressure on the Soviets to move quickly if they're going to. When the Warsaw Pact was operative, Czechoslovakia was a salient into the center of NATO positions in Europe. That's wiped out now, and the Soviets are starting from one hell of a long way back. If the Eastern Europeans are willing to allow German units to cross their territory, it would mean a long slog back for the Soviet armor. Our assessment is that they can't attack along the whole front." Pruitt glanced up from the maps. "There's just no way. They don't have the horses,

157

particularly if they have to figure on counterattacks by the German armor, which is probably the best in the world, tank for tank, right now. The Czech and Hungarian armies don't amount to much, but our intelligence reports indicate that they're well dug in and ready to fight. Morale is good and the terrain tends to favor the defense."

"My God," the president mused, "does nothing ever change? It's World War Two all over again. What would you do, General, if you commanded the Soviet armies?"

Pruitt hesitated, rolling the fat cigar between his fingers. "I'd pick one of the countries and knock it off first. Rumania, maybe. Then I'd wait for a reaction. I'd figure chances would be pretty good that there wouldn't be one, so then I'd hit another, Hungary. That would straighten out my supply lines and put me right up against the Germans in Austria. By then the Chinese attack would be resolved one way or another, and the next move would be to roll back into Poland and Czechoslovakia. I'd stop there. I don't think the Soviet Union is going to take on Germany in a conventional war."

The president shook his head. "That would take too long. It's just not politically feasible. If the Soviets hesitate and these countries consolidate their independence, it's going to be goddamned near impossible to move against them militarily."

"The president's right, Craig. The southern tier isn't as important as Poland. That's the traditional invasion route to the Soviet Union. Flat as a plate from Berlin to Moscow. If they move, they'll move there," Thompson said, stabbing his finger at the frontier cities of Kaliningrad, Brest, and Lvov.

Pruitt shrugged. "Sure, but it's also where they'd be most likely to run into massed German armor. Our

158

intelligence tells us the Poles and the Germans are cooperating militarily up and down the line. And the Poles have got a pretty fair army. I agree that an attack in the north makes the most strategic sense, but it'll take just about everything they've got to mount it. It's a tremendous risk. The German Army is going to have to make them hesitate."

"All right, General," the president said. "For Christ's sake, keep me informed. We're now reaching a point where we just can't sit back and watch the map of the world be redrawn without taking a stand."

Georg Wozniakowski paced back and forth in the modest entrance hall of the party headquarters in Szczecin while he waited for Gerhardus to arrive. The two men had agreed to meet in the Polish border city to coordinate their reaction to the expected Soviet threat. It was the same building that rioting dock workers had burned in the revolt of 1970, the only building in town damaged in the riots, as the workers had carefully doused its neighbors with firehoses to make sure that they made their point. It was the party they were attacking, nothing else. The point had been made and Wozniakowski and dozens of others in the party had accepted it. They had, for twenty-five years, fought for the socialist ideal within the Soviet system, accepting the brutality and inequities, accepting the dominance of the crude and tasteless Russians—all in the name of the greater good of the people.

Then the people had revolted, and there was no way to refuse to face it. Dock workers, miners, and textile workers were the guts of any proletarian system. When they were unhappy, the system wasn't working. Beginning after the riots, Wozniakowski, then an obscure party leader in Rzeszow, had begun

159

to form a loose network of like-minded men. Their central aim was reform of the party and the Polish economy, but their unstated final goal was freedom from the Soviet Union. They had gradually drawn in key military leaders and, finally, members of the covert opposition. They had been helped by the fact that the old party leadership was tired and had lost its self-confidence. Half-measures to reform the economy had not worked, and in 1976 there had been another economic crisis. The miners in Katowice had struck, and the government was faced with the possibility of a general strike. The army refused to move.

Wozniakowski was no more than an alternate member of the Politburo at the time, but in the panic that gripped the leadership, he moved to take control. The army and the secret police backed him. Key members of the workers' groups were part of his organization. With what seemed like miraculous ease, he had stopped the strike and pacified the country with economic liberalization measures prepared months before. The Russians had watched the performance with irritation and skepticism. It meant the virtual end of their influence at high levels in the Polish regime, since Wozniakowski rid himself of every Soviet sympathizer within the first two weeks. But his party credentials were impeccable, and the alternative would have been another Hungary or Czechoslovakia. Moreover, Wozniakowski had made it plain that any attempt by the Soviet Union to interfere militarily would have meant a bloodbath. The Soviets had ended up by accepting the new leadership.

Now, for six years he had been preparing for the final effort to free Poland. It had become obvious in the early 1970s that China and the Soviet Union would sooner or later collide in a major conflict. Poland's only hope of final freedom lay in moving when the

Russians were so preoccupied in the East that military action in the West was impossible. It had been obvious that the Poles could not do it alone. The Czechs and Hungarians were both too weak and too unreliable to be of any use. Only the Germans had both the power, the will, and the desire to shake loose from the Soviet yoke. Polish intelligence had indicated that the East German leadership after Ulbricht had been less and less happy with the role of their country as a supplier of high-quality technology to the Soviet Union in return for overpriced raw materials. They had watched West Germany move from economic miracle to economic miracle and finally to a position of political and military power predominant in Europe. And they wanted to be part of this resurgence.

In late 1976, both Germanies suddenly began to awake from a state of psychological paralysis. A new generation, free of any association with the guilt of World War Two, had moved to center stage. They were impatient for Germany to take its rightful place in the world once again. Contacts between East and West multiplied. The economies of the two nations were so closely interwoven as to be inextricably one. Television, radio, and a vast network of unofficial but persuasive cultural activities tied them even tighter.

And then Horst Beck became chancellor of Germany. His election as head of the Socialist Party had come as a shock to the West. He had, after all, been a member of the prewar German Communist Party and had been one of the most radical of the left-wing socialists after it. Even more important, he had maintained discreet, close personal ties with Willy Klein, East German party leader and prime minister, beginning in the late 1960s when the Brandt policy of détente had loosened some of the restrictions. Klein and Beck had spent three years together in Nazi concentration camps in the mid-1930s before being released to join the German Army. They had both served six years, much of it in the same unit on the Eastern front, and Soviet intelligence had more than once attempted to put this friendship to use.

Beck and Klein, both rising political figures in the 1960s and 1970s, had met at conferences, relived the old days of the party battles and the war, and discovered that nothing much had changed except the titles of their parties. They were both convinced socialists who were, above all else, Germans. At some point during the period of international flux in the early 1970s, they had made a personal pact to reunify Germany.

Three years earlier, during a party meeting in Warsaw, Gerhardus had requested a private meeting with Wozniakowski, and as the two men walked in the gardens of the rebuilt royal palace, Gerhardus had told him that East German intelligence was aware of the internal Polish organization seeking freedom from the Soviet Union. He had gone on to reveal, in guarded terms, his own desire for a free, united Germany, although at this point he had not mentioned his connections with Beck. It was the beginning of a conspiracy confined to fewer than a dozen men in the three nations. Nothing was committed to paper and meetings were carefully arranged at the myriad Eastern European conferences.

They had not envisaged an opportunity coming this quickly, but earlier in the spring Gerhardus had sought him out at a United Nations session in Vienna and told him of the Chinese approaches to West Germany for assistance against the Soviet Union. Somehow, Chinese intelligence had smoked out some elements of the Polish connection with the two Germanies. The Chinese ambassador to Bonn had informed Beck that the situation in the Far East was becoming intolerable. The Chinese would have to move, probably later in the year. Obviously, a diversion in Europe would be of inestimable value. They, the Chinese, knew of the deep German desire for freedom. They also knew of the close contacts between the two Germanies. The time was right for them to shake off the Russian yoke together. Perhaps the Poles and other Eastern Europeans could be persuaded to act in concert.

Beck had been cautious. His and Gerhardus's timetable had foreseen another decade of salami tactics until, at some point of crisis, the two could suddenly declare a united Germany and the Soviets would be too paralyzed to react. The prospective Chinese attack was just such a crisis, but the question was whether they were ready to move. The two armies would follow. The people would present no problem. The Western Europeans, never keen on a reunited Germany, would scream, but they had no power. The United States, with its atomic weapons on German soil, was the problem. Once it was agreed to take them by force from the skeleton U.S. Army in Germany, the plan suddenly ceased to be a desperate adventure and became possible.

Wozniakowski stopped and stared out into the gray bleakness of the Polish spring as Gerhardus's Mercedes limousine drew up and disgorged the new prime minister of a united Germany and Austria. The tall, slender, silver-haired German greeted Wozniakowski warmly in English, their only common language.

"Georg, old comrade, how are you?"

"Nervous," Wozniakowski said, leading the German to the office of the local party secretary just off the main lobby. Except for their security guards, the men had no staffs. "How was your trip?"

"Fine," Gerhardus said. "That new Mercedes moves as if there were air rather than a road beneath it. You must have one. I'll arrange it as soon as I get back to Berlin."

"Thanks, Willy. But I was hoping you could arrange for about five thousand tanks."

Gerhardus stared sharply at the Pole. "What's happening? Something new?"

"No. It's just that I don't share your optimism that the Soviets are bluffing about an attack. Our intelligence from the Far East tells us that the Soviet army will finish off the Chinese in about a week and turn its full weight to us. The Chinese attack is apparently the height of stupidity. Rather than entering into a war of attrition, they're wasting all their strength in assaults on the Amur-Ussuri river line and are being chewed to pieces by the Soviet airpower and artillery."

Gerhardus nodded. "They are massing their European forces, Georg. That's true. The main thrust, if it comes, will be via Brest. We are moving all our tank forces up to the border. Everything is in readiness. If they attack, we will move immediately. You must trust us, Georg."

Wozniakowski nodded. The German was right. He must trust them. He had no choice. But for the first time since the operation had started, a cold, hard knot of fear had formed in his belly. "I think it might be a better idea, Willy, if you moved certain units to the Russian border—as a show of solidarity."

The German shook his head emphatically. "No, Georg, we cannot afford the panic. If we move troops to the Soviet border, it will be regarded as a provocation, and rightly so. They fear our armor. We can't afford to put them in a position of having to react. As things stand, they are under no compulsion to move, and certainly not to use atomic weapons. But if a German army stands at their border . . ." Gerhardus spread his hands palms up.

He was right again. Wozniakowski knew that any movement by the Germans could cause panic among the Soviet military. "All right, Willy. But, remember, we are the front line here. You must be ready to move quickly if they attack. Our forces can hold them for a day and a half at most."

The two men turned to defense arrangements with Hungary and Czechoslovakia, both of which had joined an informal protective alliance led by Germany. General staff meetings were about to begin in Berlin that day.

11

The president yawned, stuffing a big fist against his mouth to stifle it. It was seven P.M. and the offices around him had gradually wound down. The world crisis was unreal to ninety-eight percent of the people of the city. Most were only peripherally aware that the confusing conflict filling the front pages could touch their lives in the closest possible way . . . by killing them.

"You see the latest figures from the Atomic Institute, Alec?" the president asked Thompson, who sat at the coffee table leafing through the latest State Department cables.

"The ones indicating that a full nuclear exchange between China and the Soviet Union would wipe out the human race in the Northern Hemisphere?" he asked without looking up. "Yeah, I saw them. I also had them Telexed to Lieu and Dimitri."

166

"You don't think their own people have the same figures?"

"Sure. But it's possible that nobody ever showed them around."

The president nodded. "Maybe they were right not to clean up their bombs. At least there are no illusions on their part that they can push the red button and still survive."

Thompson stood up and stretched, his lean body attempting to shake off accumulated fatigue. "I'm going to take Suzanne to the theater tonight. There's a new Curzon play at the Center. You can get me back within fifteen minutes if you need me."

"Okay. Try to get some rest, for Christ's sake. Nobody is coming up with any brilliant ideas in this crisis, and I'm persuaded part of the reason for it is that nobody is getting any rest."

Thompson shrugged. His relationship with the president, strained for several weeks, had suddenly improved. "You're kidding yourself, chief, if you think some brilliant tactical move *à la* Kissinger is going to get the troops back in the barracks. This is one they're going to have to fight out until they're wading in blood."

"The longer it lasts, the more dangerous it is," the president said, "especially with these goddamned Germans running around like a bunch of cowboys. What play did you say you were seeing?"

"A new one by Curzon. It's about two homosexuals who fall in love with the same girl. He calls it *Ménage à Trois.*"

"Oh, for Christ's sake," the president said, grinning, "that's perverse."

The lowering mass of Kennedy Center was ablaze with lights as the White House limousine dropped him off. He picked Suzanne out of the crowd instantly, a shimmering point of light in a silver sheath cut to the coccyx in the back.

"My God, Alec, you look bedraggled," she said, taking in his limp shirt and a suit that looked as if it had been slept in. "Would you rather skip this thing?"

He shook his head, letting his eyes flow over the fashionable Washington crowd. Kip Dean was there along with the French ambassador and James Clarence. Gordon Wiseman and his arty wife were talking to the Soviet ambassador in a corner, and four cabinet ministers were salted and peppered throughout the crowd.

Suzanne read his mind. "The world goes up in flames, but the *crème de la crème* of Washington can be found at a faggoty play."

"They're probably at the Bolshoi in Moscow and at a shadow play in Peking," Thompson said, wishing dearly for a drink.

Kip Dean strolled up, blue eyes innocently wicked. "I hear *el jefe maximo* is breathing fire and smoke because his advisors have let him down. Rumor has it that Gordon Wiseman's days are numbered as chief spook. And the chief of staff was seen leaving the White House looking like used litmus paper."

"Kip, you're losing your touch," Thompson said. "Take a look out by the White House swimming pool."

Dean's eyes sharpened. "What's out there?"

"A guillotine."

Dean grinned. "Laugh, if you will, you twentieth-century Machiavelli. But you better remember that yours is the only high-wire act left that operates without a net."

Thompson frowned. It was too early for the rumors

of rolling heads to start. The search for scapegoats came only later when the rats began to scramble for holes.

"He's just fishing, Alec," Suzanne said. "I haven't heard anything about Wiseman leaving, although, when you come to think about it," she said, looking thoughtful, "it is surprising as hell that we didn't have an inkling of what that damned Beck was going to do."

"What makes you think we didn't?" Thompson said, grinning at her, struck again by the honeyed silk texture of her skin. He was definitely going to have to pay more attention to this woman. She wasn't the type you could neglect for long.

The play opened in a chi-chi New York apartment. A tall, thin, obviously effeminate actor turned to a lovely girl curled up on a sofa to say, "What do you mean, Valerie, why am I a faggot? It's simple. My older sister seduced me when I was twelve and told me my pecker would rot off if I ever told mother."

Thompson awoke to the sharp punch of Suzanne's elbow. "For God's sake, Alec," she said giggling. "You can sleep, but don't snore."

The conversation on the stage revolved around some arcane version of cunnilatio as Thompson stifled a yawn and shot a glance at his watch. They slipped out during the second-act intermission and took a taxi to Janine's, a French restaurant on Pennsylvania Avenue that shared top billing at the moment with the Brasserie Lorraine. Thompson stopped to telephone the White House from the little foyer off the entrance as the manager snapped a quick command to the *maître d'hôtel*. The place was packed. Suzanne stood at the bar with two television newsmen who were throwing dice for a drink when Thompson got off the phone and came over. "Any chance for a table?" he said to the bartender, a Corsican ex-boxer with a broken nose who doubled as bouncer.

"Observe the *madame*," he said, indicating the blonde owner, who was leaning over a table of obvious tourists smiling a brilliant smile, a mink coat slung over one arm.

"This is your coat, is it not, *madame?* Yes? Mink, is it not, no? So hard to tell the artificial from the real these days, don't you think? More coffee." Her voice picked up speed as she overrode any possible answer. "Then you will want the check, of course. Jacques." Her voice was at once servile and imperious, gentle and hectoring. At the sound of his name, the *maître d'hôtel* appeared, as if on a string, and presented the check with a flourish to the dazed clients. Two waiters had suddenly appeared to clear the half-finished coffee and still-full brandy glasses, while another stood with a clean tablecloth half-unfolded.

As the four bewildered tourists rose to leave, the *maître d'hôtel* appeared at Thompson's elbow. "Your table is ready, sir."

"The hell it is," one of the newsmen said. "We've been waiting half an hour in this goddamned closet for a place to eat. That's *our* table."

"*Monsieur* has no reservation," the waiter said, his voice icy.

"Neither has Harry Horseshit, here," the newsman said, his face pale with rage. "Suzanne just said he didn't."

Michelle appeared at the bar, a hard, handsome blonde of about thirty-five, hair piled high in an unlikely hairdo, solid figure encased like molten steel in a black silk dress. "Listen, you, shut your fucking mouth, or get your ass out of here," she said in a husky voice made even lower by a thick French accent. "*I* decide who has reservations in my restaurant, not you. You don't like it, go." She pointed to the door with a square hand and motioned toward the bartender with her head.

"Christ, Michelle, relax, will you? We've been sitting here for half an hour," the younger of the two men said ingratiatingly.

The woman's whole body suddenly softened as she slipped an arm around the man's waist and allowed her impressive breasts to rub against him. "I know, *chéri*. It's terrible. You get the next table, you hear, Jacques?" she said, turning to the head waiter. "And next time maybe you reserve, no? Okay, Alec, Suzanne," she said, lapsing into French and leading them to the vacated table, which, in the space of seconds, had acquired a glittering array of silver and glasses.

"You two never come anymore. What the hell is the matter?" she said, dropping into a chair next to Thompson as a waiter appeared. "You want that awful Spanish sherry, *chéri?* And you, darling? A Scotch? You know, you are ruining my business with your goddamned war and politics," she said, turning to Thompson. "Nobody eats when they are worried."

"You make all your money on booze, anyway, Michelle," Thompson said, "and they sure as hell drink—especially that watered-down hootch you sell."

"You son-of-a-bitch," she said, glancing around apprehensively. "You say that again, and I'll put you in the john next time you come in here." As she spoke, she let a hand fall negligently to his leg and began to stroke the inside of his thigh in an automatic gesture as Suzanne's eyebrows lifted.

"Michelle, will you get your filthy paws off my man?"

The woman, whose eyes were flickering around the room in quick brutal stabs, glanced down and laughed. "I was only preparing him for you, darling.

171

I can't sit here with you tonight. There is chaos in the kitchen and the *maître d'hôtel* is standing there picking his nose while dozens of people starve. I see you later." She moved across the restaurant, smiling, touching, greeting, insulting, her behind weaving calculatingly erotic figure-eights as she cursed and ripped the waiters in gutter French.

"She runs the place like a concentration camp," Suzanne said. "I can never understand why you want to come here. The woman is a retired whore."

"She serves the best food in town," Thompson said, sipping the dry wine, wishing he had had the nerve to order a martini. Michelle had once told four men who had ordered a third round of martinis that she would serve them the drinks and then they would have to leave, because she would not insult her cooks by serving their food to people with paralyzed palates.

"I bet she bathes once a week, if that often," Suzanne said. "What's this thing you've got about French women, anyway?"

"I was married to one," Thompson said gently.

Suzanne colored and wound up giggling. "Jesus, I keep forgetting. You seem like the least likely married man I've ever known, Alec. She must have been miserable."

"She was. The French are a marvelous people, full of logic and order. Once they know the name of the game, they invariably play it by the rules, whether it's a revolution, adultery, or middle-class family life. I just kept changing the game too often. It made her nervous. Wasn't good for the children."

"You son is a pilot, isn't he?"

"One is, on that carrier in the Mediterranean, the *Halsey*. His mission is to drop three medium-sized nuclear weapons on certain highly important industrial targets in the Caucasus. Theoretically, he will have enough fuel to get back to his ship, always assuming that the ship is still there."

Suzanne wrapped her arms around herself and shivered. "Jesus, don't talk like that."

Thompson shrugged. "It is not a realistic mission anymore, anyway. We are not about to attack the Soviet Union. Or anybody else. All our strategic concepts are laughably obsolete. The world has moved on, and our military is sitting there staring stupidly at the biggest, most powerful pile of lethal hardware ever assembled . . . and no conceivable enemy."

"You really think things have changed that much? Do the Soviets understand this? I mean, do they have the same conception of the world?"

"Dimitri does," Thompson said, sipping the last of the sherry. "And I think he's getting through to the general secretary. The only danger right now is that somebody will make a really bad mistake in judgment and force a nuclear exchange."

"Which would mean we'd all be dead," Suzanne said.

"Yes, at least in the Northern Hemisphere. The scientists aren't sure how much of the fallout would drift south. Certainly enough to cause millions of deaths there as well, not to speak of the mutations and long-term genetic damage. Which is why it's not going to happen. There are no Hitlers or Stalins in power at the moment. We're dealing with rational men."

Suzanne shook her head. "You sound as if you might be whistling 'Dixie,' lover. I just hope you and that funny little Russian know what you're doing. I sure as hell don't trust our ballsy president and that crafty peasant who is running the Soviet Union."

A waiter placed thin slices of smoked salmon on

their plates, accompanied by French bread so crisp it crackled at the slightest touch. Suzanne ate with concentration, savoring the delicate flavor of the fish and shaking her head. "Where do they get it? It doesn't taste like any salmon I have ever eaten."

"Comes from a little stream in northern Ireland," Thompson said. "She used to know the laird in that whorehouse she worked in. He sends it over to her out of loyalty for past favors."

"Fuck you," Suzanne said, amiably spearing a slice he had left on his plate.

"When?"

"The sooner the better," she said, giggling. "I'm beginning to feel like a nun. What are we eating? I didn't hear your order."

"Lobster, made with some sort of special Corsican sauce. She recommended it on the way to the table."

The restaurant was even more packed now than when they had arrived. Tables for two had been set in the aisles for late arrivals without reservations, making the trip from the kitchen a high-risk hazard for the waiters, who threaded their way through the narrow lanes with sweat dripping off their faces as Janine moved with incessant care from one group to the next.

"God, she works hard," Suzanne said. "The place must be a gold mine."

"Loses money," Thompson said between bites of the lobster, trying to figure out just what was in the sauce. "Only way she stays in business is through Service de Documentation Extérieure et de Contre-Espionage, the French CIA."

Suzanne stared at him for a moment, not sure he was joking, when the de la Margeries appeared at the door. "Speak of the devil. Let's ask them to join us,"

Thompson said, motioning to Janine who understood instantly and solved one more seating problem.

"You did not find our little drama of pederasty and incest sufficiently interesting to stay for the dénouement, Alec?" de la Margerie said, kissing Suzanne's hand.

"No. But, then, I probably don't have the same fond memories of the monks that you have, Charles."

"My dear Alec, I went to Winchester, where I defended myself admirably from the buggery-minded masters by telling them I suffered from an obscure anal venereal disease for which there was no known cure."

"Don't be filthy, Charles," his wife said, dropping into the seat next to Alec and kissing him on the cheek. "You look tired. You should be home in bed."

"My dear, you are so naïve," de la Margerie said. "What on earth makes you think anybody but us gets any rest in bed?"

The French woman leveled her gray eyes at him. "And whose fault is that, *chéri?*" she asked with a thin smile.

De la Margerie's pale face went chalky as his wife dropped her eyes.

"Alec tells me Europeans never cut each other up in public," Suzanne said brightly.

"Another piece of American romanticism, my dear," de la Margerie said. "We just keep our voices down when we do it."

Michelle returned to the table, her voice dripping with servility. "Monsieur l'Ambassadeur, there is a little caviar left, if you like. With Wyborowa? A touch of the *pâté* from the Loire that you enjoyed so much the last time, perhaps? No?" Her whole attitude was one of anxious docility as the French aristocrat accepted her suggestions with weary indifference. His presence in the restaurant was in its way much more important to her than Alec Thompson's. Thompson brought in the political elite and the hard-drinking journalists. But the French ambassador's patronage was the ultimate culinary stamp of approval. The diplomatic corps and the large resident French community always followed his lead.

"Well, *mon chéri*, the situation leaves much to be desired, *n'est-ce pas?*" de la Margerie said. "You have once again loosed the Visigoths in Europe, and God only knows what mischief they will be up to this time."

"What the hell do you mean, Charles? *We* loosed them? They're your neighbors and allies. Why in Christ's name are we to blame?"

The Frenchman shook his head. "No, that won't work, Alec. It's been a keystone of French policy since the war to keep atomic weapons out of their hands. You don't for a minute think that anybody believes this little charade about their taking the trigger mechanisms by force, do you? Really, how naïve do you think one can be? Obviously, it was all set up in advance, even that ridiculous skirmish in Berlin where a few people were scratched."

"Two hundred were killed," Thompson muttered, drinking the rest of the wine and motioning to the waiter. He needed a brandy badly. It had never occurred to him that anybody would suspect the U.S. of collusion in the German takeover. It was so incredible that he felt like bursting into hysterical laughter.

"Yes, very effective. I would like to see the bodies," de la Margerie said drily.

"We could probably arrange it, Charles. No, seriously, they're being flown back to an airbase outside Washington. I'll have each coffin opened for you. If you like, I could even arrange for you to be present while a professor of forensic medicine proves to you that the bullets that killed them were German."

"Very funny, Alec," Claude said. "Now, would you two mind not clawing each other like a pair of cats? After that depressing play, I would like to be amused. If it's as bad as you two seem to think, we may not have all that much time left."

"You were kidding, weren't you, Mr. Ambassador?" Suzanne said, looking de la Margerie in the eye. "I mean, you can't be serious about what you just said. My God, where would the U.S. have a self-interest in setting up another nuclear power in Europe?"

"Your country has chosen China, my dear. Didn't you know? But it would prefer that the Soviet Union not know this immediately; otherwise, there would still be a possibility of betrayal. Once the serious bloodletting starts, it will be too late." He turned to Alec. "I admire your tactics, *mon chéri*. Truly brilliant. You have maneuvered your two biggest enemies into an armed conflict sure to bleed them heavily and leave them even more embittered than before. What's more, you will eventually be the mediator. At the same time, you've managed to dismantle the Soviet hegemony in Eastern Europe, the cornerstone of your policy since Acheson and Truman initiated it. And you have established the Teutonic imperium in Europe, thus getting all those messy Latins under control once and for all. Tactically brilliant. But one must wait a little to see if it is not going to be a strategic disaster."

Thompson sipped the brandy, savoring the warmth and spurious strength coursing down his throat. "Charles, you don't believe a word of it. You know it's a lot of crap, but you're capable of sending off a telegram telling your government just what you've told us. And the silly bastards at the Quai would nod

177

in total satisfaction, because that's the way they had it figured out already. You'll look like a genius."

The Frenchman smiled. "Assuming that what you said is true, and I don't concede that it is, what would be gained by my reporting the truth? They wouldn't believe me, and I would soon get the reputation for being a fool. If I'm proved right, it would quickly be written off as an accident. You must be aware, Alec, that the diplomats who become ambassadors are not the ones who are brilliantly right. They are invariably the ones who are wrong in the same way as their superiors. Nothing can be more infuriating than to have a blazingly intellectual second secretary turning in these superb political reports full of unpalatable verities. He soon finds himself in Chad, where such people belong."

Suzanne stared at him in disbelief. "You are not kidding, are you? You really think it's more important to maintain style than to sacrifice it for substance?"

"Yes, my dear, I do. You will find when you are older that style is substance. The so-called truths change from hour to hour. Evil becomes good. War becomes peace. But good manners or bad ones are immutable. So are grace, wit, elegance, and death."

"Death?"

"One comes into this world in a messy, unstylish way, my dear—inevitably. But one's manner of going is one's own choice—the ultimate style. And I should think even you would agree that it's probably the most important act we perform in our grubby, unimportant lives."

"*Merde!*" Thompson said, rolling the French "r" broadly in imitation of the lower-class accent of Marseilles.

"Exactly," Claude said. "Charles, you are talking

like a Lyceen. Please stop all this nonsense. And you, too, Alec. In any event, he did not report to Paris what he's been saying. I read it, and he said what everybody knows to be true. Your president is horrified by the whole business and is trying to get everybody to act sensibly."

"Really, Claude, you could be guillotined for what you just revealed," her husband said, looking in mock terror to his left and right. "My dear wife has come to regard diplomacy as just another toy to be played with by men who are nothing more than grown-up children."

"Only some, Charles. Others prefer more interesting toys."

Later, as Suzanne lay curled against Alec, twining her fingers in the mat of wiry black hair on his chest, she asked, "You've had an affair with her, haven't you?"

Thompson grinned in the darkness. "A gentleman never discusses such things."

"Balls," Suzanne said. "I'll bet she's good in a serious kind of way, huh?"

"Now, just what the hell does that mean?" Thompson asked as her hand moved down the line of black hair to his navel, where it clawed him gently. He was beginning to know what the French meant by *"tristesse coïtale."*

"You know, earnest and competent; not much emotion, but a lot of technique." Her hand continued its downward journey, exploring as it went.

Thompson started to laugh, remembering the days in London.

Suzanne propped herself up on her left elbow and stared at him. "I came pretty close to the nerve, huh? I mean, it was really just a good lay at five in the

179

afternoon before her husband and your wife got home." She held him now, gently demanding some signs of virility. He was beginning to feel older by the minute.

"You've read too many bad French novels, Suzanne," he said, turning toward her to find one of her small, firm breasts confronting him, the nipple, a ripe, serrated cherry.

She pushed him back. "Lie still, darling. I know you're tired, and I don't give a damn. No man ever died from this." He wondered who taught her to do it. And then he didn't care. Her mouth was like a live thing, moving down his body and taking his limp instrument and converting it into a semblance of life. He moved to turn her over, but she pushed him back again. "No, let me. I really like it this way. Be still."

Thompson listened to the seven o'clock news through the open door of the bathroom as he shaved.

"Good morning, ladies and gentlemen. This is Joseph Hartford with the latest news.

"The situation along the Ussuri and Amur rivers at the Khabarovsk junction continues to be confused today. Large numbers of Chinese troops continue to attack in human waves attempting to enlarge a beachhead several miles to the east of this large industrial city. Unconfirmed reports from the battlefield indicate that the Soviet Union has established air superiority and is subjecting the bridgehead to a withering artillery and rocket barrage. Chinese casualties are said to be heavy in both men and materiel. Meanwhile, to the south there are indications of a Russian counterthrust at the city of Vyazemski in an apparent attempt to turn the flank of the Chinese armies.

"U.N. Secretary General José Lerin has once again called on both parties to agree to a ceasefire in place and negotiations under U.N. auspices. Both sides have ignored the appeal.

"In newly reunited Germany today, troops are on the move. Two divisions of the former West German Army have joined with the small Austrian force at the border of Hungary, and a new central command structure for Austria and East and West Germany was announced. Plans for the total integration of the East and West German armed forces are well under way, and much of the combined German Army has moved up to stations along the Polish border. Rumors that the Soviet Union has given the new German state a twenty-four-hour ultimatum to dissolve itself have been denied in Berlin, where the unified German government has set up a provisional capital.

"Unconfirmed reports from Moscow say the Soviet Union has demanded the resignation of the Polish government and its replacement by a regime favorable to the Russians. The Poles have reportedly refused, and mobilization of reserves is under way.

"In Italy, President Giuseppe Sforza has escaped another assassination attempt. Four members of the Italian National Liberation Front attacked his car with grenades as he left an audience with the pope yesterday. Security guards killed two of the attackers and wounded the others. This marks the fourth attempt to kill Sforza since he took power in a *coup d'état* overthrowing the Christian Democratic Communist Coalition government.

"The oil price-war continues. The Israelis today raised their price to twenty-five dollars a barrel for Saudi Arabian and Libyan crude. The Iranians are expected to follow suit later today for oil emanating from their dependencies in the Persian Gulf. Nigeria and Algeria have announced that they will follow the Israeli lead. In Europe, the Council of Fourteen is exploring ways of retaliating against what they describe as an attempt by the oil powers to loot the economies of the developed nations.

"The Israelis are expected to explode their first hydrogen bomb at an underground site in the southern Arabian desert today. Israeli scientists say virtually no venting is expected.

"In Tokyo, Indian Foreign Minister Singh signed a treaty of friendship with China and Japan today. He later joined the foreign ministers of China, Japan, Indonesia, Australia, the Philippines, and five other Southeast Asian nations in Tokyo in negotiations to establish a Far East Common Market. The meeting is expected to adjourn tomorrow and reconvene in July in Canberra for final talks.

"And now for news on the domestic scene."

"You want to hear anymore?" Suzanne asked.

"No."

She flicked the switch as he came out of the bathroom and turned toward him, a rumpled sheet gathered about her. "You look obscenely good for a man your age," she said. "I'll bet you secretly work out with weights."

"I occasionally lift a few," he said, "but only when they're imposed on me."

"Why, you arrogant bastard," Suzanne said, throwing a pillow at him and rising from the bed in the same motion. She was totally unself-conscious of her body, which was a honey-colored machine-a-screwer, Thompson thought, remembering the fractured French phrase of an old and lecherous friend in Paris.

"What are you grinning at?" she asked, standing in front of him, hands on her hips, legs slightly apart.

"I was thinking that maybe the president and the
182

Federal Broadcasting System can wait a little longer," he said, reaching for her.

She slipped under his arm and raced into the bathroom, slamming the door in his face. "Men revolt me before twelve o'clock. Besides, my sainted father always told me it was bad for the character to indulge before the sun was over the yardarm."

12

Thompson had barely stripped off his coat when the intercom crackled. "Can you come in, Alec? Samsun and Pruitt are here. The Russian counterattack has begun."

Thompson found the president in a darkened office in front of a slide projector. "Hello, Phil. Where did they hit?" Thompson asked, shaking hands with the two generals.

"At Vyazemski, as we expected. In force. There must be half a million men in the strike group, the major part of their eastern army, and probably most of the air force, now that they've managed to contain the Khabarovsk pocket." He flicked another map on the screen. "The front is somewhat to the south of Vyazemski, where the river offers fewer obstacles. They're laying down a carpet barrage to keep the Chinese in their bunkers, rocketing every artillery position on the opposite bank and shooting up anything that moves with waves of planes. They've put in a helicopter division here," he said, touching the screen with a long, collapsible stainless steel pointer, "and they may have taken the main radar rocket control station by now. Paratroops are dropping all over the Chinese rear to disrupt communications and secure road crossings. It's probably the biggest concerted offensive since some of the Allied attacks on the Western front in World War One."

"But a hell of a lot more deadly," Pruitt said. "They're using more firepower than any general in history ever dreamed of. Their rocket expenditures alone will exceed in twenty-four hours what they used during a major World War Two offensive in a week. Logistics must be a horror story. It's going to be one bloody mess out there."

The president sat silently listening to the generals in the darkened room as he cradled the customary mug of coffee. "As of now, it looks as if the Russians are winning all the way. Is that your assessment?"

Samsun cleared his throat. "It's too early to tell, Mr. President. The offense always has an advantage in the first days of attack. No matter how well prepared the defensive forces are, they have to take the first blow. If the Chinese can sanitize the large forces of paratroops, move up their reserves quickly, and in good order and regain some control of the air, then they could give the Soviets a lot of trouble."

"What are their chances?"

Samsun shrugged. "They have not committed their air, not in any strength, which is really the biggest surprise so far. They're holding it out, obviously hoping that their anti-aircraft missiles can take out a fair proportion of the Soviet planes."

Pruitt interrupted. "The problem with planes is that the anti-aircraft missiles can't tell the difference between friend and foe. The Israelis found that out in all their wars with the Arabs. If the Chinese commit their planes, they'll have to ease off on the anti-aircraft. As it is, the Russians are using virtually none because they're so afraid of hitting their own planes. This lets the Chinese get in a fair number of effective low-level sneak air attacks without much fear of flak. But they're going to have to commit the main body of their planes within the next two or three days."

Samsun nodded. "The Soviets already have a fair foothold across the river. Satellite pictures show massed Chinese armor about to hit them here," he said, flicking the pointer over the town of Tungan. "We're a little puzzled, however, because the force is far too small for the job. They're continuing to hold back a huge reserve along a line from Fuchin to Bikin."

"What do you foresee over the next week?"

Again Samsun cleared his throat, the nervous gesture tearing at the silent darkness of the room. "All indications are that they will roll up the Chinese salient, linking up with a large Soviet infantry army backed by massive artillery at Leninskaya. They'll then attempt to broaden the armored salient with injections of infantry in order to cut off the forces to the north, which are attacking Khabarovsk. A million men, *if* they can close the ring and the Chinese can't break out." He stopped talking for a moment, shrugging slightly. "It'll be the biggest encircling movement since the early German victories in Russia."

"Don't the Chinese see the danger?" The president sounded impatient. "Are they not aware of the position they're in? It looks childishly obvious."

"We've debated that for weeks, Mr. President, from the time the plan became clear," Pruitt said. "We can only assume that the Chinese think they can hold the

186

Ussuri line and keep their salient from being pinched off."

The president stood up, motioning for the lights. "You're the professionals, gentlemen. But every time I look at the Chinese battle plans for this particular war, I'm struck by their apparent stupidity. In all my readings about war, I've never seen a plan that looked stupid until after the event. On paper they all looked great. I suggest that General Wang Chin is one of the most astute warlords of our time. He must be thinking of something that we are not."

Pruitt nodded. "He may be. There are indications that he plans to turn his invasion force around and put his main effort against the Soviet salient once it develops. But all that this would get him, even if he's successful in bloodying them, is a return to the status quo. The object of the attack, as we see it, is to pick up some territory and hold onto it, forcing the Russians to the conference table."

The president nodded. "That's our assumption. Implicit in all this is the Chinese threat that they will continue to mount similar operations until they eventually get what they want. Rather than face this prospect, they expect the Soviets to make at least some concessions. For that they need a fairly impressive initial victory. Simply repulsing a Soviet counterattack would not constitute that."

"What about that Japanese amphibious force at Sapporo?"

Samsun waved a hand, dismissing it. "They've got five hundred thousand troops there and enough landing craft to get them across. But they would have to take out the Soviet fleet and air force first, and before they can do that the battle is going to be over."

"All right, gentlemen. I'll expect you at the National Security Board meeting this afternoon. Alec, get Wiseman. Tell him I want him to do everything he can to get me a reading on the Chinese and Japanese intentions. He can burn every agent he's got, if necessary, but we have to know what's going on. If the Russians are going to win quickly and big out there, it's going to have serious consequences in Europe."

"It'll be hard to hold the Russian generals once they start. They'll cut through to the Rhine in a matter of days," Thompson said.

"I wouldn't be so sure, Alec," Pruitt demurred. "The German Army is no pushover. And if Beck's losing, there's no knowing what he might do."

"That's precisely the point, Craig," the president said, interrupting. "He's crazy enough to use his tactical nuclear weapons. And if he does, the manure will hit the fan. But I don't want to waste time on that nut now. Find out what's going on in the Chinese mind of Wang Chin, gentlemen. And I'm still concerned about that Japanese amphibious force."

General Wang Chin sat at his desk and rapidly demolished plain rice in a lacquered bowl. His doctors warned him to chew the food thoroughly, but he could not bring himself to follow their advice. As a result, the ulcer would begin to pain him again within minutes. As he ate he studied the battlefield map spread in front of him with satisfaction. It was going well, especially at the bridgehead at Khabarovsk, an unexpected bonus on which he had not counted. It was a great plus, but unless he was careful, it could turn into a disaster. The second army group commander was demanding more and more men and machines, convinced he could push the Russians back. It was impossible, of course. The bridgehead would be wiped out and the two hundred thousand men now in place would be slaughtered. But to contain it and wipe it out, the Soviets had been forced to divert an additional ten divisions from the Vyazemski counterattack. Not much, but enough. Barring unforeseen disaster, this diversion, with all the attendant demoralization inherent in last-minute, unplanned moves of large numbers of troops, would be just enough. It denuded old Korzybsky of most of his strategic reserves.

Wang Chin knew the Russian well. He had met the old man at the Soviet tank training center in Kiev in 1952 where Chin, a young general who had begun as a private in the ranks of the Chinese Communist Sixth Route Army in 1935, had risen to general by 1948 at the age of thirty. He had been in Russia filling in some of the theoretical gaps of an army career that had covered twenty years of war. The Russians were great soldiers and old Korzybsky had been one of the best he knew. His tank tactics had rivaled those of Rommel or Guderian in the latter stages of the war, and his ability to handle large masses of men without losing control was his greatest strength: that and his willpower, his willingness to commit his last reserve at the critical point, never hesitating to make the gamble that the opponent least expects. But now, almost thirty years later, he was an old man, tired and probably suffering from a serious heart condition that would not, of course, change his character. On the contrary. This was his last battle, and he would make the most of it. Chin was counting on it. The audacity and élan of the old Russian tank commander would betray him and win the battle for the Chinese. Chin, following the precepts of Sun Tsu, the greatest of Chinese military historians, would defeat his enemy by turning his very strength against him.

Once the victory was won, Chin would write a poem to draw the lesson for future generations.

Once again, he thought, with intense satisfaction, the party leaders were sufficiently confident to allow the nation to draw upon six thousand years of Chinese wisdom without fear of encouraging the reactionaries. It made things easier for soldiers like him. Armies needed tradition and patriotism and a sense of history; otherwise, it was difficult to arouse that last surge of self-abnegation that sent a man knowingly to his death for an abstract, the nation. No question about it: they died more readily for the nation than for the Communist Party. And this was what he was asking them to do—die in great numbers for a greater China. And they would do it.

Japanese Prime Minister Yashima Nagoya shivered in the spring rain that fell in a misty drizzle on the grim port city of Sapporo. But he shivered in anticipation, not from cold or fear. The five hundred thousand troops had loaded overnight and the flotilla was ready to sail. The meteorologists had been right. There was zero visibility over the Sea of Japan, and it would hold for at least another twenty-four hours. His intelligence people assured him that the Soviet defense forces were down to skeleton strength along the Amgun-Velikaya-Kema landing zone. Three divisions had been pulled out to help contain the Khabarovsk bridgehead, and most of the other troops were concentrated for the Vyakemski offensive. The Russians had not thought he would dare move. And in the beginning he had not wanted to. The risks were enormous; but so were the rewards. Over the past eight years the economies of Japan and China had become so inextricably tied that there was no possibility of holding back once Chou had decided to move. The economic logic was too compelling to ignore. Japan had to have access to the Siberian mineral deposits and natural gas over the next thirty years or its industry would atrophy. Never again would they have an opportunity to attack with the Soviet Union this weak, paralyzed by the German move in Europe. It was now or never.

He watched the gray-camouflaged ships move out one by one under the protection of the darting Japanese destroyers and missile boats. It took Nagoya back to his days as a lieutenant on a Japanese cruiser in World War II. The surge of exhilaration he had always felt at going into battle came back to him now, and he knew that he would be able to evoke that same surge among his one hundred million countrymen when he went on television that night to announce the Japanese attack. His people were sheep, but militant sheep. The young emperor would speak first, arousing them to an emotional pitch with the help of party cadres stationed at the listening halls around the country. More than two hundred thousand people would be gathered in Tokyo Stadium, and millions more would see him on the giant screens erected in the sports arenas of major cities around the country.

It was a refinement of the old Goebbels-Speer technique used so effectively in Nazi Germany. Nagoya had studied the old films and hired some of the best directors in the Japanese motion picture industry to come up with the kind of pageantry that would appeal to and move the Japanese people. His opposition had accused him of vulgar demagoguery until he had finally shut them up. They were right, of course, but what they had not understood was that to appeal to the people you isolated their emotional

191

nerve centers and hammered them. To hell with the supercilious intellectuals.

His aide stood silently at his side, conveying his urgency in an unspoken tension. Nagoya let him wait, deliberately increasing the tension, savoring his power. "Yes," he said abruptly.

The aide bowed. "Tokyo called. The Soviet ambassador urgently requests a meeting with you."

Nagoya arched his eyebrows. "Tell him to call the foreign minister."

The aide bowed again. "He insists on seeing you."

"Very well, at ten P.M. tonight, following my television broadcast."

The gray shapes were disappearing in the mist now, carrying with them Japan's prestige and its economic future. A victory would go far toward wiping out the humiliation of World War II and all the attendant indignities. This time they were going to win and win big.

General Phillip Samsun stared down at the situation map in disbelief. "You're positive, Bowman? No possible mistake?"

"None, sir," the bespectacled colonel answered. His reports had noted for weeks the increasing possibility of a Japanese intervention across the Sea of Japan. The logistics, air-support dispositions, troop movements, and ship maneuvers had all pointed to it. Both Pruitt and Samsun had dismissed the whole exercise as a bluff. That was their ass, not his.

"Well, I guess that explains the Chinese not using their air power. They've been holding it back to give cover to the landings."

"Yes, sir," Bowman said. It was the kind of obvious remark a man made when he was in shock. General Pruitt strode into the room at that moment and shouldered his way through the crowd of young intelligence experts to the map. One look at Samsun's face told him all he needed to know.

"Well, Phil, we've got our answer. Wang Chin is going for the whole ball of wax."

Samsun nodded. "Korzybsky will have to wheel part of his attacking army in the middle of a battle and retrace his steps. He won't get to the coast before the Japanese have a foothold. Even if he does, his forces won't be in position, he won't have a battle plan, and, Jesus, the confusion will be monumental, given that lousy road network and the bad weather."

Pruitt ran a finger from the Khabarovsk front down to the Amgun. "He could get a couple of armored divisions from the northern front in position overnight, maybe, except from what we hear he's ready to attack the bridgehead and wipe it out. If he stops now, he risks having Wang reinforce across the Amur and threaten his rear." He shook his head. "Beautiful, goddamned fucking beautiful."

"He's still got to fight the battles, Craig," Samsun said. "But I agree. The plan is a gem. He's sitting tight on every front and forcing the enemy to move huge masses of men in a restricted area with lousy communications to meet a series of threats without really knowing where Chin intends to strike the main blow."

"What would you do, Phil?" Pruitt asked.

Samsun grinned. "No question about it. I'd wheel that army in the salient around and attack the armored force he's pushed in from Vyazemski. Latest reports are that the point has linked up with the infantry at Leninskaya. That means most of the armor is out in the salient, probably wheeling north with a holding force in the rear. If Chin throws in everything he's got from both sides, he could freeze the

Soviets until the Japanese cut their supply lines. Then he'd just cut them up or force a retreat via Leninskaya."

"And then?"

"Hold on to the Khabarovsk salient and push an armored column across to link up with the Japanese. That would cut off the whole southern half of the Vladivostok area. The Russian armies would be in bad shape by this time. They would have to withdraw and regroup at Khabarovsk. With their communications, resupply would be a nightmare. The Chinese have the interior lines and overpowering manpower resources. If they can equalize in materiel . . ." Samsun turned his hands up, leaving the sentence unfinished.

Thompson leaned back in his chair, and propped his feet up on the desk cluttered with cables, and yawned. He had, he knew, wasted most of the day. Even in the middle of a world crisis that could conceivably leave them back in the Stone Age, the bureaucracy had continued to grind out its daily ton of crap. The president had talked four times with Kharkov, whose initial hysteria had turned into a cold rage. He was no longer threatening an attack in Europe, nor was he asking for U.S. help against the Chinese. He had accepted each call and listened quietly to the president's pleas for calm, interrupting only once to suggest that the president come to the point, since he was in the middle of directing a war. It was obvious that they had lost his attention. Thompson could picture the increasing paranoia among the Kremlin leaders as they began more and more to suspect that the U.S. was a party to the conspiracy surrounding them, despite the fact that every one of the countries attacking them was Marxian-socialist except West Germany. If they survived the crisis, it was going to be a new, pluralistic world where Communist ideology meant about as much in terms of power relationships as Christianity.

The president had conveyed Beck's guarantees that the new Germany had no further territorial ambitions. It would make no demands for the return of its prewar territories in Silesia or East Prussia and would not support any Polish claims. Nor would the Germans attempt to excrcise any hegemony over the newly independent Soviet satellites in Rumania, Hungary, and Czechoslovakia. Obviously, Poland was a special case. But the alliance was purely defensive.

Kharkov had answered with a contemptuous grunt. There was no question but that Central Europe was infinitely more dangerous than the Far East. A million men could die in the Siberian steppes and change nothing. A war in Europe could rip the world apart. But instead of working to contain the crisis, they had been busy all day talking to nervous allies in England, France, Brazil, and half a dozen smaller nations where panic was beginning to spread. Sheaf after sheaf of cables from ambassadors who feared their posts—and, more important, they themselves—would be forgotten in the crisis flooded in with absurdly high classifications smeared across the top, indicating, as one wag had put it years ago, "Burn Before Reading."

Situation papers on every conceivable eventuality were piled in a corner of his desk, but the problem had boiled down to a very simple one: Could they keep the war in the Far East from becoming a general one? Intelligence was finally beginning to function, and all indications were that the agreement between Beck and the Chinese was strictly limited to their initial moves. There were no further commitments to come to each other's assistance, which meant nothing, of course. The startling success of the German and Polish coups, the Soviet lack of reaction, and the increasingly perilous state of the Soviet armies in Asia might tempt them to further adventures. And that was when the nuclear shit would hit the fan.

The president's buzzer sounded. "The Bobsey twins are here," he said, his deep voice filling the room with contempt. Thompson joined them.

The briefing, conducted by an ashen-faced and subdued Pruitt, was mercifully short. As it ended, the president turned to Wiseman, who sat slumped in one of the oversized armchairs. "Anything to add, Gordon?"

The intelligence chief nodded. "Yes. Something is up between Beck and Kharkov. We've intercepted massive cable traffic between them over the past few hours. We can't decode it, but the volume indicates something is up. Also, there is a report from Finland that indicates a high-level meeting is going to take place in Helsinki between the Germans and the Russians within the next few hours. I'm not sure what it means. Maybe nothing. But there's no doubt about it that this Japanese attack has shaken up the Russians badly. It's conceivable that they've decided to make a deal in Europe to keep the Germans off their back while they concentrate on the Chinese."

"What kind of deal?" Thompson interrupted, frowning. "What's left for them to trade, Gordon?"

Wiseman shrugged. "I'm speculating, of course, but maybe Kharkov will offer to recognize the status quo if the Germans and Poles will pull back their troops from the frontiers and partially demobilize. This would free one hell of a lot of troops, and, more important, air power for the Far East. The Soviets just can't afford to denude their European frontier with a threat from the Germans hanging over them."

Thompson shook his head. "No, it's got to be something else. Kharkov would never trust Beck. And, anyway, the battle in Asia is going to be decided before any real reinforcements get through. They don't have the airlift capacity to affect the fighting, and that railroad is a mess. Am I right, Craig?"

The general chewed on the dead butt of a cigar and nodded. "You're right. But they still don't want a two-front war. No way. Maybe Gordon has something. Maybe they're coming up with some sort of deal to give them some short-term security."

"Have you talked to Dimitri lately, Alec?"

"Yes. He's clammed up. I think even he suspects us of having been in on this in some way. We're going to be facing massive Soviet paranoia about our motives over the next few days. They're going to have one hell of a time convincing themselves that we're not in on this."

The president nodded and turned to Pruitt. "Tell your field commanders and especially the navy to avoid doing anything provocative. I don't want any incidents or even the hint of any aggressive activity."

Pruitt nodded. "We're going to have to maintain a red alert, though. Prudence dictates . . ."

"Goddamn it, general, I don't give a shit what prudence dictates," the president said, his big fists clenched in rage. "You tell your fucking commanders to stand down. You hear me? I don't want any goddamned red alerts or any other horseshit. I want a nice, quiet, calm front put up, and I want the Soviets to be able to see it."

Pruitt stood his ground. "I'll take that order in writing, Mr. President. I will not be responsible for leaving our armed forces in a state of unpreparedness

197

when war could break out any minute." His voice was quiet, but the contained rage and frustration were just below the surface.

The president stared at him, face congested. "Pruitt, I could relieve you of your command right now."

"If you want that order carried out, Mr. President, you'll have to."

The president's secretary opened the door and stuck her head in. "It's Kharkov on the line."

The president wearily waved the generals out and took the phone. There was no personal exchange in broken English and Russian, which the rough telephonic protocol had made habitual, just the quietly precise voice of an aide to the Soviet leader speaking unaccented English. The president flipped a switch and the voice filtered through a small speaker, allowing Thompson to hear.

"The chairman sends his greetings, Mr. President, and wishes to inform you that the Japanese battle fleet and air force supported by units of the Chinese Navy attacked our fleet off Vladivostok today and sank one carrier, three missile cruisers and seven destroyers. Other units were badly damaged. A similar attack on the submarine pens in the harbor put twenty of our attack submarines out of action. The Pacific Fleet is crippled and unable to attack the Japanese landing force. The situation is grave. The chairman wishes to inform you that an order has gone out to all Soviet units to arm the nuclear weapons in their arsenals. The chairman urgently requests that you make every effort to bring Chinese and German leaders to their senses before it is too late. Good-bye, Mr. President." The distinctive click of the circuit breaker sounded on the line.

The president replaced the phone. "What do you think?"

Thompson shook his head. "He won't use the nukes. The Chinese can hit his big cities even with those primitive rockets of theirs. He'd lose fifty to a hundred million people, and for what? It's like Mao said in the early 1960s. The Chinese can lose half their population and still have four hundred million. It's a bluff, and a weak one. I think maybe Kharkov is beginning to crack. Undoubtedly the wolves are beginning to gather in the Kremlin. I think that's why Dimitri is panicking. Kharkov is his patron, and the old man may be losing his grip."

"He's a little shit, isn't he?"

"Dimitri?" Thompson sounded surprised. "I doubt if he's much different from our appartchicks. He thinks of number one first. But there's a small difference in the stakes. If Gordon Wiseman fucks up, he goes back to his law firm at four times the money. If Dimitri gets the ax, the good life is gone forever. So he's goddamned careful. It makes for a thoroughly conservative and unadventurous foreign policy. We've benefited from it for years, and the Chinese and Germans are taking advantage of it today. They know the relative paralysis of the system under pressure. Nobody wants to risk making a mistake, so they sit tight. That leaves it up to the top leadership, and there is no more insular group anywhere in the world. That's why Kharkov's message worries me. He may not perceive that situation the way we do. He may see it in far worse terms. If he thinks the survival of the Soviet Union is at stake . . ." Thompson let the sentence die and he just shrugged.

The president doodled endless circles on a yellow-lined pad. "We've got to reassure him. But I'm not sure what we can do. That oil blockade you talked about would be too late to help if the situation in the Far East is as bad as it looks."

199

Thompson agreed. "We don't have any options right now except to sit tight and hope the Russians can hold out in the Far East. Somehow, I can't see Beck making any more wild moves right now. He's already way ahead."

"You don't know gamblers, Alec," the president said. "Beck's a gambler, and the temptation to stake it all on one more throw must be tremendous right now. There'll never be another opportunity like it. Let's see what kind of beating we're taking on television tonight."

A hair-spray commercial implying that its product would guarantee sexual fulfillment faded into Suzanne Wilson's calm, reassuringly cool presence.

"Good evening, this is Suzanne Wilson with the evening news. The situation in the Far East was complicated during the day by rumors that a Japanese invasion fleet had left Sapporo and was presumably headed for a landing in the rear of the Soviet forces attacking at Vyazemski. As you can see from the map," she said, turning in her chair as she spoke to gesture toward a large schematic map of the battle area, "the Japanese forces could be a dangerous threat to the Soviet rear. The possibility of their cutting off the corridor to Vladivostok could force a halt to the Soviet counteroffensive.

"We have no firm news that the Japanese move is a serious one. Intelligence sources in Hong Kong discount it, suggesting that the most the Japanese will be willing to do is make a feint at the landing area to throw the Soviet Union off balance. However, Pentagon experts are convinced that a landing will take place early tomorrow morning. These same experts expect the Soviet Union to withdraw troops from the Vyazemski and Khabarovsk fronts to meet the new threat. This, these sources say, will dangerously weaken their counterattack against the Chinese and leave them open to a Chinese effort to pinch off their armored forces now linking up at Leninskaya.

"Meanwhile, tension remains high in Europe. Armies of the reunited Germanies are fully mobilized and poised on the eastern frontiers. Poland has called up all reserves and is on a war footing, as are Czechoslovakia, Hungary, Rumania, and Yugoslavia. The forces of the NATO alliance are on red alert, but without the German contingent, NATO, it is generally conceded, is virtually nonexistent as a fighting organ. France has put its nuclear strike force in readiness but has so far refrained from mobilizing its reserves, reportedly because of an unwillingness to cause any German nervousness at having a large French force on its virtually undefended western frontier. The French president is known to have been in telephone contact with Beck, but the substance of their conversations is not now known.

"In India, rioting broke out in Calcutta as the government attempted to distribute a new shipment of grain. Police fired into the crowds, killing more than three hundred people as starving mobs attempted to storm the distribution points. More than two million people are reported to have died in the Gujurat district in the past month, with an additional ten million in danger of starving. U.S. and European grain shipments remain piled up in the ports because the rail transport system has virtually ceased to function. Indian Prime Minister Menon in a radio and television broadcast blamed what he termed the Western imperialist powers for India's plight and called for socialist discipline. U.N. experts say that the expected failure of the monsoon for the third straight year combined with the internal chaos in India could result in a tragedy of unparalleled proportions.

"The Israeli government has announced a further increase in the price of Saudi Arabian oil to twenty-five dollars a barrel following consultations with the shah of Iran. Other oil producers are expected to follow suit shortly. The Common Market executive council has been called into emergency session to deal with the increase, which individual members characterized as legalized robbery.

"In Portugal the military dictatorship of former Colonel Porfirio Herrera executed four alleged Communist conspirators for attempted sabotage. A state of emergency continues in Lisbon, which is quiet today following a clash between left- and right-wing students on Friday. Diplomatic observers in the capital believe Herrera's days are numbered unless he can impose order in the country. The shadowy junta that backs him is reportedly losing patience with his vacillating tactics."

Thompson was about to switch off the news when the president motioned him away from the TV. A disembodied hand had slipped a piece of paper across Suzanne Wilson's desk, and she now read it.

"A late bulletin has just arrived on the situation in the Far East. A surprise Japanese naval and air attack on units of the Soviet fleet anchored in Vladivostok harbor has apparently caused serious damage to a number of ships. The exact extent of the damage is not known, but observers onshore say that at least a dozen ships and submarines were sunk. Oil storage tanks and ammunition dumps were also hit, and the military area of the harbor is in flames. We'll be back with the latest bulletins later in the program."

As the hair-spray commercial flickered back on the screen, Thompson snapped off the TV. "It's very close to getting out of control," he said. "Too many countries and people involved. Everybody's gonads are beginning to swell. And the Soviets must be getting a little desperate. This is when somebody could make a really serious mistake."

"And they almost always do," the president said.

13

Kharkov paced up and down behind the immense conference table, now covered with empty bottles of mineral water, beer, coffee cups, and the remnants of sandwiches. The nine-man war board sat slumped in exhaustion as they waited for General Korzybsky's arrival. They had been in continuous session since early morning the previous day and their old men's faces were corroded with fatigue. One of the three generals slept sitting up, his joweled face, slack and gray, slumped on his chest. Dimitri Stashevsky, acting as secretary to the board, doodled mildly abstract erotic drawings on the gray-lined pad in front of him and wondered who would be enjoying Nadia's favors once he was in exile as comptroller of the hydro-electric station in Zheleznogorsk.

The big double doors of the conference room were flung open and Marshal Korzybsky entered, followed by two aides. His old, sick face was charged with energy, and he embraced a startled Kharkov in an all-enveloping bear hug. "Let us begin immediately, Comrade Chairman. I have little time. The jet waits at the airport with motors running to return me to the front." The old man motioned to his aides, who began setting up a series of collapsible maps on an artist's easel.

Kharkov lowered his great bulk into a chair in front of the map and listened intently as the old soldier began his briefing.

"The Chinese are falling into the trap we set for them," he began. "First, like a foolish young theoretician with no knowledge of real war, Wang divided his forces and invited our counterattack at Vyazemski." Korzybsky used an old-fashioned pointer to indicate positions on a large-scale map of the fighting area. "He had an unexpected success at Khabarovsk because of Gorbykov's death." He turned to face his audience, old face creased in a brutal grin. "As always in war, accidents that seemed like advantages often lead to disaster. The unexpected success of the bridgehead has caused Wang to slightly alter his original plan. He has poured more and more troops into the Khabarovsk salient, weakening his northern position and his possible reposte to our counterattack. We are today chewing up those troops in a meat grinder of artillery and air power. They will be wiped out within hours."

"What about the Japanese landing?" Borsov, the KGB commander, asked. "That will force you to withdraw troops from both fronts, won't it?"

Korzybsky nodded. "Yes, comrade. We will be forced to bring out a few divisions to contain the amphibious assault. I would prefer to annihilate it now, but that is precisely what the enemy wants us to do. We are resisting the temptation. It is in the nature of amphibious landings that confusion reigns for the first few days. The Japanese troops will need a week to get in a position to mount any kind of offensive. I am putting fewer than ten divisions across the breakout routes to make sure that they are contained. The force is too small to represent a threat on its own. Once we have dealt with Wang's main force, we'll turn on it and squash it," Korzybsky said, rubbing his thick forefinger and thumb together.

"So you plan to continue with the Vyazemski counterattack, ignoring the Japanese threat to your rear and the possibility that the Chinese will link up with them and cut off Vladivostok?" Kharkov's voice was incredulous as he spoke.

The old general nodded. "It is the only viable strategy, Comrade Secretary. The alternative is to pull fifty divisions out of the line and attempt to crush the Japanese before they obtain a foothold. It would take a week. During that week the Chinese will have expanded the Khabarovsk bridgehead and pinched off our counterattack. We can't pull that armor back in mid-attack. I already have ten thousand tanks committed to the battle. The roads are narrow and the fields are quagmires. If we attempt to turn back, we'll have a disaster on our hands."

"How is the battle going, Marshal?" Dimitri asked.

Korzybsky turned to the map. "The point of the armored force has linked up with the much weaker army group that kicked off from Leninskaya. The armored forces have wheeled and are attacking on both flanks. They have opened a corridor through which the infantry divisions are now pouring. The Chinese are massing at Fuchin. I expect the counterattack at any hour. It will be made with the full weight of their armor, artillery, and rockets on both sides of our salient. I anticipate that they will throw all their air power into the battle, even at the risk of leaving the Japanese invasion force at the mercy of our planes." He stopped and turned to face the board. "You must understand, comrades, the Japanese attack is not militarily important. It is no more than a feint designed to weaken our main attack. The Chinese is a magician. He seeks to distract us. He thinks he can win with tricks. But war is not fought with tricks. It is won with fire and steel. We have the fire and steel. If our nerves hold, we will have peace in Asia for a decade."

"And the fleet?"

Korzybsky waved a hand contemptuously. "What about the fleet? It was a joke. Russian fleets are always jokes. I never counted on it. Planes sink ships, comrades. The Americans found that out forty years ago. Ships are not serious. They are toys. I am indifferent to what happened at Vladivostok. Again, it is a diversion. The battle will be won here," he said, placing a stubby finger over the triangle made by Leninskaya, Vyazemski, and Khabarovsk.

The war board members, former military leaders or wartime commissars, began to probe the old marshal's battle plan in detail: his artillery placement; logistics; disposition of aircraft; and command structure of his intelligence regarding Chinese intentions. Dimitri Stashevsky sat silent, taking an occasional note, watching the weary old soldier parry the thrusts of his opponents on the war board with an energy and skill that might well be his last reserves.

Finally Kharkov stood up and shook the old man's hand. "Thank you, Ivan. Please wait in the outer room. We must now discuss the decision to be taken." Korzybsky started to protest, then stepped back, saluted, and left the room, trailed by his aides clutching a mass of half-opened maps.

Kharkov looked around the table, reading in each face the same thought, and he leaned heavily on the table. "He must go. He is still in the Karsk salient, fighting a defeated enemy in a war we had already won. What he proposes is too dangerous. The risks are too great. If we win, we win dramatically. But if we lose . . ." He spread his hands out on the table, palms up.

"You think we should pull back the attack and stop the Japanese?" Borsov asked.

"Yes. We will wipe out the salient at Khabarovsk and stop the Japanese landings. At the worst, this will cost a great victory, which Marshal Korzybsky wants to crown his career. If we follow his plan and lose, it could cost us Vladivostok. A catastrophe." He turned to Stashevsky. "Dimitri, get General Vasilyev. I want him here immediately. And tell Korzybsky I will see him in my private office." Kharkov turned back to the war board. "And now, gentlemen, we must discuss Beck's proposal. I will take your recommendations to the full Politburo later."

General Witold Lulienski carefully spread the precious black pearls on a piece of toasted bread soaked in butter and savored the full, fishy flavor of the caviar. He then took a small sip of the ice-cold Wyborowa to cleanse his palate. It was a ritual of which he never tired. Some fantastic accident of chemistry had conspired to marry caviar from the Caspian Sea with the brutal virility of the Polish national drink and had come up with a taste sensation of almost unbearable beauty.

"Witold!" The girl across from him pulled at the mat of wiry black hair on the back of his hand gently, insistently. "Witold, you are not listening."

"Of course I am, Janka, Kohańyi. I always listen. It

is the curse of my life and my profession. You want to play Ophelia in the National Theater's new production of 'Hamlet.' How could I not listen? For six weeks you have hardly mentioned anything else."

He let his eyes wander around the main dining room of the actors' club. It should never have been allowed, of course, this club. It had been formed during the thaw in the late 1950s and the first manager had been a son of one of the Pomiatowski counts. He had found some old family portraits and, as a consequence, the red plush walls were covered with the degenerative visages of ancient aristocrats. Someone else had contributed the battered piano and the ridiculous Art Nouveau statuary that was scattered about. All in all, it resembled nothing more than a cheap Czech brothel between the wars. But he liked it, and the actors and writers who came there would have created a scandal if anyone had tried to change it.

Lulienski, head of Polish military intelligence, was tolerated because of the caviar. He had arranged for the Polish actors' club to establish a standing exchange of the incomparable Polish vodka for an endless supply of Beluga. Without Lulienski's intercession, obtained by a young actress now married to a member of the Politburo, the customs formalities would not have been waived. He had been made an honorary member in gratitude.

"Witold, you must talk to Jerzy. He is going to put that bitch Sophie in the role. He is infatuated with her. It's not fair. The only talent she has is in her crotch." The girl, one of the seemingly endless stream of high-cheekboned beauties with the bodies of goddesses who left the actors' conservatory each year, was beginning to enjoy her role now. Her eyes moistened in rage and frustration, her superb breasts lifted

209

against the chaste white blouse and her lips parted ever so slightly in what could have been either pain or lasciviousness or a little of both. It was, Lulienski decided, not a bad performance. Still, it would be difficult to get her the part if Jerzy Rybicki, the director of the classical theater, did not want her to have it. Things had been changing lately. The times when he could pick up the telephone and the sound of his name induced terror were gone. Now there was respect, even obsequiousness, but there were also arguments, resistance, and polite reasons why this or that could not be done. And there were pressure points and factions on the Politburo, each with his own little group of actors and writers who were protected.

Lulienski had put his finger on what was happening. The country was becoming just like it had been before the war, a nest of intrigues and self-interest. Of course, Lulienski was a cynic. He had never believed the party would be able to change the nature of the Polish people. He had always said the party would be defeated and absorbed in the end. Communism was no more than an incident in the two-thousand-year history of the strange group of people that shifted back and forth on the plain between Russia and Germany, battered, conquered, decimated, and enduring.

Lulienski had to admit that his friend was probably right. And it didn't seem to matter much anymore, even to him. The thing to do was enjoy oneself. If there was no life after death, then there was only life, and the only logic was to enjoy it to the hilt.

"Witold," the girl wheedled. "Please." Her enormous green eyes were focused on him with a concentration of will.

He nodded, pushing back his chair. "Very well, my

dear. Now, let us go upstairs for a few minutes. I don't have to be back at the ministry until two."

She shook her head. "No, Witold, I have a rehearsal. I can't."

Lulienski stood up, a heavily muscled man with the face and body of a Polish peasant. He took the girl by the arm, his big paw surprisingly gentle. He had arranged for a small room to be put at his disposal on the second floor of the actors' club. It was convenient. The ministry was just down the street. And it meant that he didn't have to find an apartment for each new girl.

"Witold, I really don't have time," the girl said, trying to keep the irritation off her face.

Lulienski guided her up the stairs, marveling once again at the smooth muscularity of her hips, barely resisting the urge to drive his hand between her legs then and there.

"Jesus Maria, Witold, let me undress," she said as he pulled her to him. "Don't, for God's sake, spoil my dress, it's new."

He ignored her protests, pulling her brutally against him and pushing her back onto the bed, enjoying her irritated efforts to preserve her dignity and her dress. She stopped struggling now and he stripped off the wisp of lace around her hips and took her, fully clothed, feeling his uniform jacket stretch across his back as his muscles expanded with the effort.

"You're hurting me, Witold. For God's sake," the girl whimpered.

The Union Club had been established shortly after the Civil War by a group of Republican congressmen as a refuge from their wives and the rowdy bars of the era. Its principle attractions in the early years were floating poker games and private rooms upstairs where discreet affairs could be conducted without fear of interruption by jealous wives, irate husbands, or blackmailing journalists. The Club, as it was called in Washington, had led a precarious existence until Prohibition dried up the traditional watering holes of the capital, and it became one of the last refuges of drinkable Scotch and a gin that did not corrode tooth enamel.

Around the turn of the century it had been taken over, as had most of the other institutions in the capital, by a group of long-term Southern congressmen and rich lobbyists, and over the years they had fought bitter rearguard actions against any changes in its traditions or mores. Only in the early 1970s was the first black member admitted, a limited number of apostate Jews having been selected during the Roosevelt administration, and women were still allowed only in an austere area off the main members' lounge. The powder room, as one member's wife once remarked, resembled the rest room in a Balkan railroad station.

The present home of the Club was a late-Victorian mansion off Massachusetts Avenue in the midst of Embassy Row. Its builder was a steel magnate who had briefly been an intimate of Chester A. Arthur, and the massive house reflected the taste of the man and his time. Ornate stained-glass windows dominated the public rooms and intricately carved woodwork alternated with faded damask walls and a profusion of Persian carpets. The Club acquired the building from a homosexual descendant of the original owner who had fallen on evil days. With it had come the massive furnishings and Art Nouveau decorations that were now a hallowed part of the Club's tradition. Two life-sized nude black marble statues, each holding a large globe, flanked either side of the entrance to the English Bar, where Kip Dean met Alec Thompson.

"Christ, Kip, how can you stand the place?" Thompson asked, glancing around at the panelled elegance and old hunting prints.

"They make the best martini in town. Bombay gin and a vermouth from the Tuscan hills that comes in unmarked casks. What'll you have?"

"A martini, I guess, but only on the understanding that anything I say is for deep background. There are times when I think you guys use gin as a truth serum."

"Truth serum?" Kip Dean's pink face turned a deeper shade as he laughed soundlessly. "My dear Alec, if anyone told me the truth in this town, least of all you, I'd have the moment enshrined in statuary and immortalized in verse. On this spot a politician bold, did me the truth unfold, or some such appropriate sentiment. No. All I ask for is a plausible lie that will titillate my readers, increase the circulation of the papers that carry me, enhance my reputation as the man with the best sources in Washington— and once in a while comes within walking distance of reality." He motioned to the waiter. "Two martinis, very dry, as usual, Walter, and some of the salmon Senator Stein brought back from Troon."

The waiter, a distinguished black man with graying hair and the profile of Thomas Jefferson, bowed slightly. "Will you be taking calls, sir?"

Dean shook his head. "Only from the president, Walter. I always accept calls from the president," he said with an evil grin composed half of self-ridicule and half of arrogance.

Thompson had known him for more than twenty-five years. Their first meeting had been at a briefing in Moscow in the late 1950s when Dean, not yet a columnist but a top reporter for the old *Washington Post*, had torn Eisenhower's press secretary to shreds with a few shrewd questions that had revealed the man to be not only a liar but a fool as well. The reporter had once gone on an infantry patrol in Vietnam and had come back an enthusiastic supporter of the war. Cynics said it had taken him back to his days as a paratrooper in World War II. After Dean's conversion to hawkdom, the generals had begun sending dozens of reporters to the front until they discovered that in most of them the experience induced nothing more than cold terror and the consequent self-hatred that comes of knowing abject fear.

"Remember that brothel in Hue—Madam Thu's, or whatever the hell it was called?" Dean shook his head in remembered appreciation of the delicate beauty of the Vietnamese whores. "You know, Alec, during and right after the war is the best time for women. You're too young to remember Europe from 1945 to about 1952. But the most beautiful women in the world were available to just about anybody. I found out something then. A pretty woman, much less a beautiful one, isn't going to suffer or go hungry. She's got a commodity that throughout history has always been in demand. And, by God, when that's all she's got, it's for sale. Here's to the aftermath of wars," Dean said, raising his glass. "To the whores of yesteryear."

Thompson smiled and drank. Dean cultivated a carapace of cynicism that concealed from all but his closest friends a deep and abiding romanticism. He had been married to the same woman for more than forty years, was an exemplary father, and had in his time been a ferocious campaigner for such diverse and unlikely causes as disabled coal miners and sexually abused juvenile prisoners. He had, Thompson remembered, spent the entire evening at Madame Thu's with a fourteen-year-old prostitute who might have been made of porcelain. They had talked, in a hilarious blend of Yale French and singsong Vietnamese pidgin, about her life and hopes. At four in the morning Dean had bowed solemnly, paid the fee, collected his glazed colleagues with Thompson's help, and led the way back to the hotel. The next day the Vietcong took the city, and they had barely managed to slip through a gap in the lines surrounding it.

The martini was superb. Thompson was no aficionado of the drink and felt a certain contempt for the fetishists who made a religion out of how it was made. But he had to agree, the Club had brought a thoroughly minor and transient art to new levels of perfection. The glass had been chilled, lemon rind rubbed on the inner rim, the mix was perhaps five to one, left just long enough in the ice to dilute the harsh virility of the gin, and garnished with the merest sliver of lemon rind. And still there was something extra.

Dean was grinning at him. "It's the ice. Most people forget about the ice. Ice made from tap water is a collection of coliform bacteria embalmed in chlorine, residual DDT, various phosphates, lead and other deadly minerals, and probably a little garden-variety arsenic. This," he said, holding up the glass, "was concocted with ice made from the water of a cold mountain stream high in the Grand Tetons."

"Impregnated with carcinogens that have been deposited on the mountain's snow from all the atomic tests, no doubt," Thompson said, taking another sip. No doubt about it. Bessie Smith had been right. Rich was better.

"I saw Henry last night."

"How is he?"

"Much better. He's lost a lot of weight, and the doctors say he'll be okay. He sends his regards and sympathy for your predicament."

"Any advice?"

Dean shook his head. "You know Henry. If he's not reading the cables, he's not going to second-guess you. And, anyway, he knows there is a whole history of relationships, small unspoken agreements, betrayals, and that indefinable rapport that develops between men of real power, even when they're on opposite sides, that have to be taken into account along with the objective situation."

"Still, he must have had an opinion. He knew Chou better than any of us."

"He thinks the Chinese mean it this time. He thinks they may feel it's almost the last chance they'll have at getting back what they regard as their part of Siberia before the Soviet Union and the United States recognize their fundamental identity of interests and band together in a worldwide alliance against the peoples of the East."

Thompson shook his head impatiently. "The Spenglerian vision—the old German fear of the eastern hordes that dates back to Attila, Tamerlane, and Ghengis Khan. It's too simple, Kip. It's," he groped for a word, "it's visceral. It isn't the real world. The Japanese are allied with the Chinese today not because they're both yellow, but because they found themselves cut off from raw materials and markets that they have to have. The Chinese accepted the Japanese because it was their only sure source of the technology they needed so desperately. It's a classic symbiotic relationship."

"Well," Dean said, "isn't ours with the Soviet Union? After all, what points of conflict do we have? They're not an economic threat to us. They're a great reservoir of raw materials for us and Europe, East and West. And they need our technology and sophistication desperately. Where is the conflict?"

Thompson finished the martini and lifted his eyes in assent to the hovering waiter. "The problem lies in perception, Kip. What you're describing may be in fact the objective reality in the world today, although I'd have to contest you on some points. But reality is meaningless if it is not perceived as reality by the players in the game. The Soviet Union is still a long way from seeing us as a natural ally."

"You mean the ideological crap they continue to spread?"

"Yes. It may be crap, given the obvious convergence that is taking place between their system and ours. But they don't perceive it as crap, and it's dangerous nonsense to dismiss ideology with an airy wave of the hand if the other side doesn't. The fact, in a real, not theoretical, sense, is that, even today, it hasn't worked to the extent we'd hoped it would a decade ago. But there is something even more important that has to be melded into the equation."

"And that is what?"

"They don't trust us, Kip. They don't think our ideology has withered, either. They believe we're out to get them. Every day in every way. Old Sutpen and the cold warriors still make up almost half the Congress, or they can swing half the votes, which amounts to the same thing. You've got to picture what kind of reporting flows out of the Soviet embassy here. You've got to understand that the Politburo has an average age of sixty-four, which means that every one of them fought in World War Two and lived through the cold war. They've got the Sutpen mentality and they don't think we've changed, either. There is an intellectual logjam that may not be broken in our generation, hindering the kind of rapprochement you're talking about."

"But you believe it."

Thompson shrugged, feeling very tired, wishing for the warmth of Suzanne Wilson's body rather than the chilly pessimism of the drink in his hand, which had suddenly lost all its taste.

"I can't afford to believe anything, Kip. You guys just don't understand how it is up there. We can't afford to let what's happening be clouded by theory. We're working with what could be the destruction of the fucking world if some guy loses his nerve and pushes a button. Nobody can afford the luxury of theories at a time like this. You've got to look at what the other side, or sides, are doing right now, today. And you can act on that. Tomorrow they may change their minds, and you cannot afford to be locked into some sort of schematic horseshit from which you can't extricate yourself! That's what's wrong with French diplomacy today. They're hypnotized by the Cartesian elegance of their formulations."

Dean nodded. "I remember what Acheson said about one of his most famous Soviet experts: 'I have his reports reduced to telegrams so I won't be convinced by the pure elegance of his style and logic.'"

"He's right. Give me a tightly reasoned, wholly logical, graceful political report, and within it I'll lay high odds is a high proportion of lies and theoretical manure. That's true of any human endeavor washed clean of inconsistencies. But it's impossible to get the facts from an embassy, Kip. They're all full of two-bit Caillières and Machiavellis, or else they're telling us what they think we want to hear in order to suck up. Plus, they're all groveling around on their bellies to the host government."

218

Dean raised his eyebrows in surprise. "I don't follow you."

"Kip, an ambassador, American or otherwise, has to have access to the top echelon of the country he's in. Otherwise he's a failure. Now, how the hell do Americans make themselves popular? They suck. And our ambassadors are all masters at it. If I send out a cable telling one of them to go into the foreign office and lay down a brutal message, it doesn't get done, not that way. Invariably it's softened in the telling or in the delivery. Often it's totally distorted by some horse's ass who says, 'Gee, I'm sorry about this nasty message, and the president doesn't really mean it, but, you know, we had to do it to placate Congress and the press.' So we send off a tough message meaning to lay our position out with real force, and what do we get? Marshmallows, because the ambassador doesn't want to offend his golfing buddies."

Dean nodded. "That's why Kissinger went to the phone so much."

"Henry's main trouble was in trying to do it all himself—he and that bunch of intellectual thugs he gathered around him. You've got to watch the bureaucracy, but you've got to be willing to use them. It's like the man said, they're the only game in town." The martinis were beginning to have the advertised effect, and it was time to take up the slack. Dean had prepared the ground, and any time now he would slip in the hook. Thompson ordered a third drink. What the hell. It was Saturday night.

"What about the war situation? It begins to look as if the Soviets may really have their balls in a meat grinder. What does our military say?"

Thompson grinned. "On deep background, Kip, they don't know their anal orifice from a cricket pitch. Everything they told us has been wrong. If it weren't so goddamned infuriating, it would be comic. I'm beginning to think that a traditional, old-style military officer may be about the most obsolete object in our government's inventory. It's just barely possible that we'd be better off if we scrapped the entire military establishment and started over from scratch with a bunch of bright young technocrats from MIT, Berkeley, and Chicago."

"That's what we used to say in World War Two. But it was the pros who won it, Alec, not the amateurs."

"Sure. I'm kidding. But Wang has a strategic plan of genuine elegance. If he's got the horses to make it go, you're going to have a whole new setup in the Far East, and one over which we're going to have very little control. Remember, it doesn't take long for self-confidence to turn to arrogance in the Japanese. They're a virile warrior people who have suppressed it for damned near fifty years. The Chinese are going to owe them something. Their commercial aggressiveness in Southeast Asia is likely to turn into something more. And we won't have the will or even the power to interpose ourselves." He shook his head. "The Chinese-Japanese combine may be the wave of the future, whether we like it or not."

"I know," Dean said. "History seems to have telescoped in our time. Until this century, it took a nation a hundred years to gather an empire and another three hundred to enjoy it. The will to power and the willingness to fight the brutal, nasty little wars that were necessary to stay on top lasted longer. Countries lost their nerves gradually and lived on their reputations for a century or so, like the old Western gunfighters with arthritic hands and cataracts in their eyes who still walked tall into old age. We did it all in fifty years."

Thompson shrugged. "You know von Klatz's theory?"

"Von Klatz?"

"German sociologist. He did a five-volume study using one of the Bonn Defense Ministry computers in which he analyzed all the elements of successful armies of the past. Know what he discovered?"

"No."

"The key factor in the success of an army has always been the willingness of the nation's upper classes to staff the officer corps. Once they ceased to be willing to sacrifice their sons, it was the beginning of the end. Vietnam was the first war we fought that was officered by the lower middle class. Remember that guy who commanded in the massacre in Vietnam? What was his name?"

"Scalley."

"Yeah, Scalley. Well, he would never have been an officer in World War One or Two or in Korea. But with the middle and upper classes opting out in Vietnam, we got the Scalleys to lead the companies. Our army became a mercenary force. It still is. And you don't go up against the Soviets or the Chinese with that kind of an army. There's no will, no motivation. The people with something to lose have to be the ones who are willing to fight for what they've got. When they lose that will, you're already in the stage of degeneracy."

"And you think we're there?"

"Kip, von Klatz put the Roman Empire's mid-stage of degeneracy at 150 A.D. The empire lasted another two hundred fifty years. With luck, we'll have whatever the telescoped equivalent is."

Dean stared at him in surprise. "You're really in great form tonight."

Thompson glanced at his watch. "I've also got to

get back to the White House. Cut the crap, Kip. You didn't get me over here to horse around with flatulent philosophy. What have you got?"

Dean took out a small Montecristo from a silver case, first offering one to Thompson, who declined. "You're right," he said as he lit the small, dark cigar, making a production of it. "Kempka picked up something from one of his sources. Don't ask me who. Seems like Beck and Kharkov are planning to meet in Helsinki. There's some talk of a deal. According to Kempka's source, it may be at the expense of the Poles."

14

"Good evening. This is Suzanne Wilson with the ten o'clock news.

"The Japanese invasion fleet that left Sapporo late yesterday evening landed a few hours ago on the coast of Asia near the Soviet Russian city of Amgun. The landing took place just after dawn following an intense, unopposed bombardment by the Japanese and Chinese fleets and intense bombing by the massed air forces of both nations. Reports from U.S. satellites indicate that the biggest air battle in history is being fought over the landing beaches as both sides pour in more and more planes.

"Indications are that the Soviet Union is breaking off its offensive against the Khabarovsk salient and wheeling its troops to meet the new threat to its rear. There have also been reports that troops have withdrawn from in front of the Chinese bridgehead across the Amur River. Moscow radio announced that Marshal Korzybsky has been replaced by General Vasily Vasilyev as commander of the Soviet forces in Siberia. Korzybsky, who is in his seventies, was a corps commander in World War Two and one of the most decorated Soviet marshals. Vasilyev, who is married to General Secretary Kharkov's daughter, is thought to be in his early fifties.

"Meanwhile, diplomatic activity in Europe continues to be intense. There are rumors of a meeting of high Soviets and West Germans." . . . Suzanne stumbled and smiled engagingly into the camera, saying, "Sorry, just plain German now—and German leaders in Helsinki. Diplomatic sources in European capitals speculate that the meeting is being held to ratify the new status quo in Eastern Europe and free the Soviets for a major war in Asia.

"The situation continues to be tense with a fully mobilized Polish Army facing Soviet forces along its entire border. The German Army has not yet moved up to support its ally, probably to avoid provoking the Soviets, but it stands ready to intervene all along the Polish-German border, should the Poles need help. Consultations between the two high commands continue around the clock, according to German sources. To the south all the former Soviet satellites, with the exception of Bulgaria, have mobilized. The Czech, Rumanian, Hungarian, and Yugoslav armies are all in combat positions."

Suzanne Wilson's gray eyes stared steadily into the camera. "The president of France, in an address to the nation tonight, said that the danger of world war is greater than at any time since the end of World War Two. He announced that all French nuclear units were to be placed on red alert, but he went on to say that France would not feel bound by its obligations under NATO or the European Community Treaty if Germany attacked the Soviet Union. He called for an immediate ceasefire in Asia and a world peace conference between European and Asian powers to be held in Paris beginning early next week.

"Meanwhile, U.S. behind-the-scenes efforts to stop the fighting have met with no success. White House sources report that the president and Chairman Kharkov have spoken no less than thirty-five times on the red line over the last few days, and similar intense diplomatic initiatives have been made to the Chinese. However, as of this evening, there has been no agreement on a ceasefire.

"In Italy tonight firemen and rescue workers were fighting through a mass of tangled wreckage in an effort to find survivors of the crash of a Soviet jumbo jet TU-144 that crashed with more than two hundred fifty passengers aboard. All are believed dead. The huge plane's brakes failed and it overshot the Rome airport runway, crashing head-on into an embankment and bursting into flames. Rescue parties believe all on board died in the ensuing explosion and fire. This marks the seventh crash of a jumbo jet since 1974. More than twelve hundred people lost their lives in these crashes. Soviet authorities have announced that an investigation team will be sent to the site immediately.

"In Spain, a series of strikes in the Basque coal mines brought the right-wing government of Prime Minister Guillermo Vilas to the verge of collapse today. The leader of the leftist Popular Front coalition, socialist Jorge Vigo, demanded that the King dissolve parliament and call elections. Vigo cited recent polls indicating that the Popular Front, made up of Socialist, Communist, and United Workers parties, had a clear majority in the country. However, rightist groups, led by the extremist Falange, demanded that the king declare martial law in the Basque area and put down the strikes by force. The biggest question mark in Spanish politics continues to be the armed forces. Since the abortive Captain's Conspiracy last year, which sought to install a left-wing authoritarian regime, Spain's military hierarchy has been reluctant to mix in politics for fear of a rebellion in the ranks. In an attempt to defuse the situation, Prime Minister Vilas, in a television address last night, promised increasing economic liberalization, including free medical insurance for all industrial workers.

"In Ethiopia, the leaders of the *coup d'état* have announced the nationalization of all foreign companies and revoked all residence permits for foreigners. Families of foreigners resident in Ethiopia were crowding aboard evacuation planes. The United States government is negotiating to send in army transport aircraft to set up an airlift.

"In Italy, a twenty-four-hour general strike of all transport workers has been called to protest an alleged insult to the head of the rail workers' union by the minister of labor, who is believed to have made an obscene gesture toward the union leader following an acrimonious bargaining session. Three hundred thousand workers marched across Italy today making the same sign. The minister has apologized and offered to resign.

"And, now, Harry Bornquist with news on the domestic scene."

Thompson flicked off the set and glanced at the memo his secretary had placed in front of him. "You'd better read this. It really looks bad."

Thompson glanced at the cryptic Buckslip from William Bucks, secretary of the interior, and began to read.

TOP SECRET

MEMORANDUM TO: Secretary of the Interior William Bucks

FROM: Chief of the Federal Bureau of Investigation

SUBJECT: Surveillance and interrogation report on Chief Warrant Officer Lawrence Henry McPherson, born March 12, 1950, Harrisonburg, West Virginia.

McPherson is in charge of preparing the minutes of National Security Board meetings.

Following normal procedure for individuals in super-sensitive positions, McPherson was placed under surveillance on April 18 at 7:30 A.M. He reported for duty at the National Security Board headquarters in the old State building at 8:45 A.M. Detailed surveillance picked him up at 12:30 P.M. Report follows.

12:30 P.M. Subject left old State on foot and arrived at Le Gourmet restaurant at 12:40 P.M. Met Miss Hildegarde Bonerth, citizen of West Germany, born in Luebeck on December 13, 1960, and a known agent under control of KGB.

13:45 P.M. Subject and Miss Bonerth proceed to Miss Bonerth's apartment on 1425 Kalorama Avenue by taxi. Following is transcript of conversation obtained through electronic surveillance installed in apartment on April 17 under permit Number 12475, signed by Assistant Attorney General Gerald Stein.

MCPHERSON: Come on, I haven't got much time. That fucking bird colonel rides my ass all day as it is. If I'm late, he shits a brick.

BONERTH: Larry, for God's sake, let me get my clothes off (laughing).

227

MCPHERSON: Christ, you are something else, baby.

BONERTH: Be still. Don't be so impatient. You act like a boy. Let me do it. Just relax.

MCPHERSON: Jesus.

BONERTH: *Verdammt*, Larry, you should learn to control yourself.

MCPHERSON: Yeah, you're right. Sorry about that, baby, but you're just too good.

BONERTH: You brought the film?

MCPHERSON: Yeah, in my jacket pocket. (Pause.) Christ, you've got a beautiful little ass on you, Hilde.

BONERTH: No. Larry, you don't have time. Your colonel will screw you good if you're any later. We can't afford to have you transferred.

Agents Harrison and Wilson entered the Bonerth apartment, breaking in the door at 14:25 P.M., and they arrested subject and Miss Bonerth, who had in her possession a fifty-frame microfilm of attached NSB board minutes. Prisoners were advised of their rights. Detainee Bonerth refused to answer any questions and asked to speak to East German consul.

Detainee McPherson, when advised that guilty plea and cooperation with interrogating officers could affect the length of his sentence, agreed to undergo interrogation.

Transcript of interrogation follows:

AGENT: When and by whom were you recruited?

MCPHERSON: That Bonerth broad. She picked me up in a bar—The Long Dong on Connecticut Avenue, I think. Must have been about a year ago.

AGENT: You were assigned as deputy chief of the NSB communications center at the time?

MCPHERSON: Yeah.

AGENT: You were responsible for the transcription and distribution of the minutes of the board's meeting among your other duties?

MCPHERSON: Yeah.

AGENT: Had you been warned of the possibility of enemy agents attempting to subvert you?

MCPHERSON: Yeah.

AGENT: Did it occur to you that Miss Bonerth might be such an agent?

MCPHERSON: No. I thought she was a good lay, period.

AGENT: You began a relationship with Miss Bonerth February 12 of last year?

MCPHERSON: You mean, when did I start screwing her? Yeah.

AGENT: In April you left your wife and moved into an apartment at 1400 Connecticut Avenue?

MCPHERSON: Yeah.

AGENT: When did Miss Bonerth first ask you to obtain copies of the NSB minutes?

MCPHERSON: About that time, I guess.

AGENT: Did you agree immediately?

MCPHERSON: I told her she was a goddamned spy and I was going to turn her in.

AGENT: What was her reply?

MCPHERSON: She started bawling and said her mother and father and brother were hostages in in East Germany. She said she had no choice but to work for the Russians.

AGENT: Did you believe her?

MCPHERSON (shrug): She offered me a hell of a lot of money.

AGENT: She gave you money?

MCPHERSON: Among other things. (Laughs.)

I am attaching a psychological profile of McPherson drawn up by Dr. James Goodfellow of the National Psychiatric Institute.

PSYCHOLOGICAL PROFILE

McPherson, son of a West Virginia coal miner and a waitress, is a strikingly handsome man with iron-gray hair, athletic build, and the natural self-possession of the born stud. He is totally narcissistic, insecure, compulsive; and obsessed by the need to prove his masculinity. There is tangential evidence that he was sexually traumatized during a two-year stint in a reformatory from the age of twelve to fourteen. He dresses with excessive neatness, but in contrast to this personal dandyism, his apartment was a foul-smelling mess. McPherson, whose IQ is 177 on the Stanford scale, has developed a highly effective personal style that fends off genuine intimacy but is quintessentially attractive to women. Despite obvious sexual neuroses, he remains fundamentally a pure sensualist unable to defend himself against his compulsions. He is subservient to his superiors and brutal to his subordinates, an attitude he characterizes with refreshing candor as "suck the officers and kick the privates."

Despite the high intelligence and a mathematical talent described by a superior as "pure genius," he is emotionally immature, seeking immediate gratification at the expense of his long-term goals, which appear to be no more than survival. He is almost existentially apolitical, and there is no evidence that his agreement to work for the Soviets was anything but a desperate attempt to escape from extreme financial embarrassment and obtain the favors of the young lady who recruited him. He was paying alimony to three wives and support to seven children at the time of his arrest.

"Shit," Thompson said disgustedly, reaching for the phone. "Lucy, get me Gordon, please."

"Yes, Alec?" Gordon Wiseman sounded tired.

"Gordon, you know that agent of yours we infiltrated into the NSB so he could defect and feed information to the Soviets?"

"Yes."

"The goddamned FBI just busted him."

Wiseman started to laugh incredulously. "I don't believe it. What did he do—try to bomb their headquarters?"

"It's not funny, Gordon. He gave them a sense of security, and I damned well want them to continue to get the minutes of our meetings."

"Relax, Alec. They have another source—on the board itself."

"You're kidding."

"No. We found out about it by accident a few weeks ago. I've had a team on him, very discreetly, ever since. We let him run, since you wanted them to have the minutes, anyway, hoping he'd break some other sources."

"Has he?"

"No. He's just a mushheaded idealist who is against war and evil."

"Thanks, Gordon."

"You're welcome. What shall I do about our agent?"

"Leave him there for a couple of days. He seems to be enjoying himself."

Suzanne shook him gently. "Wake up, darling. A beautiful, half-nude blonde just brought you breakfast in bed: burned toast; overcooked eggs; and soggy bacon with coffee that tastes like warmed-over cinders."

Thompson grinned and sat up, rubbing the sleep out of his eyes. It was eleven o'clock. He had slept almost twelve hours.

"Do you realize that you fell asleep in the middle

of one of my most fascinating monologues last night?"

"All things considered, you're lucky I stayed awake for the dialogue. Did the White House call?"

"Yes. Lucy said the president went out to play golf and won't be back until about three. She'll call you if anything comes up. She said your orders are to read the Sunday paper and relax."

Thompson reached for her, but the girl was too quick. "Uh-uh. You've got some penance to do. Men just don't fall asleep during my fascinating conversation. You are obviously not aware that mine is the face that drives millions of women mad with jealousy each night while their husbands writhe in erotic fantasies."

"Funny, I thought it was something other than your face. What was on the news?"

"The Israelis did it."

"What?" Thompson looked up sharply from the breakfast tray.

"The bomb—they blew it up in the Arabian peninsula. I forget the megatonnage, but it was a lot. Lev announced it on the radio. They're about ready to finish the delivery vehicle. He seemed sure they'd have the whole system in place by the beginning of next year." She stared at him. "Why so glum? What difference does it make? They've had atomic bombs since 1976. What does it add, a few more megatons?"

Thompson shrugged. "It just complicates the equation that much more and makes the Israelis that much harder to deal with. Militarily it doesn't mean much, but psychologically it's going to increase their already fairly massive self-confidence."

"But you were in favor of their taking over Saudi Arabia, Syria, and Egypt," she said accusingly. "What's-his-face got hold of the transcript of the

National Security Board meeting and published it, or have you forgotten?"

"No. And neither has that swabbie who gave it to him. He's still in Portsmouth," Thompson said grimly.

"That isn't the point. You favored the Israeli invasion. Why the change?"

Thompson sampled the eggs. "Not bad for a career girl."

"It's been six years. What really happened, Alec?"

"It wasn't as mysterious as it looked at the time," Thompson said. "The Israelis had made all the concessions they felt they could come up with, and the Arabs were not about to drop the pressure. They'd given up all but a small strip of the Sinai, agreed to a Palestinian state on the West Bank, excluding Jerusalem, and given back all but a small strip of the Golan Heights."

"And the Arabs still weren't satisfied?"

"Worse. The Syrians and the Egyptians were armed to the teeth with the newest Soviet weapons, including those long-range missiles that could hit every city in Israel. They had between them about twice the number of planes Israel had and three times the number of tanks. The military situation was really getting crucial," Thompson said, pouring another cup of coffee and stuffing a pipe with a foul-smelling Turkish tobacco mixture.

"Hussein's assassination and the merger of Jordan and the West Bank was the last straw, I guess," Suzanne said, surprised that Thompson was willing to talk about the old crisis. He never was before.

"That, plus the fact that the Arabs were threatening another oil boycott unless the United States and Europe put pressure on the Israelis to make even further concessions. Congress was balking at supplying Israel with still another more sophisticated set of armaments to keep up with the Arabs, and there was beginning to be a reaction against the Israelis because of oil prices. It took a long time, but it finally came."

"You saw Lev in Jerusalem two days before the attack. What happened?"

Thompson grinned at her from around the pipe. "I'll call you a liar if you ever use it, but he went along—on one condition: the Israelis had to take over the Saudi Arabian oil fields at the same time as they hit the Syrians, Egyptians, and Jordanians. We agreed to lay the Sixth Fleet off Beirut and warn the Russians to stay out."

"You went to Teheran and Ankara afterward."

Thompson nodded. "We convinced the shah to move on the emirates of Bahrein and Kuwait at the same time and offered the Turks northern Syria and parts of Iraq. Neither one of them was ever a real country. Iran took over most of the rest of Iraq, and what was left aligned itself with a reconstituted Jordan. The remnants of Syria were joined to Lebanon."

"What made you think the Israelis could bring it off?"

"We weren't sure. But the alternative was doing it ourselves. Europe was about to go bankrupt. The oil price situation had become intolerable. Our intelligence sources led us to believe that puppet regimes in Jordan, Syria, Egypt, and Saudi Arabia could be controlled. Libya and Algeria wouldn't count then. We were right," Thompson said.

"So the Israelis struck first?"

"Yeah. They took Damascus in two days, destroyed the Syrian Army as a fighting unit, and wheeled south, taking the Jordanians on the flank and rolling them up in another three days. The Egyptians were still mobilizing when the full force of the Israeli Army hit them on the seventh day. It was a surprisingly tough battle, and it cost the Israelis about seven thousand dead, but they were in Cairo in a week. It was a masterly tank campaign. Rommel and Patton would have been proud of them. Nobody was expecting the strike at Jidda and the oil fields. They went in with a damned paratroop attack and took over the oil fields virtually without firing a shot. It was all over in twenty days."

"What about the Soviets?"

"They mobilized a hundred thousand troops, and if it had gone on another week, they might have intervened. But it was all over too soon. Turkey's intervention in the north was decisive, plus their stalling about allowing overflights. They eventually did, but it was too late to help much by then."

"Weren't you surprised at how easily the Israelis were able to set up puppet regimes?"

Thompson shrugged. "The people occupying these countries have been ruled by occupying powers for thousands of years. The Israelis are efficient and ruthless. The big immigration over the last six years has pushed their population to almost six million. They had essentially demoralized populations to deal with, torn by internal dissension. Mossad, the Israeli intelligence outfit, has been brilliant at infiltrating resistance groups. You know the old Soviet maxim: 'One man with a machine gun who is willing to use it can control a hundred without a gun.'"

Suzanne shook her head. "It's all so," she hesitated, "cynical and untypical of the Jews."

"The Israelis aren't Jews—not in the sense that they've been historically perceived. It's a new race of self-confident, even arrogant, people who have been fighting for survival for four decades. It develops certain characteristics that are not especially charming but which solve problems.

235

"Christ, Suzanne, nothing lasts forever," Thompson said, reaching for her in one quick motion and pulling her down across the bed.

"My God, Alec, your face feels like sandpaper."

"You want me to shave first?"

"Christ, no. You might not be able to get it up again," she said, giggling.

15

General Wang Chin studied the battle maps in silence, following the stabbing lines of Soviet tanks as they were wheeled into position to attack the Chinese emplacements in the rear. Masses of infantry from the Leninskaya front had already begun moving into the narrow corridor to reinforce the tank forces. The main Soviet thrust would begin within hours.

Chin looked up from the maps and spoke to the staff officers gathered around him. "Our plan has succeeded. Korzybsky is fighting the only battle he knows —relentless, unremitting attack. He will throw his tanks north against the rear of our troops in the Khabarovsk pocket." Wang Chin's finger stabbed at the map. "The extent of our minefields will surprise him. But he will go on, sacrificing whatever tanks he must to break through. Our artillery and rockets must then smash the first wave of his attack and force him to commit more and more of his reserves. We must give ground gradually, allowing him to build up confidence. Then," the Chinese said, smiling for the first time, "when he is fully committed, we will counterattack with our full tank force from Fuchin and hit him in the rear, rolling up his infantry and anti-tank screen, destroying his supply lines and smashing him as he intended to smash us between hammer and anvil." Wang Chin turned to one of the staff officers on his left. "What is the latest news from the front?"

"The Russians have begun to probe in preparation for the main thrust. Special mine-exploding vehicles are cutting paths through the minefields. They are bringing up mobile track, laying units with hundreds of miles of temporary wire mesh plaques to build roads through the marshes to allow the tanks to attack on a broader front. Special tractors with immense balloon tires are stationed along the routes to rescue mired-down trucks and tanks. Heavy-duty helicopters are also coming in under our radar with fuel oil. They are moving much faster than we had anticipated."

Wang Chin nodded. No battle ever went according to plan. The Russians handled their tank masses with much more assurance than did his generals. Their communications were infinitely better, and they were drilled in the experience of World War II. But in the end that mobility would work toward their destruction, since it would mean that their tank armies would be irrevocably committed in the northward thrust when his own forces struck from the rear.

"What of the army in the Khabarovsk bridgehead, General?" one of the staff officers asked. "They are crying for air cover and reinforcements. They need ammunition and tanks, or they will be destroyed."

Wang Chin shook his head. "Cease all reinforcement. Tell the commanders they must fight to the last man. The bridgehead will be destroyed. But its destruction will ensure our victory. Order all forces facing Khabarovsk on our side of the Amur to turn south. The entire Russian offensive capability will soon be in the corridor between Vyazemski and Leninskaya. Korzybsky will attack with the entire force, and we will destroy it."

"We will lose heavily, General," one of the staff officers said.

Wang Chin nodded. "Yes. But the only important thing is the destruction of the Russian tank corps. We must sacrifice our own armor to eliminate theirs. Then the war becomes one of attrition between masses of infantry. And that is a war we cannot lose."

Thompson liked the White House on Sundays. The normally humming offices had geared down. Here and there a duty officer shuffled cables or read *The New York Times*, feet propped on a desk laden with the remnants of breakfast and the inevitable white coffee mugs with the president's seal. Only the communications section continued to operate at full capacity, feeding into the center such things as military situation reports, urgent diplomatic messages, and warnings of impending crises.

Jane Cleveland looked up from the *Washington Herald* comic strip and motioned toward the inner office. "He's waiting for you."

The president was sprawled in one of the comfortable overstuffed chairs, feet propped up on a coffee table. He wore a red jogger's suit over a rubber sweatshirt. "Christ, you look like you might have gotten a good night's sleep for a change," he said, glancing up from the sheaf of cables crumpled in a meaty hand. "Things are getting hairy out in the Far East. Have you seen these?"

"Yes. I stopped off at the communications section.

239

It looks as if old Korzybsky's plan is working. With a little luck he'll pinch off the entire Chinese salient and turn on the Japanese with his full forces."

"And all we can do is sit here and watch," the president said. "But I'd like to renew my proposal for a peace conference in Geneva. The Chinese may be beginning to panic. According to the satellite photographs, they're being fearfully mauled. It's possible that they'll accept a conference now."

"What makes you think Kharkov will?"

"He won't. But the option will be there when he is ready. I expect them to do just what you say—sanitize that salient, wipe out the Japanese landing force, and only then negotiate. But at least we'll be on the record. It's beginning to look as if that's the only place we will be. I'm not convinced that, once he wins in the East, Kharkov won't turn on his satellites in Europe. He may decide to settle Beck's hash, once and for all."

"Our cables indicate that the meeting with Beck has been delayed a day. It's off until tomorrow," Thompson said. "He may be stalling to see how the battle is going. I'll draft the message on the peace conference."

General Phillip Samsun read the biography of the new commander of the Soviet eastern armies with fascination. He was the new Soviet man, no question about that.

Born March 12, 1933, in Kiev, son of a party functionary from Leningrad. Family moved to Magnetogorsk in 1941 to avoid German advance. Father executed by Germans in the Crimea campaign while serving as commissar with Russian Marine paratroop brigade. Vasilyev was taken under the protection of the Soviet State as the son of a national hero. Attended military high school in Moscow, assigned to tank officer training school in Minsk, 1950. Commissioned 1953. Promoted to major in 1960 in normal progression. Assigned to Berlin as assistant military attaché, 1961. Promoted to colonel, 1964; assigned Warsaw Pact command staff same year. Transferred to staff college; 1965; Chinese language-training, 1966. Posted to Peking in 1969 following promotion to general of brigade. Commander, Cuban military advisory group; 1972. Promoted to colonel general in 1974; assigned command First Army, Caucasus command, 1975; deputy chief of general staff, 1976, which is present position. Married to Ekaterina Kharkova, daughter of chairman of Council of Ministers. Three children. Speaks fluent German, Spanish, and Chinese.

Samsun let the folder drop on his desk, grinning broadly. It was a classic case, of course. The man had consistently jumped hundreds of his contemporaries on the promotion list because of his high party connections. He had held command of troops only once, and very briefly, spending most of his career in the plush confines of the staff or as an attaché, notoriously a billet for dilettantes. He was rumored to be a lightweight who liked vodka, girls, and tailor-made uniforms, although there was virtually no reliable intelligence on the man's personal life other than a report of dubious veracity from the station chief in Havana that suggested he suffered from satyriasis and incipient alcoholism, an unlikely combination.

General Vasily Vasilyev relaxed in his private apartment abroad the Tupolev 263 and allowed himself a third small glass of vodka. The meeting with old

Korzybsky had been painful. The old man, sick, tired, and half-senile, had insisted on going over his battle plans at least half a dozen times as if he, Vasilyev, were an idiot. It hadn't mattered, of course. The attack had been the last wild plunge of an old tank commander still living with the smell of cordite from World War II. Vasilyev had recognized that months ago when the Chinese attack had become apparent. Fortunately, he had taken his fears to Kharkov. But the general secretary, his own father-in-law, had brushed him aside. Korzybsky had been regarded as a military genius then. But now they were all shitting in their pants and calling on him, Vasilyev, to pull it out of the fire.

But that wasn't going to help him any with old Korzybsky's staff, many of whom were a decade older than he was, men who had led platoons, companies, and regiments in World War II, and who had spent most of their lives patrolling the icy Siberian wastes. Vasilyev shuddered and reached for the vodka bottle. His tour there had been the most miserable year of his life. He'd had to do it, of course. No self-respecting general officer could rise in the Soviet hierarchy without pulling a tour in the Far East. But it had been hell, leavened only by the golden presence of Tanya. He was lost in contemplation of the compensations his onetime secretary had offered when the pilot announced they were about to land at Irkutsk.

The Far Eastern armies' staff was lined up along the runway. Vasilyev, sucking in an impressive belly, greeted each with quick military curtness, trying to remember their names, usually failing, although three had been in his class at the cadet academy.

"General, I suggest we proceed immediately to the situation room. Things are moving very rapidly. We need some quick decisions." Mikulski, chief of staff of Soviet armies in the Far East, had taken him by the arm. No point in resisting it, of course, although he would have dearly loved a nap. He found it impossible to sleep on planes.

The maps were spread across several tables and Mikulski briefed with curt phrases. "We linked with the Leninskaya armored infantry divisions thirty-six hours ago, and the bridgehead began expanding according to plan. The infantry, anti-tank artillery, and rocket regiments are emplaced along the southern sector facing the Chinese counterattack, which has already kicked off from Fuchin. The tanks have wheeled and are beginning to attack the rear of the Chinese salient."

"What are the Chinese doing?"

"Not much," Mikulski said, his voice exultant. "We've struck much faster than they expected. They're clumsy. No maneuverability. I know Wang Chin. He thought we would be slower, more cumbersome, and allowed to fight a set-piece battle with massed artillery, then throw in the tanks and hammer us against his compressed forces. But it's not working out that way. In another three days we'll have driven their forces north of the line into an impossible pocket. It'll just be a matter of time until the artillery decimates them."

"But the main Chinese attack in the south has not yet come," Vasilyev said, tracing a line across the bulge and stopping at Fuchin.

Mikulski waved his hand in an elegant conductorish gesture. Vasilyev had always disliked and distrusted the man. He was the son of a Polish officer who had fought with the Red armies in 1917 with great heroism. But the family was bourgeois. Mikulski was known as a fop throughout the army. He was also known as the most brilliant staff officer of his time.

Vasilyev grunted as he studied the concentrations. There was no question but that old Korzybsky's strategy was masterful. If he succeeded, it would be the end of the Chinese armies as a fighting force for years to come. But he was taking an immense risk. If the attack failed, the results for the Soviet forces would be disastrous. Vasilyev looked up from the map into the Pole's grinning face.

"Suppose the old man is wrong, Mikulski? Suppose the Chinese counterattack blunts the drive and they trap our tanks here in the corridor? What then?"

Mikulski shrugged. "General, in war anything is possible. Defeat is one of two choices. But one wins by audacity, not by fumbling caution. The Chinese have anticipated our attack and made their dispositions." He pointed to the heavily mined areas to the north and south of the corridor running from Vyazemski to Leninskaya. "Here, to the south, near Fuchin, they have concentrated their entire armored forces. Unquestionably, they will attack us with everything they've got. But they move their armor as if it were infantry, with infinite caution and no real punch. Our anti-tank forces will hold them until we've wiped out the forces hemmed in by the Amur and Ussuri rivers, at which point we can concentrate our entire strength, including the troops now defending Khabarovsk, and slam into them with such force that they will never be able to withstand us."

"And the Japanese?" Vasilyev placed a pudgy finger on Amgun. "Will they remain passively in the bridgehead while we ignore them?"

"No," Mikulski said. "Obviously they will attempt a breakout. But we have four divisions across the roads leading out of the landing area. It will take them at least three days to regroup and attack. By that time it will be too late for them to influence the battle."

Vasilyev scratched a razor cut on his left cheek, drawing a thin sliver of blood. "It's too dangerous, Mikulski. The risks are too great. If we win, what have we got? A million prisoners and some territory which we will simply give back at the peace treaty. But if we lose, it will mean the end of our tank armies in Siberia. The Chinese will overwhelm us with endless hordes of infantry." He held up a hand as the Pole began to protest. "I know what you will say. We will slaughter them with air superiority and artillery. But Lieu knows all this. He will sacrifice five hundred thousand, a million, two million if necessary in a war of attrition. They have interior lines. We would never be able to fight a long, slogging ground war. The logistics are insurmountable." He swept a finger along the one-track Siberian railway. "Within two months we will have used up every stockpile of ammunition and supplies we have, and the railroad cannot bring in more than a quarter of the needed replacements."

"We'll airlift in what we need."

Vasilyev snorted. "Don't be a fool. You know it can't be done. In any event, we must preserve the tank armies at all costs." He turned back to the map. "Mikulski, I cannot accept your analysis of the Japanese bridgehead. They are elite troops, and the Japanese are formidable warriors. They will break out of the landing area long before you think and take us in the rear. It's too dangerous. We must pull back from the corridor and stabilize our lines, regrouping the tanks at Vyazemski and wiping out the Japanese. The next priority is the Khabarovsk salient across the river. Throw in the reserves. Do whatever you have to, but get them back across the river. Those are my orders."

Mikulski stared at him, his thin, aristocratic features frozen in shock. "You're joking, Vasily. We're winning the battle. Even an idiot like you can see that. We've got them nailed to the wall. In forty-eight hours it will all be over."

"You will follow orders, General," Vasilyev said, turning on the chief of staff, his thick body tense with menace. He had to make it stick now, brutally, once and for all, exerting his authority and sowing fear among the others.

Mikulski slammed the long pointer he had been using down across the pile of maps. "I'll be goddamned if I will, you fucking moron. Don't you realize what will happen if we order a retreat? Those troops are in full attack formation. It will take days to get them turned around and out of the corridor. The Chinese will cut us to pieces with their artillery and rockets. There'll be chaos. We could lose half our tank force, and God knows how much artillery and infantry—all because of your stupidity!"

"General, I relieve you of your command and place you under arrest for insubordination." Vasilyev glanced around the room, his eyes falling on Mikulski's deputy, whose name came to him suddenly. "You, Kusarevich, take over the staff. Prepare plans immediately for the retreat. I'll discuss dispositions with you in two hours. And I want a coherent plan of attack on the Japanese bridgehead by morning. Our first objective is to save the tank armies that have been exposed so recklessly. Our second is to deal with the threat to our rear." He bowed slightly to the assembled staff. "Good evening, comrades," he said, turning and striding with confident purpose out of the staff room.

It had been a good job, he thought later in the comfort of the commander of the eastern armies' headquarters apartment. He had exerted his authority, letting them know in no uncertain terms who was in command. That was the important thing. As for the battle, the old man had taken insane risks. Retreat was the only sensible course. Mikulski was right, of course. They would lose men and tanks. But Wang Chin would never be able to move the immense mass of men and machines at his command with sufficient speed to trap the Soviet armored forces. A set-piece battle with Soviet forces hemmed into that narrow corridor between Leninskaya and Vyazemski was something else. It could lead to disaster or, at best, a long battle of attrition from which no victor would emerge, and his career would lie in shards about him.

No. Far better to take the safe course and retreat behind the two rivers, turning his tanks against the small Japanese invasion force and annihilating it. If he brought it off, they would have to give him a marshal's baton and everything that went with it. Vasilyev poured himself a double vodka and dipped into the caviar that had been placed at his bedside.

Georg Wozniakowski stared across the table at the German president's thick red face, a nameless anxiety bred of five centuries of war and slaughter making him slightly nauseated.

"But why does he want to meet, Herr Beck?" Wozniakowski asked in his thickly accented English. "What is there to discuss?"

Beck shrugged, a triumphant grin creasing his heavy features. "Obviously, they are in trouble. Why else? The Chinese counterattack is about to begin. They will be forced to use every plane, every reserve they have, to contain it. He's afraid we may decide to hit him in the rear when he's fighting for his life in the Far East." Beck poured two more glasses of the colorless liquid into tiny glasses and hoisted his in toast to the first secretary of the Polish Communist Party. Politely, Wozniakowski drank.

"It does not make sense," he persisted. "The Russians have twice as many divisions as we do along their frontier. Our armies are uncoordinated. They cannot be afraid of us." He shook his big head, the mop of slightly disheveled gray hair flaring as he did so. "No, he will try to divide us, Herr Beck. I am convinced that is his intention."

Horst Beck reached across the table and gripped the Pole's hand. "Listen, my friend, you always think of the past. But you must forget it. I know how many times Russia and Germany have torn Poland apart. But this is history. Now we are friends. You have my word. Germany will stand with you to the end."

Wozniakowski listened, armed by the Steinhaeger and the words of friendship. There was no point in doubting the German. He had no choice. The Politburo had already met and rejected the secret Russian offer to turn on their German allies and mount a surprise attack with the full weight of the Soviet forces at their back. They had debated most of the night. But nobody had really been tempted. Once the fighting was finished, the Soviet armies would still have been on Polish soil and the bloodbath would have begun. Still, he was sure the same offer was about to be made to Beck . . . and he wasn't sure of the German's answer.

"What have you heard from the Far East?" Wozniakowski asked.

Beck did not hesitate. "The Soviet offensive is bogged down. Wang Chin's armies are about to move. They will close the vise on the thin wedge of Soviet armor and decimate it. The Japanese bridgehead is secure. Soon they'll be moving out to attack the Soviet rear. I tell you, it is a debacle." He filled the glasses once again.

Wozniakowski preferred Klein to this fat pig in front of him. At least Klein was a man of the real left, not an apostate social democrat like this swine. But he must be polite, especially since everything seemed to be going well. "When will you leave for Helsinki?"

"In two hours, just after dark. I want a good night's sleep before the meetings. They won't be easy; of that I'm sure. I know old Kharkov. He's a wounded bear. He will threaten and bluster and try to break my will. Only when he recognizes our solidarity will he get down to cases."

"And you do not think I should accompany you— to convince him of that solidarity?"

Beck shook his head emphatically. "My dear Wozniakowski, it wouldn't be good manners. After all, he asked to see me alone. If I turn up with a phalanx of allies, he will immediately realize that there is no possibility of compromise. No, I want to hear him out. That way we'll know just how weak he is. He'll have to put his bargaining position on the table. I'll pretend to listen. Why not? Our great strength is our unity, my friend. He is the supplicant. It is always wise to know just how desperate the enemy is. It might be possible to come to some sort of agreement with him now that will freeze the status quo." Beck leaned forward, again gripping the Pole's arm. "You understand. The danger for us is not now. It will come after the war in the Far East is ended and they can devote full attention to us. It is to our advantage to get a settlement now, when the Russians are desperate. You understand, Wozniakowski?"

The Pole nodded, resenting the German's patronizing tone, but recognizing the logic of the situation.

It was, after all, what they had hoped for: a weakened, defeated Soviet Union in the Far East willing to accept an accommodation in the West. It was true that, once the war in the East was ended, Kharkov would seek revenge with a ferocity peculiarly Russian. Beck was right. But the fear persisted, almost like a pain in the gut. Maybe it was the Steinhaeger; which tasted like kerosine. He longed for the clear, clean taste of a Wyborowa. He had served the German drink out of misguided courtesy.

"Very well, Herr Beck, I wish you luck. Please keep me informed of what is going on. My people are intensely concerned."

Beck stood up and offered a meaty hand. "Be assured, my friend. You will know instantly. *Auf wiedersehen.*"

Wozniakowski watched him leave the shabby party headquarters building in Szczecin and climb into the glimmering Mercedes limousine for the short trip across the frontier to the airport. In the back courtyard an identical car waited for him, a present from the president of the United German Democratic Republic, the new name of the German state.

Alec Thompson flicked on the center television set and Suzanne Wilson's familiar face came into focus. He had missed the first couple of sentences of her broadcast.

". . . poised to attack the bridge of troops the Russians have thrown across the Khabarovsk salient. However, military experts are generally agreed that the Soviet Army has moved with surprising rapidity to consolidate its gains and turn its armor against the now-surrounded Chinese force to the north. There is a growing feeling that Wang Chin has not been able to control his troops with the same effectiveness and that the counterattack has already been dangerously delayed.

"News from the battlefield itself is confused. The Chinese continue to maintain a foothold across the Amur River at Khabarovsk, but vicious Soviet counterattacks have compressed it into a small area that is being subjected to merciless artillery and rocket attacks. To the south, Soviet tanks are attacking in waves and have broken through the first line of defense of the surrounded Chinese troops. However, Chinese artillery and rocket emplacements are continuing what is described as the most intensive barrage since World War Two. Satellite pictures show the battlefield as a carpet of exploding shells.

"Meanwhile, in Europe, rumors persist of a meeting in Helsinki between the president of the United German Democratic Republic, Horst Beck, and the general secretary of the Communist Party of the Soviet Union, Alexei Kharkov. Sources in Warsaw indicated today that the two men would agree on a now de facto division of Europe, with the Soviet Union recognizing the complete independence of its former satellites in return for pledges that Europe will remain quiet during the crucial stages of the campaign in the Far East.

"New regimes were installed in Budapest and Prague today, and indications are that similar government changes are due in Rumania. Bulgaria has reiterated its loyalty to the Soviet Union, and Yugoslavia has proclaimed strict neutrality.

"In Israel the Ministry of Science and Technology confirmed the explosion of a hydrogen bomb in the Sinai desert today. The bomb, of relatively low megatonnage, was sufficiently miniaturized to be carried by the new Israeli intercontinental ballistic missile, the Golda. Nine countries now have nuclear capability: the United States; the Soviet Union; France; Great Britain; India; Japan; China; Brazil; and Israel.

"Famine on the subcontinent has reached crisis proportions. More than two million people are reported to have perished in India within the past two months. Another million died of hunger in Bangladesh. No relief is in sight for millions more who are on the verge of starvation. U.S. grain ships are piled up in the harbors, but a three-week-old strike of railway personnel has paralyzed distribution. Riots in Bombay, Calcutta, and New Delhi have resulted in thousands of deaths as troops fired into the crowds.

"The new Marxian-socialist leaders of India have appealed for aid from all nations in the East Bloc, but to date only the United States and Canada have been able to supply grain in appreciable quantities. U.S. Secretary of Agriculture Harrison Billings warned that U.S. stocks were at a dangerous low and very little more could be spared.

"Now, Willoughby G. Pepperdine with a commentary on today's news."

"Good evening." Pepperdine's dessicated visage filled the screen in startling contrast to Suzanne Wilson. It was, Thompson thought, a brilliant juxtaposition, a real grabber.

"The situation in the Far East, as Suzanne has just told you, is still not too clear. However, it does seem fairly certain that the Soviet Union is showing a military predominance that could lead to a serious defeat for the Chinese. And this, in turn, could have grave consequences for U.S. policy, which has operated with its usual passivity during the crisis. The president and his advisors have chosen to stand aside as the map of the world is redrawn. We have, in effect, abdicated our predominant position in world politics, allowed a second-rate power such as West Germany to humiliate us, and made no effort to intercede in a conflict that could result not only in our destruction, but that of the entire world. It has been a pathetically weak performance, one not surprising to those of us who have followed the president and his advisors' course over the last few years.

"We now face a Europe totally dominated by the new United German Democratic Republic under the leadership of men who, though described as erratic, are, in fact, brilliant opportunists unlikely to allow their newfound power to lie fallow. This new German-dominated Europe will present the United States with an even more formidable and aggressive economic competitor at the same time that the Soviet Union will have become the dominant power in Asia. Everywhere our position erodes and nothing is done."

Pepperdine looked up from his script and folded his hands on the desk in front of him, his voice taking on a portentous seriousness that was the delight of nightclub imitators. "I think it is obvious that the United States is facing a crisis of unique seriousness around the world tonight. Within a very few days the old certainties of the post-World War Two era will be replaced by a fluid situation demanding creativity and decisiveness. I hope our leaders will be able to look within themselves and find it. Thank you and good night."

The president burst into Thompson's office as the broadcast ended and pointed at the screen. "Did you hear that flatulant old son-of-a-bitch? It was beautiful—well-manicured horseshit about our ineffectiveness, but not one goddamned word about what he would do if he had power." The big man slammed a sheaf of papers onto a coffee table and dropped into a chair. "He's right, though. We are not making our weight felt."

"What are we supposed to do?" Thompson asked. "Take sides in the Far East war? Attack Germany? We've been over every option a dozen times. Pepperdine and his goddamned 'creative' foreign policy is just blowing smoke up our asses. The only creative thing we can do right now is sit tight and try to influence the postwar settlement which, I have the feeling, is going to be a thoroughly messy one."

"How do you mean 'messy'?" the president asked.

"It will create more problems than it solves. It will be more a truce than a real peace. Everybody goes home mad and starts preparing for the next round."

"And the next round may be the last one. I take your point, Alec. We've got to be in a position to bring our weight to bear to avoid just that. But it's a fact of history that the man who won't fight doesn't bear much weight at the peace table."

"Normally, yes," Thompson said. "But we're still the most powerful economic and military force in the world today. When we talk, they've got to listen. The problem is to figure out just what we want among what looks like a thoroughly unpalatable set of options."

The president nodded gloomily. "A Russia totally dominant in Asia and an aggressive expansionist Germany in command of the levers in Europe. Not a particularly comforting picture."

"True. But at least in Europe the solution has a certain realism. The Germans have been the dominant power on the Continent since 1870. Only by incredible stupidity have they managed to lose. All they had to do was restrain themselves in 1914 and 1939 and, inevitably, their economic power would have dumped all Europe in their lap. This time they've waited, and it looks as if they've won. That meeting in Helsinki is going to see Kharkov try to come to some long-term agreement with Beck, something that will freeze the status quo. Beck will agree. Hell, why wouldn't he? He's being handed Eastern Europe on a plate."

"You really think Kharkov will cave in that easily?" the president asked.

"He isn't caving in. He has lost, and by now he realizes it. He's accepting a fait accompli and hoping to profit as much as he can from it. Oh, I'm sure Beck will come through with some generous economic quid pro quos, which, in the long run, will simply give German industry an even better market in the Soviet Union, as well as a pipeline into the raw materials they've got to have."

"And China?"

Thompson shrugged. "Depends on who wins. But either way, nobody is going to quit. Whatever happens, the best we can hope for is a truce."

The president heaved himself up out of the chair and stretched his big body. "Okay, go get some sleep. I've asked Jane to call me if we get any replies on my proposal for a meeting in Geneva. It's too early, of course. The Chinese may be in such bad shape that they'll agree, but the Russians won't. And Beck is probably willing to let things suppurate for a while yet. Sooner or later, though, they've got to talk, and when the time comes we've got to be there as mediator; otherwise, old Pepperdine is right. We're nothing but eunuchs in a brothel."

16

Colonel General Anton Kusarenko-Kusarevich leaned forward on the big map table and rubbed sleep from his eyes. It had taken all night, but scattered before him were the dispositions for a general retreat. It had been grim. The dozen officers who had worked with him were bitterly resentful. Virtually the entire army staff was convinced that old Korzybsky's plan was brilliant. Early reports from the battlefield had confirmed this. The slashing Soviet tank attacks had rammed through lanes cut in the minefields and enveloped the first-line defenses of the Chinese, surrounding anti-tank emplacements and leaving behind them disoriented masses of infantry.

But toward morning the reports of losses had begun to stream in. Chinese heavy artillery, crammed in great masses into the bulge between the Amur and Ussuri rivers, had laid down a withering carpet of fire. Behind this line the rockets spewed forth an unending stream of death. The tanks were getting through, but the Russian infantry was suffering massive losses and, worse, the tank trucks with vital fuel oil were going up in torches of flame across the battlefield. Efforts to resupply by helicopter had resulted in the same disasters the Americans had encountered in Vietnam. Chinese troops shot them down like ducks using hand-held rockets and laser-guided anti-aircraft batteries. Even losses of assault tanks had been much higher than anticipated.

"General Vasilyev, sir."

Kusarevich rose as the commander of the Eastern armies strode into the room followed by his staff, not bothering now to suck in his belly. He was in command. He had established that the night before. Mikulski was under arrest and the remaining generals would be more pliable because of it.

"Well, Kusarevich, where are the plans?"

"They are finished. The orders are being prepared. It will take from twenty-four to thirty-six hours to get them through to all units. The retreat can start Tuesday morning."

"Tuesday morning?" Vasilyev was shocked. The man was right, of course. Communications were bad in the East, even in peacetime. In the middle of a war they were probably hopeless. "What the hell are you using? Runners? Carrier pigeons? Get on a radio and stop the columns. Tell them to start preparations for an immediate retreat. Wang Chin may be cautious and slow to move, but when he recognizes what we are doing, even he will get his counterattack under way."

Kusarevich stood silent, aware of the stunned disbelief on the faces of his staff officers. "We can't do that, General. You can't just turn tank columns around

257

and head them back. Reinforcements are coming up. They'll get entangled. It would be disastrous."

Vasilyev stared at the map, a chilly sweat breaking out under his armpits. He had to keep himself under control. If these men discovered that he had had virtually no experience in handling large bodies of men, they would treat him with contempt, and the control he had won with such decisiveness would slip away.

"Obviously, Kusarevich, the retreat must be orderly. But I want none of the bureaucratic inertia that has come to characterize our army. Understand? I want those troops moving, and moving fast." He turned on his heel and headed for the door. "I'm going to the front, Kusarevich. I'll be back tonight. I expect the retreat to be underway by the time I return."

General Wang Chin stared down at the battle map in puzzlement. Old Korzybsky had run true to form in the first days of the campaign. The Russian tank columns had moved with devastating speed, sacrificing the first two waves to slam through with the third, methodically overrunning one position after another, leaving the demoralized remnants behind for their efficient infantry mop-up units. Their losses had been high. Chin's battlefield intelligence reported more than two thousand tanks disabled in the first day's fighting. At this crucial point in the battle, it was vital that momentum be maintained in the face of brutal losses. And it was just this fierce willpower, this reckless willingness to accept appalling initial losses in order to obtain the final victory, that characterized Korzybsky's style. And it was this on which Wang Chin had counted. For his own attack to succeed, the major portion of the Soviet tank armies had to be engaged on the northern portion of the corridor—engaged and held by the masses of infantry, artillery, and rocket emplacements that he had crammed into the small area.

Only then could he put his ponderous masses of tanks and infantry in motion to attack the rear of the much more mobile Russian force. Victory would come not through subtlety or brilliant tactics, but by sheer mass and weight. His inexperienced tank generals could not meet their Soviet counterparts in a fluid battle of maneuver such as those in the deserts of North Africa during World War II and expect to win. This was why it was essential for the Soviet northward thrust to continue.

Chin glanced up from the map as a staff officer entered and stood at attention. "Yes?"

"General Chou reports from the northern sector that the Soviet attacks have slackened. There are indications that the tank armies are preparing to wheel and break off contact."

Chin stared down at the map, his face impassive. "Inform General Chou that he must maintain pressure on the tanks at all costs. Attack with everything he has at his disposal. They must be prevented from retreating at all costs. And ask the corps commanders of the southern army to come in, please."

General Phillip Samsun rubbed his eyes as Bowman droned on. The young shit must think he was such an idiot he couldn't read the map. "Do me a favor, Colonel."

"Yes, sir?"

"Shut the fuck up." Samsun stared down at the map, glancing up at the electronic statistical chart that listed Soviet and Chinese losses. That had been some asshole's idea before his time, and he had left it alone, although it reminded him of a baseball scoreboard. The Russians were losing tanks, masses of them. But they had broken through the first Chinese line with remarkable speed. Their planes were ripping apart the Chinese anti-aircraft radar sites and blinding the missiles. Soon they would have total battlefield superiority and range at will across the cramped Chinese front. The big surprise of the war was that tanks were still effective against sophisticated missiles if used in massive numbers with a brutal unconcern for losses. It was a little like a World War I infantry attack. If you could push a wave into the enemy trenches, you were more likely than not to win. Only this was easier, the losses heavy but acceptable. And once through that front line, the tanks could roam like wild dogs, attacking the defenseless artillery sites from the rear and cutting down the men virtually without opposition. And that was what was happening.

Samsun reached for the phone. "Give me the White House."

For the first time since the crisis began, Thompson felt reasonably rested. He'd slept eight hours Sunday night alone, and this morning he'd jogged two miles along the mall, not pushing it, but feeling the alcohol and the staleness seep out with the sweat. Samsun's report on the battle was on his desk. In the initial phases it had gone much as they'd expected. Soviet tank armies had moved with brutal efficiency against Chinese emplacements hemmed in between the Amur and Ussuri rivers, rolling up the front lines and enveloping large masses of Chinese troops. It had begun to look like a classic battle of the later stages of World War II. Then, for some reason, the Russian armies had stopped. According to the latest reports, the tank armies were wheeling and moving back toward their takeoff point.

"Alec," the president said, bursting in through the door, his big body alive with tension, "what the hell is going on out there? Why are the Russians stopping the attack?"

"Nobody can figure it out. Samsun says the satellite reconnaissance pictures show they took some pretty brutal losses, but Korzybsky must have figured on that. It's not his style to break off an attack before it's had a chance. If anything, he tended in World War Two to risk total destruction by pushing on in the face of truly monstrous losses—and winning."

"But he's not in command anymore. What's the new guy's name?"

"Vasilyev. But it's unlikely he would alter the fundamental campaign strategy in the middle of a battle."

"Alec, maybe that's why he took over. Old Korzybsky may have been taking too many risks for the Politburo. Maybe they decided to replace him with somebody safer."

Thompson nodded. "It's an explanation. They may have panicked over the Japanese landing. Samsun says there are indications that the Soviets are turning their reserves around in the Vyazemski sector and moving them toward the Amgun landing area."

"What are the Chinese doing?"

"Trying to maintain pressure in the north against the retreating Russian armor. But they haven't been attacking in the south. Phil thinks they have been thrown off by the retreat. You know how cautious Chin is. He may be waiting to see what the Soviets are up to."

The president nodded. "Either way, it's not going to change the situation much in Europe. Old Kharkov will be just as hard to deal with whether he's winning or losing."

"I know. That meeting with Beck today is going to be crucial. He's not going into it weakened. He'll be a raging bull, throwing his weight around, slamming out ultimatums. What's Beck going to do?"

"He's not in bad shape. It looks as if the Germans have all of Eastern Europe lined up behind them—from Rumania to the Baltic. Maybe the satellite armies aren't worth a damn, but they can't be totally ignored. Anyway, Kharkov can't threaten a general invasion to bring them to heel. He's still too involved in the Far East."

Thompson sucked an empty pipe and stared across the room at the president, whose impatience was manifest. "I still don't see much what we can do until it ripens a little more."

"What you are saying is once Beck and Kharkov come up with an agreement we're going to have to live with it. And once the Russians decide just what they're going to do to the Chinese, we're also going to have to accept that. Jesus Christ, Alec, it means the end of American influence in the world. We will have been successfully excluded from two major world conflicts and, more important, from the settlements. Nobody is going to take us seriously from here on out if we let this happen." He shook his big head in a violent negation. "Goddamn it, I won't put up with it. I wasn't elected president to preside over the dissolution of American power and influence in the world." He got up and left the office, slamming the big oak door so hard that the pictures rattled.

Jane Cleveland stuck her head in and raised her thick black unplucked eyebrows. "And what, may I ask, was that all about?"

262

"Nothing much. Just the sound of an empire coming down around our ears."

Horst Beck was tired. The meeting had been going on for six hours with only one fifteen-minute break. He wanted badly to urinate and he needed a drink. The Russian had begun once again to repeat his threats, demands, and menaces. His translator, a young Volga German who looked like a hero out of a Goethe drama, patiently repeated after him, in German, the words, which fell like hammer blows. Beck believed none of it. Kharkov was no fool. He realized full well that, although he could destroy Germany, the result would be a totally devastated European Russia. He would not risk it. But the alternative was something else again. He, Beck, had never considered it, not even as a wild option. But now he saw that he must.

Now Kharkov had ceased the threats. His big hands were open, palms up as he outlined his proposals once again. Beck stared into the Russian's slate-gray eyes, overcome in spite of himself with admiration for the plan. It had simplicity and elegance, and it resolved some of the oldest problems confronting Central Europe in a classic way. No doubt about it, the Russian was right. It was the solution that should have been found two hundred, three hundred, years before, but nobody had had the power to bring it off. Now Russia and Germany would settle it all, finally and definitively. Some people would be hurt, yes. But they had no choice.

An aide slipped a report in front of Beck. The Russian armies were within a hair of overrunning the Chinese northern army, which was being squeezed back against the Ussuri-Amur triangle, and it would soon break. The Chinese attack to the south was stymied. Russian air power dominated the battlefield. The Japanese landing was nothing more than a confused mess of men and materiel. It would take days for it to enter the equation.

Beck glanced up from the paper and met Kharkov's eyes. There was really no choice. Wozniakowski would simply have to understand that he had not had any choice.

Colonel James Bowman glanced at his watch. He had asked his wife to dinner, and she would be waiting in the Pentagon parking lot in ten minutes. The intelligence center had been packed with brass all day, standing around poring over the maps and getting in his way. He had been forced into impromptu briefing sessions when he should have been analyzing data. Not that it made much difference. The Russians were winning going away as he'd always expected they would.

"Colonel?"

"Yes?" One of the situation analysts brought over an enlarged satellite montage.

"Something funny's going on. Look at this." He indicated a Russian ammunition dump from which a stream of half tracks had been picking up tank ammunition and carrying it to the advanced tank columns. "They've quit moving up ammunition. And take a look at this." He flipped another enlargement on top of the table. "The column attacking on the river has come to a stop. They're pulling back in some places and establishing a line."

Bowman stared at the two pictures. Obviously the Soviets had underestimated their ability to move up ammunition and had simply slowed the pipeline. But the armored column was curious. There was no reason to stop. They had rolled up the Chinese defenses, and ahead of them the enemy was hastily pulling out its artillery and establishing a line at least five kilometers farther north. In a few hours the Russian armor would be disengaged and an empty battlefield would lie before them.

"Are they out of fuel?"

"No, sir." The analyst flipped other pictures in front of him that showed oil tankers in orderly dumps behind the lines. It had been a masterly effort from a logistical standpoint.

"Then what the fuck is going on?" Bowman asked irritably. He could see the dinner with his wife going down the drain. They hadn't been getting along very well lately, and he was hoping to get things back on the rails that night.

"Beats me, sir," the analyst said. "But it sure as hell looks as if they're stopping. The whole logistical effort seems to be slowing down. In some areas they're even pulling stuff back. If I had to make a guess, I'd say they were moving over onto the defensive."

"Son, you're crazy. They're on the verge of destroying a two-million-man army. There's no way they're going to pull back. You're misreading the signs. The Russians have always been cautious. They're just realigning their logistics, probably because they poured in more stuff than they need and it's beginning to clog things up. Is Colonel Harrelson here?"

"Just got in, sir."

Bowman moved across the room to greet his relief. "Hello, Luke," he said, shaking hands.

"Jim, how's it going?"

"Piece of cake. Russians should wrap it all up by the end of the week. They're in such good shape that the latest indications show they're slowing their logistical support."

Colonel Harrelson, a rangy ex-infantry officer with

a Ph.D. in transportation sciences, raised his eyebrows. "They're burning up one hell of a lot of ammunition to be slowing down the supply line."

Bowman shrugged. "It's all yours, Luke. Pruitt and Samsun are still in the building. But, otherwise, your audience has diminished to a trickle."

Harrelson grinned. He was not the usual intelligence officer, having spent most of his career in supply and transportation.

"Okay. I'll try to keep the animals at bay."

As Bowman left, Harrelson turned to the maps. He was a methodical man, and he began with the situation sixteen hours before when Bowman's predecessor as duty officer had relieved him.

"Hello, Dimitri," Thompson said into the hollow echo of the hot line. "What's up?"

"Very good news, Alec." The Russian sounded exultant. He had reason to. "It looks as if things are going to work out."

"Meaning the meeting with Beck went well?"

"Meaning the meeting with Beck went exceptionally well. The general secretary has asked me to inform you and the president that a further meeting will be held in Paris on Wednesday morning, very early. It will be a secret session between the general secretary, Beck, Wozniakowski, the French and British prime ministers, and the new leaders from Hungary, Czechoslovakia, and Rumania."

"Sounds about as secret as a soccer match," Thompson said.

"Very good," Dimitri said and laughed. "The general secretary indicated that the president was welcome to attend, but he wishes to warn him that the situation is already settled. There will be no negotiations. He suggests that you might come as an observer. What Beck has agreed to with us will happen, regardless of what anybody else thinks or wants. Is that clear, Alec?"

"Yes, it's clear. I'm not sure you have the horses to pull it off, but it's clear. What did you decide at Helsinki?"

Stashevsky laughed. "I remember when one of your cabinet ministers made a joke about the pope: 'He no playa da game, he no maka da rules.' You didn't play the game this time, Alec, so you'll find out about the rules when the others do."

"You mean along with Rumania, Czechoslovakia, and Hungary?"

Stashevsky could hardly keep the condescension out of his voice. "Yes, I'm afraid that's exactly what I mean. Have you seen the latest reports from the Far East? It should all be over in a week. The Chinese will be broken."

"And Europe?"

"I'll see you in Paris, Alec. What about lunch at Le Roy Gourmand tomorrow? I'll be there early to prepare for the general secretary's arrival."

"Sure. One o'clock . . . if I come, that is."

"You'll come. One o'clock. I'll have my people book the table."

Thompson put down the telephone and walked to the ornate door dividing him from the adjoining office. The president was staring intently at the television tube. "That goddamned Pepperdine is going to hit us again. Look at the old bastard."

Pepperdine's dry, angular visage filled the screen.

"Good evening. The news is bad again tonight. The war in the Far East is beginning to resemble a rout as the Soviet forces prepare to destroy China's only viable army. Once again we have stood by, a hamstrung giant, while the fate of the world is decided by other, essentially weaker, powers who have a policy and the will to carry it out.

"The prospects in the Far East are grim, but those in Europe are even more alarming. German President Horst Beck and Soviet General Secretary Kharkov met today to decide the fate of that continent, and no American was present. My sources tell me that we were not even informed of the meeting." Pepperdine folded his long hands before him in a characteristic gesture and leaned forward slightly to lend emphasis to his words. "The United States of America no longer counts in world affairs. Our leaders, if you can call them leaders, have opted out. We are at the mercy of forces over which we have no control.

"It all began with our tacit acquiescence in the mid-1970s to the Communist takeover of Indochina. Once South Vietnam, Laos, and Cambodia fell, it was only a matter of time before Thailand, Burma, Malaysia, and Singapore went the same route. Indonesia was isolated and eventually became the ideological and economic satellite of the new Marxian-socialist regime in Japan. Australia, a reservoir of raw materials for the area, moved toward neutralism. Perhaps the crucial point was our passivity in the face of the takeover of Taiwan by mainland China two years after Chiang's death. It left the Philippines totally exposed and the eventual Marxian regime inevitable. What have we left in the Far East? A few island dependencies that are strategically worthless.

"And now it is Europe's turn. Our position has progressively eroded until the latest action by German President Beck has driven us from the Continent completely. The meeting between Beck and Kharkov in Helsinki was the first probing of the problem of who will assume the hegemony of that old and tired continent now that we have relinquished it.

"What we are seeing, ladies and gentlemen, is the breakup of the last remnant of the American imperium. Let us hope that our own nation will be able to survive in the world that follows, for when one imperium goes, make no mistake, another takes its place."

The president pressed the button, turning off the set with a vicious jab. "Christ, there are times when I wish we had censorship. That son-of-a-bitch is a menace."

"Dimitri called. Kharkov and Beck are meeting in Paris with the French, British, and the Eastern Europeans. They made some sort of deal in Helsinki that they're going to lay out. Dimitri says it's not a negotiating session. Beck and Kharkov are going to lay down the law."

"And they want me to attend?" The president sounded incredulous.

Thompson shrugged.

"No, goddamn it!" The President exploded. "I'll be damned if I'll be convoked to a meeting and handed decisions like a schoolboy." He stabbed at the desk console. "Get me Kharkov, Jano, now."

"What are you going to do?"

"Tell him to cancel the meeting and call a general negotiating session in Geneva, as we've been suggesting for days."

"And if he refuses?"

The president slumped in his chair, staring moodily at the coffee mug clutched in his massive paw. "Then Pepperdine may be right," he said quietly.

Wang Chin shuffled through the latest battle reports and bent over the situation map. There was no doubt now that the Soviet tank armies had begun a general retreat, moving back into the corridor in

269

orderly lines, leaving behind a few dozen suicide battalions to delay an attack by the regrouping Chinese forces they had so recently defeated. Wang Chin rubbed his eyes to fight off the fatigue. There was no question that he had made a major mistake. He should have ordered the southern attack mounted immediately when the first signs of a retreat appeared. Had he known that old Korzybsky was no longer in command of the Soviet forces, he would not have hesitated. But his respect for the old man's genius had stayed his hand. And now it was too late.

The orders had already gone out to begin the offensive, but major portions of the Soviet armored forces were already recrossing the Ussuri, linking up with the reserves in preparation for an attack on the Japanese landing zone at Amgun. Still, it would be possible to deal a crushing blow to the Soviet infantry within the corridor and perhaps capture masses of Soviet supplies.

Wang Chin called in his chief of staff. "Contact the air force commander of the northern sector. Tell him to commit every plane. He is to destroy the Amur and Ussuri bridges, no matter what the cost. I want as many Russians trapped in that corridor as possible."

Chin dismissed the chief of staff and reached for the field telephone. "Get me the Japanese high command."

General Vasily Vasilyev was feeling satisfied with himself. There was no question but that he was in command. Kusarenko-Kusarevich was just the man he'd need as chief of staff—ambitious, servile, competent. He did what he was told without wearing him out with arguments. His father-in-law was finally going to have to admit that he, Vasilyev, had what it took. The staff had worked all night on the plans for the retreat. He had gone over them in detail an hour before. There were no real problems. As Kusarevich had pointed out, the Chinese armies to the north were reeling back in disarray.

Their only problem would come if the Chinese were able to get their southern armies on the move, but there wasn't much chance of that. Anyway, with their notorious caution, the Chinese were not likely to risk their last army in an attack that seemed sure to fail. It would leave them totally defenseless.

The only problem would be to present the retreat as a victory grasped from the jaws of defeat because of the faulty plans of the old marshal. He had already begun his report. Old Kharkov would really owe him something this time. He should get his marshal's baton for sure.

17

Alec Thompson stared with distaste at the needle-nosed airplane as it taxied to a halt in front of him. The president had decided that Alec would go to Paris as an observer but would take no part in the conference. The British and French had reluctantly agreed. They pointed out that they had no choice but to meet with Beck and Kharkov, even though their German ally had refused to give them even a hint of the purpose of the conference. For once, the Frenchman had been subdued. He had attempted to persuade the president to come himself. Without the weight of the United States, he had said, there was no hope of stopping whatever it was they had decided.

But the president had refused. He would not be convoked to a meeting about which he knew nothing and to put his approval on an agreement he had not been a party to. Since the only alternative to agreement seemed to be a total break, he preferred not to go. The French and British leaders had accepted his reasoning and had agreed to coordinate informally with Thompson. But there would be no official American presence at the conference.

"Ready, sir?"

"Ready as I'll ever be."

The airman helped him into the observer's seat of the shark-like plane. It was the fastest thing in the air. He would be in Paris in a little over two hours.

Major General Hiro Yamashita inspected the airborne division assembled at the Marioka military airport with satisfaction. Twenty thousand of his nation's best men—fanatical professional paratroopers, each of whom had completed the special "Samurai" assault troop course and amphibious training—were present. In his address to them he had emphasized that no Japanese troops had fought in battle since August, 1945. It was up to them to uphold the honor of two thousand years of honorable combat. They were being asked to sacrifice themselves to assist the Chinese armies that were fighting for their lives. Their mission was suicidal, a thing every Japanese soldier should be proud to perform.

It was hopeless, of course. He knew they would fail. They were being asked to destroy the bridges at Vyazemski to disrupt the Russian supply line. The drop would be made to the east of the bridges and the assault force would form up using only the light airborne armored vehicles for the assault. It was axiomatic that paratroopers would fail in any such action. Arnhem was the textbook example. Their only real successes had been in taking lightly armed or wholly outnumbered troops by complete surprise. The best they could normally hope for with their light arms

273

and lack of heavy artillery was to disrupt the supply lines. But these bridges would be heavily defended.

Still it had to be done. The Russians must be prevented from escaping from the corridor. He saluted his men a last time and headed for the lead plane. He just hoped the old knee injury would hold up during the initial jump. It would be humiliating to be put out of action immediately.

General Witold Lulienski rubbed his eyes and regretted the vodka once again. The confidential report from Saracin, director of the Service de Documentation Extérieure et de Contre-Espionage, was categorical. German commanders along the Polish border had been told to convey a series of false reports on troop dispositions to their counterparts in Poland. A systematic misrepresentation of the military situation was to begin today at dawn at the normal liaison meetings between officers of both armies. The meetings had been set up following the break with the Soviets, and, to everybody's surprise, there had been an immense amount of goodwill on both sides, almost as if the traditional German-Polish feud was finally coming to an end.

The report could be provocation, of course. Saracin was in the tradition of great French espionage chiefs. Fouché was his idol. He was capable of any falsity, and betrayal, in the name of France. But Lulienski was at a loss to see much French self-interest in driving a wedge between the Poles and the Germans at this point. Later, perhaps, when the Soviet danger had receded, then the attempt would begin to isolate the new German colossus. He and Wozniakowski had already discussed this. But now, with the possibility of a war with the Russians, he could not see the French playing games. They had to believe that, with the Americans gone, the Germans were the only bastion that could keep an enraged Russia from moving to the channel if it felt like it. The French nuclear deterrent was, of course, a joke. In any case, everybody knew they would not fight and risk the destruction of Paris.

He fought off the temptation, then shrugged and reached into his desk for the bottle. The report was too vague. He would try to get confirmation for Wozniakowski before he left for Paris. There was no point in worrying him unnecessarily. Beck had assured him that all had gone well in Helsinki and the Paris meeting was merely a formality to legalize the division of Europe along present lines.

The vodka scalded his throat and spread its warmth outward from the stomach. He would wait. If the reports were true, there was nothing they could do, anyway.

Dimitri Stashevsky awakened against the girl's warm flesh, the gentle light of a Paris spring seeping through the filmy white curtain. He circled her waist, his right hand groping down her stomach to the triangle of hair, slipping his hand between her legs, stroking her gently. She hated to make love in the morning. But he had to have it. The erection he slipped between her hips was almost painful in its tumescence. She moaned and pulled away, lying almost on her stomach now. He separated her legs and gently began to enter from behind, trying not to waken her.

"Dimitri, stop it."

But he was in now, and he moved on top of her, driving it home, enclosing her legs as she struggled halfheartedly. "Damn you!" she said into the pillow.

"You miserable swine. Now I will drip your semen all day."

Jean Saracin popped another antacid pill in his mouth and drank it down with the foul-tasting mineral water. His stomach disgorged a taste not unlike that of sewer gas. He stared at himself in the gilt mirror that hung in baroque splendor over the fireplace in his ornate nineteenth-century office. His normally pallid face was almost yellow, which wasn't so bad. But so was his bald scalp. He sucked in his small, bowling-ball paunch ineffectually and wondered if he dared add another half inch to the elevator heels that brought him up to five-feet-four. A toupee would help his height as well, but he didn't dare begin to wear one. He had been totally bald since he was twenty-five. It would be ludicrous.

It was eight o'clock; time for the second. He took the bottle out of a small office refrigerator concealed behind a carved wooden cabinet and filled a small glass. He replaced the bottle and shut the cabinet in a careful, slow ritual before picking up the glass. He was an alcoholic; no question about it. But he maintained his discipline. Every hour, on the hour, he stoked the fire that burned within him, but only with one small glass. In the course of a day, he drank eight—nine, if you included the one when he first got up. That was precisely one third of a liter of the finest vodka. It had no visible effect on either his mind or his motor reflexes. He was careful to eat a solid lunch full of absorptive foods. He never drank more than half a bottle of wine and one brandy. By the end of the day the pallor in his cheeks had turned to a slight rose and his high-pitched voice tended to squeak occasionally. But that was only natural.

Days like the one coming up were a trial, however.

He must assist the idiot prefect in setting up the security arrangements, although it was not, strictly speaking, his responsibility. The president insisted on it. Too much could go wrong. It wasn't a normal conference, anyway. How was anybody supposed to have a secret meeting with eight heads of government? It was ridiculous, especially with the Americans involved. Anything they knew was immediately public knowledge. In any case, he would have to slip away to a bar occasionally during the day.

Saracin moved to the immense window of his office and stared out into the street below. A fine drizzle almost obscured the river. God, how he hated days like this.

It had been on such a day in the winter of 1944 that the heavy-handed young farmer had castrated him in the *préfecture de police* in Montpellier. It had been a meaningless sacrifice, his refusal to talk. The concierge had alerted the cell immediately after his arrest, and everybody had gone underground. But he hadn't been sure. So he held out. Twenty-four hours, they had told him: if you hold out twenty-four hours, nobody will ever get caught because we'll all know you've been taken.

His hand moved unconsciously toward his crotch, as if to ease the pain.

Le Roy Gourmand was a small restaurant on a side street near the Place de la République. It specialized in seafood and arcane dishes based on cheese. The proprietor, a gaunt Bordelais, was also the cook. His wife guarded the cash drawer and made out all bills. The waiters were almost all relatives. Several looked old enough to have served in World War I. The service was impeccable and the food good, without pretension. Most of the regular clients were businessmen from the neighborhood who came in at noon and occupied the same table each day. By two o'clock the place was usually empty except for a few tourists who happened to stumble onto it. In the evening it was one of the favorite restaurants of a certain type of discreetly chic upper-middle-class Parisian who would rather be caught in a cheap brothel than in a three-star restaurant.

"Bonjour, *madame*."

"*Ah, tiens*, Monsieur Thompson. How long since we have not seen you?" He and Janine had lived around the corner for several years when they were first married. The restaurant was new then and much cheaper. He had occasionally come down with a pot and bought enough of a special stew for the impromptu parties they had given. The stew was no longer on the handwritten menu. Madame had shrugged when he asked about it once.

"Too cheap, Monsieur Thompson. Too many people ate the stew, for which we could charge almost nothing. But, if you insist, come early and you can eat with the waiters. For them we have stew.

"And how is your wife?"

"Fine," Thompson said. He had never mentioned the divorce. The woman would not have approved.

"Your friend is waiting." She gestured toward a back room where six tables were set off by a clouded-glass partition on which was engraved a Rubenesque nude that some irreverent customers maintained had been modeled after the proprietress.

"Dimitri, how are you?" Thompson said, shaking hands with the Russian with genuine affection.

"Fine Alec. And you? You look tired."

"You would, too, if you'd ridden that goddamned air force jet I came over on. You people could be a

278

little more considerate in calling your conferences. Then I could have slept on the presidential jet."

"Still, an opportunity to spend a few days in Paris is worth it, no?" the Russian said, spreading out his hands.

"For a sybarite like you, maybe." The two men ordered, allowing the antique waiter to suggest crayfish and a Dover sole with a bottle of the house's own Sancerre. As he talked, Dimitri's eyes scanned the other diners.

"We are all right here, do you think?"

Thompson shrugged. "What difference does it make? You're not going to tell me anything the French don't already know. And I don't have anything to say."

The Russian looked pained. "Really, my friend, you mustn't be bitter. It's true that this time we have you, how do you say, by the short hairs." Stashevsky was inordinately proud of his command of American slang and profanity. "But think of the times you put us in embarrassing positions over the past six years. I won't even mention Israel."

"Okay," Thompson said. "But this time you've outsmarted yourself. You're making some sort of deal with the Germans that is going to turn them loose in Central Europe. Believe me, Dimitri, you'll regret it sooner or later."

"Yes. Thank you for the advice." Stashevsky's voice was chilly. "I lost most of my family to them in World War Two. But in this instance it was you who did not control your Germans—you who allowed reunification."

"Oh, for Christ's sake, Dimitri," Alec said, sampling the wine. It was superb, dry without being acidy. Perfect for the fish. "Klein and Beck have been intriguing for years. You surely don't think we were behind it?"

"No, but it was an unforgivable intelligence goof. You'll agree, I hope. Neither of us realized that our principle ally in Europe was about to betray us. Incredible." He touched glasses with Thompson and sat back to enjoy the wine.

Thompson shook his head. "You guys will never get over the conspiratorial mentality. I never pay any attention to our intelligence. In the first place, it's almost always impossible to check it out against the facts, and, second, if you have to rely on intelligence to find out what the opposition is thinking, then you're not doing your job." He leaned across the table. "Have you ever had a problem figuring out what our intentions were in a given situation?"

The Russian shook his head.

"Obviously not. You know what our interests are, you've studied our personalities and our psychology, just as we have yours, you know the military imperatives, and you can forecast our actions within a fairly narrow range. You don't have to rely on some asshole with a long-distance microphone, a satellite, or a sophisticated bug."

"That's true," the Russian murmured. "But, tactically, it can be very important to know about timing and such things. Although we have both always known that the two Germanies would reunite given the slightest chance, we didn't know when the attempt would come."

"It was a failure in perception," Thompson acknowledged. "You get into the habit of classifying people and situations, and it's hard to break out. The Germans have always refused to accept their classification as a second-class power. We made the mistake of believing our own superpower myths. But would you have believed it if your intelligence had told you the scenario? I doubt it. Stalin didn't believe in Hitler's attack on Russia in 1941. Hitler refused to accept his intelligence assessment of the Allied landings in Normandy. You didn't believe we'd encourage the Israelis to take over the oil fields in 1977." He shrugged. "We're back to judgment."

The crayfish came smothered in a delicate cheese sauce. The Russian isolated one and lifted it to his mouth, closing his eyes in expectation. "My God, what degeneracy. When socialism comes to France, we shall have to retain a few places like this as museums." He put his fork down and stared across the table at Thompson. "And what do you expect from our little conference?"

Thompson shrugged. "You've agreed on some sort of European condominium. The details are not important. You're drawing a line and agreeing that your writ will run to the east of it and the German's to the west."

"Excellent," Stashevsky said, sipping the wine and smiling.

"The wine, or my analysis?"

"Both. But your analysis is useless until you know what the condominium is."

"What difference does it make? You'll tell us tomorrow. Our reaction will be delayed a day. That won't change it."

"What reaction?" the Russian asked, glancing around the room. Every table was taken. Next to them four balding merchants discussed the price of cotton goods and the depressed state of the retail market. One table over, a man and his wife sat in morose silence, methodically putting away their second bottle of the house's red wine. Across from them a balding, porcine man in a loud checked suit was host to three

281

young women, obviously his employees, who sat in simpering admiration at his every word. Two aging homosexuals debated at endless length over the menu, and adjacent to them a young couple exchanged caresses under their table, virtually ignoring the food.

Thompson grinned. "Don't look so worried, Dimitri. I haven't had the table bugged."

"A reflex action. It is, of course, impossible that any of these people could be other than ours, since only you and I knew of the rendezvous until a few minutes ago. And, as you say, what difference does it make?" He smiled, revealing a set of capped teeth that reflected the light like mirrors. Russian dental technology was still in the Stone Age.

"You still haven't answered my question. Assuming we and the Germans have agreed to divide Europe between us, what can you do about it? What options do you have?" He leaned on the table, brown eyes boring into Thompson's. "I will answer you, my friend. You have none. America is a world power, yes. If you choose to take everyone else with you in a suicidal war, you can do it. In South America you can usually get your way, although painfully. But in the rest of the world, you march to the sound of someone else's drum: the China-Japan axis in Asia, and the German-Russian one in Europe." He leaned back and smiled. "Our postwar policy will have succeeded when the last American soldier leaves European soil in the next few weeks. It leaves us confronted not by a colossus, but by a pygmy. Make no mistake, the Germans will soon realize who is the master here. Once the war in China is won, we will turn our attentions to them." He held up his hand as Thompson started to speak. "Don't be alarmed. I'm not talking of war. I'm talking about power and its uses. Germany is not a continental power and never will be. It lacks the basic resources and the necessary geography."

"You mean that in a nuclear exchange every German would die and half the Soviet Union would survive." It was the basic equation they all worked with.

Dimitri nodded. "Obviously it's not going to happen. But the Germans know and we know, which is why they will back down in any serious confrontation. We will simply turn the screw little by little until they bend beneath us."

"You mixed a metaphor, Dimitri."

"I beg your pardon?"

"How is Nadia?"

"Fine. And Suzanne?"

"Probably irritated as hell. I didn't tell her I was on my way to Paris."

"Nadia is with me, of course."

"I know. Has she recovered from the operation?"

Neither man had ever met the other's lover, but their respective intelligence services provided detailed information on each of the women. Stashevsky now raised his eyebrows in appreciation and acknowledgment of his colleague's depth of information.

"Yes," he murmured. "She is fine now. Will you be seeing your former wife here in Paris?" It was his turn now, and he savored his colleague's start of surprise.

"In Paris?"

"Yes. Her husband is back home in Marseilles, but she has come up for several days of shopping. She's staying at the Hotel Drouot . . . in case you are interested." The Russian glanced at his watch and stared down regretfully at the neatly cleaned plate. "I must be getting back. The general secretary will be arriving shortly. There will be another interminable meeting, although everything is long since settled."

The two men shook hands on the steps of the restaurant and took separate taxis. Inside, the porcine man in the checked suit stood up and watched over the clouded glass until they disappeared before dropping his napkin and moving quickly to the table they had just vacated. He fumbled momentarily with the base of the vase of flowers, dismantling a small metal object that he then dropped in his pocket. His three companions, no longer giggling, had already left.

Thompson sprawled in the office of the United States ambassador to Paris and waited for the satellite transmission of the morning news from Washington. Suzanne Wilson's calm voice preceded the image.

"Good morning. This is Suzanne Wilson with today's news.

"The situation in Asia continues to be confused. The Russian offensive in the Khabarovsk salient has ground to a halt despite the apparent lack of serious Chinese resistance. Western military experts are speculating that logistical problems forced a temporary regrouping because of the rapidity of the advance.

"Meanwhile, there are rumors of a major diplomatic initiative in Europe. The Russo-German conference in Helsinki obviously resulted in an agreement between the two powers, but no details have been announced. France, Britain, and other Common Market powers are known to have protested to their German ally at not having been informed either of the conference or its results. The new united German government continues to ignore the Common Market diplomatic machinery in what seems to be an obvious attempt to solidify its predominant position on the Continent.

"In the United States the president has once again called for a conference of all the concerned powers to meet in Geneva at the earliest possible moment. The conference would be preceded by a ceasefire in Asia that would in no way prejudice the final negotiations. France, Britain, and most of the smaller European powers have agreed, but there has been no answer from Germany, Russia, or China. Informed diplomatic sources here doubt that such a conference can convene until a more stable situation has evolved both in Europe and the Far East.

"Guerrillas have again attacked a border post along the northern frontier of South Africa. Four border patrolmen were killed and seven wounded in the surprise attack. Units of the South African Army, flown in by helicopter, repulsed the attack and killed twenty of the guerrilla force, which retreated across the border into Rhodesia. South African Prime Minister Pierre Vorndran warned that any further incursions would result in a preemptive strike by South African forces across the border at the guerrilla camps.

"Another oil spill occurred in the Norwegian oil field in the North sea. A small cargo ship slammed into an oil rig in a dense fog last night and broke the oil line. Five hundred tons of oil were dumped into the sea before it could be shut off. Three members of the rig's crew are missing and are believed dead."

Thompson flicked off the set and turned to Ambassador Samuel Morgan, who sat behind the massive desk trying to look stern. "I must say, Alec, you're acting most strangely. I've been waiting to see you for hours. First you go off to lunch with somebody, then you sit here in my office looking at television. *Ce n'est pas sérieux.*" His French accent was atrocious.

"My apologies, but I am not here to talk to you. I want the logistical support of your embassy, nothing else. Now, here's what I need."

Morgan raised his hand in unconscious imitation of an imperial gesture and interrupted. "I won't put up with this. I expect to be kept informed of what's going on. And as for my staff, they're far too busy to be taken off their work unless I feel sure that it's worthwhile."

Thompson stared at the man, wondering in what kind of world he lived. For the fifty-five years of his life he had been surrounded by a soft cushion of millions, if not billions, of dollars. No real contradiction had ever bruised the carefully nurtured ego reflected in the petulant, watery eyes and jutting chin, which, remarkably, gave no impression of forcefulness.

"Sam, listen carefully, because I cannot afford to waste any time. You and your embassy are at my disposal. You and your staff will do as I ask. I intend to tell you nothing of what's going on for the very good reason that you drink too much, and when you drink, you talk; in fact, you talk too damned much at all times. So you will now pick up the phone and get your political and economic counselors in here; also the press attaché, administrative officer, and head of communications. Since you have the only red line to the president, I'm going to have to ask you to vacate your office for about the next twenty-four hours."

Ambassador Samuel Morgan had turned the color of the off-white walls of his office. "You can't talk to me that way, goddamn you. I contributed a million dollars to the president's campaign."

"Yes. And you bought seven years in Paris, where you have fucked up royally. If you don't want to end your tour today, I suggest you do as I ask."

"The president . . ." Morgan started.

Thompson got up and moved to his desk, picking up the red phone and dialing seven numbers. Almost

286

immediately Jane Cleveland's cool voice came over the line. "The president's office."

"Let me talk to him please, Jane."

"Sure. How's Paris?"

"Full of dancing girls and bubbly."

"I'll tell Suzanne. Here he is."

"Alec, how is it going?"

"All right. I talked to Dimitri. He practically confirmed that they'll be coming in here with an overall agreement. I doubt if there is much you can do. Kharkov seems to have it wrapped up. You might try once more with him. Maybe we could get the venue moved to Geneva and at least get the semblance of negotiations."

"To save my face? If it were at a lower level, and if I could run for office again, he might do it. He'd have to think that he'd need me at some future point. But not this way. Let's face it, Alec, he's got no incentive not to savor this one to the hilt. I won't be around much longer, and there isn't a goddamned thing I can hurt him with now. No, I won't do it. Let it ride. We'll just have to hope we can live with whatever they've come up with."

"Sam wants to talk to you." Thompson passed across the phone.

"Hello, Mr. President." He stopped and Thompson heard the president's voice booming hollowly out of the phone.

"Hello, Sam, good to hear your voice. Do all you can to help Alec out, will you? He's over there representing me, so regard anything he says as coming out of this office. How's Mary? Good. Look forward to seeing you here soon." The connection severed.

Ambassador Samuel Morgan looked up helplessly. "He didn't let me say anything."

18

Colonel Alexei Popov had lost his voice. He had been screaming into the radio of his Tu-70 tank for seven hours attempting to hold his regiment together in the night retreat. They had been told to pull back through the infantry battalions that were supposed to clear the roads to allow them through. The moron who had given the order had failed to realize that the fields on either side were a quagmire. The special flexible steel treads laid in the first hours of the offensive to give the tanks and mechanized troops a footing had by now become twisted masses of useless confetti that clogged the tanks' treads and pierced the truck tires. The commander of the infantry division ahead of him had flatly refused to move his trucks off the highway for Popov's tanks. He had orders to extricate his men and the heavy artillery he was assigned to protect beginning at dawn. To hell with Popov's tanks. On either side of the tank column miles of newly emplaced artillery and rocket batteries continued to fire at a leisurely pace, one shell every two minutes, to use up the ammunition piled high around them.

It was beginning to get light in the East. Within an hour the Chinese reconnaissance aircraft would be able to spot his concentration of men and vehicles, and the mass of artillery to his rear would begin to lay down a carpet of shells. Colonel Popov made his decision. He whispered an order into the microphone and the lead tank ground forward, nudging the first truck gently to the side, lifting and flipping it off the road onto its side.

General Wang Chin sipped pale green tea and studied the infrared television photographs of the battlefield just received from the Chinese Red Star satellite. The Chinese offensive had kicked off at dawn and was already in trouble. The third corps had moved out ahead and drifted across the line of attack of the second. Their tanks were hopelessly entangled and the battlefield was a mass of screaming commanders attempting to extricate their attack columns from the mess. Precious hours had been lost.

General Yamashita's paratroops had met with unexpected success in their attack on the Ussuri bridges. Four spans of pontoons had been knocked out before massive Russian reinforcements had been brought up. Latest reports indicated that Yamashita was dead along with half his force. The remnants were holed up in the small town of Shermetyevo, blocking a major road junction and fighting to the death in the shattered remnants of the town.

Satellite pictures showed that most of the Soviet armor was now clustered along the banks of the Ussuri, waiting for the Soviet engineers to repair the bridges. Massed anti-aircraft artillery and rockets were decimating Chinese air attacks on the bunched armor. The battlefield was a charnel house of blackened vehicles and bodies. Behind the line, squads of Soviet military police were rounding up deserters, shooting commissars and officers who could not explain their absence from their units, and gradually bringing order to the retreating masses of men and vehicles.

Wang Chin stared at the map, his stomach knotting up in frustration. A magnificent opportunity was slipping through his fingers. For a few hours the superb Russian war machine had become a helpless, struggling mass thinking only of flight. And his bumbling commanders had let them escape.

General Vasily Vasilyev stood at attention, telephone in hand. His father-in-law's voice crackled over the field telephone. "What is the situation, Vasily? Your reports from the battlefield are not clear."

Vasilyev controlled the tremor in his voice with an effort of will. Old Kharkov would have his head if he wasn't persuasive. "We are successfully pulling back from the Leninskaya-Vyazemski corridor. There have been losses, Comrade Chairman—heavy losses. But there was no alternative. To have continued the attack would have meant the destruction of our entire tank armies."

Kharkov interrupted him, his brutal voice smashing over the telephone line. "How many tanks have we lost?"

"Five thousand—most of them in the offensive itself. We should soon be able to concentrate fifteen thousand at Vyazemski for an attack on the landing zone at Amgun. We will annihilate the Japanese and end the threat to our rear, Comrade Chairman."

"How many men have you lost?"

Vasilyev hesitated. "Before we finish the withdrawal, our losses will rise to two hundred thousand, Comrade Chairman. It was inevitable that we would suffer, given the rash idiocy of the marshal's plan. We are lucky not to have lost the whole army."

"Vasily, listen to me." Kharkov's voice had lost its bluster. He almost wheedled. "No one must know of those losses. You understand? You must understate them by half. And, Vasily," he said, his voice hardening, "if you expect to survive, you had better be right about your ability to destroy that Japanese bridgehead."

Jean Saracin had his eighth vodka of the day and switched on the tape. His English was good, and most of the conversation at Le Roy Gourmand had been in English, although the American had occasionally switched into Russian to make sure his Soviet counterpart understood the subtlety of what he was saying. The transcript was there, impeccable, as always. But he liked to hear the words, study the intonation. Often, there were startling implications in the way a man said something that could distort the apparent meaning wildly. There was little of that here, although a great deal was left unspoken, as always between two people who understood each other thoroughly.

Unfortunately, there was almost nothing useful. The president would not be happy. He would probably grumble something about needing a twentieth-century Fouché again. Still, it had been a technical tour de force. The taxi driver who had picked up Thompson at the embassy had been one of his men. He had murmured the name of the restaurant into his radio, and the mobile surveillance team had moved into the restaurant well ahead of the two subjects. The bug had been emplaced unobtrusively, the electronic pickup truck parked easily within range, and the team had kept them under visual control throughout. Very professional.

And, of course, there was one interesting possibility on the tape. He picked up the telephone. "Get me the Hotel Drouot—Madame Janine Vaugiraud.

"Madame Vaugiraud?"

"Yes."

"Madame Vaugiraud, my name is Saracin, Jean Saracin. I am the chief . . ."

"Yes, *monsieur*, I am well aware of your position. My husband is not prefect in Marseilles for nothing. What is it you wish?"

"It is an affair of state, *madame*—of the utmost importance to your government and your nation." He liked the nice note of pomposity mingled with threat in his voice. Women could never resist intrigue.

"I don't understand, *monsieur*."

"It concerns your former husband, *madame*. I wonder if I could trouble you to meet with me for a few minutes. A member of my staff is waiting in the lobby of your hotel. I will take very little of your time, *madame*. You will pardon me for not calling on you at your hotel, but you will understand that it is awkward to leave my desk just now." He let the steel show through, enjoying the slight anxiety that must be present at the other end of the line.

"Very well, *monsieur*."

He was surprised at the icy calm of her voice. But, then, he shouldn't have been. He had, after all, read her dossier.

Thompson stared at the remnants of a hamburger, a greasy bag of crumbled potato chips, and the empty beer bottles scattered over the elegant cocktail table. He wasn't used to operating without a staff. Since

Henry's day, the foreign affairs advisor to the president had moved about the world in the manner of a medieval potentate trailed by a horde of courtiers. The big plane with its private bedroom, air force stewards, instant communications, and a dozen staff members, left him free, in theory, to concentrate on the big picture. In reality, it was just another one of the perquisites of the governing elite, an ego trip in lieu of the immense salaries paid by private business.

Still, it was a pain in the ass not having his staff. His own people had learned to dose their servility with frankness and had lost the paralyzing fear that permeated most of the middle echelons of the State Department when he came into view. His carefully cultivated reputation for icy ruthlessness was useful most of the time, but it also got in the way. Without an advance team it had taken an hour longer than necessary to set up the procedures for getting cables and telephone calls to the president, arranging to keep the press at bay once they discovered the conference was meeting, which they inevitably would, and making sure that nobody let him sleep through a crisis because they were afraid to disturb him, as had once happened during the Israeli war.

The system was at fault, of course. It was strange that a country as informal and relaxed as the United States maintained the most constipated foreign service in the world. A mass of hilarious pomp and circumstance surrounded the person of the ambassador, a man with the civil service rank equivalent to a postmaster in a medium-sized city. People leaped to their feet as he entered, murmured "Mr. Ambassador" in reverential tones, and resisted violently any effort to strip the office of its incrustations of baroque ritual. A nation settled by men who refused to uncover in the presence of kings was rapidly being populated by people who genuflected to clerks—and liked it.

The futuristic phone whistled softly. Thompson moved to the large console behind Morgan's desk and contemplated the flashing lights uncertainly before picking it up. "I'm sorry to disturb you, Mr. Thompson, but there is a lady on the line who insists on speaking to you." There was an embarrassed silence. "She says she is your wife."

"Put her on."

"*Bon soir, chéri. Comment ça va?*"

"Hello, Janine. What are you doing in Paris? Your last letter said you were vacationing in Corsica."

"We were, but Herbert was called back, and I got bored. I came up to shop."

"How did you know I was here? Not more than four people in Paris are supposed to be in on it."

She laughed, and Thompson suddenly felt again the pain of the lost years. "Jean Saracin, our own little French Himmler, told me. He wants me to seduce all of America's secrets from you."

"And you said you would?"

"I am a patriotic French woman. What could I say?"

"Where are you?"

"At the Drouot, room twelve. I always stay there when I come to Paris alone. Do you remember, *chéri?*"

"Yes."

Nineteen fifty-four had been a vintage year for despair in France. The defeat at Dienbienphu had very nearly ripped the nation apart, adding to the bitterness and alienation of a French army that felt itself more and more betrayed. Mendez-France became prime minister, ended the war in Indochina, and urged the French to drink milk. They were never to forgive him. The European Defense Community, Europe's last hope at real unity, died in a paroxysm of intra-party wrangling in the French Assembly. In the south more than a hundred people died after a baker used seed grain treated with insect poison to make bread. He was guillotined after confessing he had known the grain was dangerous. And none of it had mattered.

He had sat in the June sun in the cafés immortalized by Hemingway and Miller, drunk dry white wine, and watched the girls go by. After three years in Korea, the city was unreal, its colors artificial, as if painted on a stage. The natural texture of life was mud, and its color a brownish gray. The movement and life of the city sometimes made him dizzy after the quiet immobility of the hospital. A kind of anomie had set in. Years later he had read that men coming out of war resented the quiet and dullness of peace. They missed the intensity and perception that danger and tension brought, and they resented the dull grayness of life without it.

He had taken a room on the Quai Voltaire in the Hotel de Suede, a fourteenth-century building across from the *préfecture de police*. It had five floors, each with three miniature rooms. There was a john on alternate floors and one bath for which you had to pay. The price was two dollars a night. That included breakfast, coffee with the taste and consistency of weak ink, and superb croissants. A young maid brought it each morning, not bothering to knock, entering and edging between the bed and dresser to put the tray on the miniature night table. There was no room for a chair.

Once she had come upon him half awake, an erection lifting the sheet in a comic arc. He had turned quickly on his side, but she had begun to giggle, almost dropping the tray as she circled the bed. Then she was in with him, smelling of coffee grounds, bread crumbs, and stale perfume. It had become a morning ritual that summer. She demanded nothing, accepting his modest presents and offering her body with a friendly joy. To the end of his days the first taste of French breakfast coffee would bring her back to him. Then one morning another maid brought the tray. The manager of the hotel had explained later. Hélène was only fifteen. She had run away from home, a farm in the Perigord. Her father had finally traced her through the Social Security registrations and taken her back. The manager, an émigré Swede married to a sour French woman, had shrugged.

"It will not help. She will wind up a *prostituée*. She has the mentality."

A month later he met Janine.

He had been attending a lecture of the great André Manfried at the Ecole Libre des Sciences Politiques. Manfried was lecturing on American politics of the 1860s. His exposition on the Civil War years was a classic. His uncle had been ambassador to Washington, and he quoted at length from that noble gentleman's dispatches. What he described, and Manfried's own analysis of the events of 1861–65, had the same fascination as a house of mirrors. Reality is there behind the distortion, but impossible to find unless you already know it. At one point the old man, spade beard quivering, located Colorado somewhere on the east bank of the Mississippi. Thompson had grinned broadly, hiding his face quickly behind his hand. You didn't smile in a French professor's class unless the signal had been given.

The girl on his right had shot him a furious glance. When the lecture ended, she had turned to him and, in impeccable, if archaic, slightly British-accented English, proceeded to chew him out.

"If you cannot show common courtesy to one of the towering figures of French scholarship, *monsieur*, I suggest you refrain from attending his class. Your behavior was insolent, insufferable, and boorish."

"But he located Colorado on the east bank of the Mississippi."

"*Et, alors?*" she said, lapsing into French, puzzled.

"It's like," he groped for a sufficiently impressive comparison, "putting Marseilles in Lorraine."

The girl stared at him for a moment and started to giggle. The idea was too ridiculous to contemplate. She had luminous green eyes, and underneath the antique cardigan, tweed skirt, thick rayon stockings, and flat shoes, she seemed to be reasonably attractive. She had agreed to have a coffee with him.

They had fought almost from the first minute. She was viscerally anti-American, pointing out to him his and his country's faults in the haughty accents of the upper-class French with a certainty born of total ignorance.

He didn't argue. He had long since learned that to argue with a woman is to prove that you do not love her, which no doubt accounted for the attraction of the strong, silent male. She lived with an aunt in the upper-class Sixteenth Arrondissement, which considerably complicated the tactical problem of getting her into bed. She had to be home by ten o'clock or the old lady raised holy hell. And despite a verbal adventurousness that bordered on the pornographic, she shied like a skittish horse from allowing herself to be lured up to his room or off on a weekend.

After a month of delightful but sterile fencing, Thompson had begun to grow weary of the game. She was an exotic, fun to fool around with. But she wasn't

297

about to get involved. Then one Sunday afternoon he came to pick her up at her aunt's apartment, an immense, high-ceilinged penthouse on top of a building put up shortly after Hausmann had ruthlessly widened the boulevards of Paris to give the cannon an unrestricted field of fire and make revolution more difficult.

"My aunt had to go to Bordeaux. We've got the apartment to ourselves. I invited Claude and Charles. We can dance and listen to jazz. I bought some of the new Bessie Smith records."

He had groaned inwardly. The French could sit in rapt silence for hours and listen to the Dixieland and Blues he had been born with and long since exchanged for Bix, Charley Parker, and Chopin. Also, he had learned to dislike Charles de la Margerie, whose insolence and veiled insults had begun at their first meeting.

They had gathered in a small study, dipping into a large can of her aunt's caviar, the first Thompson had tasted, and drinking ice-cold Polish vodka from tiny crystal glasses. A cold rain outside turned to sleet, beating against the window to the purple tones of Bessie and the down-home growl of Big Bill Broonzy. Claude and Charles had left early, and Thompson, pleasantly tight, had sat on the floor, back against the ornate sofa, letting the music dig into him. It hadn't been as bad as he'd expected.

"You are drunk, *chéri*," Janine had said, standing over him, frowning, fists on her hips, legs apart. He had reached out, slipped an arm around her knees, and collapsed her onto his lap. She had fought him for a while, halfheartedly, then given in with a sudden reciprocal passion that had taken him by surprise. The next weeks were lost in a haze of happy eroticism. Janine had confronted her aunt at the end of the first week and announced she was moving in with

Thompson. The old lady had raised her eyebrows and shrugged and said she would appreciate it if her niece would make an effort not to become pregnant and keep up appearances by moving back into the apartment when her mother came to Paris.

They had shared his closet-sized room, bathed together in the nineteenth-century tub on the first floor, talked all night in the cafés of the Latin quarter, and made love. Above all, they made love.

Years later, during the bitterness of the divorce, she had turned her green eyes on him, her face suddenly softened. "We should have ended it that spring, *chéri*. Then it would have been perfect. You would have gone back to America, and I would have married my French bourgeois, and we would have taken the lovely unspoiled memories with us to our grave."

19

"Goddamn it, Alec!" Ambassador Samuel Morgan was enraged. "I am the president's personal representative to the French government. You are insufferably rude in not taking me to your meeting with the French president. And I insist that you at least inform me of what comes out of it." He stopped, his jaw hanging loose in frustration.

"Look, Sam," Thompson said, "try to understand. You have no part in this. No ambassador does. That's the way we handle it. The more people who get involved, the more chance there is of a leak. I'll tell you what you need to know, Sam; otherwise, just try to stay out of the way."

"Then I'm nothing but a goddamned messenger boy."

Thompson shrugged. The man was right, of course. Governments had never realized the flexibility the telephone conveyed until the early 1970s when an impatient Henry Kissinger had begun picking it up and talking directly to those of his counterparts who spoke English. At one stroke the paraphernalia of conventional diplomacy had been wiped out. It also eliminated an immense amount of misunderstanding.

Ambassadors, by the very nature of their craft, had to maintain their personal contacts in the country to which they were accredited. A tough, brutal message from Washington was almost invariably weakened, if not in substance, then in tone and by explanations that very often dulled the edge and killed the impact. Almost as bad, reporting to Washington tended to build the ambassador's image and confuse issues. Political officers, only too human, tended to support one party or another because of their own personal predilections, and the self-interest of the United States often was lost in a fog of ideology. Kissinger, with his uncanny instinct for recognizing his and his nation's limits, had once again converted American diplomacy to the art of the possible instead of an instrument propagating the revealed religion of Jeffersonian democracy. And he had done it virtually alone, without the immense, unwieldy apparatus around him.

"Sam, I'm going out to dinner with my ex-wife. I'll let your duty secretary know where I can be reached."

"But, Aloo, what if the president calls?"

"Tell him I'm *à la recherche du temps perdu*."

Gordon Wiseman reread the two page analysis of battle messages. Satellite recordings of battlefield command messages, many in the clear, had finally begun to make a pattern. They made no sense, but the pattern was clear. Attack. Retreat. Attack. It was obviously a prepared strategy, probably to suck the

301

Chinese into a premature reaction. He picked up the phone. "Get me Phil Samsun at the Pentagon, please."

Colonel Alexei Popov's tank column had formed a battle line facing north with the last of its fuel. The tanks were immobile, awaiting the attack. The Chinese heavy artillery barrage had walked over them leaving few casualties, but it was now smashing into the tangled mass of vehicles and men from which he had painfully extricated his column when the order came to return to the front. He was technically under arrest. The commander of the infantry division had ordered him shot when his tanks had begun to clear the road. But that was hardly important now. Somewhere behind him in that chaos was a tanker convoy with diesel oil. If it didn't come up, the Chinese would pick them off like ducks in a pond. The situation was the same up and down the line. Radio lines were filled with desperation calls for ammunition, fuel, and reinforcements. The roads were chaos, and the Chinese artillery had finally awakened. Murderous rocket fire bracketed every crossroads and assembly point.

In the south the Chinese counterattack must have begun. He hoped the fools in the high command had had sense enough to turn some of the tanks around to meet it. That had been the original plan: attack brutally in the north, throwing them off balance; punch through to the river, then wheel, using the reserve armor as the point, and meet the counterattack from the south. It would have worked, too, Popov thought, despite the fact that the Chinese were ready for them. The enemy's inexperience in tank warfare and their inability to deploy rapidly had worked the same as total surprise.

Then those fools in the high command had fucked

it all up. He'd heard that the old marshal was back in command. Maybe now they could depend on somebody knowing what was going on.

"Colonel," the voice said over the radio in a hoarse crackle, "They're beginning to attack."

Popov saw them then—a mass of Chinese infantry moving in a human wave. The anti-tank teams mounted on jeeps carrying wire and radar-guided missiles were embedded in the thick masses of men. Popov turned his glasses to the rear. The Russian infantry, imprisoned in its trucks, had not come up. The tank line was utterly exposed with about five minutes' running time in its tanks. He had been told to stand his ground. No retreat. Somebody had to give the rear time to get untangled and form the front again. Popov closed the tank turret and began shouting orders into the radio. There wasn't much ammunition. There was no point wasting it on the limitless Chinese mass advancing on them. "Fire only on the vehicles."

Vasilyev pored over the satellite photographs of the Japanese landing zone. They represented the controlled chaos of any military operation, but behind the seeming disorganization he could discern the beginnings of a disciplined fighting organization taking shape.

They were pitifully short of tanks, and Soviet air superiority was already established. The Japanese Air Force, superb in quality but hampered by second-rate equipment and low numbers, was no match for the hordes of MIG's with which he was now able to blanket the battlefield.

"Kusarevich," he said, turning to the chief of staff, "we must attack immediately. We cannot wait until the remainder of the tank forces are extricated from the corridor. Form up the tank divisions for an imme-

303

diate drive on Amgun. The chairman is adamant. The Japanese must be destroyed without any further delays."

"General, it can't be done. The men are exhausted. Half the tanks are crippled. Our fuel supply system is in chaos. It will take the military police days to round up stragglers and reform them into fighting units. There is no way we can attack that landing zone in less than a week."

Vasilyev approached his second in command, bloodshot eyes inches from his exhausted subordinate's face. "Kusarevich, you don't understand. For the first time in your career you are being presented with an opportunity." He waved a hand at the battle map. "We must destroy the Japanese, Kusarevich—quickly. Otherwise, this battle will go down in history as one of the worst defeats of Soviet arms since Borodino. We don't have any choice. To retrieve the old man's sanity, we must move and move now, or we will not have another opportunity." He paused dramatically. "I have reason to believe the chairman is on the verge of replacing me."

Kusarevich stared at him. How had he gotten himself into the hands of this vainglorious idiot? Mikulski had been right. Whatever he touched would turn into disaster. "Very well, General. I will form up an army to attack. But I warn you, it may lead to disaster."

"Hello, Janine."

"*Bonsoir*, Alec." She kissed him on the cheek, leaving a whiff of Ma Griffe around him.

"How are you?"

"How am I?" She laughed. "I am forty-six, *chéri*. My behind is spreading. I cannot paint out the lines in my face. I became a grandmother last year. It becomes more and more clear to me that I shall die. And how are you?"

"About the same."

"No, I don't think so. You have power. You are busy. You don't think about yourself so much. That makes it easier. There is a great exhilaration in being powerful and famous, no? No doubt many young women find the combination attractive, although, of course, you don't really need that, *chéri*," she said, taking inventory. "You don't gain weight. You no doubt continue your ridiculous sports. No, you are a decidedly attractive man in the manner of a predatory, if aging, wolf."

"You don't look so bad yourself."

"What are you doing here?" she said, ignoring the remark.

"Your report for Saracin?"

"The man is a despicable fool. Do you know that he threatened Herbert's career if I didn't cooperate? Something about making him a sub-prefect in the Drome."

"What did you say?"

"Well," she said, smiling, "I wasn't sure how much power he had, so I agreed to go out with you even though I pointed out to him how much I loathed you." She reached across the table and put her hand on his, pulling gently at the wiry black hair curling from beneath his cuff. "However, any sacrifice is preferable to the Drome." She glanced around at the restaurant. "My God, you are a sentimentalist, *chéri*. When were we here last?"

"About a century ago." Bofinger's was a nineteenth-century restaurant near the Place de la Bastille that specialized in seafood.

"God, it looks just the same—a joke by Gaudi out of Dali."

"It's a national monument—the purest evocation of Art Nouveau in all France."

"Don't talk of monuments. I'm beginning to feel like one."

She had hardly aged, Thompson thought. A few lines around the luminous green eyes, a few more pounds, which she had needed, anyway, and a certain weariness behind the gaiety.

"How are the boys?"

"Big Alec is still hunched over his piano in Vienna. I only hope he surfaces once in a while to find a girl." Her face hardened. "And your young militarist is still intent on killing himself on that carrier."

"*Plus ça change, plus c'est la même chose,*" he murmured. She had never forgiven him for allowing their younger son to go to Annapolis and become a flyer. Not that he could have done much about it. The boy had been obsessed with planes from the time he was ten years old.

"I am resigned to it. Do you know the statistics? One in ten is killed within the first five years. Another in the next. Four are alive after twenty. What will that girl he married do if he is killed?"

"Janine, it's what he wanted to do. He's not a child anymore."

"You're all children," she said, her voice sharp with bitterness. "As I grow older, I become more and more convinced that men are not serious. They wish to go through life playing games. It must be dramatic. You cannot accept the dullness of reality. So you fight wars and play with dangerous toys."

"Since when did you become a women's liberationist?"

She shook her head, the cloud of dark hair, already graying when he had met her at eighteen, tumbling about her face. "I may be a bitch, Alec, *chéri*, but I am not stupid. If you fight, you fight on your own terms, not those of the enemy. Those poor women have elected to fight you with your weapons on your terrain. Nothing is sillier than that. I have often thought it was a clever plot on the part of the American male to free himself from the pitifully little responsibility he accepts in any case."

"What are you doing these days?"

"I paint when I have the time. And I still do ceramics, although the competition from the young ones is ferocious. I have a show in a month, which is why I am here. But I have no time—the prefect's wife, you know," she said. "I must go to all the stupid public functions and waste my time making polite conversation. Still, it is nice as one grows older to have the young ones being servile."

"Lovers?"

She raised her eyebrows. "That is hardly your affair, *chéri*. But since you ask, no. It is too tiring. Also, I find men depressingly the same as I grow older—except you, of course, Aloo. You were always an original."

He suppressed a smile, remembering the times during their marriage when for no apparent reason he had suddenly found himself engulfed in a soft cocoon of affection, flattery, and sensuality. It had been a decade before he realized that invariably this sudden abnormal outpouring had been followed at the strategic moment by some special demand usually involving money. He had once told her she didn't really need to go through such elaborate charades. Why not just ask? There had been a memorable fight, and she had not spoken for days.

"Stop looking so insufferably self-satisfied," she said. "After all, we are not married, *chéri*. One can afford a few weaknesses when one knows that nobody will be there to take advantage of them the next day."

"Love, marriage, and sex defined as war," he said, grinning at her across the table. "Even you never really believed it."

"No. But you must admit we had fun."

"While it lasted."

She shrugged. "Nothing is forever, *chéri*. What are you going to feed me?"

He ate his second heavy French meal of the day, wishing it were hamburger, and listened to a marvelously comic description of a day in the life of a French provincial governor.

Over coffee she turned serious. "What am I going to tell Saracin, that *bon-marché* Fouché?"

"What does he want to know? It's no secret why I'm here. Christ, spooks are all the same. They keep looking under rugs when it's all on the table. I have no secrets, Janine. Tomorrow Europe is going to be carved up, and we're not invited to the feast. We'll have a look at what happens and decide what we can and will do."

"You don't sound very happy. Is your career going badly? All I read about you is what a tough, clever diplomat you are."

"The press," he said with amusement. "Newspapermen are probably the most vain breed alive. You stroke their preening little egos once in a while and they're in your pocket. Henry knew that better than anybody. He must have given more 'confidential' briefings in eight years than all the other secretaries of state in history. And in not one of them did he give out anything that any halfway decent newsman couldn't have figured out on his own."

"And you do the same thing."

"I try." He glanced at his watch. "Are you going to sleep with me?"

Her eyebrows arched in a frown. "I haven't decided. I'd like to, of course, but I wonder if it's worth the complications."

Later, in the little room at the Hotel Drouot, he ran his hand down the velvety skin of her back, pulling her back from sleep.

"Umm, yes, *chéri?*" she said.

"Know something?"

"What?" she asked, giggling, knowing what was coming.

"You're still not a bad lay."

"Neither are you."

The president of France received him in a small office in his private rooms at the presidential palace. Although approaching sixty, he looked ten years younger, his spare athletic frame superbly draped by the best tailor in Paris. He extended his hand and greeted Thompson in his elegant, upper-class French. "Delighted to see you. And how is the president?"

"Concerned. He sends his regrets at not being able to attend. He felt sure you would understand."

The Frenchman nodded. "I do, completely. But I'm not sure that I agree. It's always unpleasant to be confronted with a fait accompli over which one has no control. But in this instance, I think his presence might have given us some leverage in guiding events. Without him . . . He shrugged, holding his hands out, palms up. "I am under no illusion and neither is Harold that we can have a decisive influence on what either the Russians or the Germans do. It is a very bitter time, Monsieur Thompson. I must tell you that the carelessness of your military in allowing seven thousand atomic warheads to fall into the hands of

309

that man Beck is utterly unforgivable. It is the kind of historical accident that simply should not be allowed."

"The question is, what are we going to do now?"

"It depends on what the Soviet Union and Germany have in mind. I assume that Beck and Kharkov have come to some sort of agreement on the division of Eastern Europe into spheres of influence. We are probably helpless to prevent this. Only the threat of a nuclear holocaust by the United States would make them pull back, and that is not credible. Nobody believes you would commit suicide over Eastern Europe."

"What are the long-term German goals?"

The Frechman shrugged. "Hegemony in Western Europe. Even disunited, Germany was by far the most powerful economic unit. Now, joined and with atomic weapons, it bestrides the Continent in just the way we have attempted to prevent it from doing since the days of Frederick the Great. I am a realist, Monsieur Thompson. I know when I have lost. And, believe me, any hopes France ever had of playing a decisive role on the Continent—let us not even speak of the world—are finished. We are finally, irrevocably, a second-class power. My foreign office is feverishly developing plans for a military rapprochement with the Soviet Union, the classic maneuver in the face of Prussian resurgence. I think it is a foolish and perhaps dangerous idea."

"You don't think the Soviet Union is interested?"

"Interested, perhaps, but too realistic to take it seriously. If we attempted such a demarche, we would alienate the Germans irrevocably without giving ourselves any but an illusory protection. No, I fear we have no choice but to acquiesce in whatever we are being offered—unless, of course, you have other suggestions."

"No, although the situation in the Far East looks more promising than it did two days ago."

"You mean the apparent Chinese victory?"

"Yes."

"Something very odd is certainly going on. There are even some indications of dissension in the Politburo. But I don't believe the Russians will allow themselves to be distracted by internal upheavals at a time like this. Kharkov has undoubtedly made some very serious mistakes for which he will eventually pay, but not now. I don't think we had better bank on anything like that."

Thompson suppressed a yawn. He hadn't expected much from the Frenchman, but the man's passivity was disconcerting. He had obviously decided to make his peace with the Germans at virtually any cost. It was obvious that he had discounted any American power to move events in Europe.

The conference opened at two-thirty in the afternoon in a small château on the outskirts of Paris used by the French government for secret meetings. The principals sat in no apparent order of precedence around a hollow oblong table. Their advisors and Alec Thompson lined the wall in chairs carefully placed to avoid damaging the priceless Chinese wallpaper. Kharkov and Beck sat together at one of the narrow ends facing the French president, and the lesser powers were scattered on either side.

The slender Frenchman cleared his throat, glanced at the bank of simultaneous translators in a cramped glass booth, and opened the meeting. "Gentlemen, this conference is, to say the least, unusual. France has been asked to host the meeting by the governments of the Soviet Union and the United German Federal Republic. I assume their purpose is to reassure us as to their future intentions, given the radical revisions that have taken place in recent days. Before turning the meeting over to them, however, I would like to make several points. First, France, better than most countries seated at this table today, has reason to know the consequences of national arrogance. Power, used brutally and without consideration for one's neighbors, becomes a political poison that more often than not leads to the sickness and destruction of the one who uses it. Far better the wisdom of restraint in strength which, historically, is more likely to lead to lasting and peaceful settlements. Second, it is with great regret that I note the absence of the president of the United States. This great power cannot be excluded from any major settlement in Europe today. Its leaders have called for a ceasefire in the war raging now between the Soviet Union and China and a major world conference, to be held as quickly as possible in Geneva to settle outstanding differences and, above all, avoid the danger of a nuclear holocaust in which virtually the entire human race would perish. I wish to associate myself, my government, and my nation with this call for peace." He paused. "General Secretary Kharkov has asked for the privilege of opening the conference."

The Russian, his big peasant hands clasped tightly in front of him, nodded to the Frenchman across the empty space between them. "Thank you, Mr. President, I will try not to waste your time. My nation is at war with a brutal and unprovoked aggressor. I must return at once to direct its efforts. This meeting was called to announce to you certain painful decisions that the unilateral reunification of Germany made necessary. I will not conceal from you the unhappiness of my government at the treacherous actions by the governments of East and West Germany that resulted in a breach of all postwar agreements and in a criminal abrogation of solemn commitments."

Beck turned angrily and opened his mouth to speak, but Kharkov plowed on, his big body tense with concentration. "However, we in the Soviet Union are realists. The betrayal of trust by my former socialist colleagues in East Germany was a bitter blow. But it was not totally unexpected. Our great wartime leader, Josef Stalin, warned in 1945: 'Once a German, always a German.' This anachronistic nationalism is a part of the German character, and we have always accepted it. We accept it now, since the only alternative is that nuclear holocaust of which the French president spoke so eloquently. However," Kharkov said, looking up and searching the table for Wozniakowski, directing at the Pole a look of venomous hatred, "there were others involved in this action for whom the Soviet Union is unable to find any excuse, either in history or in politics. The socialist government of Poland, for so many years protected and aided by its brother Slavs in the Soviet Union against the German threat, turned upon us with treachery and cowardice when we were under attack in the East. They stabbed us in the back like common criminals, endangering the very existence of our nation at a time of great danger." Kharkov paused and took a sip of the mineral water in front of him.

"I wish to emphasize here today that the Soviet Union has always held toward the Polish nation the most sympathetic and brotherly feelings. This nation has suffered greatly in history. It was reconstituted following World Wars One and Two only with Soviet aid and assistance. Its destruction was solely due to the perfidy and treachery of its German neighbors.

This makes its recent actions in combining with Germany against us even more incomprehensible. My government has decided that Poland has, by its lack of faith and its perfidious actions, forfeited its right to exist as a nation." Kharkov leaned back in his straight-backed chair as exclamations broke out around the table. The French president hammered a gavel for silence. Kharkov resumed.

"We have come to this conclusion in concert with the government of the United German Federal Republic with which we have agreed to a peaceful partition of the Polish nation." Kharkov gestured to an aide, who unveiled a map stand behind him. "The lines of division will be as indicated on this map. This decision was arrived at with the greatest reluctance by both the Germans and us. However, it was agreed that an independent Poland attempting to play one of us against the other was a danger to world peace that could not be allowed to continue."

The Russian turned to Wozniakowski.

"I speak now to my former comrade who, although he has betrayed me, is still the leader of a great people whom the Soviet Union does not wish to see destroyed. German and Soviet troops will cross their frontiers in six hours' time. Any resistance is futile and will be mercilessly crushed. I say to my former comrade, save your nation, give orders immediately for the surrender."

Wozniakowski had risen from the table, his face an ashen mask. "I address myself to President Beck. Is your government in accord with these statements?"

Beck left off the compulsive doodling that had covered the lined pad in front of him with tanks and planes. "I have no choice, Georg," he said, spreading his hands. "They would have attacked you no matter what we did. It would have meant our destruction

314

as well. I cannot allow all of Silesia and parts of East Prussia to be lost to Germany forever. You must understand. There is no choice. I can assure you that your people in the area taken over by Germany will have complete autonomy."

Wozniakowski gathered up the papers in front of him and passed them back to an aide. "Very well, gentlemen. But I must tell you now, I will not advise my nation to surrender. Poland will fight as it has always fought every attempt to destroy it. And I can assure you, gentlemen, that if defeated it will rise once again when the amoral aggressors are defeated." He turned to the French president. "You will excuse me, but I must return to my country immediately."

Kharkov cleared his throat as Wozniakowski left. "If I may continue, the situation in Eastern Europe is irrevocably altered by the illegal reunification of Germany. We are faced with an impossible situation in which competition for the goodwill and allegiance of the small countries between us can only lead to the danger of war. We must be realistic. A border must be established firmly at this time to reduce the danger of ambiguity and the possibility of war. In the interests of a just and lasting peace in Central Europe, it has been decided by the United German Federal Republic and the Soviet Union that the nations of Bulgaria, Rumania, and Hungary will be permanently within the Soviet sphere of influence." He looked up, seeking out the leaders of the three nations around the table. "This means, comrades, that your governments will be adjusted immediately to take this reality into consideration. The unnatural nation of Czechoslovakia, established artificially by fiat following World War One and a serious threat to peace ever since, will cease to exist. Slovakia will become a province of the Soviet Union. The Czech portion of this nation will be annexed to the new United German Federal Republic with proper safeguards to protect its language and culture, as in the case of Poland."

Kharkov stopped and looked around the table once again. "This is a final solution. There is no longer room on the European continent for small powers that continually cause tensions by their pretensions and increase the possibility of a major war in which we would all die. These decisions have been made in the interests of the peace and security of us all. I hope they will meet with your approval. If they do not . . ." He shrugged, letting the sentence die.

The French president hammered his gavel, gradually restoring order around the big table. "Are we to understand that this decision is final and irrevocable? You are not here to discuss, but to announce?"

"That is correct."

"You associate yourself with the general secretary's statement, Monsieur Beck?"

"Reluctantly, Mr. President. I see no alternative. The present situation is totally unacceptable to the Soviet Union. If we do not associate ourselves with this decision, it could mean nuclear war. None of us wants that. I regret deeply the necessity for Germany to violate the territory of two of its friendly neighbors. But, given the situation, I see no alternative."

The French president glanced across at Thompson, slumped in his chair, legs extended. "It is highly irregular, but we have among us a representative of the American president. Is it possible, Mr. Thompson, that you have a message?"

Thompson stood up. "No, I have no message. I am certain that the United States government will not, however, accept the naked aggression of two powerful nations against their helpless small neighbors. It is a return to the law of the jungle in world politics that can lead to the destruction of us all."

Kharkov broke in. "What has happened here today is a direct result of the indecision and irresponsibility of the United States: your carelessness in Germany; your indecision in the Far East. Tell your president, Mr. Thompson, that a nation that refuses to face its responsibilities will not long remain a world power." The Russian stood up. "I must now return to my country."

20

General Wang Chin bent over the radio receiver in his central operations room and listened to the excited voice of the Second Army commander. "We have linked up with the northern sector. The Russians are retreating on either side of us in the corridor. More than a hundred thousand prisoners have been taken. The Soviet tanks are without fuel. The crews are abandoning them and fleeing. It is victory, Comrade General, victory for our great nation over the foreign devils."

"Control yourself, General. You see only a portion of the battle. The Soviet Army has lost less than twenty percent of its effective strength. Most of its tanks have already recrossed the Amur and Ussuri rivers and are reforming in defensive formations. Our bridgehead at Khabarovsk was finally destroyed this morning. It cost us more than two hundred fifty thousand men. Do not be rash. Re-form your divisions and wheel in the direction of Leninskaya. Attempt to destroy as many of the Russian stragglers as possible, but under no conditions are you to cross the Amur. The Third Army will wheel right and move to the Ussuri, where it will form a defensive line."

"But what of the Japanese, General? We must pursue across the Ussuri River or the Japanese bridgehead will be destroyed."

"Follow your orders, General." Wang Chin shut off the phone and moved back to his inner office. Lieu would have to be told. They were in no condition to aid the Japanese, who were preparing to move off the beaches. His fuel was exhausted and ammunition was dangerously low. The Russian Air Force had driven his planes from the sky. The artillery and rocket barrages had won the battle, but in the process they had used virtually every shell available. Masses of trucks were moving up with replacements, but by the time they arrived the Soviet armies would have reformed behind the river barriers and any offensive would be suicide.

"We must surrender, Georg," General Daniel Lulienski said. "If we don't, there will be a slaughter. We have less than four hundred thousand men against two million. It is hopeless."

Wozniakowski shook his head. "If we surrender, history will consign us to the garbage dump along with all the other spineless peoples of history, Daniel. We must fight, even if it means the destruction of Warsaw. The people must carry down to defeat the knowledge that we did not submit like sheep the way the Czechs have already agreed to do. Only with the memory of martyrdom will they have the moral strength to resist in the future."

"The Czechs have surrendered?"

"Yes. My message to the Czech government suggesting joint action has been rejected. German and Russian armies are already marching in to take over. We will be completely surrounded, Daniel."

The general moved to the telephone. "Then I must change the troop dispositions. We are almost completely defenseless to the south. It is 1939 all over again."

Wozniakowski turned to an aide. "Get me the cardinal, and call a meeting of the Politburo immediately. Arrange for a television appearance in place of the regular evening broadcast. The cardinal will join me. The people will have to be warned. Also, arrange for emergency food rations to be delivered to the special depots and for the children to be evacuated from the cities according to the war plan."

Colonel Alexei Popov was dying. His shattered tank, one tread ripped from its wheels, lay skewed across the dirt road, its 120-mm gun pointing upward in an impotent erection. He lay across the gunner's lifeless back, unable to move. The Chinese heavy rocket had scored a direct hit, penetrating the armor and exploding inside the body of the tank. He had been in the open turret surveying the battle, and the force of the explosion had turned his legs into a pulpy mass of bone and muscle.

When he had regained consciousness he heard the Chinese troops flowing around the crippled tank, chattering excitedly as the sounds of the battle receded. He had called out once, but his voice was too weak to penetrate the iron cocoon of the tank. Now he was alone with only the toy-like pop of distant guns to break the silence. The pain was unbearable. He could no longer control the tears streaming down his cheeks. In a last effort of will, he disengaged the grenade from the dead gunner's belt, hesitated a moment, then pulled the pin.

General Fabian von und zu Feiersdorf strode into the general staff bunker grinning broadly. "At ease, gentlemen. This meeting is a mere formality. You all know the order of battle." They gathered around him at the battle map spread on the long trestle table. "Manteuffel will force the Oder here at Frankfurt and lead the thrust on Posen. Hugo, you will cross at Goerlitz and make for Breslau. Von Wittsleben will attack through Ostrava as soon as his army is in position. I don't need to stress the need for speed. We have an agreement with the Soviet Union, and we will abide by it scrupulously, gentlemen. But I am not so sure that they will. You must reach the agreed line of demarcation with all the speed you can make." He looked up from the map and surveyed his officers. "We are winning today, gentlemen, the victory that was denied us in World Wars One and Two. The German nation will finally, thanks to its soldiers, occupy the place in Europe and the world that it deserves by virtue of its courage, energy, and dynamism."

The electronic clock on the shelf behind the president's desk bleeped a hollow chime. It was midnight. A mass of intelligence reports was scattered over the cocktail table and on the floor around it. Gordon Wiseman, Thompson, and General Phillip Samsun nursed large mugs of coffee as the president stalked back and forth across the room. "Goddamn it, Alec, there has to be something we can do. We just can't sit here and let them be raped. Look at that." He gestured toward a map of Poland, heavy grease-pencil marks indicating the lines of the German and Soviet attacks. "They've stopped the Russian thrust cold at

Brest. And at Przemysl they're counterattacking. Do you hear? Counterattacking! Against troops that must outnumber them three or four to one."

Samsun cleared his throat. "The Germans have overrun the First Polish Army around Gorzow. They'll be in Posen by tomorrow. The two southern columns are also moving rapidly. It can't last long, no matter what they do against the Soviets."

The president stared at him, his heavy face contorted with fury. "Goddamn you, Samsun, you sound as if you want the Krauts to win. I'm sick and tired of the way you and the rest of the goddamned generals keep making excuses for the Germans. They're tearing the guts out of an innocent country in concert with the Soviets. Don't you understand that? What the hell makes you think they'll stop there? What makes you think France, Italy, and Britain won't be next?"

There was a tense silence in the room as the big man stopped pacing and stared down at them. Thompson finally put his cup down and met the angry stare.

"We all understand, Mr. President. But there is nothing we can do about it. Poland is a tragedy. Nobody denies it. But its destruction doesn't alter the balance of power in Europe. Our vital interests are not affected. It just cleans up a messy situation in Central Europe that would have caused unending problems for the Russians and the Germans if Poland were allowed an independent existence. Neither one could afford for it to become the satellite of the other. The real estate is too strategic. Splitting it up has been the only viable solution for two hundred years. It's a historical imperative."

The president glared down at him, jaw loose, before recovering. "You know something, Thompson, I've been listening to you and your fucking historical imperatives for years, while American power has gradually dribbled away like an old man's piss. It just may be that there are some moral imperatives that take precedence over the neat, surgical little world of geopolitics that you find so elegant and inevitable. The only advice I seem to get from you anymore is to accept the inevitable. And the inevitable always seems to be an American defeat."

Thompson stood up and faced him, nursing the big coffee mug in both hands. "You get my honest opinion. When you don't think it's worth listening to, you can tell me to shut up or get another advisor, Mr. President. But as long as I'm in the job, I don't intend to take anything off of what I say just to please you. There has been no American defeat in any of the events of the last ten days. Two of our most powerful opponents have fought a major war, and the more powerful of the two seems to be bleeding badly. In Europe a situation that existed in all but name has been legitimized. Germany has been the dominant power on the Continent for more than a decade. Its frustration at not having that recognized was building to a dangerous point of tension. What happened was inevitable and probably a hell of a lot less damaging to our interests for having happened now rather than later."

"Our interests? What the hell are our interests? We seem to be an impotent old man playing with himself while the world burns down around him."

Thompson shrugged. "You became president at a time when American power was in decline. It was never as great as we imagined it to be, and it began to erode as early as the 1960s when phenomena such as Castro and the Vietnam war escaped our control. The SALT talks marked the end of our nuclear predominance. The economic dislocations of the 1970s ended our economic hegemony. By the time you took over we were first among equals, no more."

"And now we're sucking hind tit."

Thompson put down the coffee mug and faced him again. "No Americans are dead, Mr. President, if you except a few soldiers in that Berlin garrison. None of our vital interests has suffered. The German-Soviet cooperation we're seeing is transitory. When this is over, they'll be enemies. The same is true of the Chinese and the Russians. We have no fundamental quarrel with any of these powers. If we're shrewd and keep our nerve, we can become the balance wheel of the postwar settlement. What we're seeing is the breakup of the post-World War Two condominium that we dominated more or less by the accident of having emerged from the war as the greatest economic power of our time and because of the anomaly of the atomic bomb and the transient superiority it gave us. If we're clever enough, we can also dominate it."

"And just how do you propose doing it?"

"The way it has always been done—by being smarter. Metternich used Austria, a second-rate power in his day, as a fulcrum to control the destiny of Europe for almost half a century. Bismarck, the leader of Prussia, another relatively weak power, took over from him. They didn't do it with overwhelming power. They did it by recognizing and using their allies' and enemies' strengths and weaknesses. The days when we could dominate by raw economic and military power are gone. They've been gone for a decade, but history is a slow learner. Only now has it become apparent."

"And what do we do now?"

"It depends on how this war in Asia resolves itself.

If Phil and Gordon are right and the Russians have suffered a major defeat, then it may be in our best self-interest to work to contain this new Chinese-Japanese alliance. I'm not sure it isn't, anyway. The power potential of Japanese industry in conjunction with the raw materials and manpower of the Chinese mainland is awesome. But there is no hurry. We can wait until the war resolves itself before we move."

"And what would that move be?"

"You've called for a conference in Geneva. Once we're all seated around that table, the trading will begin. The world is going to be divided up into spheres of influence. We'll have a major say in just how it's divided."

"Well, I hope you're right, Alec. I hope you're right."

Vasilyev watched the battle from a log bunker above the ruins of the coastal city of Amgun. The attack had caught the Japanese by surprise as they moved out of the landing zone. Great masses of tanks followed by hordes of infantry still exhausted from the battles in the Leninskaya Vyzomski salient had thrown themselves into the Japanese columns. Kusarevich had described it as a tribal assault rather than a military exercise. But luck and numbers had been with them. The Japanese had reeled back under the impact of the first blow and managed to set up a defensive perimeter around the beachhead only because of the disorder of the Russian forces.

Then Amgun had become a killing ground. Soviet heavy artillery dominated the heights, and swarms of MIG's blackened the sky. The Japanese Navy littered the shallow harbor, charred evidence of its gallantry in attempting to bring off a portion of the trapped invasion force.

"General," said a grimy-faced infantry major who stood at attention at the entrance to the bunker.

"Yes?"

"A message from the Japanese commander. He wishes to discuss surrender terms."

Mr. Thompson." Jane Cleveland shook him gently. "Seven o'clock." She handed him a big mug of coffee.

"Thanks, Jane. What day is it?" He had not bothered to go home. The last meeting had ended at four A.M. The president had offered him a bedroom upstairs, but he had preferred the couch.

The secretary smiled. "Friday. Must be Washington, huh?"

"Yeah. Let's see what Suzanne has to say about the world." Jane Cleveland flicked on the center television set as Thompson fumbled in his drawer for an electric razor. "Have I got a clean shirt kicking around?"

"I think there is one left," the woman said, moving to a cabinet on one wall and bringing out a neatly laundered blue shirt. "It doesn't fit your tie, but what the hell."

"Thanks, Jane," Thompson said, taking another sip of coffee, trying to wash the furry taste out of his mouth.

Suzanne's cool image flickered on the screen.

"Good morning. The situation around the world today is increasingly grim. In the Far East the Sino-Soviet conflict seems to have resulted in a bloody stalemate. Latest reports indicate that the Soviet armies have been thrown back behind the Amur and Ussuri river boundaries with great losses of men and materiel. The Chinese bridgehead at Khabarovsk has been wiped out, and the survivors of the Japanese invasion force have surrendered at Amgun. Soviet and

Chinese leaders are rumored to be meeting in Djakarta to arrange the details of a ceasefire along the entire line.

"Western military experts have evaluated the battle as a standoff, although Sino-Japanese losses in men and materiel were probably larger than those of the Soviets. It is the consensus of these experts, however, that the campaign represents only the most serious of a series of incidents over the past fifteen years and that permanent peace along the Sino-Soviet border is unlikely to result from it.

"In Europe, Czechoslovakia has capitulated and has been occupied by Soviet and German troops along the agreed demarcation line. In Poland, the gallant Polish Army, with most of its forces concentrated on the Soviet frontier, has put up a surprisingly strong fight. Initial Soviet attacks have been repulsed, and there are even reports of successful counterattacks. However, in the West, three German columns have ripped through the lightly defended frontier areas and are approaching the Polish cities of Wroclaw and Poznan.

"The president has once again called for a ceasefire in place and a peace conference of all the major powers in Geneva. So far there have been no replies to his plea for an end to the fighting. The secretary general of the U.N., José Lerin, has polled the U.N. Security Council members, requesting a meeting of the Council, but both the Soviets and the Chinese have refused to attend.

"In Europe, both the French and British prime ministers have associated themselves with the president's call for a conference. The leaders of Brazil, Nigeria, and Australia have also joined in the demand that a ceasefire in place be negotiated immediately.

"Meanwhile, in Bangladesh, another major flood struck the delta yesterday, killing an estimated twenty-thousand people and leaving more than a million homeless. The government in Dacca has called for a worldwide relief effort."

Thompson punched a button, and as the image dissolved, Gordon Wiseman came through the door, yawning. "Hello, Alec. Heard the latest?"

"Which one?"

"You know the Germans have been having a little trouble coordinating their joint air forces, what with the East Germans flying MIG-27's and the West Germans with their F-18's."

"What happened?"

"The Poles painted German markings on their MIG's and sent just about their whole air force over Germany. Before anybody could figure out what was going on, they'd shot up about a hundred fifty planes on the ground."

"Jesus!" Thompson expelled his breath.

"Serves the sons-of-bitches right," Wiseman said. "But that's not the worst of it. Everybody got jittery and for about ten hours the West German Air Force was shooting down any MIG they saw—including dozens of East German planes. Beautiful."

"What are they doing now?"

"The MIGs are grounded," Wiseman said. "It won't matter, of course. The Germans will be in Warsaw tomorrow."

"What about the Russians? Are they still stalled?"

Wiseman shook his head. "No. They finally broke through at Brest. They put out long flanking movements, which the Poles just didn't have the horses to counter. It was inevitable. The front in the South is collapsing. We hear they'll surrender soon to save Warsaw."

Lucy Stein came in and handed Wiseman a note. He read it quickly and handed it on to Thompson.

"They've destroyed Warsaw—more than a thousand Russian planes using a combination of explosives and fire bombs. The place is an inferno."

Thompson stared at the piece of paper and had difficulty breathing. "What in God's name for, Gordon?"

The intelligence chief shrugged. "Punishment, I guess. The Soviets feel betrayed. An effort to destroy the capital so it will be easier to control the people later. You know how it works with them. Get the center. Kill or neutralize the intellectuals. Instill terror. One man with a machine gun and the will to use it can control a hundred who are defenseless. Why are you surprised?"

"They've guaranteed the hatred of the Polish people for the next hundred years."

"Alec, you're still a romantic. It doesn't matter. This isn't the nineteenth century, when revolutions were started by a few people with pistols and a willingness to die. The world is being recolonized. It was inevitable. Poland is just one of the first victims. Mark my words. Over the next couple of decades everybody is going to have to choose up sides. There aren't going to be any nonaligned countries anymore. The power centers are forming up: the United States and the Western Hemisphere; Germany and Europe; the Soviet Union and the Sino-Japanese conglomerate. Any nation that expects to survive is going to have to join one of the groupings. There isn't any other way."

The president's buzzer sounded and Thompson heaved himself out of his chair. It was going to be a long day.

Lieu Shen drank the bitter green tea in small, delicate sips as he read the reports from the front. Victory had been within their grasp, but the Chinese generals had been too inexperienced in the handling of large masses of troops to take advantage of the opportunity. Even so, the results were gratifying. The Russians had lost more than three hundred thousand troops, a bloodletting they would not soon forget. It was true that Chinese losses in men had been even greater, but that was of no importance. A nation of eight hundred million could afford a pinprick, but the Soviet Union could not stand many more wounds such as this one.

It was a pity that Teng would not be able to savor the result. He had suffered a stroke and fallen into a terminal coma during the night. He would have been disappointed, of course. They had hoped to win it all in one quick move. As it was, they would have to be patient. Already Wang Chin was preparing the next attack. It would come in one year, two at the most. And once again the Russians would be forced to bleed. And they would finally realize, as the Americans had in Vietnam, that there would be no end to it.

There was only one problem. With Teng dead, Lieu Shen was the only one left to complete the victory. Fortunately, the pain had diminished over the past days. Perhaps the organism still had enough control to stave off the inevitable. Or perhaps the drugs were finally beginning to work more effectively. In any case, he was grateful for the remission. Now, more than at any other time, he needed that ability to concentrate totally, that ferocity of will that had brought him through all the bad times.

Because now the danger was greatest. Now, on the verge of victory, they could still lose it all.

"Georg, we must surrender. There is no hope. It is a senseless slaughter. We have proved our point. Now we must stop." General Witold Lulienski, his face dark with a two-day beard, watched the general secretary of the Polish Communist Party across a table filled with war maps in the concrete bunker of the army general staff. Above them the Polish capital was a smoking ruin.

"Yes." Wozniakowki's whole body seemed warped, as if a distortion in the bone structure had twisted him off center. Tears were streaming down his cheeks. "Witold, I have destroyed Poland. This time the dream is dead. They will wipe us off the face of the earth."

"That is what every generation that witnessed a Polish disaster thought, Georg. But each time we have risen to defeat them. We will again. The people are with you."

Wozniakowski pulled himself together. "We must pull the armies in the East across the river into the German zone. I have a message from Beck. He promises to be generous and warns that Kharkov will send his prisoners to Siberia."

"Yes, I know. I have ordered the Western armies to surrender at midnight. The Germans will open their lines to us. In the East we will continue a fighting retreat and pull the armies back into the German zone. The highways are already clogged with refugees. You must surrender yourself to Beck tomorrow, Georg."

The Pole shook his head. "No, Witold, not to Beck. I have sent a message to Kharkov. It is to him I will surrender."

Pruitt was briefing as Thompson entered the Oval Office. The president nodded curtly and turned back to listen as the paunchy general moved his pointer across the map. "It's over—this round, anyway. A

Mexican standoff, if ever there was one. But there's no question that the Soviets suffered the most—not in men, maybe, but in their gut they know they lost."

"Why, General? Why have they lost? Seems to me they bloodied the Chinese badly and have crippled the Japanese Army for several years."

"True, Mr. President, but I can only cite you the old joke about a Russian-Chinese war."

"Which one is that?"

Pruitt grinned. "The Russians attack. On the first day they capture two million Chinese. On the second day they capture ten million. On the third day fifty million." The general stopped.

The president frowned. "What's the joke?"

"On the fourth day the Russians surrender."

The president nodded. "Okay, I take your point. The Chinese can accept losses of this magnitude indefinitely. They may even regard them as a way of reducing population pressures. But the Soviets can't. What is their option, Pruitt?"

The general shrugged. "I'm not sure they have one. A nuclear attack is out of the question, since the Chinese have developed a response capability that would take out the major Soviet population centers. It's a grim prospect: another Vietnam war along a seven-thousand-kilometer border . . . only much more bloody and massive with a power that outnumbers them four to one." He shook his head. "I don't see a way out."

"When do you foresee the next round?"

Pruitt shook his head. "Hard to say. The Chinese never act according to norms we can forecast. But it will come. And the Russians know it."

"Do you agree, Alec?" the president asked, turning once again to Thompson.

"Yes. It's going to be a fuse point for the forseeable

future. The Chinese won't drop their demands, and the Soviets can't concede to them. It's something we've been living with for two decades already, and we'll just have to keep living with it."

The president's mouth tightened into a thin, hard line. "Goddamn it, Alec, every time we talk lately, that seems to be your favorite line: 'We've got to live with it.' Well, maybe we don't have to live with everything. Maybe the power of this country can be brought to bear in such a way as to come up with some solutions to problems. I'm getting a little sick of being a spectator."

Thompson sipped coffee from the large White House mug, trying without much success to control the tremor in his hand. "When you came in, as president you said you wanted to diminish the American presence in the world and draw back from responsibilities that you felt we no longer had the power to sustain. You wanted to cut our losses and maintain those power points that were essential to our interests but avoid getting involved in peripheral conflicts such as Vietnam or Angola. You wanted to concentrate on strengthening the country internally—rebuilding the economy, instituting an equitable tax system, curbing crime, cleaning up the environment, health care, aid to education. Well, Mr. President, you succeeded. Nobody questions that you've done a magnificent job. Your successor is going to inherit a country with more unity and with more people getting a fair share of the goodies than during any period in history."

"I know all that, Alec," the president said. "We're talking about foreign policy."

"So am I," Thompson said. "You took the resources you could have put into guns and used them for butter. Now, when you need the guns to back up a more aggressive foreign policy, they're not there. Make no mistake, Mr. President, you make foreign policy with guns, not words."

"Good evening. This is Suzanne Wilson with today's news. It has been ten days since a ceasefire along the Amur-Ussuri riverfront ended the Sino-Soviet war in Siberia. The peace conference called by the president to end this war and redraw the map of Europe opened in Geneva today with all the major world powers in attendance. The Soviet Union, in its opening statement, has demanded an undertaking by the Chinese government that no further attacks will occur along the Asian frontier. Chinese Premier Lieu Shen in his reply reiterated his demand that the Soviet Union return the territory taken from China by fraud and force over the past three hundred years.

"Meanwhile, the partition of Poland and Czechoslovakia was formally ratified at a meeting between Soviet and German leaders in Geneva just prior to the opening of the conference. The United States, France, and Britain have protested what the president described as this 'illegal and high-handed action' but diplomatic sources in Geneva believe the protests are pro forma.

"And, now, before going on with the evening news, here is Willoughby G. Pepperdine with an analysis of the international situation."

"Good evening. What is happening in Geneva today is the culmination of more than twenty years of the erosion of American power. In retrospect it is easy to see that it all began with the unsuccessful invasion of Cuba in 1961. That failure signaled to the world that the American thrust for power had reached flood tide and had begun to ebb. The fiasco in Vietnam—our unwillingness to play the ruthless role there that our position as a world power demanded—inevitably led to a weakening at the seams in the fabric of world power. As nineteenth-century Austrian historian and political scientist Oswald Schlumberger put it so succinctly: 'A power unused atrophies.'

"We, in the United States, led by men of small vision and less intelligence, never grasped the geopolitical reality that a nation either rules or is ruled. We were unwilling to understand, because it was an unpleasant reality, that any great power, if it is to survive, must continually involve itself in dirty, nasty little wars and soiled backstairs intrigues to replace hostile regimes with those that support our goals. We were too squeamish to support the dictators and semi-criminal leaders who would have helped us perpetuate our power. In a battle with a ruthless and utterly cynical enemy, we retreated into pious platitudes and the morality of Sunday school class.

"Our self-indulgence and unwillingness to sacrifice either our principles or the lives of our sons led to the rapid erosion of our real power and, even worse, to a psychological paralysis in the face of the virile and aggressive intentions of our competitors for power. More important than any of this, however, was the perception on the part of our adversaries that we had lost our will—that indefinable lust for domination that drives great powers to the heights, and the loss of which condemns them to defeat and eventual oblivion.

"Today we are faced with the results of that policy. To use Lenin's famous phrase, 'What is to be done?' With courage, ruthlessness, utter attention to geopolitical realities, and an end to mush-headed moralizing, we may yet survive as a great power. But if we continue on our present course of adolescent immaturity hidden by a mask of idealism, we shall wind up on the garbage dump of history many decades before that inevitable end becomes necessary. And now back to Suzanne and the news."

"Thank you, Willoughby. An oil fire in the Gulf of Mexico is raging out of control off Brownesville, Texas. Fourteen members of drilling rigs are known to have perished and another thirty are missing. Fire-fighting helicopters are moving special diving teams into the area in an attempt to shut off the oil flow.

"Riots have broken out again in the streets of Lima in protest over a twofold increase in the price of bread. National guard units fired into a crowd of pro-testors, mostly women, killing two. President Gomez has declared martial law and warned that looters would be shot on sight.

"Sweden's socialist premier, Lars Torgerson, has called for the independence of Namibia and con-demned the latest repressive measures taken by the South African government. Torgerson, in a message to the U.N. General Assembly, proposed that the U.N.-sanctioned boycott of South Africa, now largely ineffective, be enforced by the warships of major powers.

"In the United States a large cache of heroin was found in the suitcase of a member of the Haitian delegation to the United Nations. Members of the Drug Enforcement Administration said that Hippo-lyte d'Artagnan has been suspected of smuggling the drug for many months. The Haitian government has protested Mr. d'Artagnan's arrest, terming it a viola-tion of his diplomatic immunity.

"Tornadoes raged over eastern Kansas and parts of Nebraska and Missouri today, leaving damage in their wake estimated at forty million dollars. Ten people were reported dead and several dozen are missing.

"And here is a late bulletin. William Madarios, a

student on the campus of the University of California at Berkeley, burst into a coed dormitory today firing two pistols. Three students are dead and five are seriously wounded.

"Madarios was later killed in a shootout with the city police. No motive for his attack on the dormitory has as yet been discovered.

"And that is the news tonight."

Washington D.C., September 10 (World News Service)—The office of the president today announced the resignation of Alec Thompson, presidential advisor for National Security Affairs. Mr. Thompson, who held the post for almost seven years, has accepted a position as Childers professor of international relations at Washington's Georgetown University.

In his letter accepting Mr. Thompson's resignation, the president expressed regret at his leaving and praised his "searching insights and immense contribution in the field of foreign affairs over the past seven years."

Mr. Thompson's successor has not yet been named, but persistent rumors indicated that Dr. Willoughby G. Pepperdine, former Harvard professor and commentator on international affairs for the Federal Broadcasting System, has the inside track.

"Well, professor, how does it feel to be out of the rat race?" Suzanne leaned across, pulling gently at the wiry black hair on his chest.

Thompson grinned up at her. "Who says I'm out of it?"

Suzanne sat up abruptly, her breasts taut in the shadowed morning light of the bedroom. "What the hell does that mean?"

"Senator Clarence called me yesterday."

"And?" She had her hands on her hips, staring down at him.

"He's kicking off his campaign for the presidency next week."

"What's that got to do with you?"

"He wants me to head his brain trust on foreign affairs, and, incidentally, to write his speeches. He mumbled something about how for once the country ought to have a really professional secretary of state."

"Alec, what did you say?"

"I told him I was on my honeymoon."

Pinnacle Books proudly presents

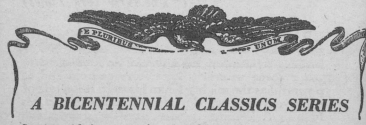

A BICENTENNIAL CLASSICS SERIES

Starting with four great American historical novels by Bruce Lancaster, one of America's most distinguished historians.

_____TRUMPET TO ARMS An exceptionally crafted romance spun beautifully amidst the fury of the American Revolution. (PB-887, 1.75)
"Explosive in style . . . *Trumpet to Arms* is always easy to read and strikes a note as stirring as a call to battle."
—The Boston Globe

_____THE SECRET ROAD A fascinating, yet little known account of the exploits of Washington's Secret Service. A gripping story of America's first espionage unit. (PB-889, 1.75)
"A veteran craftsman at the top of his form."
—The New York Times

_____PHANTOM FORTRESS A masterful treatment of the career of General Francis Marion, known to history as "The Swamp Fox." (PB-905, 1.75)
"History that is good and galloping, for competent scholarship underlies the romantic story."
—New York Herald Tribune

_____BLIND JOURNEY An absorbing tale of romance and adventure that moves from 18th-century France and its grandeur to the carnage of revolutionary America. A story no one should miss. (PB-915, 1.75)
"Romance, adventure . . . full pulsing life. Bruce Lancaster's best."
—The Boston Herald

Check which books you want. If you can't find any of these books at your local bookstore, simply send the cover price plus 25¢ per book for postage and handling to us and we'll mail you your book(s).

PINNACLE BOOKS
275 Madison Avenue, New York, New York 10016

"I think we may be going a bridge too far."
—Gen. Browning, Deputy Commander
Allied Airborne Army, to Field
Marshal Montgomery (Sept. 10, 1944)

A BRIDGE AT ARNHEM
by Charles Whiting

Arnhem. The most daring and sophisticated airborne operation of World War II; unparalleled in its size and scope. Somehow it turned into a debacle which caused the Allies twice as many casualties as D-Day.

How did Arnhem go wrong? And why was it touted as a great victory when it was, in fact, a dismal failure?

Ace journalist Charles Whiting answers these and other questions and brings the tragic story of Arnhem vividly to life in this important new book.

A BRIDGE AT ARNHEM　　　　P635　　$1.75